Cautiously she eased herself out of bed, pulling at the sheet so that it came with her. Out of the corner of his eye he saw her and advanced on her with mischief in mind as part of her back and legs became exposed. She dodged quickly but one corner of the sheet held firm and tripped her. She went to the floor with a thump. He knelt beside her as she rolled herself defiantly into a cocoon, the sheet ripping as he did so. He caught her and held her, laughing.

"No, Ross! Don't!!" . . .

THE
ANGRY TIDE

A Novel of Cornwall
1798–1799

Winston Graham

BALLANTINE BOOKS • NEW YORK

For Jean

Library of Congress Catalog Card Number: 77-90809

ISBN 0-345-28046-6

This edition published by arrangement with Doubleday & Company, Inc.

Manufactured in the United States of America

First Ballantine Books Edition: June 1979

BOOK ONE

Chapter One

It was windy. The pale afternoon sky was shredded with clouds, the road, grown dustier and more uneven in the last hour, was scattered with blown and rustling leaves.

There were five people in the coach; a thin clerkly man with a pinched face and a shiny suit, his thinner wife, their half-grown daughter, and two other passengers: one tall gaunt distinguished-looking man in his late thirties, the other a stoutly built clergyman a few years younger. The tall màn wore a brown velvet jacket with brass buttons, mostly undone to show the clean shirt and the shabby yellow waistcoat beneath, tight buff trousers and riding boots. The clergyman, except for his collar, might have passed for a dandy, with his green silk patterned suit all to match, his silk cloak, his scarlet stockings and black buckle shoes.

The clerkly man and his wife, a little overawed by the company they were in, made only whispered asides to each other as the coach lurched and clattered over the potholes. Although silence obtained now, there *had* been conversation, and they were aware of the nature of the company they kept. The tall man was Captain Poldark, a man recently come to eminence in the county and a member of Parliament for the borough of Truro. The clergyman was the Reverend Osborne Whitworth, vicar of St. Margaret's, Truro, and absentee vicar of St. Sawlewith-Grambler on the north coast.

There *had* been conversation but it had lapsed into a none too friendly silence; indeed, the interchange from the beginning had had an edge on it. Captain Poldark had joined the coach at St. Blazey, and Mr.

Whitworth shortly afterwards at St. Austell and at once had said:

"Ho, Poldark, so you're back; well, well, I expect you'll be glad to be home again. How was Westminster? Pitt and Fox, and all that. My uncle tells me it's a regular gossip shop."

"It's what you make it," said Captain Poldark. "Like so many other things."

"Ha! Yes. So my cousin-in-law George said when he was up here. Bitter blow you struck him then, you know, depriving him of his seat. Whetted his appetite, it had, those twelve months as a member. Very down in the mouth for a while, was George."

Captain Poldark did not speak. The coach smelled of dust and stale breath.

Mr. Whitworth eased his tight trousers inelegantly. "Mind you, Mr. Warleggan is no laggard in furthering his own affairs. I have no doubt you'll be hearing more of him before the year is much older."

"I shall wait with interest," said Poldark, looking down his strong nose.

"We need all the able men we can muster," said Whitworth. "Now more than ever, sir. Domestic discontent, Jacobin clubs, naval mutiny with red flags hoisted, bankruptcies everywhere, and now this Irish rebellion. Have you any news that it has been put down?"

"Not yet."

"The disgraceful atrocities of the Catholics must be duly punished. The stories one hears match the worst excesses of the French revolt."

"All atrocities are duly punished—or at least avenged. One never knows who begins them—only that they set off a train of consequences that never end."

Mr. Whitworth stared out of the window at the lurching greenery of the countryside. "I know of course that your Mr. Pitt favours Catholic emancipation. Happily there is little chance of its going through Parliament."

"I think you're right. But whether it's something to

be happy about I rather question. Do we not all worship the same God?"

Mr. Whitworth's nose was a different shape from Captain Poldark's, but he had no difficulty in looking down it—at the presumption of a man prepared to question his judgment on his home ground—and there for a time the conversation lapsed. However, the young cleric was not one to be discouraged by small rebuffs, and after the coach had been stopped for five minutes while the coachman and some of the outside passengers moved a fallen bough, Whitworth said:

"I have been spending two nights with the Carlyons. Do you know them?"

"By name."

"Tregrehan is a very comfortable and spacious residence. My father and mother knew the Carlyons and I have kept up the acquaintance. They have a very fine cook, a treasure indeed."

Captain Poldark looked at Mr. Whitworth's swelling stomach but made no comment.

"Their spring lamb—exceptional tender . . . with, of course, asparagus and roasted calf's heart. It is the conjunction of dishes which makes the table. Upon my word, though, I don't know whether that was better than the boiled fillet of veal with some sweet sauce of their own devising, and a sage and rosemary stuffing. Constantly I tell my wife, it is not the ingredients, it is the way those ingredients are put together."

"I hope your wife is well." Here at least was common ground.

"She has a mopish temperament. Dr. Behenna believes it now to be a disorder of the spleen. My son, I'm glad to say, is in fine fettle. Never have I seen a stronger two-year-old. Barely two-year-old yet. A handsome, beautiful boy . . ." Mr. Whitworth scratched himself. "Very different from the poor overlooked nashed little creature the Enyses have produced. Thin and weakly of body, they say, with a head far too big, and it dribbles from its mouth all the day long. . . . I'll swear this coach is full of fleas. I have a delicate skin, peculiarly susceptible of fleas and come up the size of a guinea at the least bite."

"You should try Dr. Leach's Fumigatory Powder, sir," said the clerk, greatly daring. "It is used in the noblest houses."

Whitworth stared the clerk down. "I'm obliged to you, sir. I had heard of it."

The coach lurched on.

II

Ross thought: my life seems to run in repetitive patterns. Long years ago—I forget how many—I came back from Bristol in just such a coach, a young man, limping and scarred from the American war, and had just such company. A clerkly sort of man and his wife, but then they had a baby to hold, not a thin pockmarked girl. But I shared the coach too with a clergyman, Halse—an old man now—whom I disliked almost as much as I do this one. And we sparred in talk and got out disgruntled with each other. The time of year was different, October then; yet today the leaves are lying about from yesterday's storm as if it were autumn already. And the only major difference perhaps is that then I was poor—and to be shocked when I reached home to discover how poor I really was—and now I am prosperous. And then I was about to receive the even greater shock of finding that the girl I loved was going to marry my cousin. And now I have a wife . . . Well, yes, I have a wife . . .

But then I was young and full of astonishing vigour. Now I am thirty-eight, and not so young. And not perhaps so resilient.

And all my life seems to run down similar avenues —just as it is doing now. Twice in my rash impulsiveness I have raided prisons and taken prisoners out—once in England, for which I was bitterly attacked by my own class, once in France, for which

5

I have received equally unmerited praise and admiration. Apart from the odd adventure here and there I have loved only two women in my life and they have both turned to other men. I have opened two mines. I have two children. The catalogue could go on and on.

Perhaps it is the natural outcome of getting older, he thought, this sense that life is repeating itself. Perhaps this sensation occurs to everyone if they live long enough. Indeed, if one considers the routine and uneventfulness of most people's lives, it may be I ought to consider myself fortunate that my life has been one of such variety.

But that's not quite the point. You're blunting the point of your own argument—

"What?" Whitworth had asked him something. "Oh, no, the House will not rise for six or seven weeks yet."

"Then you're returning early?"

"Business affairs," said Ross. "I have been away long enough."

"Ah, yes, business affairs." This struck a responding chord in Osborne Whitworth's heart. "By the by, now that you know Viscount Falmouth so well . . ."

He paused, but Ross did not acknowledge or deny the fact.

". . . now that you *must* know Viscount Falmouth so well, as you sit in his pocket—or in his pocket borough anyway—perhaps you would care to use your good offices with him on my behalf, since I am seeking the living of Luxulyan, and, although the living is not in his gift, he is sure to be well in with the patron; and merely his name on a letter would carry weight."

"I'm sorry to hear you are leaving Truro," said Ross maliciously.

"Oh, but I'm not," Ossie Whitworth assured him. "The recently deceased vicar of Luxulyan seldom lived there. I wish to augment my sparse income, which barely, you'll understand, suffices for day-to-day living and providing subsistence for my wife and growing family. Ministers of the Church have sti-

6

pends quite out of keeping with the demands that are put upon them. It is really—if unfortunately—essential for a man in Holy Orders to possess two or more livings in order to survive."

"You already," Ross pointed out, "have two livings. That in my own parish of Sawle became yours two years ago."

"Yes, but it's a miserable poor one. The expenses incurred in maintaining it almost eat up the increment. Luxulyan is richer, and the landowners and gentlemen far more generous. The south coast, you know, is always better found than the north."

There were some cries of protest from the outside passengers as the coach passed under low-hanging trees. One branch scraped the nearside window. The clerk and his wife had exchanged glances at the turn of the conversation, which Mr. Whitworth had had no hesitation in introducing before them, as if they did not exist. But Captain Poldark, apparently, was saying no more on the subject. The clerk could not help but feel that the Reverend Mr. Whitworth might have couched his request in more tactful terms.

Ossie peered out of the window. "Well, I am nearly home, thanks be to God. All this lurching and ducking is enough to turn a man's bile. I swear I was at sea only once but it was no worse than this. That rascal Harry had better be waiting to take my bag. Ah, yes, there he is." Ossie raised his stick and gave three loud knocks on the roof of the carriage.

They came to a stop, the wheels crunching on the soft ground, every iron bar and leather trace protesting as the motion ceased. The coachman jumped down and opened the door, taking his hat off as he did so, hoping for a tip.

Ossie was in no great haste to descend. He scratched again and began to button his coat. "Mind you, I might at some time be able to do you a favour, Poldark. You may not know that my uncle, Conan Godolphin, is a close personal friend of the Prince of Wales; and sometimes a friend at court—literally at court—can be of signal advantage to a man in the Commons. Especially a distant country member without title or social connections, such as yourself. Uncle Conan knows all the great Whig families and many influential noblemen, so there could be such a thing as a *quid pro quo* in all this."

"Indeed," said Ross after a minute. "A *quid pro quo,* eh?"

"Yes. That's what I would suggest."

"I'm not sure what it is you do suggest."

"Oh, come, Poldark, I think I have made my meaning clear."

Ross said: "You have a curate-in-charge at Sawle. Odgers is a hard-working little man. When you were appointed to the living you increased his stipend from forty pounds a year to forty-five pounds a year."

"Yes, that's so. It was a generous gesture and in keeping with the times. Though, living as he does off the land, almost, and with scarcely any expenses, I conceit it difficult to imagine what he does with the money."

"Well, I can assure you he does not live well. He grows vegetables to sell in the local market. His wife scrimps and saves and patches, and cuts down garments from older children to younger, and the children themselves lack any refinements of dress or education such as a clerk of the Church would reasonably hope they might have. You have told me it is hard for a clergyman to subsist. Well, on forty-five pounds a year he lives scarcely better than a farrier or a smith."

"Then I can only say he must mismanage his affairs disgracefully! I have long thought him an incompetent little man."

Ross eyed the speaker without favour. "The *quid pro quo* I might envisage, Whitworth, would occur if you were to increase Mr. Odgers's stipend to one hundred pounds a year. I should not require your uncle's good offices, but would be quite willing on those terms to ask Lord Falmouth to intercede on your behalf."

"A hundred pounds a year!" Mr. Whitworth began to swell, an ability he had when angry. It was more often a characteristic of certain animals and birds, but Ossie was peculiarly capable of it. "D'you realise that the *total* stipend from Sawle is two hundred pounds? How could you expect me to remain vicar if I paid half of it to an uneducated curate!"

"Well," Ross pointed out, "he does all the work."

Ossie Whitworth picked up his hat. His manservant, Harry, had now taken down the valise and was waiting beside the coachman with a foolish grin of welcome. "That is what an uninformed person would suppose."

"It is what I suppose, since I am a close neighbour of your church."

"God's my life, I'll wish you good afternoon, Captain Poldark."

Ossie climbed out of the coach, brushing the lapels of his coat with his free hand, as if dismissing not merely the material fleas that plagued him but the unjustifiable suggestion advanced. He did not glance back into the coach, nor did he tip the coachman, but walked off down the narrow lane towards St. Margaret's vicarage and the arms of his unwelcoming wife. Harry brought up the rear, tall and bowlegged behind the stocky stride of his master. A glint of river showed between the stooping trees.

The coachman climbed back onto his seat, clucked to his horses, flicked the whip, and the coach creaked and lumbered forward on the last mile of its journey to Truro.

III

Demelza Poldark had been entertaining Rosina Hoblyn to tea. Rosina, who only limped a little since Dr. Enys had cured her lipsy leg, was still unmarried after the tragedy of her near marriage to Charlie Kempthorne, though now twenty-five, and charming in a sweet and gentle way. Her younger sister, Parthesia, was wed to a farm hand and a mother already. Rosina had always been the quiet one of the family; perhaps it was an attitude of mind imposed on her early by her lameness; and she still lived at home with her mother and father and made something for herself out of millinery work.

Demelza had discovered her only a few months ago, and with her usual zest for friendship now put all the work she could in her way. She found the girl companionable as well as industrious. So Rosina had been making sun bonnets and caps for the children and had walked over from Sawle with them to see if they suited. While she was there they had taken tea and Demelza had ordered a straw hat for herself. Then she had walked a little way back with Rosina in the glimmering evening light, noting everywhere the ravages of yesterday's storm.

At Wheal Maiden she stopped and said good-bye but did not at once return; instead stood watching the girl's retreating figure as she plodded off across the bleak moor in the direction of Sawle Church. A waste of a nice woman, she thought, pretty, industrious, with surprising taste and manner considering who had fathered her—the glowering Jacka. Heaven knew, she *ought* to have a fellow feeling, considering that her own father would have made Jacka seem by comparison a gentle, reasonable man. They had that much in common, she and Rosina, they were "sports," untypical of their parents, somehow "better," if better meant having ideas and tastes above their station.

Though, again, heaven knew how much of this would ever have surfaced in herself—or had any opportunity to surface—if it had not been for a chance meeting with Ross at Redruth Fair so many years ago. But for that encounter, what possible hope would she have had?—a drudge, terrorised by a drunken father and smothered by a clutch of younger brothers, for all of whom she had had to act the mother at fourteen. Perhaps her father's conversion to Methodism would have taken place anyhow, perhaps she would have been able to make some niche for herself in the poverty-ridden, grindingly hard world of the miners. But nothing, nothing compared to what she had—even if the most important part of what she now had she was no longer sure she wholly retained.

At least the material part was wholly there, was here to be seen and appreciated all around her. A farm (estate if you liked to call it that) which provided many of the necessities of life; a mine which provided all the rest and the luxuries besides; a farmhouse (or manor house if you liked to call it that) of which one "wing" (it only had one) had recently been extended and rebuilt; four indoor servants to do her bidding, with all of whom she had instinctively established a nice relationship of half friendship, half respect; two unique and beautiful children; a superb position to live, at the foot of a valley and, as it were, peering over a low wall into the sea. And her twenty-eighth birthday just gone—not too old yet, not fat, not skinny, not lined, no birth creases across her belly, all except two of her teeth, and those back ones, and the front kept white by rubbing them every morning with a marshmallow root. She mixed now with the highest people in Cornwall, not merely the gentry but the nobility, and they accepted her—or appeared to accept her—as one of themselves. She also mixed with the miners and the fisherfolk, and they accepted her too.

And Ross. She had Ross. Or thought she had. But he was far away. And for too long had been far away. And here was the worm in the bud, the rot in the deeps of the heart.

To try to take her mind off it she sat on a granite stone—a part of the old Wheal Maiden house that had not been utilised by the Methodists—and stared again after the retreating figure of Rosina, so distant now as to be almost out of sight. The sky was brilliantly clear after the inflamed temper of yesterday; even the few dark clouds to the south over Sawle Church's leaning spire were retreating with the advent of dusk. It was understandable that folk should suppose some similarity between themselves and the climate and imbue the wind and the storm with human

11

characteristics. Yesterday the weather had been in a vile rage; it had cursed and sworn and quarrelled with everyone and thrown the crockery; now it had blown itself out, the temper was over and in the reaction it seemed tranquil in its exhaustion. You couldn't believe it was the same person.

The trouble with Rosina, Demelza thought, was that she was betwixt and between. With the skill of her fingers she was able to dress in humble good taste; she had even taught herself to read and write; but these skills and small evidences of a wish to be different set her above the ordinary miner or fisherman with his untutored manners and blunt approach to life. They were probably as much put off by her, thinking themselves inferior to her, as she by them, thinking the opposite; and it was hard on her, for she met no one else.

Of course, Demelza thought, she herself had two brothers, both crossed in love. Sam, the elder, had fallen in love with the loud, jolly, lusty Emma Tregirls, and she with him; and only his religion stood between them. But she could not swallow his intense Methodism, which filled his whole life, nor, being an honest young woman, was she willing to pretend that she had. So she had moved and become a parlourmaid at Tehidy ten miles away. In some respects Rosina would suit Sam much better than Emma, if only he could be persuaded to see it that way.

But people never fitted into convenient pigeonholes. Also, it had been at Demelza's suggestion, seeing them in complete deadlock, that Emma had gone away, with the agreement that they should meet again in a year's time. It had been through Demelza that Emma had got her new position. It would be anything but fair, therefore, to try to fit Sam up with another wife before even the year was out.

That left Drake, the younger brother. Drake was in a much worse state, having fallen in love with Elizabeth Warleggan's cousin, Morwenna, and then seen her married off to the Reverend Osborne Whitworth, vicar of St. Margaret's, Truro, by whom she now had a two-year-old son. Drake was in a worse state, but because it was hopeless, he might be a more suitable subject for speculation. Morwenna was out of his reach for ever. The marriage bond, once undertaken, was indissoluble, and, however unhappy Morwenna might be as the vicar's wife, one could never see her running away from him and setting up house with Drake in defiance of all the laws and conventions of the land.

So Drake's case was hopeless, and for nearly three years he had known it to be, and for nearly three years he had lived in a state of utter depression and had never looked at another woman. And two years ago Ross had bought him a small property and a blacksmith's shop a mile this side of St. Ann's, so now he was a respectable tradesman and one of the catches of the neighbourhood. But he never looked at a girl. At least he never looked at one in the way young men were accustomed to look. He was emotionally frozen, physically frozen, doomed to sterile bachelordom, his memory totally dominating his present thoughts so that they remained fixed on a girl long since lost. What was more, one couldn't be absolutely convinced that it would have been a good match even had it ever been able to take place. Morwenna was a reserved, shy, genteelly educated girl, a dean's daughter, far more "above" Drake than Rosina was above the average miner. Could one have seen her as a blacksmith's wife, cooking the meals, washing the clothes, scouring the floor? Surely it would all have gone stale very soon.

Of course Drake was still only twenty-two; three years was nothing in a man's life at that age. But Demelza distrusted a vacuum; there seemed to be a risk in it; and she thought Drake might get set in his melancholy. He was always very pleasant but she terribly missed his *gaiety*. In the old days it had bubbled from him in an irrepressible way. Of all her brothers he was the most like her, seeking and finding pleasure in all the small things.

So. It was perhaps risky to try to play the matchmaker. It was also probably useless. The spark came from nowhere, and no one could supply the spark. But there was a long word that Demelza had heard used recently and, when she discovered what it meant, one she especially liked the sound of. It was "propinquity." You didn't actually *do* anything. Or nothing obvious, that was. Nothing that anybody could possibly object to. You just arranged things so that propinquity took place. Then you waited and watched to see if there was any result.

And she alone probably of all people in the district was in a position to contrive such propinquity. She must bend her mind on how best to achieve it.

A gentle breeze blew out of the west as she got up to go. A solitary horseman was coming across the moorland. She turned and began to walk home, her mind comforted by the thought of what she might arrange. Once before, long years ago, she had brought all sorts of trouble on herself by trying to arrange meetings between Ross's cousin Verity and a Falmouth sea captain with a bad reputation. She really should know better than to meddle in other people's lives. Yet hadn't there been justification finally, after all the trouble, at the very end? Wasn't Verity now married to her sea captain, and happily married? Wasn't that the best result of all?

She stopped to lift her skirt and look at the back of her knee where something was tickling. Sure enough, it was an ant who had wandered off his stone wall and was exploring impermissible regions. She flipped him off with her finger and let her skirt fall. But she did not go on. A peculiar feeling in the pit of her stomach. What horseman would come this way at dusk? And was there not something familiar about the way he sat his horse? Oh, rubbish, he would have written. He would have sent word. Gimlett would have had to meet him in Truro. Parliament did not end its sittings for weeks yet. It was one of the Trenegloses. Or some visitor they had invited. There was nowhere else to go on this track at all. The hamlet of Mellin? Nampara House? Mingoose House? That was all, before the waste of sandhills to the northeast.

She turned back to the brow of the hill. She stood on the brow of the hill beside the chapel, shading her eyes, though what light there was was behind her. The figure was appreciably nearer. She had never seen the horse before. The rider she had.

She began to run down the hill, shoes scuffing on the rough track, hair flying, to meet him.

Chapter Two

Some hours before the second weary traveller reached home, the first one had arrived at his destination, St. Margaret's vicarage, Truro; but no light-footed, long-legged, eager young woman had come running to greet him.

This was not a disappointment, for he had not expected it. Nor would he ever expect it from *his* wife, for she, alas, was insane.

It was a terrible cross the Reverend Osborne Whitworth had to bear. Having been bereaved at a very early age of his charming, if feckless, but doting first wife, he had married quickly again, anxious not only to provide a new mother for his two orphaned little girls but to furnish a new life-companion for himself, a young woman who would be at his side for his mutual society, help and comfort in prosperity and adversity, a young woman, moreover, who would help him to avoid the sin of fornication and be of one flesh with him as an undefiled member of Christ's body; and in so doing, no doubt, conceive and bring forth more children—particularly a son—in the fear and nurture of the Lord and to the praise of His Holy Name. In making his choice it had not seemed anything but natural to him to look also for a girl with some connections and money to her name.

So, reverently, discreetly, advisedly, and soberly, he had picked on Morwenna Chynoweth, a tall, shy, dark-skinned creature of eighteen; shortsighted, not pretty by any ordinary standards, but with a perfectly beautiful body. She was genteelly born, too, the daughter of the late dean of Bodmin, and her cousin was George Warleggan's wife. The Warleggans being not at all genteel, in spite of all their efforts to appear so . . . but they were very rich and becoming ever richer, and after some hard bargaining George had settled a sufficient sum on Morwenna to make the marriage a practical proposition. Quite clearly he was aware of the advantages to himself of being associated with a family as distinguished as the Whitworths, who themselves were related to the Godolphins.

So the marriage had been arranged and had taken place, and the small matter of Morwenna's objections had been confidently set aside. After all, no girl of that age knew her own mind; and for a creature virtually without expectations the offer of such a union was like opening a gate to a new life. No person in her senses could refuse. And as for the physical side of the matter, Ossie had been confident enough of his own male charms to be sure that her awakening would rouse in her a quiet adoration. Of course it didn't matter much if it did not, for carnal desire and pleasure were male characteristics and the female was sufficiently gratified by the attention she received without further reward.

So it had begun, and for a while Ossie had not noticed any danger signals. She had sumitted five times a week, and, although on occasion her attitude and her facial expressions had been far from flattering, he had not taken too much notice of them. Then she had borne him a child, and a male child at that, a healthy, vigorous, thrusting, heavy, greedy baby whom Osborne had instantly recognised and acknowledged as his very own son and spiritual heir; but she herself had suffered at the birth, and it was at this stage that the first signs of insanity began to show. Her slight aversion to the procreative act had become a rabid

16

one, and, aided in the first place by the advice of that insufferable charlatan, Dr. Dwight Enys, she had begun to refuse her husband his appropriate and proper rights.

But worse, far worse, was to come. She had persuaded him to hire her youngest sister, Rowella, to come to the house to help look after the children, and then, delusive insanity growing hourly, had imagined that some sort of a liaison was developing between Rowella and Osborne himself and had screamed at him one night with lunatic eyes and hair hanging like seaweed that he must never—never, mark you!—lay hand on her again. When he was about to ignore this demented command she had shrieked at him that if he were to take her against her will she would the next day—the very next day, mark you!—kill, murder, put to death the child of her own womb, John Conan Osborne Whitworth.

It was a cross heavier than any man should be asked to bear, and the Reverend Mr. Whitworth was seriously considering what steps might be taken to lift the weight from him. A rich man—a really rich man without religious obligations—would no doubt easily find a way. But he, Osborne, was in the wrong calling. When one worked in God's service one was *supposed* to bear unhappiness bravely, and it would be no aid to his further career if it was thought by his brother clerks in Holy Orders that he had acted prematurely or selfishly in having her—well—put away. One of these days he must go to Exeter to see the bishop, pour out his heart and see if he could get the bishop on his side. That would be the great step forward, but it must be approached cautiously. That fool Dr. Behenna was no help, arguing as he did that Mrs. Whitworth suffered nothing worse than depressive spells of melancholia.

So, plodding down on his heavy legs behind his manservant, down almost to the river's brim where the ancient church and its vicarage seemed to stand with their feet in the tree-lined mud, he made no conversation, and when he entered the drawing room on

17

the first floor he found Morwenna sitting by the window sewing in the slanting sunlight.

She rose when she saw him. "Osborne. You are a little earlier than I expected you. Will you take tea?"

"The coach left earlier." He walked across to the mantelshelf on which stood three letters that had come for him in his absence. "Where is John?"

"In the garden with Sarah and Anne."

"You should not leave him unattended. There is the hazard of the river."

"He is not unattended. Lottie is with them."

(Lottie was the girl engaged to take the place of Morwenna's slut of a sister, who had been married off in disgrace to a local librarian called Solway. Rowella Solway. Lottie was pockmarked and inefficient but anything was better than the impudent, debased creature who preceded her.)

Ossie took out his watch. "I suppose you've finished dinner," he said grudgingly. "What have we in the house? Nothing, I'll be bound."

"We have spring chicken and a tongue. And part of a leg of mutton. And custards and some tart."

"And all very ill-cooked and totally lacking in flavour," said Ossie. "I know. It is not until one has dined at one of the great houses that one realises the uncouthness of the food one is expected to eat in one's own home."

Morwenna looked at her husband. "Did things not go well with you at Tregrehan?"

"Well? Of course they went well! Why should you suppose different?" Ossie turned his letters over. One, he knew from the copperplate writing, was from that gout-ridden old buffer Nat Pearce, no doubt inviting him to whist. A second was from one of his churchwardens, probably voicing some pettifogging complaint. On the third the name and address was printed in copperplate lettering with a fine pen, the seal on the back of plain sealing wax and bearing no impress. He looked up and met his wife's gaze. She was so untidy these days, her hair not properly combed; her frock looked as if it had been slept in. Another sign of

the creeping dementia. He really must bring pressure
to bear on Behenna. Ossie was not sure if he *really* believed her threat to kill John provoked by his hus-
bandly attentions; but—but—he had never dared to
call her bluff. However, if she continued to go down-
hill and began to suffer delusions—such as her wild
fantasy that he had been carrying on with her repulsive sister—if that happened she might well imagine
that she had been molested against her will, and *then*
was John safe?

"Did you have a tiresome journey?" Morwenna
asked, forcing herself into a solicitude she did not feel,
seeking some reason for his being so out of temper.

"Tiresome? Yes, indeed it was tiresome." Reminded, Ossie scratched himself. "Those coaches are a
disgrace; they're alive with fleas and silverfish and
wood lice. They never use a fumigant or even seem
to brush the cushions. Next time I shall hire a post
chaise. . . . And that impudent squireen Poldark was
aboard."

"Poldark? Do you mean Ross Poldark?"

"Who else? There's only one, isn't there? God be
praised. As arrogant, as presumptuous, as ever."

"I suppose he was returning from London, from
Parliament."

"Of course, and home too soon. George was not
so neglectful of his duties when he was a member.
No doubt Poldark had trouble in his mine, or something of that sort." Ossie broke the seal on the third
letter.

"Did he say so?"

"Did he *what?*" Ossie stared at the letter.

"Say that it was something wrong with his mine?"

"No, of course not. Not in so many words." The
writing was not printed and he knew it very well. It
was as tidy and precise as Mr. Pearce's, though not
so ornate. Against all reasonable judgment, his heart
began to beat noticeably.

Dear Vicar,
I hope you will forgive me for addressing you

after so long an interval; but I am in hope—indeed I mention the hope each night in my prayers —that the passage of two years will have brought about an amelioration of those hard feelings that you once had for me. (Though never, I assure you, did I ever feel anything but gratitude towards you and my sister for the kindly and comfortable home you gave me, nor to you for the attention and affection you showed.)

But I have tried many times to see Morwenna and every time she has refused me admission, and once when I attempted to speak to her in the street she turned coldly away. I do not suppose, judging from this, that I shall ever again be welcome in your house or in your church. I appreciate, too, that having married so far beneath me, this is an added bar to any full reconciliation. Yet we live in the same town and must continue to, and I would so like to feel that any real enmity that existed is at an end. (My cousin, Mrs. Elizabeth Warleggan, receives me from time to time, and should we chance one day all to meet there together, embarrassment would be avoided if we could greet each other without obvious coldness or distaste.) If you have influence with Morwenna, I pray you will use it to this end.

Vicar, it is two years now since I left your house to marry Arthur, and at the time, inadvertently, I carried away some books of yours among my own. These are two volumes of Latimer's discourses and the collected sermons of Jeremy Taylor. I have often wanted to return them but have wondered how best I might do this without seeming to presume. If I come to your door I know I shall be turned away. If you would write me a line I could leave them with Arthur in the Library, or, since you are often in the town and passing by my door at number seventeen Calenick Street, could I ask you to call in for them? I am usually at home in the afternoons and would look on this as a special sign of your condescension and forgiveness.

I remain, sir, your respectful and obedient servant and sister-in-law,
    Rowella Solway

"What's that you say?" snapped Ossie.

"You have not told me," said Morwenna, "whether you wish to eat now or would prefer to wait until suppertime."

Ossie stared at her as if he were confronting Rowella. What impertinence, what impudence, what presumption! The girl was outrageous, mentally as deformed as her elder sister, to write such a letter. And morally depraved and spiritually lost. And physically repulsive. She was a *worm,* as voluptuous as some slimy thing crawling from under a stone, a *serpent* to be bruised beneath the heel. That she should dare to write to him!

"Are you not well?" Morwenna asked. "Perhaps you have a summer fever."

"Nonsense!" With an effort Ossie turned away and stalked to the mirror, adjusted his stock. His hands were unsteady with anger. "Tell Harry I will eat at once."

II

Dinner was a little later at the Great House in Truro, indeed had only just finished, and Elizabeth, graceful as a wand, had just risen to leave the two gentlemen to their port.

It had been a polite threesome, conventionally polite throughout a meal carefully chosen and designed to impress. Indeed Elizabeth, with her deep rooted knowledge of what was done and not done, had dropped a hint to her husband that, where no large dinner party was intended, this meal was too elaborate and too obvious in its design. But George had chosen to ignore her. His new friend *must* be impressed at this, their first dinner party together, by the wealth, the taste, the epicurean knowledge of his

21

host. It was all very well if you were a gentleman sprung from generations of other gentlemen, perhaps you could afford a sloppy meal in untidy surroundings. Many of George's so-called superiors ate like that: Hugh Bodrugan, John Trevaunance, Horace Treneglos; and he despised them for it. *He* chose to eat differently, to behave differently, to have other standards than theirs, and if he entertained an important guest he chose to demonstrate what money could buy.

In any case, his guest knew him and knew his origins. The show was not put on to deceive anyone. You could not pretend in the town and the county in which you carried on all your business activities. Besides, this friendship might lead to big things, and it was necessary to do all honour to it in the beginning.

Elizabeth had yielded.

Their guest had celebrated his fortieth birthday a few days ago. He was a tallish man with his own greying hair brushed back in wings behind his ears; a thin-faced man, good-humoured, but with small eyes that were both sophisticated and acquisitive. Christopher Hawkins of Trewithen, lawyer, member of Parliament, onetime High Sheriff of Cornwall. Fellow of the Royal Society, baronet and bachelor and boroughmonger.

After Elizabeth left and a manservant had poured the first glass of crusted port a short silence fell and endured while the two men sipped appreciatively.

George said: "I'm glad this opportunity has arisen for you to visit us in our house. We'd be happy if you would stay the night."

"I'm obliged," said Hawkins, "but I'm two hours from my own home now and there is business I want to attend to in the morning. This is admirable port, Mr. Warleggan."

"Thank you." George forbore to say how much it had cost. "However, another time I hope you will be able to arrange your business so that you can spend a night or two with us, either at Cardew, where my father lives, or at Trenwith on the north coast."

"The old Poldark home . . ."

"Yes. And Trenwith before that."

Hawkins took another sip. "A long time before, surely. Didn't the last Trenwith marry a Poldark about a century ago?"

"I believe so," George said shortly.

"Of course that's not an unusual progression. The Boscawens married a Joan de Tregothnan and made their home there. The Killigrews married an Arwenack. Let me see, there is a Poldark left, isn't there?"

"Geoffrey Charles. Yes. He's at Harrow."

"Francis's son, yes. Not to mention, of course, Ross Poldark, a few miles to your east. And he also has a son."

George regarded his guest carefully, to try to fathom whether the name of Ross Poldark had been introduced into the conversation from malice or inadvertence. But Sir Christopher's face was not an easy one to read.

"Geoffrey Charles will naturally inherit Trenwith when he is of age," said George. "Though he'll have little or no money to maintain it. When my father —if anything happens to my father Elizabeth and I will move to Cardew, which is a much more considerable house and has perhaps something the same aspect as your own, being set among fine trees and looking towards the south coast."

"I did not know you knew my house."

"I know it by repute."

"That must be altered," Hawkins said courteously.

"Thank you." George decided that Ross Poldark's name might have been introduced into the conversation for a third reason and decided to turn it to account. "Of course I envy you one thing more than any other, Sir Christopher."

Hawkins raised his eyebrows. "Do you? You surprise me. I thought you had all that a reasonable man could possibly want."

"Perhaps a man is not reasonable when he has once possessed something and then lost it."

"What? Oh . . ."

George nodded his formidable head. "As you know, I was a member of Parliament for more than twelve months."

The manservant came in again but George waved him out and poured the second glass of port himself. The two men sat in silence beside the littered table, which glinted with silver and glass in the subdued light from the window. Although they were much of an age they were so different, in appearance, in clothes, in expression, in build, that a consideration of age hardly seemed to be relevant. Hawkins thin, shrewd, sophisticated, cynical, greying, looked a gentleman through and through but one who knew all the ways and the wickedness of men. Human nature, you felt, would never surprise him. Beside him George, in spite of everything, looked heavy and a little uncouth. The pale lemon silk neckcloth seemed inappropriate around the strong bull neck. The finely tailored velvet coat did not hide the strong muscles of arm and back. The clean, well-kept hands, though not overlarge, had a breadth about them that suggested manual labour. (Not that he had ever done any.) He too wore his own hair, and there was not a trace of grey in it; but the first inch or so grew up vertically from the scalp instead of lying along it.

Hawkins said: "You came in at Truro under the wing of Francis Basset, Lord de Dunstanville. When Basset composed his differences with Lord Falmouth you lost the seat narrowly to Poldark. It was natural enough. Finding another seat in a Parliament as yet six months old presents difficulties. But, if you are anxious to return, has Basset no suggestions to offer?"

"Basset has no suggestions to offer."

"Has there been some area of disagreement between you?"

"Sir Christopher, there is little in this country that can remain private. To such a public personage as yourself, with so many avenues of information open to you, it can hardly be a secret that Lord de

Dunstanville does not offer me the patronage he did. We are still on civil terms but cooperation, at least on a parliamentary level, has ceased."

"May I ask why?"

"There were—as you say—areas of disagreement. May I ask if *you* always find yourself in accord with Francis Basset?"

Hawkins smiled thinly. "Scarcely ever. . . . But if you have lost the patronage of de Dunstanville, and made, I imagine, an enemy, at least for the time being, of Lord Falmouth, your choice is limited."

"Not in a county returning forty-four members."

Sir Christopher stretched his legs. They were dining on the first floor but the sound of carts rattling over the cobbles outside sometimes impeded conversation. "As you know, Mr. Warleggan, I have three seats myself, but they are all notably occupied."

"Yet I'd appreciate your advice."

"Anything I can do I will do."

"As you know, Sir Christopher, I am a wealthy man, and I have a fancy to indulge my wealth. Do you know what Lord de Dunstanville is reported to have said at a recent dinner party at his house?"

"Reliably?"

"I have it from a guest who was present. He said: 'Mr. George Warleggan's grandfather was a blacksmith who worked a forge in Hayle and hadn't a shilling to his name. But Mr. George Warleggan, by industry and good luck, has acquired a fortune of two hundred thousand pounds.' "

Hawkins eyed his host with a narrow assessing gaze but did not speak. George looked up and met his eyes. "The only misinformation in that remark, Sir Christopher, is that my grandfather's forge was not in Hayle."

Hawkins nodded. "Well, your fortune is a matter for some congratulation, then, isn't it. Francis Basset must have thought so too. No one even as rich as he is can afford to despise wealth in another."

". . . That's as may be." George leaned forward

to fill the glasses again. "But since I have money and wish to use it I would be very much in your debt if you would advise me how I might best re-enter Parliament." He paused. "Naturally, any favour I might do in return . . ."

Upstairs a child was crying. (Valentine, as if saddled with some incubus at an early age, often had bad dreams.)

"Had you approached me before the election of last September, Mr. Warleggan, your question would not have been a difficult one to answer. The government usually has seats to sell at three to four thousand pounds."

"Then I was member for Truro."

"Yes, yes, I understand. But at the moment—"

"I am not," George said, "so much concerned to buy a seat as a borough. I don't wish to be at the beck and call of some other patron. I want to be the patron myself."

"That would be much more expensive. And of course it is by no means a straightforward operation. One has the voters to consider."

"Oh, the voters . . . Not in some of the boroughs. Which do you control, Sir Christopher?"

"I have an interest in Grampound and St. Michael. Voting powers there are vested in those inhabitants who pay scot and lot—"

"What does that mean?"

"Roughly, those who pay a rate towards the maintenance of parish affairs."

"And how many such are there in each borough?"

"Officially it is supposed to be fifty in each borough but in effect it is fewer than that."

"And how does the patron influence the voters, if that is not too crude a way to put it?"

"He owns the properties they occupy," said Sir Christopher dryly.

"Ah . . ."

"But one has to have a care, Mr. Warleggan. Where overt bribery is seen to exist elections are frequently declared void on appeal to Parliament,

26

and the offending member or his patron may be sent to prison."

George turned a couple of guineas in his fob. "No doubt you would instruct me in the niceties of such matters. In return, if there should be any way in which I could assist you, either in banking or in furthering such interests as you may have in smelting, mining, or shipping, pray let me know. It would give me pleasure if I were able to assist you."

Hawkins stared at the dark red eye of his port. "I'll inquire for you, Mr. Warleggan. Circumstances are always changing—there may be a chance at any time to purchase such controlling interests—or there may not. It is very much a matter of luck, of foresight, of opportunity. But most of all, of money. That will open many doors."

"Money I have," said George, "and will lay it out as you advise."

Chapter Three

The other weary traveller had arrived home. He had dismounted and they had walked home together while dusk accompanied them and then overtook them like a rising tide. The children were just abed and Ross said not to wake them; it would be a surprise for them in the morning. He had been to see them sleeping and had accepted his wife's assurances that they were in health. Downstairs again and all bustle and pattering feet and the clink of knives and plates while supper was brought in and they ate it together.

Through the meal they talked of the casual homely things: Jinny Scoble had another daughter, whom she had called Betty. Jack Cobbledick had hurt his foot on a harrow and was laid up in bed. The two pigs, Ebb and Flow, in the normal progression of nature, had had to be disposed of, but two more, from Flow's first litter, had taken their place, had been given the same names, and the children were becoming reconciled. Jud Paynter had got so drunk last week that he had fallen into one of his own graves and had had to be hauled out. Ezekiel Scawen has passed his eighty-fourth birthday and claimed not to have had a tooth in his head for sixty years; the Daniels had made him a cake. Tholly Tregirls had had a brush with the preventive men but had got away without being recognised. Verity had written last week and said the measles were very bad in Falmouth—

"Dwight," said Ross, who had been doing most of the eating and little of the talking. "Caroline's baby. What is wrong with it?"

"Sarah? What d'you mean?"

"Is that what she's called? Of course, I remember now, you wrote me. Is she deficient? Mentally, I mean."

"No, Ross, *no!* There is no reason to suppose so! But Caroline had a bad time and the baby was small. She is still small and rather frail. But why did you suppose? . . ."

"That dangerous donkey in cleric's clothes, Osborne Whitworth, said as much in the coach from Par today. He suggested the child was witless and dribbled from its mouth all day."

"All babies dribble, Ross. Like old men. But I don't think Sarah is worse than any other. It must have been spoken out of malice."

"Thank God for that. And the marriage between those two—does it prosper?"

Demelza raised her eyebrows. "Should it not?"

"Well, I have had fears sometimes. They are such total opposites in everything they think and do."

"They love each other, Ross."

"Yes. One hopes it is a sufficient cement."

After that Jane Gimlett came in to take away the supper things and they moved into the old parlour, which looked and smelt and felt the same to Ross as it had done since childhood. He noted, however, the re-covered chair, the two new vases, with flowers in them: bluebells, tulips, wallflowers. In those years when Demelza had been growing out of servitude and childhood to become his companion and then his wife, almost the first evidence of the changing relationship had been the appearance of flowers in this room. He remembered with great vividness the day after he had first slept with her Elizabeth had called, and Demelza had come in in the middle of the conversation, bare-legged, rough-clothed, unkempt, with a sheaf of blue-bells on her arm. And she had offered them to Elizabeth, and Elizabeth, probably sensing something, had refused them. She had said they would fade on the way home. And after she had gone Demelza had come to sit at his feet, an instinctive movement as it were to claim him.

Well . . . life had changed a little since then. Demelza had changed since then.

He lit his pipe with some difficulty from the small smouldering fire; drew at the smoke, sat back.

"You're thinner," he said.

"I am? Maybe a little."

"Are you fretting for Hugh?"

She stared at the fire. "No, Ross. But perhaps a little for my husband."

"I'm sorry. I should not have said that."

"You should have said it if it was in your thoughts."

"Then it should not have been in my thoughts."

"Perhaps sometimes we can't help those. But I hope all this time in London you have not been thinking I have been grieving, for someone else."

"No . . . No."

"You don't sound very certain."

"No. What I *have* thought, ever since last September, is how difficult it is to fight a shade."

The candlelight flickered with air from the open window.

"You don't need to fight anyone, Ross."

He looked down at his pipe. "Compete with."

"Nor compete with. For a time . . . Hugh came into

my life—I can't tell you why—and into my heart, where before there had only ever been you. But it is over. That is all I can say."

"Because he is dead?"

"It is *over*. Ross." She blinked as if removing mental tears. "It is over."

"Yes . . ."

"After all . . ." She got up, dark eyes glinting, and moved to poke the fire.

"Yes?"

"It was not a worthy thought."

"But say it—as I did."

"Is this the difference between a woman and a man, Ross? For after all, all my life with you I have had to fight—not a shade but an ideal—Elizabeth. I—have *always* had to compete."

"Not for a long time now. But perhaps you're right. What's sauce for the goose . . ."

"No, no, no, no, no! D'you b'lieve I allowed myself to feel a heartache for Hugh out of retaliation? You surely could not! What I mean is, because it happened you say you have to compete with some memory. This I have to do and have had to do all my married life. It shouldn't be allowed to wreck all that we still have."

His pipe was not drawing properly. He laid it on the mantelshelf and stood up. He seemed to have grown bigger since he had been away.

"Should it be allowed to wreck what we still have? No. We decided that last September. But this parliamentary frippery in which I am engaged came at a fortunate time. We have been apart, we've had time to think, and I believe time to reorder our thoughts, and to some extent our lives."

She took a breath. "And what has been your conclusion?"

"What has been yours?"

"No, I made mine last September. There is *no* difference. There *can* be no difference—for me."

"Well, as for me," said Ross. "As for me—well, of course I have seen all these beautiful women in London."

"Indeed you must have."

"I believe the women of London are the most beautiful in the world."

"Tis quite likely they are."

"What have you been doing while I have been away?"

"What have I been doing?" Demelza stared at him in indignation at the change of subject. "Seeing to your mine and your affairs, of course; trying to bring up your children in the way they should go! Doing all the ordinary things of *living* and *breathing* and—and looking to the farm and the rest! And—and *waiting* for your letters and answering 'em! Living just as I have always lived—but without you! That's all I've been doing."

"And how often has Hugh Bodrugan tried to creep in your bed while I've been away?"

Demelza burst into tears.

She made for the door. "Leave me go! Let me alone!" she cried as he barred the way.

He held her forearms and she looked as if she was going to spit in his face.

He said: "It was meant as a joke."

"Twas a poor joke!"

"I know. We can no longer joke, can we, because it is all too tender and raw between us. God help me, there was a time, and not so long ago, when every tiff between us ended in laughter. That is all lost."

She said: "Yes, that's all lost."

He held her for a few moments more, and then stooped to kiss her. She turned her head so that his lips only found her hair. "Leave me alone," she whispered. "You're a stranger. I don't know you any more."

He said: "Perhaps the fact that we fight shows that we still have something to lose."

"A marriage without warmth, without trust—a trust that we've both betrayed; what good is that?"

"You don't ask me how I have disposed of my spare time in London, what women I have had."

She wiped her eyes with her hand. "Perhaps I've no right to."

"Well, after all you're still my wife. And since you are my wife I'll tell you. In the early months on different occasions I invited two women into my rooms. But before they had even undressed I sickened of them and turned them out. They left shouting derisory curses at my head. One accused me of impotence, the other called me a trike."

"What is that?"

"No matter."

"I can look it up in the dictionary."

"It won't be in the dictionary."

"I can guess," said Demelza.

There was a pause, while he released her arms but continued to prevent her moving away from him.

She said: "Those were harlots."

"Yes. But high-class ones. Very select."

"And what of the real ladies, the beautiful ladies?"

"They were—in circulation. But I found none to my taste."

"You tasted them?"

"Only by the eye. And that generally at a distance."

"It seems you've been a monk."

"Only because you are more beautiful than all of them."

"Oh, Ross," she said weakly, "I do so *hate* you! I hate you for *lying* to me! Say if you wish that you want me to be a wife to you again. That I will be. But don't—pretend."

"If I were to pretend you might take it for the truth —but because it's the truth you disbelieve me, eh, is that it?"

She shrugged but did not speak.

He said: "Oh, in a picture gallery I cannot say that three out of five men would not pick a different picture from mine. It is not just looks, it is what's behind 'em; it's the familiarity of knowing someone intimately and yet wanting them all over again; it's the total commitment of personality; it's the ultimate spark between two people that lights the flame. . . . But who knows whether it will warm them or burn them up?" He stopped and frowned at her. "I had no idea when

I came home how we were to meet. I have no idea at this moment whether we shall ever laugh together again—in *that* way. I want you, I want you, but there's anger and jealousy in it still, and they die hard. I can't say more. I can't promise that tomorrow it will be like this between us or like that. Nor can you, I'm sure. You're right in saying I'm a stranger. But I'm a stranger who knows every inch of your skin. We have to go on from there—in a sense to start again."

II

Ross was up at four next morning. He left Demelza, her breath ticking gently like a metronome, went out of the bedroom and down the stairs. Day was breaking outside, but the dark hadn't yet left the house; it skulked in corners waiting to trip you up.

He went out and stood under the shadowy lilac tree listening to the sleepy chirp of the finches and the sparrows. Somewhere up the lane a blackbird was in full song among the nut trees, but about the house they had been slow to wake. The air was white and pure and soft and he inhaled it like ether. Then he slid round the house while a cow lowed at him and a pig grunted, climbed the stile and was on the beach, sand soft and churning at first, then hard where the tide had been.

It was not yet far out. The waves were small but explosive, bursting into little flurries of self-importance as they turned. He threw off his robe, kicked his slippers away and went in. The sea was like a surgeon, icy and probing: although it was mid-May his body froze before it responded to the stimulus. So for five minutes, and then he was out again, breathless but glowing, as if his flesh was made new. He wrapped himself in his robe as the rim of the sun peered slanting over the sandhills and set fire to the first chimney top of Nampara.

Reminiscent mood—he had swum like this after his night with the woman Margaret following the ball in

Truro, and the day before he first met Demelza. He had swum then as if to rid himself of some miasma attaching to the night. Not so this time. No expense of spirit in a waste of shame. A trivial event, of course, for God's sake: he had resumed intercourse with his wife, for God's sake. Fit subject for ribald dialogue in one of the fashionable plays in London.

Yet it hadn't quite turned out as expected. What *would* one have expected? In spite of his brave words, perhaps the casual. Or more likely the fiercely resentful, a claiming of a right long since in abeyance and nearly lost. But in the event it had never progressed beyond the tender. Somehow a much-derided emotion had got in the way and turned it all to kindness. Whatever happened now, however they met today, or tomorrow, in whatever form constraint or hurt or injury or resentment reared its head, he must remember that. As she would, he knew. If only one could altogether exorcise the ghosts.

When he got back to the house all were still sleeping, though the Gimletts and the rest of the servants would soon be astir. His children slept on. Demelza slept on. He dressed and went out again. The sun was still shining but clouds were marching like rioting miners out of the western sky. He walked up to Wheal Grace. The engine was tirelessly working, pumping up the water that for ever accumulated in the sump. Two tin stamps clanged. He had intended having a chat with whichever of the Curnow brothers was in charge of the engine but at the last moment changed his direction and walked towards Grambler. He felt full of energy and the sort of elation that came rarely now. All this was total contrast with the noisy, sooty streets of London. But perhaps contrast was a necessary part of appreciation.

Henshawe, the grass captain of Wheal Grace, lived at the far end of the poverty-stricken straggle of cottages and hovels that made up Grambler village, and was up and about, as Ross knew he would be.

"Why, Cap'n Ross. I'd no idea you'd be back so soon. Going back to the mine, are you? I'll walk with you so far as her, if you've the mind. But how about a dish of tea first?"

So it was nearly six before they left, and the cores were changing as they reached the mine. Those miners who knew him well clustered round him, talking and joking and asking questions and telling him local gossip; but he noticed an element of reserve that had not been there before. Apart from that independence of mind natural to Cornishmen, who were not accustomed to bowing low to their squires in the way of up-country folk, was the fact that many of these men had been his companions in boyhood. Joshua, his father, unlike Charles, Francis's father, had drawn no barriers when Ross was young, so the boys had gone line fishing together, had wrestled, had picnicked, had played wild games in the sandhills, had later sailed over to France in company to bring back brandy and rum. Even after Ross returned from America, a scarred and limping veteran of twenty-four, it had always been an easy relationship, the differences of station acknowledged but largely ignored. Now there was a change, and he realised why. By accepting Viscount Falmouth's invitation and being elected for one of the seats in Truro he had "gone up" in the world. He wasn't just a J.P. who sat on a bench and solved local problems and dispensed local justice: he was a member of Parliament, and Parliament, for better or worse, made new laws for the land. They probably thought privately that there weren't many laws necessary except the laws of God.

He had not yet broken his fast and was hungry, but it seemed the right moment to get a hat and a candle and go down with the new core. That, if anything, would re-establish the old camaraderie; besides, Henshawe's news was not of the best and he wanted to see everything for himself.

But it had to be postponed. The others were filing down, taking it in turn to step onto the ladder that would take them two hundred feet below ground, where they would spend eight hours of the bright day, and he was waiting for Henshawe, when a lighter

footstep made him turn. It was Demelza, with Jeremy
and Clowance.

"Captain Poldark," she said. "I have two friends
for you."

Then he was engulfed.

III

"I did not know whether to tell you or not," said
Demelza. "Captain Henshawe came and told me, and
as he does not write very easy I thought perhaps I
must pass it on."

It was nearly dinnertime and they were sitting together on the old wall beside the stile, looking onto
Hendrawna Beach. The day had turned cold, and
Demelza was wearing a cloak. The children were
on the beach, but they were far away at the water's
edge and Betsy Maria was looking after them.

"I don't think from a first look it is quite as bad as
Henshawe supposes. It's true the south lode—the
one we found first—which has brought up such riches—
is wearing unexpected thin. It took everyone by surprise, for it began in great depth and there was no
reason to suppose it would not be so uniform over
most of its breadth. But it is not so. Nor is the quality
so good as it was. But with care there is still a year or
more's yield even if there is no 'on lode' development.
But the north lode—virtually a floor—is yet barely in
full development. Or seems so. After being so deceived in one perhaps one should qualify one's assess-
ment of the other. But there is—must be—ample for
a number of years, and that is surely all any mine
venturer can hope for."

"Perhaps it was wrong to bring you back, then."

"I didn't return solely for that reason. Nor even
principally. I was—fatigued of London. You've no
idea, Demelza, unless you have experienced it, the constant noise, the bustle, the smells, the chatter, the
clamour, the lack of air. Even one day, even half a

day such as I have now had, makes me feel a new man, made over again."

"I'm glad."

It being new moon, the tide was now far out, so far that the firm sand stretched for great distances, intangibly bordered by a smear of surf. Betsy Maria and the two children were token figures not identifiable.

Demelza said: "It is a long time since you have talked to me as you have done last night and this morning. Perhaps it is all the speeches you have been making in Parliament."

"Speeches. Huh."

"But tell me about it. What is it all like? Your lodgings have been comfortable? You didn't write so just to deceive me?"

"No, they were good rooms. Mrs. Parkins is a tailor's widow. George Street is off the Strand, near the Adelphi Buildings, and quiet after the noise of the main streets. Eighteen shillings a week I paid—did I tell you?—carpeted and furnished. Mainly I ate at the coffeehouses and such. But Mrs. Parkins made me a meal when I asked. It's a way from Westminster, but there were always ferries at the foot of the steps to take me there."

"And where you meet—in Parliament?"

"A hybrid, born of a chapel for a father and a bear pit for a mother. You go to the chamber, you approach it, through Westminster Hall, which is a fine lofty building, but the chamber itself is much like Sawle Church, except that the benches face each other instead of the pulpit and are banked so that each may see over the one below. At times it is insufferably crowded, at others near empty. The business usually starts at three and can go on till midnight. But the business itself is most of the time so parochial that one wonders it could not have been settled locally. A bill is introduced, say, for creating a new road through the village of Deptford. The next is for dividing the parish of St. James in the city of Bristol and building a church. The next is for draining low ground in some parish in the East Riding of Yorkshire. What, I frequently asked myself, was I doing in such a place and what could I contribute half so well as minding my own affairs in the parish of Sawle?"

Demelza looked sidelong at her husband. "But there are important things too, surely?"

"There are important debates, yes. Pitt has introduced a tax on incomes to counter what he calls shameful evasions and scandalous frauds. It is to be two shillings in the pound on incomes of over two hundred pounds, and he hopes to raise ten million pounds towards the war. But he spoke at inordinate length."

"Did you vote for it?"

"No. I think it is too great an invasion of privacy."

"And the slave debate?"

"What of it?"

"Mr. Wilberforce introduced one, didn't he, in April?"

"His motion was narrowly defeated. By eighty-seven votes to eighty-three."

"And you spoke in it?"

Ross turned and stared. "Who told you that?"

"I think," Demelza said, shading her eyes, "that we should go and meet the children. Otherwise they will be late for dinner."

Ross said: "I hardly *spoke* in it. It was an intervention that lasted barely five minutes and was unpopular with both sides of opinion."

"It didn't read so."

"It was not in the *Mercury*."

"No. But in another paper."

"What other paper?"

"I did not see the name. Unwin Trevaunance cut the piece out and sent it to Sir John and Sir John gave it to me."

Ross rose. "Shall I call the children?"

"No, the wind is in your face. Let's walk out."

They tramped over the rough grass and stones and were on the beach.

"Why was it not well received, Ross? Reading it, it

said just what I believe you think, and I could hear you saying it."

"I met Wilberforce twice in February," Ross said. "He is a likeable, warm, religious man, but strangely blinkered. You know the saying that charity begins at home. Well, not with him. Quite the reverse. Charity with him begins overseas. He will work up a fine rage about the condition of the slaves and the slave ships —as who would not?—but can see little in the condition of his own countrymen to take exception to. He and not a few of his followers are supporters of the Game Laws; he favours all Pitt's measures to curb freedom of speech, and wishes to keep the wages of the poor down. I got up that day," Ross said, frowning at the sea, "with no prepared speech, which was lunacy, but you must know that when one man has finished speaking a number of others rise and it is for the Speaker—who is like a chairman—to choose whom he fancies. Maybe he picked me because I was new in the House. I was taken aback. It is a strange experience, for it is like speaking from the body of a church, with all the congregation lolling and sprawling and gossiping all about you. You are adrift in a sea of faces and hats and top boots and hunched shoulders . . ."

"Go on."

"I am going on—as I did that day. I have to tell you that I did not stumble or stutter, for the challenge, instead of overawing me—as it should have done by rights—annoyed me. But I had come to my feet to support—of *course*—Wilberforce's bill. As Canning had. As Pitt had. As any man with any compassion in his bowels would do. The arguments against were—abominable in the ingenuity of their twisted reasoning."

"As you said."

"As I said. But, after speaking three or four minutes I—I felt it necessary to *jolt* all those men, *all* of them, if I could, with a realisation of the evils that existed under their very noses. It was not, I said . . . But you have read it."

"Go on."

"It was not as a committed Christian that I spoke—for everyone in the House no doubt would claim to be that—perhaps particularly those who spoke against the motion, since the Society for the Propagation of the Gospel itself owns slaves in the Barbadoes. This manifested itself in its worst form in the abominable slave trade but existed also in lesser but no less evil forms on the doorstep of everyone of us in the House that day. There were, I said, in England one hundred and sixty crimes for which a man might be hanged; yet by the laws introduced over the last two decades many a man was now so poor that he could not live except by crime—if feeding his belly and his starving family was still to be considered such an offence. Grievous as it was, intolerable as it was, that human beings, black or white, should be bought and sold in slavery, was the House aware that new slaveries were springing up in England; that, for instance, children employed in the mills of the North of England were dying in their hundreds of overwork while their parents, denied work of any sort, contrived to live off the tiny earnings that their children brought home?"

"That is better than it said in the paper," Demelza said. "And then?"

"Rightly I was called to order—for I was veering right away from the subject of the debate—and thereafter soon sat down. I have not spoken with Wilberforce since, but he has given me a couple of cold nods, so I do not think my intervention was looked on with the greatest favour."

They walked on. The children had seen them coming now and were running to meet them.

"And Lord Falmouth? Do you see much of him?"

"I have dined at his house once and we have supped over at Wood's Coffee House in Covent Garden, where the exiles meet two or three times a year. It is called the Cornish Club. I think we have come to be a little on each other's nerves, but I have to tell you that he has not attempted to influence my conduct

40

in the House so long as I support Pitt on most major issues."

The children were racing now. Jeremy had outstripped Clowance's fat little legs, and Clowance, it seemed likely, was going to go into a sulk.

"And you are home, Ross, for all the summer?"

"All the summer. And I hope you have something good for dinner. Last night—and the air this morning —has made me hungry."

Chapter Four

Since the persecutions instituted by Mr. Tankard at Mr. George Warleggan's suggestion ceased, Drake Carne's business had prospered. Even in times of war, even in times of scarcity, even in times of depression, people needed a blacksmith, especially one who could also make a serviceable wheel. Drake had had the great advantage when he began of taking over a going concern, even if run down; there had not been any need to create a new connection in the face of opposition. "Pally" Jewell had been there forty years before him; the difference was a young man in place of an old.

It was sourly observed of Methodists that they prospered more than other men. The reason was simple: once they had truly laid hold of the faith they eschewed gambling, wenching, and, for the most part, drinking, so that, aside from their religious meetings, they had not much else to do but work. While regarding this world's goods as of secondary importance, Wesley had never for a moment forbidden his followers to prosper, so long as they did so in a godly and modest and sober way. And this was happening to Drake, and faster even than most; for the loss of Morwenna left him without the solace of a wife and the distraction of a family. He worked. From dawn till dark—and often after by candlelight, he worked. With the shop went six acres of land, and this he farmed, mainly growing animal feed, which he sold to the big houses round. (Not, of course, to Trenwith.) He kept chickens and goats and a few geese. When for any reason business slacked off he made spades and shovels and ladders, and the mines bought them from him. Recently he had taken on two undersized boys of twelve, the Trenwinnard twins, as assistants. He was putting money in the bank, not because he felt it was any use to him, but because he had to put it somewhere.

Sam, his brother, still came every Tuesday and Saturday and stayed and talked a while and prayed with him. Drake had broken away from full participation in the life of redemption, and, although still a member of the Connexion, he had never returned to it in the way Sam would have liked and nightly prayed for. Sam, whose religion had been the cause of his failure to win Emma Tregirls, pursued it with unremitting zeal, and saw no cause to abate his conviction that divine love ruled and must continue to rule the spirits of those who dwelt in Christ. He would gladly and joyfully have married Emma unredeemed; Emma, though she loved him, could not accept the fact that she needed redemption.

One day Drake received a note from Demelza asking him if he could spare a few hours to put in a new fireback she had bought for the library. "I have not seen you *at all* this month," she wrote. "We have been so Busy haymaking the Storm all but ruined one field but the rest was in and thanks be the ricks stood the strain. Ross is back from London looking so pale as if he had been living in a Vault but well and he has already made his mark upon the House of Commons. Though he denies it. Have you time to take a meal with us? You know four people who would like it among them your loving sister Demelza."

The boy was waiting—it was Benji Ross Carter, now thirteen, with a scar on his face, though on the other cheek, not unlike that of the man he had been named after—so Drake said he would be over about four the following Wednesday. On the Wednesday, having left the forge in the care of Jack Trewinnard, the elder by half an hour, he walked to Nampara and saw to the fireback.

It was a simple fitting and one, Drake would have thought, any handyman could have managed; but he fixed it, and then drank tea with his sister in the old parlour which remained, in spite of alterations and extensions, the life centre of the house. Demelza was looking very well and specially pretty—she bloomed at regular intervals like a perennial flower—and the children clambered all over Drake for a while and then were gone. Ross was still up at the mine.

Drake said: "A fine pair of children you have, sister."

"Grufflers," said Demelza.

"Please?"

"Grufflers. That's what Jud calls them."

Drake smiled. "They have a betterer start than we had."

"Their father is a small matter different."

"And their mother."

"You never knew Mother, did you?"

"Not so's I recall. You was—you were always mother to the six of us."

"I knew her till I was eight. Then I—came in for her family. When you're young like that you don't think, you don't compare, you don't wonder. As you get older it's different. Oft I've puzzled since why she ever wed Father. She was an orphan—I b'lieve she was a love child—but her aunt brought her up on their farm. She used to send me to sleep when I was little talking about the ducks and the hens and the geese. She was pretty. At least I think so. Till she was dragged down with all us children and all that poverty. I never knew Father come home in the evening till he'd drunk what he'd made."

"Father ever good-looking, was he?"

"'Tis hard to say for sure, isn't it? It's hard to see

when people are old. Was Dr. Choake ever good-looking? Was Tholly Tregirls? Or Jud?"

Drake laughed. "I must go, sister. Thank ee for the tea. Will Jeremy go away to school soon?"

Demelza wrinkled her eyebrows at the thought. "I am trying to teach him what I know and then he can maybe have a tutor for a while. I shall never hold him in if he has the wish to go away, but at seven or eight it is savage for a boy to be torn from his home. Ross did not go till after his mother died, when he was turned ten."

"Of course," Drake said, "and Geoffrey Charles, he was eleven when they sent him to Harrow."

This was such a sore subject that for a few moments neither spoke.

"Here's Ross now."

Then there was pleasant talk for a space, while Ross refused fresh tea and gulped a cup from the old pot standing up and asked Drake to come to the mine one morning, for they had recently received a consignment of tools, screws, nails, and wire from Bristol, and he suspected the quality was inferior but was not sure enough to be able to complain.

Drake said he would come next Monday at seven, and was edging his way towards the door, when Demelza said:

"I believe Rosina Hoblyn is just leaving. D'you know her, Drake? She's from Sawle and lives with her family. She does needlework and millinery for me."

Drake hesitated. "I expect mebbe I seen her about."

"I've given her a stool—you know the old one, Ross, that was in the box bedroom. It will be useful for her at home, but as she is a little lame it is a long way to carry it." Demelza went to the door and called. "Rosina."

"Yes, ma'am." Rosina came to the door, needle in hand. When she saw the two men she looked surprised.

"Are you ready to go? That must be near finished."

"Oh, it is. I was but adding a stitch or two, here and

there, waiting for you to come see twas right and proper."

"D'you know my brother, Drake Carne? He's going your way; he lives at St. Anne's, so it'll not be out of his way at all, and he can carry the stool."

Rosina said: "Oh, ma'am I can manage that. Tis no great weight; and I'm used to fetching and carrying water and the like."

"Well," Demelza said, "Drake is going that way and is about to leave. You do not mind, Drake?"

Drake shook his head.

"Then go get your bonnet."

The girl disappeared, and soon came back, carrying her work basket and the stool. This was handed to Drake, who took it, and they set off, over the creaky wooden bridge and up the may-lined lane out of the valley. Ross and Demelza watched them go.

Ross said: "Is this another of your matrimonial experiments?"

Demelza narrowed her eyes. "That little limp stays with her in spite of all Dwight has been able to do. She's a nice girl."

"A more flagrant contrivance I never saw."

"Oh, no, it was not! I don't think so . . . Since they both happened to be here at the same time . . ."

"At your invitation."

"Ross, Drake needs a wife. I don't want to see him dry up in his youth from disappointment and loneliness. I want to see him—in joy again, as he used to be. He's my favourite brother."

Ross poured himself another cup of tea. The teapot just filled his cup with its last drips. "There's something in what you say. But have a care: matchmakers often burn fingers."

"I shall do no more. It is just—putting them together once or twice—that's all."

Ross swallowed his second cup. "Does Drake ever mention Geoffrey Charles when you see him?"

"He mentioned him today. Why?"

"He'll see a big change in Geoffrey Charles if he comes home this summer. I took him out when I was in London. I didn't tell you, did I? I took him to Vauxhall. It seemed a suitable thing to do."

"George would not like it."

"George can rot. We listened to music and, avoiding the harlots, sipped a glass of wine in the gardens; then we went into the Rotunda to admire the statuary. I took him back at seven. He has changed. He is very—grown up. Next term, he tells me, he will have Lord Aberconway as his fag."

"Well, that is what happens to boys, isn't it? They grow up very sudden. There's nothing you can do about it. But I'm sorry if it isn't a good change."

"Well, I'm not saying he's disagreeable now—far from it—he's *very* good company. It's just that these years at Harrow have turned him into a worldly-wise young man. Do you know more than anything what I felt as he walked beside me? That his father had been born over again. I knew Francis from childhood, of course, but it is in his teens that I remember him most vividly. Geoffrey Charles has become the living repeat of his father. And as I liked Francis—most of the time—so I like Geoffrey Charles. He's witty—lively—perhaps a little unstable at the moment—but good company for all that."

"But not good company for Drake."

"I don't think it will work between them any longer."

II

On the way up the lane and then across the moorland towards Grambler nothing was yet working between Drake and Rosina. Rosina was wearing a yellow bonnet and a faded but clean yellow muslin dress with a white frilled hem, from under which small black boots appeared regularly as she strode beside her tall companion. Her limp was hardly noticeable on level ground. With the stool over his shoulder Drake was trying to pace himself to her speed. He was wearing green barragan trousers and a coarse shirt open at the throat, with a green neckerchief.

The silence had lasted such a long time that at last he forced himself to break it.

"Going too fast for you, am I?"

"No, no, tis just right."

"You've only to say."

That ended conversation for a time.

Then, after moistening her lips experimentally once or twice, she said: "I go over most once a week now. Tis easier for Mistress Poldark if I'd go there to work than she sending it over. Mending and patching I do for her an' all."

"I never seen my sister make much sewing," Drake said.

"No. She d'say she's not handy with a needle. But she have the ideas. Oft when I go there she have the idea and I make it up just as she want."

"Who learned you?"

"Mostly myself." Rosina pushed a strand of hair out of her mouth. "Being laid up so long, see, you start to work with your hands. Then I borrowed a book on it from Mrs. Odgers."

"You can read?"

"Yes. Mother would bring home laundry from Trenwith, and often twas wrapped in newspaper. Mind, I don't read easy."

"I could neither read nor write till I was past eighteen. Then my sister learned me."

"This sister?"

"I've only the one. Several brothers."

"Sam is your brother, isn't he? The preacher. I seen him about often. A rare good man."

"Are you a Methodist?"

"No. I just go church Sundays."

They had reached the outskirts of Grambler. Both knew that if they once walked through the village together and as far as Sawle the news would be everywhere that Drake Carne was courting at last, and it was to be Rosina Hoblyn.

"Look," said Rosina. "I can manage from here. There's no weight to the stool, is there?"

He hesitated, the busy wind pushing and thrusting at him. "No. Tis of no moment. That is, if you don't have the mind to wish otherwise."

"If you have not I have not," said Rosina.

III

So exercised in mind was the Reverend Osborne Whitworth in matters closely concerning himself that he did not open Nathaniel Pearce's letter until two days after his return home. Of late Ossie had been finding excuses for refusing the old man's invitations to whist because like as not when the day came Mr. Pearce would be laid up with gout and have to cancel, or when he played be too absentminded to return his partner's lead. For a time Ossie had borne this because of the chance of meeting the notary's influential clients, but now he felt he had met them all and knew them well enough to do without an intermediary. But when he did finally read the letter it was not after all an invitation to whist. Mr. Pearce was ill and urgently wished to see him.

Ossie delayed another couple of days, and then, being in Truro on other business, stopped outside a door bearing a wooden sign on which was printed: "Nat. G. Pearce. Notary and Commissioner for Oaths." As he mounted the shaky stairs which seemed ready to collapse under the attack of worm, following the slatternly pimpled woman who had let him in, Ossie wrinkled his nose at the stale smell in the house, a smell which became more pronounced as he was shown into the bedroom. Used to smells associated with occasional and reluctant sick visiting, Ossie did not have a tender nose, but this was distinctly unpleasing.

The Notary and Commissioner for Oaths was sitting propped up in bed in a nightshirt and nightcap. His fat face with its terrace of chins was the colour of a mulberry just before it comes ripe. A coal fire burned in the grate and the window was tight shut.

"Ah, Mr. Whitworth, I had thought you had forgot me. Come in, my boy. You will regret to see me in this state. I regret it myself. Everyone regrets it. My daughter weeps tears nightly and says her prayers at my bedside. Eh? What's that? Speak plain, please, this gouty condition has affected my hearing a little."

"I have been busy with parish affairs," shouted Ossie, not accepting the chair he was offered and standing with his back to the fire. "There is a great deal to be attended to, with Whitsunday but two days off, and matters in Sawle needing my attention. I have also had business in St. Austell. In what way may I assist you?"

"One thing," said Mr. Pearce, "one thing about you my boy, is that I can always hear what you say without your having to raise your voice. Eh? I suppose it's you being a cleric, you're used to preaching and the like. Well . . ." He blinked his bloodshot eyes a couple of times. "Was it Thomas Nash who wrote a poem— 'I am sick, I am like to die'? Well, I am sick, Mr. Whitworth, and doubt not at all that Dr. Behenna is right in taking a deleterious view of my chances of recovery. I'm sixty-six, my boy; though bless my soul it seems no time since I was your age. Life is like— like one of those hobby horses you ride at a fair— round and round you go enjoying every moment, and then the—then the music stops . . ."

Ossie lifted his coattails so that with his hands behind his back each tail was draped over one arm. He observed that Mr. Pearce was emotionally moved. Indeed tears trembled and fell onto the bed sheet. The old fool was clearly very sorry for himself.

"Gout? That's nothing. You told me once you've suffered from it for twenty years. A little fasting and you'll be up and about again. Did you forswear any luxuries for Lent? Tell me that."

"The gout?" said Mr. Pearce. "That was what you said, wasn't it? Ah, the gout I have had in the limbs for half of a lifetime; but now it has risen to my heart. There are times in the night—I tremble at the thought of them—when I stretch up—and up and up

—hoping for the next breath. One of these days, one of these nights, my boy, and the next breath will not come."

"I wish I could help you," Ossie said coldly. "I'm sorry if you are so sick."

Mr. Pearce remembered his manners. "A glass of canary? It's on the side there. Noblemen have seen fit to congratulate me on my choice of a canary. Help yourself, will you?" Ossie did so. "No, alas, I may not drink it afore sundown, Behenna says; though what difference it will make in the end, the good God knows. . . . And talking of the good God, Mr. Whitworth, I'd remind you that I am in your parish. St. Margaret's extends to take in this corner of Truro, even though all the rest belongs to St. Mary's. Anyway, I could not bear the comforts of the sour Dr. Halse."

Ossie for the first time realised why he had been called. Offering solace to the sick and the bereaved was one of the duties of his office that he was least attracted to, but when driven into a corner he made some show of it. For the most part, since he had a good memory, this consisted of quotations from the Bible: obviously nothing that a mere parson could say could be so apt or so authoritative. But Mr. Pearce was an educated man and clearly would not respond to the first quotation that came to mind.

In the end he shouted: "Job in the time of his tribulation said: 'If a man die, shall he live again? All the days of my appointed time will I wait, till my change come. Thou shalt call, and I will answer thee: thou wilt have a desire to the work of thine hands.'"

Silence fell. Mr. Pearce said: "I believe a glass of canary *will* be helpful to me, my boy."

It was poured. It was drunk.

Mr. Pearce said: "You're a parson, my boy. You're in Holy Orders. The bishop has laid hands on you. So you ought to know. If anyone does, that is. Eh? Eh? What did you say?"

"Nothing," said Ossie.

"Ah, well, I suppose that's about what anyone

would say confronted with such a question. All the same, d'you know, I'd be interested. Do you believe what you teach, Parson? D'you believe in an afterlife? My daughter does. Oh, yes. She's a Methody and considers that it is only important to repent here and now and all the rest will be added to you after you die. That's fundamentally what the Bible teaches, isn't it, not regarding which particular branch of religion you swing from. Repent and you'll live again."

Ossie said: " 'Thou hast hold of me by Thy right hand. Thou shalt guide me with Thy counsel, and afterward receive me to glory. Whom have I in Heaven but Thee? My flesh and my heart faileth. But God is the strength of my heart, and my portion for ever.' "

"You dropped your voice," said Nat Pearce, Notary and Commissioner for Oaths. "Tis unusual in you, my boy; you've one of those voices that *carry*. But, I don't supposition that what you have had to say is quite in my particular field. Maybe you'll find a fox, but tain't the same one! D'you know, I would wish to repent if I could believe there were something to it, for I've not been so well behaved these last few years. Tis pressure of circumstance that has been at the bottom of it all."

Ossie moved reluctantly to the chair and lowered himself into it. "St. James says: 'Blessed is the man that endureth temptation; for when he is tried he shall receive the crown of life.' "

"Eh? Yes, that's very well." Mr. Pearce raised a swollen mulberry of a hand and scratched among the ruffles on his chest. "But I haven't altogether *endured* temptation, my boy. I have *yielded,* here and there, and that is the point, ain't it? I'm not at all easy in my mind, and I don't fancy passing on to meet my Maker with a burdened conscience. I'm terrible uneasy. You truly believe there *is* such a Being, do you? You believe these tales of hellfire and eternal damnation? Upon my soul, I don't know what to think."

"God is eternal," said Ossie. "God is omnipresent. God is the supreme judge. There can be no turning away. If you go down into the nethermost parts of hell

He is there also. There is no escaping Him. Is it the sins of your youth that trouble you now?"

"Youth? Whose youth? Mine? Nay, nay. Did I sin then? Maybe. If so I have forgot. I have forgot what they were. Nay, my boy, tis the sins of age that trouble me. Those of the past ten years."

Ossie took out a handkerchief and breathed into it. "What sins can you have in mind, Mr. Pearce? Gluttony? Sloth? Concupiscence? I detected you once, I believe, cheating at whist."

Mr. Pearce had his hand behind his ear. "What? Oh, that. If it had only been at whist, my boy . . . If only at whist . . ."

"Then pray what is wrong? I haven't all day to listen."

Mr. Pearce coughed, trying to clear the phlegm gathering in his throat. "I have—from time to time, my boy, indulged in a little speculation. It seemed harmless enough. There was money to be made, d'you know—in India—in Italy—in some of our burgeoning industries. It is difficult for a country solicitor to accumulate wealth, though all his life he attends on it. Alas, in the main, my little speculations were unfortunate. It is chiefly the war. Italy was overrun. Madras was seized for the French. Some of our English industries have failed for lack of outlet, with all Europe closed against them. So, money was lost instead of made. Eh? Eh? I say money was lost instead of made."

"So you are less well off," Ossie said, never one to jump quickly to another's meaning. "What is there to that?"

"Alas," said Mr. Pearce. "I have to tell you, my boy, that—that some of the money I speculated with was not . . . well, not my own."

IV

Half an hour later the Reverend Mr. Whitworth, having offered what contemptuous comfort he could to his ailing and contrite friend, went into the stables of the Red Lion Inn to pick up his horse; but there, feeling the impulsive need of further refreshment to sustain him before his ride home, he waved the ostler away and stooped through the gloomy passage that led to one of the parlours and ordered a pint of porter. So little light came from the latticed windows after the brightness outside that it was not for some seconds that he recognised the man sitting at a table near him.

He at once got up and moved to the other table. "Dr. Behenna. May I join you?"

"Certainly, sir. I'm at your service." Behenna was a man of forty-two, the principal surgeon of the town, authoritative, stocky and well dressed. Many a simple man would have trembled at the sight of these two together, for between them they encompassed all that anyone could know of the body and the soul. On the whole Behenna was the greater feared, for his denunciations and judgments were the more immediate. Hellfire was at least at one remove.

Behenna was drinking porter too, and for a few minutes their conversation was casual: neither man was accustomed to lowering his voice, and two corn merchants were at another table and well within earshot. Behenna began to inveigh against the spread of apothecaries in the town who, without any qualifications except a board over their shops, saw fit to prescribe for all and every ailment man was heir to.

"Look at this," he said, spreading a broadsheet on the table. "This is what they distribute and advertise, sir. 'Dr. Rymer's-Cardiac Tincture and Analeptic Pills,' 'Roberts's Medicated Vegetable Water for Scrofulous Wounds. For the Evil, Leprosy, Pimpled Faces, Flushing, and all Morbid Affections,' 'Dr. Smyth's Specific Drops for Weakness of the Natural Functions. In tin or flint bottles, according to size.' What are we coming to, Mr. Whitworth, that the surgeons of the town should be expected to suffer such quacks and medical jockeys in their midst?"

"Indeed said Ossie, fingering the broadsheet indifferently. "Indeed." The corn merchants were about to go.

"It would be a good subject for the pulpit," said Dr.

Behenna, brushing a fleck of porter from the front of his brown velvet jacket. "They should be denounced by the church, and in no uncertain terms. It is become a scandal."

"Indeed," said Mr. Whitworth again. "I think I could do something along that line. Not Whitsunday, when it would be inappropriate, but within a few weeks perhaps."

"That would be very obliging of you, sir, for many of the common people—*most* of the common people—are gullible to a degree, and few can distinguish between a skilled physician who has devoted all his years to the study of human suffering and an ignorant charlatan who will sell them a bottle of coloured water and call it the elixir of life."

"It so happens," Ossie said, as the corn merchants left and no one else entered, "it so happens that I would welcome the benefit of your advice—on another matter—a matter which I did broach with you once before but to which you returned no altogether positive answer."

The surgeon sniffed at the top of his gold-banded cane. The end of his last sentence had been talked down by Mr. Whitworth beginning his, and Dr. Behenna, not accustomed to being overborne in this way, was slow to change tack.

"What subject is that?"

"My wife," said Ossie.

There was considerable conversation going on in the main taproom, but this room was a little backwater. Indeed there was a quality of liquidity about the light, for the flawed and discoloured panes in the windows cast deceptive colorations on table and bench and chair, on mugs and glasses, on hands and clothes and facial expressions, so that they were at once muted and inscrutable.

"She is unwell again?"

"I think she is well enough of body, Dr. Behenna, but far from well of mind. I have marked a noted deterioration in her general behaviour."

"How, sir? In what way?"

"She has periods of profound melancholy when she will speak to no one, not even the children. Then she has spasms of savage excitement, when I tremble as to what she may do next. I have noticed a marked decline in her mental powers."

"Indeed? It's less than four weeks since I visited her. I must call again shortly."

Ossie took a deep draught of porter. "You know the problems that I face, as a responsible minister of the Church. You know how I spoke to you at Christmas. I cannot see how the situation can go on very much longer as it is." He dabbed his mouth with a large linen handkerchief.

"I know, Mr. Whitworth. But you must appreciate what I told you then. Even supposing you were able to get Mrs. Whitworth committed to an asylum, the treatment is nil. The inmates are sometimes chained. When they will not eat they are forcibly fed—and then not infrequently choked to death. I do not believe your wife would long survive."

Ossie contemplated this agreeable thought for a moment. "It is always considered, it is well understood," he said, "that insanity is a visitation of judgment upon the wicked. No good man, no good woman is so visited. You will remember how Christ drove out the evil spirits."

Dr. Behenna coughed. "But there are degrees of visitation, and one hesitates to think of Mrs. Whitworth as being possessed by an evil spirit."

"I don't know what else. I don't know what else. Since Christmas, however," said Ossie, "I have been giving thought to another course that may be open. A compromise course. There are in fact in Cornwall one or two private madhouses where the less seriously afflicted are taken in. There is one I have been in touch with at St. Neot. Such a recourse would not need the sanction of a court; Mrs. Whitworth could be conveyed there privately and kept there privately—in comfort. Fed and looked after by persons competent to fulfil such duties. Taken away from the strain of life in a busy vicarage. Given the constant and full medical care that she so obviously needs."

Behenna looked at his companion.

"I would hardly have thought such places afford—hm—quite what you say. But there it is. It would cost you money, of course."

Ossie bowed his head. "That I would have to face."

"And in a sense deprive you of a helpmeet, Mr. Whitworth. Although I appreciate the problems you have to face—"

"Great problems. I am a man, with all a man's natural needs. It is not good that a man should suffer deprivations of the kind I am forced to suffer. You, of all people, must know it is detrimental to his health and well-being."

"Possibly—"

"There can be no 'possibly' about it, Dr. Behenna. It is the gravest possible hazard to his physical and mental equilibrium—"

"It could so be argued. What I was about to say was that I understand Mrs. Whitworth fulfils most of her household duties adequately. And this, if she were put away, you would altogether lose. You could not re-marry."

"Certainly not. The marriage bond is sacred and in-dissoluble. No, no . . . I should be forced to engage a housekeeper."

The two men looked at each other, and then Behenna bent his head to his drink.

"A housekeeper . . ."

"Yes. Why not? After all, I understand that you employ one, Dr. Behenna."

The doctor put down his tankard. He wondered where Mr. Whitworth had heard of his private arrangements. Of course nothing was private in a small town.

"Well, yes, I do."

Two drunken men, arms twined, tried to get in through the door but failed. After some stumbling and argument they backed out, not encouraged by the stare of the clergyman sitting at one of the tables.

Behenna shrugged. "Well, my dear sir, who am I to say more on this subject? As Mrs. Whitworth's husband you are entitled to have her sent away if you wish. I doubt if anyone could object. I suppose she has a mother living? . . . But you have the prior right . . ."

Ossie frowned. "Dr. Behenna, I am in Holy Orders, and therefore my position is somewhat delicate—more delicate, that is, than if I were an ordinary common member of the secular community. It is not a matter of having the agreement of her relatives that concerns me, but of obtaining the sanction of my bishop. Or if not the sanction, then at least the sympathy. If I took this grave step of having my wife put away; and I do not question that it *is* a grave step—she might very well be incarcerated for life—I should be reluctant to have the matter brought to his notice if the decision had been taken solely on my own initiative. The opinion of the surgeon attending on my wife would therefore be of the utmost value and importance. That is why I request it."

There was silence for a minute or two.

"Ecclesiastes," said Osborne, finishing his drink. "Chapter thirty-eight, verses one and following, I believe it is. I have never used a passage from the Apocrypha as my text, but no one I am sure would object. 'Honour a physician with the honour due unto him for the uses which ye may have of him, for the Lord hath created him.' Something of that sort. It would be very suitable, in that context, to bring up the subject of the true as distinct from the false physician. Don't you think?"

Dr. Behenna twisted one of the brass buttons on his coat. "Your wife has never shown any *positive* signs of violence, has she?"

"She has repeatedly threatened the life of our son. I told you. Isn't that enough?"

"It is certainly a very grave sign. Though such threats could well be empty."

"How can one tell?" said Ossie. "Does one have to wait until the dastardly crime has been *committed?*

And upon an innocent defenceless child? I never have a moment's peace."

Behenna finished his own drink. "I understand how you feel, Mr. Whitworth. I'll come to see Mrs. Whitworth again. Would Tuesday be convenient?"

Chapter Five

News reached Cornwall that week of a raid that had been carried out on Bruges. Locks, it was reported, had been totally destroyed in the port, the canal and basin drained dry, buildings had been blown up, invasion barges destroyed. Weak behind her defensive moat, England could still make the effective gesture of defiance. The young cleric Sydney Smith declared that he now considered war between the English and the French no longer a temporary quarrel but as the expression of a natural antipathy between the races such as existed between the weasel and the rat. He did not specify which in his view was which.

In February the Directory had instructed General Buonaparte to inspect the invasion fleet with the hope that he might lead it against England, but, having observed Hoche's failure of the year before, and, being aware of what had happened to the combined fleets of Spain and Holland when they met the British last year, Buonaparte had turned it down as too much of a gambler's throw. Instead he had gone south again, no one in England for a while knew where. But just before Ross left London, news had come in that the General was in Marseilles assembling a fleet and an army.

Now, a secret report reached England that a great fleet had left Marseilles with the General on board, that the fleet consisted of 180 ships and that it carried 1,000 guns, 700 horses, and 17,000 of France's best troops. It so happened that the recently promoted and recently knighted Admiral Nelson was in command of a fleet which had been sent to the Mediterranean last autumn even though invasion fears were then at their height, a bold, indeed rash, move which had been opposed by the admirals but decided on by Lord Spencer at the Admiralty, who overruled them. It could now be a fortunate decision, always supposing that the two forces should encounter each other somewhere in the wide reaches of the Mediterranean. A frigate had been dispatched to inform the admiral of the enemy's move.

This information, while it allayed some immediate fears of invasion in Cornwall, did not remove them; for Hoche was still somewhere about, and France had the forces to mount two expeditions at the same time. While he was in London, Ross had been to observe the preparations to meet an invader in Sussex and Kent. If the French landed drastic measures would at once be taken there to remove or destroy anything they might capture. Ross felt that in Cornwall not enough preparations of this sort had been made and set himself to put his point of view to the local Volunteers and Vigilantes.

In June a council of another sort was held—this in the Warleggan family. Nicholas, George's father, had been in indifferent health for some time and spent more and more time at his country seat. As a consequence the management and direction of Warleggan interests had fallen wholly to George. His uncle Cary was immersed in day-to-day administration and took a greater active part in the affairs of the business: George usually decided policy.

It was a grey, warm, damp day, when Truro, lying among its rivers and its mists, was at its most enervating, that Nicholas chose to limp into the main office of the bank and try to pick up the reins he had dropped a year ago. George gave him an account of what had been happening while Cary, sweating thinly under his skullcap, provided details and extra figures if Nicholas wanted them.

Presently Nicholas, staring at the great ledger in front of him, said: "You've been making heavy personal drawings, George. Eighteen thousand pounds in the last three weeks. May we know what enterprise you are favouring?"

George smiled: "Not so much an enterprise, Father, as an investment for the future. My future."

Cary hunched his shiny coat round himself and said: "Very dubious investment, Nicholas. Very dubious indeed. An investment in self-aggrandisement, if one may venture to put it that way."

George looked at his uncle dispassionately, as if seeing him without any sense of blood relationship. "I have been buying property, Father. In St. Michael. A few houses. A few farms. A posting house."

"Derelict," said Cary. "Tumbledown."

"Not altogether."

"But this very large sum? . . ."

George said: "Last year, because of a stupid and contrived agreement between two of our so-called nobility, I lost my seat in Parliament. This you well know, my dear father, since you fought with me to the end, allowed our friend Poldark to take my seat. Well . . . that is done. Unless we arrange to shoot him on the highway we cannot unseat him. But I see no reason to be deprived of a place in Parliament for any length of time. I enjoyed the experience. Seats are for sale. I am buying one."

"Not a seat," said Cary. "A borough. You can get a seat for two or three thousand pounds. Trying to buy a borough will cost you five or ten times that before you're finished."

"Agreed," said George. "But who has a seat for sale just after an election? Life is short: I don't wish to wait. With a borough—if I get it—I have control. I can also dispense patronage: a parsonage for one, a customs appointment for another, a profitable contract for a third. One comes to possess influence and power of a new kind."

"St. Michael is scot and lot, isn't it?" Nicholas remarked. "From what I know of them they're very difficult boroughs to control—and expensive. The costs do not finish when you buy the property, George, they go on and on. People—the voters, such as they are—tend to form themselves into groups and sell themselves to the highest bidder."

"I'm a rich man," said George. "I can afford to indulge myself. This fellow Barwell, who made a fortune in India; he too is prepared to pay for his indulgences. My fortune came from nowhere but the county in which I was born; and I intend to represent that county. There is no more to be said, dear father, there is no more to be said."

"Nor is there," said Nicholas, frowning at the accounts. "I do not for a moment deny your right to spend this money as you please. Indeed I'm in favour of your attempt to get back into Parliament. So long as you know the pitfalls . . ."

"I think so. Sir Christopher Hawkins has made them clear."

"He's selling the properties to you?"

"In part. In other cases he's negotiating the sale."

Cary said: "D'you know that lampoon about Hawkins and his home? It was going the rounds a year or so ago.

> *A large park without any deer,*
> *A large cellar without any beer,*
> *A large house without any cheer,*
> *Sir Christopher Hawkins lives here.*

Cary sniggered.

"Nevertheless we'd do well to keep him as our friend," said Nicholas. "Having quarrelled with the Boscawens—irrevocably, I fear—and being on less amiable terms than hitherto with Basset, Hawkins is a necessary ally in high places."

"I'm bearing that very much in mind," said George.

Further conversation was prevented for a time by a fit of coughing that attacked Nicholas. Cary watched his brother with an eye like a cockerel.

"Have you tried snail tea?" he asked. "When I had

the influenza some bad last winter a year gone and my chest was raw as a brush, it had a soothing effect. That and camphor behind the ears."

George fetched his father a glass of wine, which he sipped. "Upon my soul," Nicholas said, "I never was troubled in all my life with any affection of the bronchia until the time I came to Trenwith, George, when Valentine was born. I caught a chill in that draughty bedroom you gave me, and I truly believe that old witch of a woman, Agatha Poldark, cast some spell upon me there that will not disperse."

"Agatha cast an evil spell on us all," said George sourly. "Even Valentine. If another child is ever born to us I shall make certain the confinement takes place either here or at Cardew."

Nicholas wiped his eyes with a red bandana handkerchief. "Is there something of it in the wind?"

"That was not what I said."

"All the same, boy, one child is scarce enough to make sure of the inheritance. Twould be better—"

"*I* was enough," George said shortly.

"Talking of inheritance," said Cary, playing with the feather of his pen. "You both know, I reckon, that Nat Pearce's illness had developed a putrid tendency and the surgeon gives him no more'n a few weeks to live?"

Nicholas shook his head and sighed. "Old Nat. Is that so? Why, he's barely three years older than I am. I've known him since I was twenty or so. His father was a lawyer before him but died young and Nat inherited the practice almost so soon as he had gone into the business." He dabbed his mouth and coughed again. "Of course in those days he was far too superior for the likes of me. It is all a long way back—before ever we had anything of this—and yet tis not forty years."

"Things've altered in more ways than one," said Cary. "Nowadays I *own* him, Mr. Nathaniel Pearce."

"Much change you'll get," said George. "He's in debt all round."

Cary picked his nose and carefully assayed the

mining samples he had dug up. "Nephew, if you can spend your money one way, buying ramshackle property at big prices in order to put two letters after your name, I too can be extravagant in my own way. I conceit I know more about this town and the doings of its inhabitants than any other man alive; and Mr. Pearce's business I have reason to know particular well. And I can tell you that when Mr. Pearce dies certain persons in this town will be in something of a taking when the details of all his affairs come out."

George narrowed his eyes. "You didn't tell me this. D'you mean he has been using for his own ends some of the monies entrusted to him?"

"That is what I do mean."

"How do you know? Did he tell you? Are the Boscawens involved?"

"Unfortunately I suspicion not. Or to a very small extent. Mr. Curgenven, their steward, keeps too close a watch on all transactions, legal and mercantile. But there are others."

"Can you name them?"

"There is the Aukett trust. When Mrs. Jacqueline Aukett died she left three grandchildren, who were minors, and Mr. Pearce was chosen to administer the trust. Then there's the Trevanion family trust. And there's another bound up with Noakes Peto and the mills he left . . ."

Silence fell. Nicholas's breathing sounded like a kettle just beginning to sing on the hob.

George said: "Uncle Cary, are you being selective? Is it just chance that all the people you mention banked at Pascoe's?"

"Not chance," said Cary. "Not chance. For in these cases Pascoe's Bank, or Pascoe himself, have been a party to the trusts."

Nicholas closed the ledger and drummed on the top of it with his broad fingers.

"You're not supposing, Cary, surely, that there could be any risk in this to Pascoe's Bank itself?"

"I'm not supposing and I'm not *not* supposing. It would depend on what other pressures could be exercised at the appropriate time. Don't forget I have Pascoe's son-in-law in my pocket."

George said: "I know that he still banks with us, but am unaware of the details."

"Soon after he married Pascoe's daughter he told me he had a thought to change banks—first having discharged his debts to us out of his wife's marriage portion. But I talked him out of this. I persuaded him to remain, by playing upon his vanity and his cupidity."

"That may not have been difficult," said George. "But tell us how nevertheless."

"St. John Peter does not really like to be beholden to his father-in-law, whom he tends to despise, as a mere banker, so I suggested to him that I should renew his accommodation bills with us at a very low rate of interest. I told him we were anxious for reasons of prestige to retain his name among our customers. Some fools are vain enough to believe anything. I pointed out to him that the money we could offer him would bear two percent less interest than his new money—his wife's money—would be earning for him in Pascoe's. He would therefore gain by continuing to deal with us and at the same time neither his wife nor his father-in-law would know the extent of his then debts."

"And he accepted that?"

"Being the man he is, why should he not? And since then, doing as he does, the bills have increased in size and number."

"You think long, Cary," George said. "This must have been in your mind for years."

Nicholas Warleggan was still ruminating on his last remark. "Pearce isn't big enough—his affairs aren't big enough—to shake Pascoe's Bank. Pascoe survived the crisis of '96, when we all felt the wind blow. He might have been vulnerable a few years ago; but now he must have big reserves."

"Nobody in banking has big reserves, Father," George said. "Not even us if the cards were called.

But it depends what pretty surprises Cary has up his sleeve."

"Pascoe, Tresize, Annery and Spry," Cary muttered contemptuously, and shuffled his old coat about his shoulders as if it irked him. "That's his reserves. St. Aubyn Tresize has a good name, maybe, money in land, a few wharves in Hayle—but no real *weight*. Frank Annery is a notary with some connections. Spry is a Quaker, and like most Quakers is a warm man. But warm men do not fancy a cold wind."

Outside there was the noisy tramping clatter of hooves and the shout of grooms, as a string of horses was led back to the stables of the Fighting Cocks Inn after their daily exercise.

"What is St. John Peter's indebtedness to us?"

"About twelve thousand pounds."

George said: "What does the fool do with his money?"

"Hunting mainly. He's Master of the Rame Hunt, and keeping up that sort of style is costly. Also he has taken up with some woman with expensive tastes in St. Austell."

Silence fell.

Cary said: "As a matter of interest Ross Poldark has a substantial balance at Pascoe's. Upwards of four thousand pounds last month. Aiming at one bird, we might wing another."

Nicholas said: "I wonder that you know all this, brother."

Preliminary movements at the corners of Cary's mouth suggested that he might have thought of smiling. "Pascoe employs a clerk called Kingsley. He is underpaid and is now able to afford a few small luxuries that he has not enjoyed before."

"I also wonder," said Nicholas, "where all this is going to lead, what the value is of this continuing rancour. We are too big now, have too many interests to need to waste time and money paying off old scores. Yours is the right way, George, to wish to get back into Parliament. That is looking ahead; preparing for the future. A member has many opportunities for advancing his interests. But Pascoe's Bank? Ross Poldark? Do they merit the trouble you may have to take?"

Cary was about to reply but George spoke first. "I know you are the most magnanimous of us, Father, and that is an admirable thing to be. I too can be magnanimous at times, but preferably to my friends. I am a little surprised too in view of what you said just after the election, when Lord Falmouth had treated you in so cavalier a manner and had succeeded in forcing Captain Poldark into Parliament in place of your own dear son."

Nicholas nodded and reached for his stick. "That's so. But it was spoke in the heat of the moment. Perhaps when one has been as ill as I have been this winter one comes to have—different views, different perspectives." He heaved himself up. "No matter. It was but an observation. I'll go and seek your mother out. That is, if she is back from her shopping."

II

Mrs. Nicholas Warleggan was not yet back from her shopping, whither she had been accompanied by Mrs. George Warleggan.

Elizabeth's relationship with her mother-in-law was delicate and not of the easiest, for Mary Warleggan had not grown into her position but had remained the simple countrywoman she had been at the time of her marriage forty years ago. At that time, being the only surviving daughter of a small but substantial miller, she had been marrying beneath her in taking the son of a blacksmith, especially old Luke Warleggan's son, however upstanding and strong he might be and whatever his aspirations. But Nicholas— who never in his life had been called Nick and fought any man or boy who so addressed him—had soon borrowed money on the mill and on the land, and when his father-in-law died had sold it, every stick and stone of it, and had moved with his wife and small son from Idless to put up one of these new foundry places and smelting works beside Carnon Stream. There he had begun importing pig iron from Pentyrch and Dowlais near Cardiff, and wrought iron and faggot iron from Bristol. From these were made the tools necessary to supply the mines and the cottages: screws and nails, grindstones, fire grates, wire, red lead, pig lead, pots and kettles and basins. Thence sprang new ventures, the building of wheels for tin stamps, the manufacture of alloys from local tin and copper, and eventually the erection of complete steam engines for the mines. Learning to find good assistants to whom you paid good wages they could not hope to get elsewhere but from whom you expected the utmost in efficiency, Nicholas had spread his interests about the county, and, as a result of the credit he extended to mines, he found himself drawn into banking. An office opened in Truro soon became the centre of his activities, and Cary, who had been managing the foundry for him, was brought in to superintend their financial operations, and thus found his true mission in life.

So had begun their fortune, and Nicholas's son, inheriting the drive of his father and developing a new and sharper eye for the profitable venture, had so far increased that fortune that, in the fulness of time, Mary Lashbrook, the small miller's daughter, found herself the mistress of a great porticoed mansion seven miles from Truro with thirty bedrooms and five hundred acres of pasture and timber. More embarrassing still was the fact that her only son had chosen to marry this beautiful young impoverished widow whose family had almost the longest pedigree in Cornwall. (There had, indeed, been a terrible moment two years ago at a dinner at Trenwith, to which Nicholas and Mary Warleggan had mercifully not been invited, a dinner given for the great Sir Francis Basset—as he then was—and his lady and some others of the higher aristocracy, when in the course of conversation Basset had observed casually that his family had come over with the Conqueror, and Jonathan Chynoweth, the ineffectual burbling Jonathan, had at once said: "My dear sir, that is hardly a matter for congratulation. I have records of my family for two centuries before the Conquest. We Cornish look on the Normans as usurpers.")

So it was perhaps understandable that common ground between the two Mrs. Warleggans was hard to find. If Mary had ever been able to persuade herself that Elizabeth truly adored George as she did it might have made all the difference. But Elizabeth was too cool, too detached, too patrician to share in the sentiments they would then have shared. You could not discuss George's health with her, or whether he was overworking or if his moods meant that he needed a bilious powder. Valentine was the nearest meeting point, but here again Elizabeth had all the modern mother's fads and did not take too kindly to superstitions that she felt were out of date.

Not that Mary believed there was any real lack of goodwill on Elizabeth's part. For instance this afternoon. Elizabeth could have made an excuse and allowed her to go to Mistress Trelask's alone. Instead they walked together in the misty clammy afternoon, over the cobbles, slipping and tripping here and there, skirts held in hand, among the common folk, some of whom recognised them and curtsied or pulled a forelock. And at Mistress Trelask's Elizabeth was not only useful to Mary in helping her to choose between two paduasoys, but ordered a bonnet herself, and after it was over said:

"You've never met my cousin, have you? My cousin Rowella who married Mr. Solway, the librarian? She is but in the next street. Shall we call on her and persuade her to give us tea?"

So up they went, Mrs. Warleggan knowing well how Rowella had married far beneath her, and secretly admiring Elizabeth for not being ashamed of the fact. So they came to the door: it was one of six small houses in a terrace, poorly built, the thatches in need of repair, the window frames crooked, the brick mouldering already; and out of the door as they approached it came a thickset fashionably dressed, plump-faced young man whom a stranger would only just have recognised as a clergyman.

"Why, Osborne," said Elizabeth. "Is Rowella in? We were about to call."

Chapter Six

Ross had seen Dwight and Caroline several times and had seen and admired little Sarah, who indeed was little, and pale, but intelligent and alert. Caroline said nature was compensating for so tall a mother by giving her a pygmy. Dwight said he would wager that Caroline at four months old had been no bigger, and scarcely so good-natured. Caroline replied: "There you are wrong, Dr. Enys, it is only since marriage that my nature has changed for the worse." But, in so far as one could perceive her true feelings behind the defensive flippancy, she seemed happy in her motherhood and spent much time with the child, neglecting, as she said, "horses and other more important matters."

Dwight was none too well but drove himself relentlessly in his care for his patients. Sometimes it was not his health so much as his spirits that seemed down, and, on the first occasion Ross had a word alone with him, he tackled him on the subject.

Dwight said, "Caroline taxes me too. She accuses me of being a born pessimist, which is not true; but I think it is a necessity in my profession to foresee the way in which an illness might develop, and, if possible, to try to prevent an outcome that is bad. If I know that a child with measles may develop pneumonia, as many do, and die of it, am I a pessimist to recommend that the child be treated in a way best calculated to avoid this?"

They were riding back from Truro together, having met by chance half a mile out. Dwight had been to inspect progress on the building of the new Miners' Hospital which was now in course of construction near the town; Ross was returning from a meal with his friend and banker, Harris Pascoe, where as usual they had tried to solve the world's problems.

"Financially," Pascoe had said, "England is better off . . . or the government at least is better off, than it was a year ago. These great gifts from the nobility and the business houses towards the prosecution of the war! The Duke of Marlborough five thousand pounds. The City of London ten thousand pounds. And three m-mercantile houses in Manchester— three only!—to subscribe thirty-five thousand pounds. Voluntary subscriptions already total one and a half million. It eases Pitt's burden."

"He looked ill when he spoke last in the House."

"I believe his romance has f-foundered. He hoped to marry Miss Eden but the matter has gone awry. Some say he was so short of money that he lacked the courage to put the question. Well . . . sometimes integrity can exact too high a price. A man who has been first minister of this country for so many years . . ."

"Ireland is a terrible trouble," Ross said. "What a story! Persecution, insurrection, conspiracy, betrayal. There's no end to it."

"And in the meantime I wonder where General Buonaparte has gone."

"To the east probably."

"But where east? Egypt?"

"It is possible. He must have his eyes on India."

"Ross, are you sorry you have chosen to represent Truro?"

Ross frowned. "Not sorry. Not yet. But—restive."

"Have you ever been anything else?"

"Well . . . the needs of mankind are so great, the process of satisfying them so slow. I mean, of course, the fundamental needs—even while we are fighting a war for our very existence. The days are ending, I think, Harris, when nation fought nation without involving the mass of the people. Now, especially since Carnot, war is a word which involves everyone. England, all of us, are fighting France, all of them, so it is more than ever important that the poor and the dispossessed should feel they are no longer forgotten and unregarded. They are just as much a part of England as the noblemen and the mercantile houses."

Harris looked at the colour of the wine in his glass. "Produce of France," he said. "Once we saw them as a nation of benighted papists. Now we see them as revolutionary atheists. I wonder at heart how far they are different from us. Were you able to obtain any silver change in Truro this morning?"

"None. None at all."

"People have started hoarding it. One cannot keep pace. Have you seen these—Spanish dollars, taken as prizes, reissued at the Mint with our own King's head stamped over the other?"

"They offered me such but I refused."

"No need. They are legal tender. At four shillings and ninepence each. But I suspect they will disappear like all the rest. Do you suppose your mine will dry up in its riches as quickly as it began?"

Ross smiled. "I see you keep well informed. We shall be rich for a year or two yet, and maybe much longer. The north is a keenly lode and hardly yet explored. I've also ordered a resumption of work in the direction of Wheal Maiden."

"You have a l-large balance with us at the moment, Ross: close on four thousand pounds. Have you thought of putting some away in Consols? They were back to seventy-one last week."

"It's an agreeable feeling to have it all readily available in your bank. I'm looking for something else in which I can take an interest, like Blewett's shipyard at Looe; like the Daniell furnaces. The more I spread my interests, the more insulated I am against the vagaries of Wheal Grace."

"Now that you are a member of Parliament your name will carry weight. Oh, don't pull a face, it's true whether you like it or not. There will be men looking to add your name to theirs in many enterprises."

Ross said: "I shall be like a rich heiress—suspecting the intentions of my suitors. . . . Seriously, Harris, is all well with my cousin?"

"Who? St. John Peter?" Pascoe shrugged. "He leads my daughter a dance."

"The young fool. I'd like to knock his head in. What can one do with such people?"

"Wait perhaps until they grow into old fools. Joan says very little, but one hears reports."

"Does he still bank with the Warleggans?"

"Yes. But he has hardly touched Joan's money. He must have some personal arrangement with them. I don't know of its nature."

Ross grunted in some discomfort. "I wish I had influence with him. But sweet reason has never been his strong point. I wonder about his father, whether I might have a word with him."

"I don't think it would have any good outcome. St. John always speaks of his father in the most disrespectful terms."

Ross grunted again, and silence fell. "Talking of the Warleggans . . ."

"Were we?"

"In a fashion. Happily I have seen nothing of George as yet. I suppose he is in Truro?"

"Oh, yes. They all are. George, I believe, is in the process of buying himself back into Parliament."

"The devil . . . With Basset's help?"

"No, no. George has been buying burgage property in St. Michael from Sir Christopher Hawkins. I have no details, but I gather a substantial number of properties are likely to change hands."

"That may give him an interest in a borough, but surely there are sitting members?"

"Yes; a man called Wilbraham, and a Captain

Howell. Warleggan hopes no doubt to persuade one or the other of them to resign. It's not impossible if the money is right."

Ross stretched his legs. "I must go, Harris. Why will you never come to see us? It is the same distance either way."

"I have to be here most days," said Pascoe. "None of my partners is active, and I had hoped, as you know, that Joan's husband might have come in in an active capacity, but, as you also know, he looks on banking as usury and will have no part of it."

They went downstairs. The bank was busy with market-day customers. Pascoe opened the side door.

"George," said Ross, bending his head to go through. "Could he not find less expensive ways of gaining a seat?"

"Oh, yes. But what he hopes no doubt in the end is to control both seats at St. Michael. Then, who knows, he might spread his fingers further. With seats to put at the government's disposal, he would be in a strong position to ask for favours in return. While Pitt is so scrupulous in his personal life, he has no hesitation in buying support for his policies."

"Say no more," Ross commented. "I have a queasy stomach."

II

So it came that he met Dwight and they jogged home together in the wind and an occasional flurry of mist. June had been a damp month. The sun had got permanently lost in a south-westerly air current that blew before it unending canopies of cloud. Demelza had wanted to know where it all came from. Did somebody manufacture it, she asked, just over the horizon?

So perhaps in this tiring weather it was not surprising that Dwight should seem quieter even than usual, more withdrawn. Ross minded it not at all: the soft air was so fresh after the stinks of London. He needed sun for his hay and drier winds to keep the blight off his potatoes, but he was not in a mood to complain of that.

Presently Dwight said: "All is well between you and Demelza now?"

"What? Should it not be?"

"Well, Ross, I am your closest friend, aside from being your doctor, so I ventured to ask, knowing there had been—a few difficult times last year. It's not my wish to intrude."

Ross checked his horse. "If by difficult times you mean Demelza's passion for Lieutenant Armitage, then, yes, I grant you, they were difficult. What do you do about a young man, a brave one, in many ways an admirable one, but sick—and as it turned out mortal sick—who attempts—and succeeds or fails, I know not—to make a cuckold of you? And what do you do about a wife whose loyalty has hitherto been absolute, and you see her like a sapling blown in a hurricane, bowing to the ground, perhaps uprooted by it?"

"Oh . . . I'm not sure if—"

"But perhaps you know more than I? Caroline was Demelza's only confidante."

Dwight smiled and pulled his hat on more firmly. "We are all very close to each other, Ross. It is a very peculiar relationship. Sometimes I think you know Caroline better than I do. In that case, do you suppose for one moment that any confidence Demelza made to her would *ever* be passed on to me?"

Ross nodded. ". . . You have to face the fact, Dwight, that a jealous man is a suspicious one."

"Armitage is dead. Whatever it was, however little or however great, it is over. There can be nothing now. Hold what you've got, Ross. You're so lucky. Above all forget. If you let it fester . . ."

"D'you know, in spite of everything—for many people think we are the most devoted couple—my relationship with Demelza has never been anything but a fiery one. In eleven years we have survived a number of storms—most of them, perhaps, of my making. Now we must try to survive one of hers."

"Which is always harder."

"To be sinned against rather than sinning? Of course. Put in those terms it makes me ashamed. But you are not dealing always with the rational emotions. Feelings spring from the depths of one's entrails—to master those when they come needs a control, an iron control, of one's tongue, one's eyes, one's very thoughts . . ."

They were near now where their roads separated, Dwight to fork left towards the declivity in which stood John Jonas's Mill, with four cottages on the rise beyond and the finger of a worked-out mine pointing to the sky; thence a mile of moorland to Killewarren; Ross straight on to Bargus Crosslanes and past it to Grambler and Nampara.

Ross said: "We are talking of my problems, Dwight. I think we have not yet dealt fully with yours."

"Why d'you say that?"

"You said, 'You're so lucky.' While acknowledging it as the truth I sense some extra meaning."

"Oh, I think I meant as compared with the most of my patients that I see, rich and poor. They're a sorry lot and make me feel health is the first condition of life. Without it—nothing."

"Well, I assume since they are your patients they are likely to be ailing to call you in. I confess I meet a number of healthy people about. Of course it is a prime essential; and those who have it don't appreciate it until it is lost. But this seems to have a personal implication. Hasn't it? You've told me you're not unwell yourself. There's a darkness of spirit in you, Dwight."

They had both checked their horses at the fork in the path. Ross's Sheridan was restless and anxious to be home.

Dwight said: "Sometimes perhaps we can talk of it."

"I have no appointment. Let us get down for a minute. Is there some way I can help?"

"No . . ." Dwight patted his horse's neck. "There's

no need to get down. It can be said in a few words, if you wish it. Sarah will not live."

Ross stared at him. *"What?"*

"Have you observed that the child has a slight bluish tinge to the lips? It is little noticeable but, being a surgeon as well as a father, I noticed it. She has been born with a congenital defect of the heart. A murmuration. Perhaps even a perforation—that I don't know —one cannot be sure."

"My *God,*" said Ross. "My God. My God!"

Dwight narrowed his eyes and stared at the colourless day. "When one sees, as I do, hundreds of children brought into the world in poverty and squalor and deprivation, many of them attended by some clumsy midwife who mishandles the mother, bites the cord with her teeth, and gives the child a drop of gin to keep it quiet, and they all, or almost all, in the first place, in the first months of life, whatever happens later, they almost all are perfect in every way, it is very strange to contemplate the paradox of a rich child, attended by her own father and brought up with all the care and attention of a princess, that such a child should be flawed, and flawed in a way it is beyond the skill of man to cure."

It was a long speech, and it came out so quickly that Ross realised his friend had had these words, or similar, in his mind night and day over the past months.

"Dwight, I don't know what to say. I suppose . . . Caroline doesn't know?"

"No. I can't tell her. I have thought of every way. Of trying to break the news gently—even of writing. It's *impossible.* It must take its course."

Ross caught at his reins harshly to keep Sheridan quiet. The horse shook its head and a drip of foam fell from its mouth.

Dwight said: "You mustn't tell Demelza. Not that *she* would say anything, but she could not keep it out of her face."

"Dwight, this is the worst thing that has happened to us—to us as a quartet—since Julia died. But forgive me—my knowledge of medicine is limited to a few crude facts. Can you be so sure?"

"Yes—unhappily. At least, nothing is certain in this life, but there is hardly anything could be more certain. I have seen it a half dozen times all told—as it happens, more often when I was a student in London. The complaint is readily detectable. One puts one's ear to the child's chest. The normal heart beat is a gentle *thump-thump*. Sarah's heart goes *hush-hush*."

"Let me ride a way with you, Dwight."

"If you wish. But not as far as Killewarren, or Caroline will wonder you don't come in. And your face at the moment would betray you."

Ross wiped his gauntlet glove across his nose, and they moved off slowly in the direction of Jonas's Mill. Sheridan was difficult to turn away from home.

After a while Ross said: "But she seems—bright, alert, in every way well. Is there nothing else to show?"

"Not yet. There may not be. It is simply a question, Ross, of waiting for the first infection. Whether it comes this year or next, her heart will not have the resources to meet it."

Chapter Seven

In July, Drake Carne had two visitors, one regular and expected, the other irregular and unexpected. The first was his brother Sam, whom God had chosen— and Sam felt this in all humility—to help to draw lost souls nearer to the gates of Paradise. He had received again and again the impress of the Seal and the earnest of the Spirit in his heart, beholding, as in a glass, the glory of Christ. Yet humbly witnessing, never claiming for himself more than he could offer to others. Employed as a tutworker at Wheal Grace, he spent every leisure moment either in class or in prayer with his fellow Wesleyans or helping in some practical fashion with the problems of the poor and the sick in Grambler and Sawle. As a stranger to the district, having come from Illuggan little more than four years ago, he had been regarded with suspicion at first, and with not a little hostility from those who were not of his religious persuasion. But good works had worn the resistance down and he was now about as popular as any man who didn't drink in the kiddleys could be.

Sam visited his brother twice weekly, though, as his commitments ever grew, the visits tended to become shorter. He had twice refused Drake's offer of a partnership in the blacksmith's shop, saying that his call lay elsewhere.

On this Tuesday Sam stayed longer than usual, helping Drake fix the shafts into a cart. When they were almost done he said: "Brother, it pleasures me to hear tell you are going with a young woman again."

"Give me another heave," said Drake. "Now, if you'll hold 'n steady while I drive in another nail." This was done. "Rosina Hoblyn, you d'mean? I've seen her thrice—and all but once by accident. Tis oversaying it to say I'm going with she."

"Well . . . it is not for me to direct ee, Drake; though I will say I would gain pleasure to see you wed to a fitty young woman. Tis hardly natural to spend all your life alone. You know how I've grieved that you've not come back fully into the Society; but I know too how you've suffered these last three year gone, and twould raise my heart just to feel you was making the first steps to climb out of the pit."

Drake stood back and frowned at the cart. "Tis level or not level, brother?"

"Tis level."

"This side? You think this side too?"

"Aye . . . Drake, you're still some young, yet already you're in a good style of trade. Day after day, month after month, you've risen early, wreaked late and eaten the bread of carefulness. It is not in you to seek riches, but modest riches will come your way. To what end, brother? I ask myself, and you must ask yourself, to what end?"

"That is what I never do ask myself," said Drake.

"Not yet. For you have been sore stricken. But in time the sorest wounds must heal."

"Must they?" said Drake.

"I ask your pardon, brother, if I tread on delicate ground. But if I do, ye must know tis out of love and affection that I do. There comes a time I d'b'lieve when tis necessary to look about the world and see what tis your duty to do. Not your inclination, maybe, but your duty. For looking to help others is the best way of looking to save yourself. If now—if now you became convinced through prayer that twas your Christian duty to alter your condition in life by exchanging the state of a single for that of a married man, then I would say there are few young women who would be more comfortable to you than Rosina Hoblyn."

"You would, eh?" said Drake.

Sam eyed his brother. Although a man still of slim build, the years at the forge had given Drake great physical strength. His were the sort of muscles that hardly showed except when they were being used. They were being used now when he lifted the end of the cart bodily onto a low trestle and began to knock out the wheel pin.

Drake said: "You think I'd make Rosina a comfortable husband if I didn't love her?"

"Love might come, brother. If you shared in the love and worship of Christ, love *would* come. Then if your marriage was blessed with the precious fruits of little children, your soul would become like a watered garden and you would know the truest fulfilment of life."

"And Morwenna?" said Drake.

There was silence. It was a name never mentioned by either of them. The silence was shattered by a single blow of the hammer, and the pin fell to the floor. Drake began to lever off the wheel.

"Morwenna is wed," said Sam.

"That I d'know all too well."

"And is a vicar's wife and has a child of her own . . ."

"And is in hell."

"Drake, ye cannot know this."

"I know this. Would ye, then, brother, counsel me to find my own heaven and leave her in hell?"

"Ye can do no other. It is grieving, Drake, over what cann't be undone. You are bespoiling your life, grieving, grieving, grieving . . ."

"Oh," said Drake. "Sometimes I forget." He put the wheel down and sighed. "Tis shameful to me now how oft I forget. No ache, no misery lasts for ever. But to take another *woman*. That would be more shameful still, and twould not be fair on Rosina. I could never bring to her a full heart."

"Perhaps you would—in time."

"And in the meantime what do I say to she? That I would wed her for a convenience, that I need someone to keep my home and breed my children? Is that what I should say?"

Sam bent to retie his boot. "Perhaps I shouldn't've spoke. Perhaps twas better not to have asked. But I have a concern for ee, brother, and I want the scales to fall from your eyes, the gall of bitterness to be eased and sweetened. For if Christ wills, ye have a long life to live."

As Drake passed by he touched his brother's shoulder. "Leave me be yet a little, Sam. If I have a long life to live, then leave me be a little yet."

It was one of the few fine days of a second damp month of summer, and old Pally Rogers, his spade beard grizzled in the wind and the sun, rattled down the hill in his cart, raising a hand of greeting as he passed by.

Drake said: "It seem me many folk d'live their lives without any of the trouble that come to we. What of yourself, Sam? You have all this concern for my misfortune, but what of your own?"

"My own?"

"Well, what of Emma Tregirls. Now she've left the

Choakes and gone Tehidy—miles away. Are you not just the same as me?"

Sam nodded. "Yes, brother. We both have a soreness of the heart. But mine is balmed by the grace of the Holy Spirit. Nightly I pray for Emma. Nightly I pray that she may see and discover the bond of iniquity by which she is enslaved. If that d'happen, then there shall be double rejoicing; rejoicing for a spirit which has obtained an interest in the blood of Christ, and rejoicing that so splendid a human being, while changed from glory to glory by the spirit of the Lord, shall also come to me as my wife, and that we shall cleave and be as one flesh and discover together the liberty of perfect love, carnal and eternal."

It was Drake's turn to look at his brother, the tall fair-haired man with the lined young face, the kind, intent blue eyes, the shambling walk. Sometimes, Drake thought, Sam's sentiments came out just a little too smooth as if from a sermon he'd prepared. But he knew this not to be so: if the words came a bit too easy, this was from constant teaching of the Bible to his classes; Sam spoke them from the deepest convictions of his heart.

"And you're happy 'bout that, 'bout leaving Emma go?"

"I have faith," said Sam.

"Faith that she'll come back?"

A shadow crossed Sam's face. "I didn't leave her go. She went and I could not stay her. I would have wed her whether or no but she wouldn't come to me, she said, unsaved and she wouldn't—or couldn't—find salvation. I have faith that Jesus will order my life—and hers—in such a way as may be best to further His will."

Jack Trewinnard came skidding into the yard with a bucket in one hand and a hoe in the other. When he saw Drake had company he hastily wiped his nose on his sleeve and went out through the stable.

Drake said: "Well, brother, I reckon there is little to be said on either side, is there? I know Demelza feels as you do about Rosina, for twas she in the

first place who contrived that we should meet. Rosina,
I grant you, is a goodly person, neat and clean and
of a nice presence, and she would do her most for any
man she was wed to. And I have some taking for
her as a person. She's—kind. And pretty. But . . . it
must all wait a while. It is—too soon. If there ever
could be anything it is too soon. You must give me
leave to live my own life, Sam. Twill be better for all
concerned."

II

Drake Carne's second and more unexpected visitor
came right at the end of July. Drake had been out to
get a basket of fish from Sawle and had left the young
Trewinnards in charge, and he did not at first recognise
either the thoroughbred grey horse or the tall handsome young man chatting to his two assistants. The
young man turned and saw Drake and let out a shout.
It was Geoffrey Charles Poldark, fresh home from
Harrow.

They had not met last year at all. Elizabeth and
George had arranged that Geoffrey Charles should
spend the summer holidays in Norfolk, and at Christmas the weather had been so bad that the Warleggans
had not come out to Trenwith. In the interval a charming, untidy, impulsive boy had, but the influence of
schooling and the alchemy of adolescence, been transformed into a pale, carefully dressed, languid young
man.

They shook hands, and then Geoffrey Charles put
his hands on Drake's shoulders and gazed at him quiz-
zically.

"Well, by God, so you are here just as I left you,
as if I'd scarce turned my back. And who are these
little urchins? More brothers of yours?" Apart from his
turn of speech his voice was quite different: it had completely broken and only squeaked occasionally on a
higher note.

"Geoffrey Charles. But you're some changed! I

scarce would've known you. Back for some time, are ee? Well, tis real good to see ee after all this while!"

"We came last night, Mother and I. Uncle George is wrestling with some property acquisition and thinks to join us next week. So you are prospering? Damn me, I can see you are."

They talked for a while, Drake standing, Geoffrey Charles sitting on the low wall, elegant leg idly swinging. There was constraint between them such as there had not been before. Two years ago they seemed to share the same enthusiasms, now they had nothing in common.

Presently Geoffrey Charles said: "What is amiss with your eyebrow, Drake? It looks like the Greek letter zeta lying on its side. . . . Is this from the wrestling match I hear you had with Tom Harry?"

"No, that was my brother Sam," Drake said.

"What, the Methody? Does he wrestle, then? I wish I'd seen it. I'd like to see Tom Harry taken down a peg."

"Sam lost."

"*Did* he? And did you lose too?"

"In a manner of speaking. I was set on by three of them."

"Three of our men?"

"Twas hard to be sure."

Geoffrey Charles stared at his friend and his leg stopped swinging.

"Tell me, Drake. I'm your friend."

"I'll not involve you in nothing."

"I know . . . you did it once, and once is too often. Well . . . a nod and a wink, as they say. I'm a little short of authority yet, Drake. Servants at Trenwith don't yet flinch at my footsteps. But I will be able to make Master Harry's life a shade unpleasant for him from time to time, I rather believe. It will be a little contribution to the cause of friendship."

"Tis over and done long since," Drake said. "I've not seen sight nor sound of any of them for pretty many a day. It should all be forgot. Let's talk of other things. Your school . . . Your new friends . . ."

"My school." Geoffrey Charles yawned. "It is a decent enough sort of a place now that I am become used to it and now I'm no longer a fag. One does not need to work very hard except to pick up a little Latin and Greek by the way. My tutor for the first year was a noted flog-bottomist and brandy drinker called Harvey. 'Come forth, sir,' he would bellow, 'and let thy breeches down!' I suffered notably under him; but now I have a cheerful old buffer of forty-odd who cares little for my welfare so long as I do not interfere with his. When I go back I shall have a fag of my own."

Drake picked up his basket of fish, which was attracting the flies, and carried it into the house. When he came out again his visitor had not moved but was picking at a fancied spot on his green velvet riding jacket.

"And," he said without looking up, "next term I shall take a mistress."

Drake stared. "Please?"

Geoffrey Charles saw the expression on Drake's face and burst into a broken-voiced laugh. "You know what I mean?"

"I'm not sure as I do."

"A mistress. A woman. A girl. It is about time."

Drake said woodenly: "I hoped as you didn't mean that."

"Why not? It's—part of life. And, I'm told, a not unpleasant part. Have you ever had a woman, Drake?"

"No."

Geoffrey Charles slid off the wall and patted his friend's arm. "I ask your pardon. I suspect good taste is not part of our curriculum . . . But as for myself . . . Well, it may not be next term, but soon, I hope. I shall look around. Quite a number of the older fellows at the school have their little *amours*. And it is a tradition in our family to be blooded at an early age. . . . I see I have offended you."

"I'm not my brother's keeper."

"Well said, by God! And now we must change the subject again, eh? But to what? I hear that Uncle Ross condiddled Stepfather George out of his parliamentary seat, and Stepfather George will never forgive them for it."

"Them?"

"Him and Aunt Demelza."

"What had Demelza to do with it?"

"Well, I only overheard my stepfather talking once about it, but he seems to think—or has got it into his wooden head—that this agreement between Lord Falmouth and Lord de Dunstanville was reached through some intermediary role played by Aunt Demelza. I cannot imagine how. I didn't know she even knew either of them!"

"They were visiting last year. But I cann't suppose how she could have had any influence with two such great personages."

"Well . . . Uncle George believes what he wants to believe. Anyway, tomorrow, before he comes, I shall ride over to Nampara to see them all. I hardly know my two young cousins—or whatever they are. Second cousins, is it?"

Drake had been hesitating over the question for some time, but now it had to come out. "And Morwenna? Did you see her?"

"Briefly. After London, Truro seems more than a trifle provincial, and I was at pains to come out to the sea so soon as ever I could prod Mother into moving. She—Morwenna—seemed . . . well. Better than last time. But she was busy entertaining some rural dean whom Mr. Whitworth had invited."

There was silence. Drake bit his lips. "The—her baby . . . he is well?"

"Oh, yes, a monster. He is going to be as big as his father. And he greatly lacks discipline. Mr. Whitworth is a martinet with everyone else, but his son can do no wrong in his eyes, and soon, I suspect, will rule the roost." Geoffrey Charles picked at the spot on his coat again. "I tried to get a word alone with Morwenna but it was not possible. I'm sorry."

"No . . . Perhaps tis just as well." Drake looked across at Geoffrey Charles's raised eyebrows. "What is the good of trying to prolong something which is long since over? She have her own life to lead, and a busy one tis, as I well d'know. She's settled, married, a vicar's wife, a mother. There's naught but more sorrow in trying to keep alight the old memories. She wouldn't thank ee to try to do it and I mustn't *want* ee to do it. I've got my own life here and—and I must think on that. What's past is past, Geoffrey Charles, bitter bitter though that may be."

Geoffrey Charles watched one of the Trewinnards wheeling in a barrow of kindling wood. "How d'you tell t'other from which of those two?"

"Jack have a scar on his hand and another on his knee."

"So that if they both put their heads up over a wall you could not tell?"

"It don't matter. If I call for one they both come running."

"Drake, it is good to hear you say this about Morwenna. Now I'm a trifle older I can see how much you were—committed in those days—especially during that long dark winter. D'you remember those primroses you used to bring? But it's gone. All that time is gone. You do well to speak as you have done."

Drake nodded. "But we're on a dark subject again. Tell me more 'bout yourself and 'bout London. How long will ee be at Trenwith, do ee think?"

"Till mid-September, I'd suppose. So you'll be seeing more of me."

Drake said: "I cann't be like your school friends, Geoffrey Charles. Tis not in me to—to talk of women the way you do. I think mebbe you have grown out of my world. After all, I'm Methody too, though much lesser so than Sam. I'm here working at my forge—a tradesman making a way for himself. But you are the young gentleman—the next squire—off to school in London and then no doubt to Oxford or Cambridge or such like. You'll meet many other gentlefolk and many fine young men with ideas fitted to their station. I'm not of that world, nor never shall be."

Geoffrey Charles nodded. "Agreed. Damn me, I

agree with every word you say. My horse is restive, so I must be off. You are right, Drake. By God, you are right. We should be total strangers. But all my life, Drake, I hope to belong to two worlds—the world of eminence and fashion, if it will accept me—and, ecod, if I can afford it! The world of beaus and macaronis and saucy girls and *willing* ones; and a little gaming here and there, and a little drinking and a little loving . . . But also, also, by God, I belong to this blasted acreage on which my ancestors built Trenwith several hundred years ago; and this world includes St. Ann's and Grambler and tottering Sawle Church and grumbling Jud Paynter and preaching Sam Carne and one-armed Tholly Tregirls and doe-eyed Beth Nanfan the daughter of Char Nanfan, and others and others and others. But among them all, the one from whom I demand the most unremitting friendship and trust is blacksmith Carne of Pally's Shop, in the valley below St. Ann's. So there you are. You must take it or leave it. What do you say?"

He hopped on the wall and mounted his grey, and half unhooked the reins but stayed a moment to see what effect this long speech had had on Drake. Drake did not say anything but reached up his hand and the two hands were clasped for a moment. Then Geoffrey Charles uttered his broken, half-masculine laugh and went off up the valley.

III

At about the time of this meeting Dwight received a letter. It was signed Daniel Behenna and Dwight stared at it in surprise. Although they were only on rare occasions rivals, Dwight having at his wife's request confined his practice to the country districts round their home, the approach of these two medical men to their joint profession could hardly have been more different, and their contacts at any time had been little more than icily polite.

Sir [said the letter],

You will no doubt recall the occasion two years ago when for a period you attended a patient of mine, Mrs. Morwenna Whitworth, the wife of the vicar of St. Margaret's, Truro. At that time she was suffering from the ill-effects of a prolonged and difficult parturition. Later, as you will remember, the Whitworths dispensed with your services and recalled me.

Mrs. Whitworth is again now ill, but this appears to be a condition of considerable mental disequilibrium, on which I would consider your opinion to be of value. Few of us can begin to plumb those influences of an atmospheric, cosmic or telluric nature which affect the human brain, and I would only say to you that if we could consult together on the symptoms which this unfortunate woman now evidences there might be a happier outcome for her than otherwise appears possible.

I have the honour to be, sir,

> *Your obt. servant*
> *Daniel Behenna*

It was an odd letter, Dwight thought. Not Behenna's natural style—unless his natural style was to write letters out of keeping with his character. It was indefinite —the one failing Dr. Behenna never betrayed—and it seemed—perhaps only seemed—to ask for help.

Dwight replied:

Sir,

I have the favour of your letter of the 18th. I shall be pleased to attend to this patient, in a consultative capacity, and I shall be privileged to discuss her condition with you, both before and after my visit. The one stipulation I would make is that when I see Mrs. Whitworth it shall be alone.

If you are able to agree to this, will you kindly

arrange a time and date and I will endeavour to meet it.

I am, sir, your obt. servant,

Dwight Enys

He rode over a week on the following Wednesday, met Dr. Behenna in the vicar's study, where ten minutes of stiff conversation appraised him of the facts; then he was taken to the upstairs parlour where Mrs. Whitworth was waiting to receive him.

This she did as a dear friend, tears welling in her eyes but not falling as she took both his hands, smiled briefly but brilliantly as she sometimes could, and then indicated the chair in which he might sit while they talked.

They talked for forty minutes. Once Morwenna burst into tears but rapidly stayed them, apologised and blew her nose and turned to him, ready for the next question. He found her more vehement than she had ever been before, and at times her eyes were wild and straying. But she replied to all his questions, even those designed to catch her, with quickness and certainty. When there was nothing more to ask Dwight made an examination, felt her pulse, sounded her heart and chest back and front, pulled back her eyelids, felt the grip of each hand, the thrust of each foot, stared at her fingernails, her scalp, the veins and tendons at the back and front of her neck. Then he shook her gravely by the hand, putting his other hand over hers, picked up his bag and left.

In the downstairs parlour his colleague and the vicar were waiting for him. This was a very trying occasion for Mr. Whitworth. His dislike of Dwight Enys was deep-rooted, and had only been too solidly confirmed when he had attended upon Morwenna before. It had been a great relief when for reasons of his own health Dr. Enys had stopped visiting patients as far from his own home as Truro. Ossie had hoped never to see him again, certainly not inside his own house and pronouncing a medical opinion upon his wife. Ossie was very annoyed with Behenna, and had not yet preached his sermon in praise of physicians. Behenna had seen Morwenna three times for which obviously he would charge—without committing himself to a final opinion either way. He fully saw and understood the gravamen of Mr. Whitworth's complaint; he admitted that Mrs. Whitworth was in a very unstable state of mind; but he said he felt himself unfitted to write such a definitive letter as Ossie wanted him to write without the confirmatory opinion of another surgeon.

This was nonsense in Osborne's opinion, coming from the self-opinionated man it did, and the name of the doctor who should be invited to endorse that opinion was so distasteful that the vicar almost threw the whole idea overboard. Only his feeling as to the rightness and justice of his cause made him persist.

So now it had come to this: two surgeons and a husband gravely standing among the tall clerical furniture discussing the mental condition of the tall dark distressed girl in the room above.

Dwight said: "Dr. Behenna, Mr. Whitworth, since you are both here I assume you'd wish me to address you both. I have examined Mrs. Whitworth and talked with her. I would have preferred to have spent longer, but I don't suppose this would in any substantial way have affected the outcome. I find your wife, Mr. Whitworth, in a very nervous, highly emotional and uneasy condition. She is quite clearly suffering from prolonged strain, and I would not like to predict that at some future time she could not become—at least emotionally unstable. But to me she seems—at this present—entirely sane. I have done my best in the short time at my disposal to discover any symptoms of hallucination, catalepsy, *folie circulaire,* morbid melancholia, inhibitory mania, inability to concentrate, or other indication that she is losing her reason. I have found none."

The only sound in the room was Ossie's heavy breathing. "And is that all you have to say?"

"No. Not all. In my opinion she is in better physical health now than she was two years ago. Physical, that is. But quite clearly, Vicar, you have a wife who suffers from certain neuroses, and in that sense must be regarded as delicate. Possibly she always will be. I cannot say. But clearly she needs—care ... kindness ... consideration ..."

"Are you suggesting she does not receive this?"

"I'm suggesting nothing. The fact that she is in better physical health than two years ago may imply that your care for her welfare is not all in vain."

Dr. Behenna took out his handkerchief and blew his nose.

Ossie said: "And what of her threats to murder our son?"

Dwight stared out on the garden, where the trees hung heavy over the river.

"She has never made any move to hurt him?"

"Did she deny she had made these threats?"

"No ..."

"Well, then!" Ossie said.

"I appreciate your dilemma, Mr. Whitworth, and I sympathise with it. But do you not think this is the sort of threat she would be unlikely ever to carry out?"

"How do I know? The very existence of this threat is proof enough to me that she is insane, that in fact she is an evil woman. I would remind you, as I reminded Dr. Behenna, that the Church looks on insanity as God's judgment upon the wicked. Christ rebuked the unclean spirits and drove them out. No good man or woman should be prone to such a visitation."

Dwight said: "I'm not in a position to argue theology with you, Mr. Whitworth, but I'd remind you that that theory has recently been much shaken by the illness of the King and his becoming mentally distressed to the point of being put in a straitjacket. From this I understand he has now happily recovered. But I believe it would be considered a treasonable doctrine to argue that the King's insanity had been brought on him by his own evil ways."

Ossie swelled in the silence.

Behenna, feeling that his own future as family doctor to the Whitworths was at risk, said: "The problem, Dr. Enys, as you no doubt know is that Mrs. Whitworth is refusing Mr. Whitworth the exercise of his proper conjugal rights by uttering this threat every time he attempts to claim them. Neither legally nor morally has she any sort of excuse to do this. They are bound together as man and wife by the sacrament of the Church. No man shall put them asunder. And no wife can deny her husband what she has promised him at the time of their marriage."

Ossie licked his lips. "Exactly!"

Dwight glanced at him and his glance was not polite.

Ossie said: "You use these words, these *words*—neuroses and the rest. Can you suppose I am not suffering at the same time? It is against the will of God that such a situation should continue!"

Behenna said: "I must agree with you on that, sir."

Dwight said: "Dr. Behenna, I don't deny the problem. Nor would I attempt to minimise it. But is this a problem that we can take any professional steps to solve? We are asked if we will write a letter confirming Mr. Whitworth's view that his wife is *non compos mentis* and may therefore be put away. My answer is no, as yours surely must be. Though overstrung, Mrs. Whitworth is as sane as most women I attend daily—and altogether more charming. It is not our province to pronounce upon the success or failure of a marriage —thank God, for I see many in disarray. Sir," he said to Ossie, "I can't help you. Nor would I if I could in this respect. Perhaps I come of a different persuasion, but my view is that if a husband cannot win his wife by kindness, sympathy, little attentions, and a show of love, then he should go without her. If that is not your view, then I cannot alter it. But it is a dilemma that you must solve yourself."

He picked up his bag and inclined his head at the two other men. "I see that my horse is waiting, so I'll not keep him any longer."

He left. Dr. Behenna left five minutes later. Mr. Whitworth never preached his sermon on the excellence and worthiness of physicians.

IV

At about this time, unknown to the people of Cornwall, but more important to their destinies than the Ross Poldarks or even the Lord de Dunstanvilles of their world, two men were active in the Mediterranean. One of them, a French general, had just led his troops to land at Alexandria, had taken the city, routed the Mamelukes, and was now master of Cairo. A small man in a badly fitting and ill-kept uniform, with hair falling thinly and untidily across his brow as if he had just been wakened from sleep, a man with a powerful bony nose, a fierce mouth and piercing eyes, whose sallow complexion was more often than not disfigured with a skin complaint and whose French accent was markedly Corsican; a man whom his army adored and would follow to the ends of the earth. The other was an English admiral, a man of frail and sickly constitution, with lank sandy hair turning grey, who had lost an eye four years ago and an arm last year, who now had to have his food cut up for him and frequently waved the stump of his arm about when excited or angry, who had just after numerous mishaps and misdirections arrived back in the vicinity of Alexandria for the second time, to observe the masts of the French fleet at the mouth of the Nile in the roadstead alongside the island of Abukir; a man whom his shipmates adored and would also follow to the ends of the earth. These two men, or a part of the forces under their command, were about to do battle, and on the outcome would depend the future of most of Europe and North Africa, and Asia beyond.

Chapter Eight

There were few men in Great Britain who more frequently preached the virtues of self-control than the Reverend Osborne Whitworth, and no area in which he more sternly applied it to himself than in the control of his own self-critical faculties. Charles II had once said: "My words are my own and my actions are my ministers'." Ossie would have agreed with this but made sure he was presiding over an acquiescent cabinet.

Yet even he had taken a time in finding a justification for resuming his meetings with Rowella Solway. She had been so wanton, had deceived him and tricked him so basely, had cheated him of money and had ruined his relationship with his wife, which until then had been a thoroughly harmonious one. She had trailed her vile feminine lures in front of his eyes when he was suffering the voluntary deprivation of carnal satisfaction because his wife had given birth to a son and was ill thereafter; she had enticed him up to her room and there had taken off her bodice before him, exposing herself in wanton wicked nakedness, and then, when in the overmastering grip of accumulated passion, he had fallen into her trap, she had virtually blackmailed him into a continuation of the liaison under threat of exposing him to her sister—and later, much later, most dastardly trick of all, had pretended she was with child by him and so forced him—yes, forced him, her vicar and her brother-in-law—to pay her an enormous sum of money in order that she might marry a worthless, gutter-bred librarian —with whom, no doubt, Ossie would not be surprised to learn, she had been carrying on all the time.

At the time of this marriage and later, Ossie, had he

been a Catholic, would have been prepared to pronounce anathema on her, and as a Prostestant rather of the High than of the Low school he would have been very willing to consign her to the nethermost parts of hell. And, though a man of sedentary habit, he would have been glad to take an energetic hand with the stoking.

So it had gone on for many months; but his estrangement from Morwenna, the necessity of seeking his solace elsewhere—a very difficult operation in so small a town without setting the tongues wagging—the infrequency with which he could safely do so, and often the unsatisfactoriness of it all when it took place, had turned his mind reluctantly to that slut who had so enticed him and then so entranced him. First it had been the concoction of dire punishments that should befall her—that she might catch all the poxes on earth and her teeth drop out and her nose fall off; that she should be bitten by a mad dog and run foaming through the streets until she twitched herself to death in a muddy gutter; that abscesses should form in her ears or lightning paralyse half her body: that . . . And then, unfortunately, his mind had turned upon punishment he might inflict on her himself: that he should tie her down and stick pins in her . . . But this, *most* unfortunately, was the wrong sort of fantasy, because it led to other fantasies in which he played a more integral part.

And then one day he had accidentally met her and, instead of the usual lowering of eyes and heightening of colour, with the hurried froufrou of skirt and flopping of low-heeled slippers to take herself as quickly as possible out of his sight, she had very briefly met his eyes and as briefly smiled. And thereafter on the rare occasions when they met she *had* smiled shyly at him; almost forgivingly—*forgivingly,* mark you!—and once or twice the smile had held a hint of provocation. So to the letter on his return from Tregrehan, and a month later, provoked out of his natural hostility and caution, he had called to pick up the books.

And nothing could have been more proper than

her behaviour then. She had produced the books, which had been ready waiting and parcelled on the window ledge. She had inquired most anxiously about Morwenna and the baby. She had told him of her own life and her desire to do a new translation of Seneca's Commentaries, of Mr. Solway's ambition to enlarge and improve the County Library and his desperate shortage of funds. She meant, of course, she said, funds for the *Library*. As for themselves, they were very poor, as Mr. Whitworth must observe. Mr. Solway's salary of £15 a year had recently been increased to £16, but even so he worked every evening at home doing copy work for a notary—that was, every evening except Thursdays, when he spent the evening with his father and mother. Of course, she said, without the vicar's generous gift to set them up and the income from it to support them, they could not have lived at all. She remembered him, she said, every night in her prayers. Every night, she said, and somehow the way her eyes squinted down her long nose and her lower lip trembled subtly transformed her statement from a religious to a secular one.

And Ossie found himself breathing deeply and thereafter quickly took his leave. But not before he had promised to try to bring Morwenna to tea on the following Thursday; and if not, if she would not come, to come alone. And he had come alone, and again conversation had been circumspect until, quite suddenly, in the middle of the talk, Rowella had exclaimed: "Oo, my shoe is hurting me," and had pushed each slipper off by pressing the heel against the floor. She was not, as it so happened, wearing stockings, and her feet as she flexed the toes looked like small white animals arching their backs to be stroked. Ossie had stared at them with the greed of a starving glutton being offered a plate of his favourite food; and had thereupon suggested that he might perhaps call again next week, but this time in the evening.

So it began. Rowella was not a "nice" girl like Morwenna; nor was she a woman who saw respectability as the main objective of life, like her mother;

she had the intellectual talents of her father without his religious convictions; and deep inside her like a hidden source of misdirected energy pulsed the blood of her grandfather, Trelawny Tregellas, who could never resist a speculation and had gone bankrupt more often than any other man of his day. Grandfather Tregellas walked the tightrope of monetary hazard, and the risk seemed part of the attraction. Granddaughter Rowella, being a woman, was developing a talent for risks of another kind.

As for the vicar of St. Margaret's, his was the greater hazard. Yet he suggested to himself, and persuaded himself, that it was not so. First of all, this was a temporary measure. Along with the hope that his wife might soon be committed to a place of correction went the conviction that a suitable "housekeeper" could then be found who would look after his children and his house and not be averse to looking after his own comforts too. This would make Rowella no longer a necessary figure in his life.

When, however, medical sanction for such a move was not forthcoming he rethought the whole situation and began to make different plans. If he were doomed to go on living with his wife, then she must take the consequences. Whatever her insane aversions might lead her to think, she still possessed the same beautiful body she had always had, and sooner or later she would have to provide for him. He began to inquire for a suitable nurse for John Conan Osborne Whitworth. If he could not employ a housekeeper then he would look for a nurse. For her, looks would not matter, he decided. She must be *strong,* strong and utterly reliable, and so devoted to her charge that she would not leave him night or day. When he found such a woman and found she was wholly to be trusted, then he would call Morwenna's bluff. It was not a wholly unpleasant thought.

So this was still a temporary measure—this renewal of an old aberration—and as such less dangerous than venturing among the dockside cottages where the town whores lived. As a clergyman there was nothing suspicious about his visiting a former parishioner who was also his sister-in-law. Far worse to be surprised coming away from those dreadful derelict cottages. Also there was no risk of disease. Also it was *infinitely,* a hundred times more exciting. Rowella was like that. Half the time he could have strangled her, but night and day he thought about her. And if she had a baby this time, there was no risk of his being called the father.

Of course it was more expensive—a major drawback—although Rowella was careful not to set her demands too high. Arthur Solway was delighted to receive a gift for his library from the vicar of St. Margaret's of £20 "for books." He also noticed that Rowella had several new pairs of shoes. And she had had made for herself two new nightgowns that were really, almost not quite nice, being of a sort of soft woollen material printed like a tiger skin and only reaching just to the ankle. Arthur enjoyed his young wife both in bed and out, but his was a limited capacity for enjoyment, limited almost as much by his careful, tidy mind as by his physique. But since her knowledge of money matters was so much more extensive than his he was content that she thought them able to afford these little extravagances.

Once a week, then, every Thursday, Mr. Whitworth visited Mr. Pearce, who, although pronounced to be dying, clung obstinately to his life and his life's secrets. Morwenna was surprised at her husband's attentiveness to the old man, but Ossie explained that although Mr. Pearce was bedridden they were able to play French ruff together, and occasionally piquet. In fact he timed his arrival at the notary's office for just before sunset and left as soon as it was fully dark. It was only three minutes' walk, then, and there were few people about in the cobbled streets. A glance up and down the hill, a discreet knock at the door, and presently the door would open with four slim fingers grasping it so that it should squeak the less. Arthur Solway always stayed with his family until ten, so Rowella made sure that her guest should be up and away again by nine-fifteen.

II

Things at Wheal Grace were moving to adapt to the new situation: as each setting time came round tributers were abandoning the less profitable pitches they had been working on the south lode and striking bargains for ground on the north lode. Tutworkers like Sam Carne and Peter Hoskin, after being on timbering and crosscutting for a year, were back on shaft-sinking and driving to link up with the old Wheal Maiden workings. No one was laid off: there was work for all; but Ross was glad he had not expanded as he had been tempted to do in the first flush of enthusiasm, especially as the price of tin had not risen as much as people had expected with the continuance of war.

He shared the summer with Demelza and the children; and sometimes the old companionate laughter broke through. There were abrasive moments—sudden sharp jagged rents in their composure that showed the dangers still latent, but nothing irritable, nothing petty. Ross sometimes wondered if there had ever been a couple who got less on each other's nerves than they did. There might possibly be outright war—never skirmishing.

As September came in he began to look with distaste at the thought of returning to London. Of course there was no obligation for him to attend the Commons regularly. Most M.P.s, unless they were place men nominated by the government, drifted in and out of London much as they chose, calling in at the House as one would call at one's club, discussing the government of the country with their friends, and voting here and there on issues that personally concerned them. But it was easier for most of them than it was for Ross. Three-quarters of the Cornish M.P.s were not Cornish at all and lived in and around London. Two at least boasted they had never been to Cornwall. If you lived in Twickenham or Guildford or Tunbridge Wells it was much easier to be casual about it, coming up to Westminster one day and, if it suited you, home the day after the next. For Ross it was five days' hard travelling there and five back; expensive and vastly tedious. The Lords Falmouth and de Dunstanville and others of their calibre owned their town houses and migrated with their families to London for a part of each year. Ross couldn't take Demelza and the children into furnished rooms—or if he could he didn't want to. Nor did he fancy asking Demelza to come and leave the children at home.

In August they brewed two casks of strong beer at Nampara, and Jeremy, usually up to mischief, and always seeking to do a favour to his friends, the new Ebb and Flow, gave them the beer grounds out of both barrels. When Demelza went out the pigs had collapsed in a drunken stupor and Jeremy was in tears thinking he had killed them. The animals slept all through the rest of that day, two palely hairy snoring mountains whom no one could rouse, and next morning by a happy coincidence—Ross thought—Sir Hugh Bodrugan called hoping to find Ross up at the mine, to admire his Berkshire wonders and to see if he could squeeze Demelza a couple of times in tender places.

It didn't work out that way. Demelza was there, and apparently on her own, but was even more adroit than usual at keeping him at arm's length. She led him through the house into the kitchens, where he had never been before and where he was peered at fearfully by a couple of serving wenches and an older woman, until they passed through the still room and out into the back yard, where Ross was sitting on a keg helpless with laughter while Gimlett tried to persuade the pigs out of their torpor. First he would get Ebb on to his two front feet and try to lever him up onto the back two. Whereupon the front two would cross, like a dandy at a street corner, and the whole ponderous bulk would slowly collapse snout down onto the straw and the cobbles. Flow was in better shape and able to stand on all legs, but the legs had no cohe-

sion and she lurched from side to side as if she were
on a boat in a rough sea. Every now and then she
thumped into a wall and all but went down. Her snout
quivered and turned, and once in a while she would
open her mouth in a cavernous yawn.

"Ecod," said Sir Hugh. "They've got the staggers!
Tis a complaint not uncommon in horses, but never
have I seen the like in pigs! Mistress Demelza, you
cured my valuable horse once with your spells. Tis
time you said something over these or they'll be dead
before dark!"

"Do you smell nothing?" Ross asked.

"Of course I smell something, sir! Find me the farm-
yard devoid of stinks and I'll ask for a new nose. It is
all part and parcel of animal life, though Connie's pet
menagerie, I'll grant you, reeks like a jakes when you
open it first thing in the morning!"

"Does it ever reek of the taproom?"

Sir Hugh stared from under his beetling brows.
"Nay, now, come to think of it . . . Damn me, have
they got at the ale?"

"My small son tried to kill them with kindness."

"Damn me, where can I sit down?" He glowered
heavily about him and found another barrel. There he
sat down and began to laugh. In all their acquaintance
Demelza had never seen him properly laugh before.
(Perhaps one didn't when one was feeling concupis-
cent, as he always did when he saw her.) It was a
horrible sound, compounded of a lion's roar and a
donkey's bray, and it produced scared faces peering
out from the kitchen and raised Jack Cobbledick's
busy head from the barn beyond. It even brought Flow
up short. She stood for a few moments steady on all
four trotters, staring at this extraordinary hairy ap-
parition that was bellowing at her, then she turned
about, tail wagging like an eccentric worm, and disappeared into the darkest corner of her sty.

After a while Sir Hugh Bodrugan limped back into
the parlour, demanding Demelza's arm to support him.
There he refused a light canary but took a glass of
brandy and sprawled in their best chair, his short

101

stout legs stiff in front of him, a tear still escaping now and again to trickle down his cheek.

To his disappointment Ross joined them and, in spite of hints, showed no signs of going up to the mine. Presently Sir Hugh, making the best of a bad job, observed that he was glad now that Ross had refused him a part of Wheal Grace, since he heard it was likely to be closed within the year. Ross said that he knew Sir Hugh liked a little flutter: would he care to wager a thousand guineas that Wheal Grace would still be open when the new century came in? Sir Hugh, never quite at his ease with Ross—you never knew how the feller would jump; totally undependable and bad blood somewhere—downed his brandy at a gulp and extended his glass for more.

"Nay, sir, for that's no more than I would have lost if I'd made the investment." This unassailable piece of logic convinced Sir Hugh that he had had the last word, so he changed the subject. "Things are looking up on the war front, eh? France nearly at war with the United States. Mad Paul becoming anti-French. They say we shall be in negotiations with him before Christmas. And this rebellion in Ireland coming to a dismal, bloody end."

"And Hoche dead," said Ross.

"Who?"

"Hoche. General Hoche. At thirty-one. As great a general as Buonaparte. It means the risk of an invasion of England is so much the less."

"And what of Buonaparte? What mischief is he up to?"

"The latest report by overland courier from Constantinople is that he landed in Egypt in July, took Alexandria, and was known to be moving on Cairo."

Sir Hugh scratched under his wig. "You young fellers know it all, don't you. And now, of course, you being a member of Parliament . . . What d'ye do in that place? Talk, I suspicion. Hot air, sir. The production of hot air. If hot air would run your mine, Poldark, I guess there'd be plenty to spare in Westminster, if ye could but bottle it like one of these gases and release it where it could be of use to you! Sir Horatio What's-it should take it on his ships and blow it out through his fourteen-pounders!" Hugh Bodrugan rumbled with the subterranean amusement that Demelza was more used to. "But maybe I have local news for you. Are you invited to this Warleggan party that's to be held at Trenwith at the end of the month?"

"Did you suppose we should be?" Ross asked.

Hugh rumbled again. "No. Seeing how the wind blows, sir, I would imagine not. But tis to be quite a considerable affair from all reports. Many of the county, as you'd suppose—the Trevaunances, the Tregloses, the Teagues, the Choakes, the Devorans, the Hawkinses. But also some odd characters from up-country—a number of M.P.s I'm told. What George Warleggan lacks in breeding he makes up in enterprise. I learn he's going to enter Parliament himself again soon. Rather him than me. I'd no more sit in that noisy chapel day after day listening to fellers talking through their hats than I'd sit on the closestool after my business there was discharged!"

"You put it well," said Ross. "So I take it you're not going to Trenwith."

"Me? Not going. Why, blast me, I've no wish to powder and flig myself up like a macaroni, but Connie wants to go, and, by God, if Connie wants to go, I rather suspect we shall be there!" Sir Hugh Bodrugan began to palpitate with laughter.

"You find the prospect amusing?" Ross asked.

"Nay, I was thinking of the pigs. Next time we have a little party—which God knows is infrequent enough these days—I've a mind to try the potion on a couple of porkers of my own. Twould be a valuable source of entertainment for us all!"

III

Nights are seldom warm in Cornwall, but in the last week of August a quiet spell descended on sea and land, and the usual breezes did not get up. Walking

home from Grambler in the afternoon Ross met Paul
Daniel and said: "When's your next night fishing,
Paul?"

"Tonight, sur. Tes the right sort of weather and
there should be a fair chance of catching 'em inshore."

"And rabbiting after?"

" 'S I reckon."

"Watch you don't go on Treneglos land. Now Mr.
John is in charge he's more particular that way."

"We keep to the coast, sur. In the main, that is."
Paul Daniel cocked a wary eye at his questioner.

Ross smiled. "How many are you tonight?"

"Oh . . . Dozen or more. Zacky Martin, Henry
Curnow, Jud Paynter, Bone, Tregirls, Ellery, Hoblyn;
you know 'em all."

"Jud? Isn't he too old?"

"Not too old to hang on the end of a line—and to
use 'is cunning."

Ross looked up at the sky. "Would you accept another recruit?"

"Mean you, sur, do ee? Well, twould be handsome.
Just like old times."

"When d'you start?"

" 'Bout eleven, I reckon. Curnow don't get off mine
till ten, and tis low water at midnight."

"I'll be there."

Line and net fishing in Cornwall had been indulged
in for centuries: it was a valuable source of food; and
it existed not in the tiny fishing ports and harbours
where seiners could go out commercially, but on the
long beaches where the sea thundered and the sand
was flat and uninterrupted for miles. On these beaches,
on which the sea rushed in and receded twice daily
over great areas, where no rock or shelf existed to
break the Atlantic surf, where necessarily the water
was shallow and the sand firm, there was a fair share
of marine life: the mackerel, the flounder, the bass,
the skate, even the gurnard, could be caught in nets
and lines artfully put out.

As a boy Ross had had his share of this kind of
fishing. Encouraged by his father, by Tholly Tregirls,

and to a lesser extent by Jud Paynter, he had been in and out of the water at all hours and all seasons, from the times when a harvest moon had cast warm mellow shadows of the men working on the beach to cold February nights when hail had pelted on one's bare skin like peas from a shooter.

In line fishing a strong line with perhaps fifty baited hooks was carried down to the beach at low tide, someone swam out with a heavy stone to anchor it; and hours later, after the tide had been in and out again, you garnered the result by pulling in the line and seeing what had been caught on the hooks. Net fishing was more complicated. You took down to the beach a fine small-mesh light-weight net made of thin twine or even cotton; the upper length of the net was tied with corks to make it float, the lower length with one-ounce weights to keep it on or near the bottom. One man, or if the net were a big one, two, swam out with the leading line while another man or so held on to the trailing line. After the swimmers had gone out to sea, perhaps three or four hundred yards, they would turn and swim parallel with the shore and then come in again, with the leading line still in their hands —or round their waists—so that they had described roughly a semicircle in the sea. Then, once they were ashore, they would begin to draw in the net and hope —usually rightly—that they had caught some fish in their trawling. This again was always done at low tide, partly because that was where the fish were, partly because the surf then was lighter.

It was net fishing that was in progress the night Ross joined them, and not one but four parties were on the beach. As a boy he had often wondered what moved the fishers so that perhaps for four or five perfectly good days there was no activity at all, and then suddenly they would all go down and make a night of it. He had never met anyone who could give a reason for the decisions arrived at; some tribal instinct moved.

On this occasion the nearest net was just below the now derelict Wheal Leisure mine on Treneglos ground, and a light had been lit near where the old adit came out. The light came from a beer cask, which long years ago had been filled with paraffin wax, and a rope dipped in saltpetre thrust into the centre. Every now and then more wax was added; sometimes the rope wick was renewed; but the old barrel seemed to go on for ever. This when lit was like an enormous flaring candle which gave not only light but a little warmth to the beach, and round it there were always a few fishermen taking their noggins of rum. Drink was as much a part of the scene as fish.

As Ross approached the scene a worn half-moon was just rising over the sandhills like a counterfeit penny that had been bitten in half. Three men were squatting by the barrel and one had a bottle up-ended to his mouth. Needless to say, this was Jud Paynter. Dressed in brown patched corduroy trousers, scuffed leggings over heavy boots, a shirt, a coat, and a sacking about his shoulders, with an old felt hat down over his ears, he looked dressed for a December vigil in his graveyard rather than a night's fishing in temperate September air.

"Ah, Jud," said Ross. "Busy as usual? And who've you been teeling this week?"

Jud did not allow the sudden materialisation of his late employer out of the shadows to disturb the rhythm of his Adam's apple. He put the bottle down and wiped his mouth on the back of his hand. Then he licked the back of his hand to make sure no flavour was lost.

"Aw, Cap'n Ross. Ye will have yer little jest, eh? Prudie say to me, Cap'n Ross he always d'have his little jest, she say."

"How is Prudie?"

"Aw, she've the toothache and as sour as a grab 'cause of it. She d'sit glumped up in a corner, making grief w' everything I do, like twas my fault! Glad to be out of 'n, I am. Else I'd not be here in the dark 'alf of the night messen my proper sleep!"

"But having your proper tot too, I see."

"Well, Cap'n, tes the only comfort I d'have, see. That and a drag o' baccy. I'm old, and no misment.

Tes cruel hard work setten folk underground. Harder'n planting taties. Harder'n seeking tin! Ted'n right I should 'ave to do it. Ted'n proper!"

Ross opened his bag. "I've brought two jars of rum to add to the store. But not all for you, Jud."

Jud showed his two teeth in what looked like a snarl but might charitably have been taken for a smile. "Thur be fine antics over to the big 'ouse, Cap'n. Seen 'em, 'ave ee? Lumpous great coaches! Fair dring of folk coming and going. Old men in gossan wigs riding ascrode gurt horses! And poor folk like Grambler folk standing goggle-for-gapes a-watching of it all. Tes all to pass off tomorrow eve, I reckon. Goin' are ee, Cap'n?"

"No," said Ross.

"There now," said Jud, squinting cunningly up at Ross. "Reckon tes a proper disgrace what that there Warleggan man done. What have he done? I'll tell ee. All them fences. All them keepers. They edn God's laws. God d'say, thou shalt not move thy neighbour's landmark. Ted'n Christian!"

"Where's Paul?"

"Here, sur, just comin','" said Ellery, who had politely got up from his squatting position when Ross arrived.

Walking towards them across the beach were Paul Daniel and his eldest son, Mark—known universally as Young Mark to distinguish him from his still-mourned uncle—and Jacka Hoblyn, Rosina's father. Young Mark was naked and dripping.

"Even, sur, even sur, even sur," they said as they came up, and Paul added: "We done one drag; a poor catch, but the tide've still to fall. Zacky and Henry are sorting and clearing the net."

"You've not used the bigger net?" Ross asked.

"We thought to try un next. But tis 'eavy for a youngster, so I thought to take 'n out myself."

"How are the others faring?"

Paul peered up the beach to where groups of dark figures were just discernible in the ochreous light that a ground haze had given to the low moon. "Don't think they've drawn yet. Zacky d'say there'll be a better catch at the far end."

There had been a moderate surf at high tide, but now, nearing dead low, it was a thin white line like a painter's brushstroke dividing two elements.

"I'll take it out myself," said Ross. "Jud shall come and hold the end for me."

There was a moment's hesitation. Jacka sniffed and rubbed his knuckle across his nose.

"I think twould be better wi' two, sur," said Paul. "This net's a tidy weight just so soon as he gets damp."

"It's no heavier than many a one I swam out with twenty years ago."

"Nay, sur, but—"

Ross glanced round at the men. "And d'you think I'm so flabbed and potbellied I can't do the same thing today?"

Jacka glowered and spat.

Paul said: "Been in the sea this year, 'ave ee, sur?"

Jacka muttered: "All this London tra-ade. Reckon there edn no sea London ways, es there?"

Jud took out his pipe and began to stuff it with some obnoxious mixture of his own. "Nay, Cap'n, think again. Ee be zeer wi' all this high living. Ted'n time yet to be measuring ee for a windan sheet. Go ee for a forestroll along the beach and leave the swimmun be."

Ross smiled in the dark. Whatever concern the others were showing for his health, Jud was only thinking that if Ross went he was to be employed as the anchor and must stand on the edge of the water with maybe his feet in an inch or two of it, with the rope round his waist, and wait while the net was carried out and then have to help to pull it in when Ross landed with the other end further down the coast. If Ross didn't go he'd probably be allowed to sit by the guttering tar barrel to smoke his pipe and drink his tots in peace.

Ross said: "The care that you all have for me touches me deep. You know I'm but three or four years younger than Paul and Paul is a thought shaky on his feet these days and could hardly wrestle with his own shadow; and I know my life is soft and comfortable, for I spend all my days in London sprawling in the salons of rich and beautiful women, so gladly I'd acknowledge your concern for my health and safety and take no part in the swimming tonight. But for one thing. I cannot bear to disappoint Jud."

There was a mutter of laughter that gradually grew. While he was speaking Ross had realised that the sarcasm he was using, the prolonged nature of the phrases, were something not suited to his present audience—that in a sense he *had* changed so it was with a touch of relief that he heard the point of the joke go home.

He began to take off his clothes. "Come on, boy," Jack Hoblyn said, grasping Jud's arm. "Put the jar down—twill still be here in 'alf an hour."

Protesting, Jud was hauled to his feet. Protesting, he was allowed to thrust a piece of straw into the tar barrel and from it to light his old clay pipe. Then, hat pulled firmly on head, he shuffled off in the wake of Ross and Paul Daniel, who insisted on carrying the net as far as the water.

There they paused a while, surveying the whispering sea, staring up-beach at the other figures, considering where best to cast. Sometimes you would tell by the water lying on the sand in shallow patches, or by the turn of the small waves. Presently Jud was urged into the wet sand, the rope tied round his waist so that some sudden pull shouldn't jerk it out of his hand. Ross took off his shirt and gave it to Jud to keep, accepted the weight of the net on his shoulder and stepped naked into the sea.

The water was cold but bracing, the frothy little waves spattered him with cold showers of spray as he stepped through them, up to knee, up to thigh, up to waist, and then presently he was waterborne.

As soon as he was swimming he wondered why he had not done this before. It was not merely his absence in London; years had passed since he had come fishing in this way. It was different from the polite bathing of daytime, the walks on the beach with the children, the gallops on horseback with Demelza; this was essentially masculine, essentially earthy—if one could use that expression—essentially utilitarian and plebeian, of the common folk who tilled the soil and searched the sea and lived plain and hard. Like his father, and unlike Francis and Francis's father, he had always had something in common with this world—it was a part of himself, just as much as his intimate breeding as a Poldark was a part of himself. That he had married a miner's daughter had confirmed the union, not created it.

He had been slipping the net off his shoulder and through his fingers as he swam; now he lay on his back to get his breath and raised his head to see how far he was from the shore. Jud's figure was like a rubbing post in the middle of a field, sentinelled and alone. Paul had moved along the beach to where Ross might be expected to come in. He was out perhaps two hundred yards. The sea was quiet calm, just a gentle rise and swell as the slow waves moved towards the shore. Another hundred yards would be enough: that would about extend the net.

He went on and then turned to swim parallel to the shore and as he did so found himself in a powerful current that wanted to take him the other way. He realised he was in a vellow.

A vellow is a strong current which develops here and there along the Cornish beaches at low tide, caused by and causing shallow declivities in the sand, and is irresistible when it takes hold. To a stranger they are fatal, for he tries to swim towards the shore, exhausts himself, and is carried away and drowned. To a swimmer familiar with the beaches they are not dangerous, for he allows himself to go with them and then when their force begins to wane he swims out of them and comes ashore where they allow him.

As this current caught him and tried to bear him away Ross vividly remembered a time in March when he was sixteen or seventeen. He was down on the beach with his father and a few others on a cold gusty night, and he had carried the net about as far out as he had on this occasion. An exceptionally strong vellow had caught him and, as was the custom, he had dropped the net and gone with the current. He had eventually come in more than two miles further up the beach and had had to walk back naked with the wind cutting at him and stinging his body with sand. When he at last arrived his father was standing by the tar barrel watching two men sorting fish from one of the nets, and all he said was "Well, boy, you've been a long time."

So the correct thing, the only thing, to do on this occasion was to unhitch the rest of the net, signal to Jud—if he happened to be watching—and go with the current till he felt it releasing him. But he was very fresh, not yet at all cold, and more than a trifle irritated by the obvious concern of such as Paul Daniel that he might have grown soft, living in London. However much he might claim he was in a vellow there might be one or two who would consider Captain Poldark had gotten a bit short of wind and decided to give up his netting while he could.

So he began to swim against the current and did not release the net. He did not make for the shore but tried to carry out his original design of bringing in the end of the net near to where Paul Daniel would be waiting.

He soon realised that he was making no headway at all. By swimming hard up the beach he was about remaining in the same place. The part of the net he still held was pulling heavily on his shoulder. The waves, in the way they did in such a case, had got up, so that he could not raise his head far enough out of the water to see the figures on the shore. The current wanted to take him out. In fact it was taking him out whether he wanted to go or not. It depended very much on the size of the vellow as to how far he might be carried before he could return, but obstinately he would not drop the net. It seemed to him that if Jud held to his end there must be a limit to the extent of the drift.

After ten minutes or so he began to feel cold. It was nothing, but he realised that one felt cold quicker at thirty-eight than at eighteen. He had gradually let out more of the net, so that the weight of what he still carried was really quite small. But it was more than it should be. He was not alarmed. You don't live so close to the sea so long and in such close contact with it that you ever envisage it as an enemy. Naturally you respect its tantrums but you know how to deal with them. Or think you do.

He lay on his back for a few minutes, admiring the half-moon. As it rose above the sandhills, so it had paled. The half-bitten coin had turned from copper to orange; now it was lemon; in another half hour there would be scarcely any colour. Little lips of waves glinted and glimmered with it. It sprinkled its light on the water, making the shadows dance. He was really rather cold. Demelza was in bed and asleep, so were his two fine children. Nampara drowsed in its comfortable fold of the valley just over the shoulder of the Long Field. Probably from here if you raised your head you would be able to see the chimneys. "Sir, before I proceed to reply to the arguments adduced in support of this motion by the hon. member for Stockbridge, I beg that the clerk may read the address of this House to his Majesty of the 6th of last April, which the hon. gentleman alluded to, but declined reading . . ." Ross Poldark, Esq., M.P. How his father would have laughed. Respectability! My dear Ross! What can you be thinking of? But then his father, after a wild and wanton youth, had married a girl he truly loved, and then after a brief married life Grace Poldark had been taken from him, in great grief and in great pain, and Joshua had gone back to his old ways.

But Ross had not lost his wife; and his family and to some extent his mine prospered, so perhaps for him, though respectability was not to be sought, if it came unsought it was not totally to be derided. "Mr. Speaker, sir, the hon. member for Ilchester has implied that slavery is a condition that Christianity can condone. May I inform the hon. member . . ."

Suddenly he was in calm water. None too soon, for he was beginning to shiver. Very odd; it did not often happen this way, that one came out of a vellow while still struggling against it. Triumphantly, the end of the net still in his possession, he began to swim towards the shore. It was not far but it took him much too long. He ploughed on, the chill striking deeper, until his knee unexpectedly grated on sand. He stood up, feeling the waves breaking past him. He stumbled and almost fell, then got into shallower water and took a firm grip of himself. Must not shiver. As if nothing undue had happened, he made for the two figures waiting for him. He saw that one was Paul Daniel, the other Jim Ellery. They were in peculiar attitudes, crouched as if in great pain from an attack of colic. As he came in they tried to stand up, and Paul, his face a mask of anguish, took the rope from him.

"Well, sur," he said weakly, "you sure done a proper job there. Got caught in a vellows, did ee? I suspected so much. But you never let go of the net! So Jud—the vellow was so strong. And he couldn't untie himself in time . . . He—got—drawn—in! . . ."

Ross stared out at the now friendly sea. Not too far out, but far enough to have to swim, was Jud, hat firmly still on head, pipe in mouth, smoking vigorously with the effort, like some aqueous monster of the deep that breathed fire from its nostrils. Obviously he was still trying to untie the twine from round his waist.

But he was better not to try, for the current then would bear him out.

Paul Daniel sputtered a couple of times into the moonlit dark: "Sur, if we pull gently on this rope, mebbe we shall not draw the fish this time; but presently, if God so will, we shall save Jud Paynter from a watery grave!"

Chapter Nine

That they should entertain a large party at Trenwith was George's idea and not at all Elizabeth's. One of the most beautiful manor houses in the county, with three or four reception rooms of the most elegant and handsome design, it suffered from an inadequacy of attractive bedrooms. The Tudors were, on the whole, like that. About fifteen bedrooms, apart from the servants' quarters, offered themselves, but of these the best were occupied by George and Elizabeth, the second-best by her parents, and the rest were all so heavily panelled and small-windowed as to be very dark, and some were small and odd-shaped and poky.

It was a house eminently designed for the afternoon party or the splendid dinner occasion, not for guests who stayed the night. Yet its isolation was such that only a small number of local friends could come and leave in a day: others had to be put up and had to make do with what was offered them. Fine for the Tudors, to whom a bed was a bed and what did the rest matter? Not so fine for late Georgians, who, two hundred and fifty years after, expected a bit more.

This worried Elizabeth more than George. She was the hostess; on her depended the comfort and the pleasure of the guests; and some of these people she had not even met, being friends of George's whom he had come to know in London. Four were actually coming *from* London, an enormous trip at enormous trouble and expense. (Cornish people thought little of going east, Londoners seldom if ever came west.) They were expected to stay several days before moving on elsewhere. Apart from the inadequacy of the bedrooms there was the inadequacy of the servants.

But George would not have it otherwise or elsewhere. Their Great House in Truro was even more inadequate, and he would not invite his friends to Cardew as she suggested. George, like many men who have risen in the world ánd aspire to rise further, was a little embarrassed by his parents. At Trenwith in any case the nuisance of Elizabeth's parents had to be borne; but they at least stood out instantly recognisable for what they were, like silver spoons against pewter, and could be borne with the better.

There was going to be a big dinner party on the Thursday. There was to be music from the tiny cramped minstrels' gallery but no dancing in the hall below, because when Geoffrey de Trenwith finished it in 1509 he had also had built and fixed permanently into the flags of the hall floor one of the longest and most formidable oak dining tables in the world, and, short of digging up the floor and sawing the dining table into small pieces to get it out through the door, there was no way of moving it.

On the Tuesday and the Wednesday the distant guests arrived; on the Thursday the weather was mercifully fine, so in the morning they were able to occupy themselves strolling about the grounds; at around midday the local gentry came. Old Sir John Trevaunance, now approaching his mid-sixties and still a bachelor, with Unwin Trevaunance, the M.P. for Bodmin who, chronically extravagant and chronically short of money, lived grudgingly off his brother's doles, which were as grudgingly granted. Sir Hugh Bodrugan —fligged up, as he called it—with his young and hard-swearing stepmother, together with their rather raggle-tail nephew Robert, who was also their heir but never sure how much, except for some land and a rotting mansion, he was likely to be heir to. Lord Devoran, Ross's friend, with his strongly built, stocky-legged niece Betty, who immediately looked round to see if there was any promising-looking man she might sleep with. Dr. Choake—very lame these days and only really comfortable on a horse—with his feather-brained lisping wife Polly, who now wore a wig to cover her greying hair and was indulging—so gossips said—in an *affaire* with her groom.

Sir Christopher Hawkins, cynical, quietly dignified, arrived alone. Gossip rumoured many things of him but proved nothing. John and Ruth Treneglos followed. John was having some sort of trouble with his eyes that made him screw them up and unscrew them as if they were constantly exposed to the sun; Ruth, though still only a little over thirty, was becoming fat; perhaps as a result of their litter of children with which she had presented her husband in the last ten years. Last year, in the fulness of time, Mrs. Teague had been gathered to her ancestors, but all Ruth's four sisters had been invited—all unmarried and all likely to remain unmarried and doomed to live on together in their mother's house, becoming narrower of outlook and more acid as the years progressed. (George had asked them because he was short of women and they were at least well-bred.) The Reverend and Mrs. Osborne Whitworth were invited too.

So were Dr. and Mrs. Enys. Dwight had been very reluctant to accept, and, when Caroline had argued that a refusal from so close a neighbour would give unnecessary offence, had suggested that perhaps they could accept and then he could be called away by the sudden illness of a patient. Caroline said, "My dear, I have a husband. Everybody knows it. This is an occasion when you can observe marital attendance on me with practically no effort—except the effort of putting on a new suit of clothes. Besides . . . Unwin will be there." So Dwight went.

Of this group the Devorans, the Whitworths, and Sir Christopher Hawkins would have to be offered accommodation for the night. Notable absentees were the Poldarks, and Lord and Lady de Dunstanville. The four visitors from London were Mr. John Robinson, Mr. and Mrs. Hanton, and Captain Monk Adderley.

Mr. Robinson looked seventy or more, and when he arrived the last part of the journey had so upset him that he retired at once to bed and was seen no more until the party was in full swing. He, George explained, had for years been a close associate of Pitt, had helped to arrange and manage the seats at times of elections, had calculated losses and gains, and had negotiated with the borough-mongers as to which seats he could be safely promised on Pitt's behalf. He had played no such part at the last election, having pleaded age to be excused; but he was still a man of influence. What he didn't know about the internal working of the Commons was hardly worth knowing. And his friendship and advice to a man aspiring in that world was inestimable.

Mr. and Mrs. Hanton had no connection with Parliament, and Elizabeth estimated that Mr. Hanton's genteel pedigree was about as long as George's own. But Hanton had built up investments in the East India Company, had himself been back only two years from Bengal, had bought a considerable estate in Surrey, and had banking and industrial interests in the Midlands. Like the Warleggans, Hanton had difficulty in throwing off traces of his ancestry. His being invited to a party of this quality was a subtle piece of flattery which would engage his friendship, a friendship which could be as valuable to George—on a different level —as John Robinson's.

The fourth guest, Captain Monk Adderley, was the most surprising of the four, for Elizabeth could not at first see advantage to George in the association. Adderley was twenty-eight, very slim and erect, his manner mild and courteous, his reputation formidable. He had served in the army for eight years, chiefly in India and China, where, it was rumoured, he had fought several duels and killed two fellow officers. He had been discharged from the army after suffering a serious head wound in another duel. The ball had carried away part of the skull, and the silver plate put in when he was trepanned was thought by some to have affected his reason—though no one could have supposed it from his perfect social demeanour. For the last few years he had represented the one rotten borough in Shropshire, Bishop's Castle. He was known in Parliament, on the rare occasions when he paid it a visit, for his strong anti-Catholic and anti-French views.

It was a little startling, when one observed him, to discover that his father was a rich Bristol merchant of no great genteel pretension. Indeed, the only duel it was said Monk had ever refused occurred soon after his twenty-first birthday when his behaviour had so enraged his father that the old man had called him out. Monk had refused to fight on the grounds that his father was not a gentleman.

George Warleggan and Monk Adderley? Elizabeth, pursued with the utmost tigerish courtesy by the young man, wondered for a little. George's value to Monk was not difficult to see, for the young M.P. was known to be deep in debt. The other value appeared as the days progressed. Whatever his origin, Adderley had been completely accepted by Society. He had adopted the aristocratic attitude and gone one better. He drank, he gambled, he womanised, all in the most exquisite taste. He belonged to the best clubs, and was remarked as a figure everywhere. What better friend could George have if he intended to return to London?

Perhaps too there was an attraction of opposites. Adderley had the sort of glamour that George could at once admire and despise: the military bearing, the effeminate dress, the drawling voice, the careless contempt of money, the frivolous conversation, all wedded to such a ferocious reputation.

Dinner began at three and went on till six. In spite of wartime scarcities and appeals for the patriotic conservation of food, nothing had been spared today. They dined and wined at Geoffrey de Trenwith's great table, and when the ladies retired the men sat on drinking their port and talking and arguing and laughing together. The music was playing from the gallery, but discreetly, so that it should not make conversation difficult. At eight tea was served, and many of the men retired to the winter parlour to play quadrille or whist or whatever else took their fancy. The ladies took a stroll in the gardens and admired the ornamental lake, from which the last raucous toad had long since been banished. Geoffrey Charles, in his best suit, lounged along with Dwight Enys, who had never had any taste for cards and was talking to the only person in the household in whom he took a personal interest —though put off a trifle tonight by Geoffrey Charles's deliberately bawdy conversation.

As darkness fell the chatting groups began to move indoors. Dozens of candles were lit, and trembling light fell from the high mullioned windows across lawn and shrub and lake; the music rose and some people essayed to dance in the hall in spite of the table. Having seen her mother and father safely to bed—another responsibility—Elizabeth skimmed down the stairs, conscious that the crisis of the day was past. There was, no doubt, chaos in the kitchens, but it was all hidden away. Supper at eleven would be a light meal: cold boiled fowls, some bacon, a tongue, a cold leg of mutton roasted, mince pies and syllabubs with canary and other light wines, so that should not be a trouble. Just as everyone else was coming in she chose to go out, to have a little peace and quiet on her own.

The best place to walk was on the long lawn below the handsome drawing room on the first floor. The grass, she knew, had been cut and brushed that day, so should be too short for the dew to wet her slippers, and the light from the oriel window of the drawing room would light up where she walked. All she needed was five minutes to draw the evening's breath and then she could return to the fray. Especially she wanted to be alone.

Her relationship with George had never been more cordial. The horrors of last year and the year before, the near breakup of their marriage over his suspicions about the parentage of Valentine, had blown over; one never knew for *certain* what George was thinking but one gathered most from his attitude to Valentine, which had become attentive again and as warm as George was capable of being. His attitude to her was as possessive as ever but with, she fancied, a new trust, she was no longer followed wherever she went in Truro; and Monk Adderley's feline attentions did not seem to upset him.

She was happy to have Geoffrey Charles back— shocked by his blaséness so young yet charmed by his manners and his new elegance. He was still seeing Drake but there had been none of the old clashes about it between him and his stepfather. Life was better than it had been for a long time.

She bent to look at a large moth that was fluttering on the edge of a white oxeye daisy, and as she did so someone moved in the shadows. She started back.

"Good evening, Elizabeth," said Ross.

"My *God!*" said Elizabeth.

"Neither God nor the Devil. Just a trespasser unfortunately surprised."

"What are you doing here?"

He shrugged. "Trespassing."

"To what end?"

"Well . . . this is partly my house, you know—in sentiment at least. My father was born here, I was accustomed to come here all my childhood and youth. I'm—what you might call the senior Poldark today. It occurred to me, in a flash of whimsy, to discover for myself the sort of party that you were giving—and to which we'd not been invited."

"You must be *mad!*" she said in horror. "Coming here—risking so much!"

"I think . . . I think, Elizabeth, eleven months a member of Parliament have had a constraining influence on me. I have been—conforming. It seemed to me it was time for the good of my soul not to conform quite so much to the accepted pattern."

"But if you're seen . . . for God's sake go!"

"No . . . I think I'm safe tonight. George would not risk a major scandal in front of all his fine guests. Not that I want any trial of strength—ever." Someone moved a candle into the window of the lower room, and the light fell on his face, showing up the bony places, the trace of scar, the heavy eyelids. "Nor did

I seek word with anyone; but when you came out I could not resist speaking to you."

She said, relaxing a little: "I came—just for a breath of air."

"Is Geoffrey Charles here?"

"Yes. He was in the garden just now. But I pray you, don't attempt to speak with him tonight."

"I've no such intention. I saw him in London."

"Yes, he told me. It—pleased him greatly." She fingered her scarf. "No doubt you found him very worldly-wise, Ross. Blasé. In one so young."

"It means nothing. Francis was the same. He'll grow out of it."

"Do you think he's like Francis?"

Ross hesitated, measuring the tactful answer. "In the better ways, yes."

There was a little burst of laughter from an open window, and someone moved in front of the candles.

"Valentine?" Ross said.

"He's well. Now please go."

"And yourself and George? I must ask that."

"You've no right . . ."

"After our conversation of a couple of years ago . . ."

"That was not of my seeking. It should never have happened."

"But it did."

She said: "Then forget it. Please forget it."

"Gladly. If you'll tell me how I may. It has been unquiet on my mind ever since."

She hesitated. "It is over—done with."

"I'm *very* glad. For everyone's sake. The suspicion . . ."

"Will only rise again if it has cause. Such as your coming here now—"

"Ma-am, is this gentleman annoying you?" A light voice, affected but not at all feminine.

A man came out of the shadows. A tall etiolated man with the short hair of a soldier, tight smiling lips, and the palest of blue eyes that looked almost sightless in the shadowy light. He wore a suit of cream satin, with scarlet buttons and a scarlet neckcloth. It was impossible to tell how much, if anything, he had overheard.

"Oh!" said Elizabeth, and paused a moment and swallowed. "Not—not at all. No, it is not so at all."

Ross said to the man: "Why should you suppose it likely?"

The newcomer whispered: "Sir, I have not the honour of your acquaintance."

"Capt—Captain Ross Poldark, my cousin," Elizabeth said. "Captain Monk Adderley."

"Your servant, sir. I confess when I saw you talking to Mrs. Warleggan I took you for a threadbare troubadour who had come to sing outside our windows on this pleasant night and was being dismissed without his proper *pourboire*."

"I sing ill," said Ross, "and accept pourboires with even less grace."

"That's a pity. I always accept what women have to offer, on principle."

Elizabeth said to Adderley. "Come, we must go in. The ladies—the other ladies—will be missing you." When he did not move she took his arm.

"Stay," said Adderley. "The name Poldark means something to me. Are you not in the House?"

"I am," said Ross.

"A new member?"

"That is so. I don't recall having met you there."

"Nor is it likely. I attend so seldom. Monk Adderley laughed gently, a melodious but mannered sound. "They are all so tedious, those old men, and they take themselves seriously, which is almost the worst fault a gentleman can have."

"*Almost* the worst," Ross agreed. "Good night, Elizabeth."

"Good night."

"Your name came up in some connection," said Adderley. "Some light connection. I don't remember precisely how. I belong to Lord Croft, by the way. Who owns you?"

"No one owns me," said Ross.

"Well, damn it, my dear, you sit in someone's interest? These Cornish boroughs are as rotten as a basket of bad eggs."

"Lord Falmouth's interest," said Ross.

"Ah, well, then. And are you not one of the eggs, eh? That's what I mean. Call and see me sometime when you're in town. Everybody knows where I live. We'll throw a dice together."

"Thank you," said Ross. "I shall look forward to that. With anticipation."

As he turned away he did not catch Monk Adderley's aside to Elizabeth, but he supposed it to be derisive.

II

When he got home Demelza was waiting up for him in the parlour, though she was making some pretence of sorting through Clowance's frocks. She was wearing a tight-waisted frock of navy blue lawn, with a paler sash. Her hair was down, but she had trimmed it a few days ago, so it only just reached her shoulders.

"You're abroad late," Ross observed.

"Clowance is bursting out of everything. She'll become a real roly-poly if we're not careful."

"Wait another couple of years until she begins to grow upwards; then she'll be as thin as Jeremy." He pulled off his neckcloth and frowned at himself in the mirror.

"Have you been fishing again, Ross?"

"It could be so described. In troubled waters."

The ribbon in one of Clowance's frocks was frayed. Demelza picked at it. "Have you been to see Elizabeth?"

"Not exactly. I went to look at my old home—to see what sort of company the Warleggans were entertaining, that there should be so much fuss and talk about it. Naturally I didn't go in."

"It was—risky, Ross."

"Not risky. I know the secret ways too well. Francis

and I used to explore the shallow tunnels together, those that had been made and abandoned by men dead before Queen Anne."

"But . . ." She hesitated. "It is not what you would have done a year ago."

He looked at her. "No . . . No . . . Although I've had several clashes with George since he came to live at Trenwith, I have never sought them. The last was when Drake was arrested—and then, of course, the elections of last year . . ." He nodded slowly. "But you're correct in supposing I was willing to live and let live. There was room for us both in the world—I thought. And still do. I—I was seeking no clash, no encounter, going there tonight. It was just—as I said, an impulse to see . . ."

"And you saw?"

"A little. I found Elizabeth walking alone in the garden and spoke to her. She was not overpleased to see me—and that is understandable. Her marriage to George seems to have become peaceable at last. So she says, but not why. One can only speculate why and hope that it is permanent. Clearly she wants it to remain so—and uncomplicated by jealousies—however unfounded—that might spring to life again from his discovering me on his property, talking to his wife."

"And you, Ross?"

He shrugged a little impatiently. "I've told you—explained to you—too often. There's nothing new to add."

She folded the rest of the frocks and stood a moment knee on chair, heel raised.

Ross said: "But another man came on us when we had spoken a few words. I've forgotten the name Elizabeth gave him, but he made the back of my hair stand up."

Demelza came across to him. "It's the wrong sort of thing to do, Ross. Oh, I don't mean because of Elizabeth now. I mean because it's in the spirit of enmity, of—of challenge. You said a few years ago that we had all we wanted. You said—exactly—live and let live. . . . Is it because I've failed you since then?"

He patted her hand. "Perhaps we've failed each other—just a little anyway. But don't magnify this, don't blow it up and out of proportion—it was a single act of—of unreason, if you like. You have to face the fact—must have faced it long ago—that I am not always a reasonable man."

Demelza sighed. She could say no more to this. "I hear you near drowned Jud last night by being unreasonable in another way."

"Jud never even dowsed his pipe! He swims well enough and always has. But you should have heard his language when we pulled him in by the line like a stranded fish! And he'd kicked off his *boots*—he'd lost his *boots*—which made him most furious of all. There he stood with his bare toes sticking up and water dripping from him all ways, even from the brim of his hat, fairly frothing with indignation!"

"Demelza said: "I'll give him an old pair of yours."

"What's worse," Ross said, "they've dubbed him with a new name today. They're calling him Jud Pilchard. I'm afraid he'll burst a blood vessel in annoyance."

"It is the small boys he doesn't like," she said. "They call after him from a safe distance. It was long enough before they stopped asking him about the Archangel Gabriel."

"By the way," Ross said. "Jacka Hoblyn had a serious if respectful word with me later in the night. He wishes to know if I have any idea as to my brother-in-law's intentions towards his daughter."

"And what did you say?"

"That I had no idea. Drake has seen Rosina four times, I believe, but if he has no serious intentions Jacka does not want him to keep other eligible young men away."

"There *are* no other eligible young men! If Jacka's not careful he'll spoil everything! Drake's not one to be hurried or driven, especially with the other sadness still in his heart."

"Well, it's time for bed. Past time." Ross snuffed the candle above the window seat and drew back the curtains, opened the window to release a moth, shut it again. Demelza put out the other two candles, picked up the fourth, and stood waiting for him, the door half ajar. The flickering light showed up her dark eyes and pale skin, the thoughtful expression, the velvet chair at her side with its foliate back, a half-empty glass of wine, the black bottle beside it. Conversation had moved rapidly, as it was wont to do, from the grave to the ridiculous. It was a saving grace in their relationship, but now it did not ameliorate enough.

She said: "Ross . . ."

"What?"

"No matter."

He came to the door and put his arm round her as they went out. They climbed the stairs together, companionable, it seemed, at one. But there was an ache in her. "I've failed you," she'd said. "Perhaps we've failed each other," he'd replied—not lightly, but almost as it were in passing, as if it must be an observed and accepted fact between them. Perhaps it must. Perhaps he was right. But it should not be so said.

It should not be so said.

Chapter Ten

The eighth of October, which was a Monday, dawned for Sam Carne much like any other day. He rose early, prayed on his knees for half an hour, worked in his garden as soon as it came light, and then had a sparse breakfast before walking across to Wheal Grace, with his tools on his shoulders and his croust, which today was bread and cheese with a piece of cold boiled bacon, in the pouch of his jacket.

He went down with Peter Hoskin, and they reached the forty-fathom level and stooped off through muddy passages and the dripping echoing caverns to the same old tunnel they had been working away at two years ago. Now that the south lode was proving deceptively thin, Ross and Henshawe and Zacky Martin had decided to try again to link with the old Wheal Maiden workings. They had considered the risk of unwatering the old mine, but Maiden had always been known as a particularly dry mine, being on a hill; and various adits still drained away into the Mellingey Stream. Also, before Wheal Grace, another mine had been begun on the hill and all the slime and deads from these excavations had been emptied into Maiden and filled up the main shafts. Ross said he thought there was more likelihood that Sam would start working upwards, as became a religious man, and finally force himself up through the floor of his new chapel.

Some hope had been raised by the recent discovery of two or three pockets of promising ground near the end where they were working; and before they came to their usual spot they passed two couples, Ellery and Thomas, and the youngsters Aaron Nanfan and Sid Bottrell, who were stoping these small lodes. Once they got to the end there was a fair amount of ground to go at, for they had used a charge last thing before leaving yesterday. They stripped off their shirts, folded them on a convenient piece of rock, and began to work.

Peter Hoskin was a great chatterer. He talked whenever Sam was near enough to hear, and sometimes when he was not. Not that Sam minded; but today he didn't listen. His mind was on Emma Tregirls. Twelve months had bone by since Demelza had got her a position as a maid at Tehidy. More than twelve months. Sam had agreed to the year's separation, for he had no choice. But now the year was up. If he did not hear soon, should he write to her? But Emma could not read, and the thought of some other tweeny spelling out his love letter was distasteful. He thought perhaps he should go over and ask to see her. Having been born nearby, he knew Tehidy like the back of his hand, but it was such an enormous house and one could hardly walk up to the front door and ring the bell.

He decided that that was what he would do, precisely that—or a side door anyway. He'd ask for a day off next week and visit his stepmother and his brothers. Perhaps he could persuade Peter Hoskin to come at the same time and visit *his* family. There had been an occasion—a sad occasion—when they had walked together on family business before.

The morning went quickly, and towards the end of it Peter's sharp eyes spied another streak of keenly ground almost over their heads. The other four were called up to examine it, and it was agreed that Zacky Martin should be invited to inspect it tomorrow to get his agreement that it was worth overhand stoping. Afterwards they all tramped back past the wheelbarrows and the picks and the hammers and the keg of gunpowder and the fuses and the rubble and the planks to a cooler corner, where they ate together.

It was a noisy meal, for they were lusty men, and the two youngsters seemed to enjoy the sound of their own voices, their own laughter echoing and re-echoing round the cavern, two hundred and forty feet below ground level. In spite of his religion, for none of these men was a Methody, Sam was popular in the group. When he chose to be he was good company and once in a while could be persuaded to imitate the voices of other people, which he did well. Like children, once they'd enjoyed an experience, they wanted it exactly the same again, and it didn't matter that Sam had imitated Dr. Choake or Jud Paynter last week; he had to do it again.

So there was a lot of laughter that day, especially about Jud's fishing expedition and what Prudie had said. Then it sobered a bit as they talked of the big party the Warleggans had had and the food they'd eaten and the liquor drunk: Char Nanfan and others had been asked to go and help, so they knew all about it. Then Ellery began to tell of Tholly Tregirl's bulldog; but by then it was time to get back to work.

It was an hour later that Sam took his pick out of

the relatively soft ground he was attacking and found the end moist. At first he thought it an ordinary leakage of water such as might occur at any time. Then he bent forward so that the candle in his hat showed up where his pick had been. A little rill of water was escaping into the tunnel.

"Peter!" he said. "Come here! Look at this!"

Peter was just pushing the barrow away, but the urgency of Sam's voice made him set it down and come back. He stared.

"God and His angels!" he said.

While they watched the rill had doubled in size.

"You'd best go back. Go back warn those others. Get out of here!"

"Yeh, but d'ye think—"

"Go on. Hurry! Get 'em up to grass!"

Water was coming now as if out of the spout of a thin drainpipe and shooting three feet from the rock. Every second the aperture was enlarging. It looked as if they had found Wheal Maiden, and it wasn't dry after all.

They were at forty fathoms and must have struck the lowest tunnels of Maiden. If these excavations had not drained away, a great quantity of water might have built up in this part of the old mine, through the shafts and tunnels, almost up to surface level. And now at last it had been granted an outlet.

Not stopping to grab his shirt or his tools, Sam ran back after the others, shadows lurching as he ran, with the water pursuing him and gurgling about his ankles. Less than a hundred yards from where they'd been working, a winze, or underground shaft, had been driven to the level below, where both the valuable lodes of tin were being worked. Fifty yards beyond that was the first air adit with a wooden ladder as far up as the twenty-fathom level and a tunnel beyond.

Sam caught them up in the cavern where they had had their croust. "Go up!" he shouted. "Warn 'em up there!"

He began to climb down to the lower level, shouting as he went. Before he was half down a wall of water fell on him, knocking him against the side of the ladder. Half drowned, half stunned, he fought for the next rung and the next and at last found himself at the bottom. The water was already roaring in its fall, like thunder. Because the winze had been driven three fathoms deeper than the next levels he was able to jump out of its way and gain a brief lead. But at the rate it was falling it would fill the bottom of the winze in two or three minutes.

He began to grope and run along the tunnel, which was narrow here and dark. He had lost his hat and therefore his candle and it seemed minutes before he stumbled over a barrow and broke into a cobbly gunnis and thence into a vaulted chamber where tiny points of flickering light showed where the miners were working. The lights were like glowworms, only yellow instead of green. As he came in there was a brief explosion and a wafted pungent smell of dynamite, where men had set off a charge.

He began to shout, to shout at the top of a voice trained for prayer meetings; but no revival in the great Wesleyan amphitheatres had brought him to such a vehemence as this. Work stopped; the men nearest to him downed tools and came back to him.

However reluctant some of them might have been to receive his Message aboveground, they took in this one very quickly indeed; miners live in constant danger: fire, falls, and flood are their greatest fears, and Sam spoke of the last. In seconds they had dropped everything and were pushing and filing back the way he had come, into the narrow tunnel which was their only way of escape. He went on, shouting his warning to the farthest away. But they came quickly too; no need to convince them, only to say the word; he passed them by, every one, warning them of the flood they'd have to face, of the danger of the deep well that by now would have been created by the sump of the winze: that to try to climb the way he had come down would be suicide: they must swim across the winze to the north tunnel on the other side, where the ground rose slightly, and fight their way up it till they reached the main shaft. If they reached that they were probably safe—though one of them must warn the workers on the northern lode.

Soon the cavern was empty and dark: Sam cast his eyes around it—no one remaining—then he followed in the wake of the last candle. He had gone no distance before he was in swirling water up to his waist, then to his armpits; the struggling men ahead of him made the water rise higher by the displacement of their bodies in the confined space. Air was short as water rose—pockets of it seemed to explode in his ears. The danger was the winze: men could not swim across more than perhaps two at a time: as he reached it he bumped against the man in front of him: there were more than a dozen waiting to take their turn, and the water pouring down from above was now carrying with it stones and planks of wood and any rubbish that it could sweep along. To swim into and through that waterfall, with only a half confidence that the tunnel at the other side would offer them any real escape, needed nerve and determination. One man funked it and decided to try the ladder up the winze. He got about twenty feet and then fell with a great explosion into the water, just missing one of the swimmers, and was lost to sight.

"The Lord is my light and my salvation," shouted Sam, his voice carrying above the uproar. "Whom then shall I fear? The Lord is the strength of my life; of whom then shall I be afraid?"

Five were left—then four, then three, then two, each one submerging and beginning the swim underwater to minimise the weight of the waterfall from above. Then it was his turn.

"The Lord is my light!" he said to himself, took a deep breath and sank his head into water that was already up to his shoulders. The thump on his back told him he was under the waterfall. The distance was nothing—ten strokes—but at the other side he came on legs, flailing in his face. Was the other tunnel blocked with men or was it in fact *lower* in the water to begin? Were they just kicking and drowning? His blood was pounding and his lungs heaving. A foot caught him in the chest and kicked him further off. He stroked his way cautiously back, surfaced now, taking a grateful breath, for the waterfall was at the other side of the winze. A man was floating face down; he caught his hair and pulled him towards the place where the beginning of the next tunnel ought to be. But it was pitch dark and he was no longer sure.

Then a voice, echoing in the dark. He made for it. "Sam—is that Sam? Where's Bill?"

His groping foot caught on the edge of the tunnel, a hand grasped his and pulled; behind him he held on to the hair. Men were shouting now farther up. He came to his feet, banged his head against the roof of the tunnel, water floated into and out of his mouth; his nostrils were just above the water. He held on to the hand.

The hand began to pull. They'd formed a chain. The ground must be rising gently. But as the tunnel rose, so did the water, so that step by step they were no better off. Someone in front must have stumbled, for he heard a choked cry and a splash and commotion; but presently they moved ahead again.

The ground rose abruptly by about a foot and mercifully the roof rose as well, so that Sam was head and shoulders clear. Distant from them, the way they were going, was a faint glimmer in the utter blindness of the dark: someone from the north lode, maybe, had come to help.

Sam shouted at the man in front of him: "Can ye give me a hand. Bill—I think tis Bill—is in a bad way."

They heaved the unconscious man over on his back and supported his head above water. It was probably Bill Thomas, but you couldn't be sure. Sam didn't even know who was helping him. They got the man onto Sam's back and proceeded again, step by step. Here and there the water deepened or the tunnel roof was lower, and Sam had to put his face into the water so as not to scalp the unconscious man on the rock roof above him.

The light grew nearer. It might not mean everything in the way of safety but it meant eyesight.

Sam had forgotten that a longish excavation had been stoped just near the main shaft, but now he saw candles bobbing on the other side and realised there was another swim ahead. He and his helper—it was Jim Thomas, Bill's brother—launched themselves together and began to ferry their burden across. At the other side was Zacky Martin, who had come down at the alarm, and a half dozen others, up to their waists, crowding the narrow tunnel ahead. Sam and Jim were hauled out of the water and Bill taken from them.

Now it was better—now they were through the worst—words and news exchanged—who was missing? —how deep was it in the south lode?—the north was four feet or more but everyone was coming safe out of that. There'd only been two men prospecting still deeper—one of them had got up, somehow, clinging like a monkey, the other had been swept away; but there was a chance he might come up through one of the old winzes still further north. Who was left behind in the south? None, said Sam. Or if there is they'll not come out alive. Then we'll best go up, said Zacky bitterly. There's naught more to do down here.

So another tunnel, but now water only waist high, and men to help. Sam was feeling all in now and he realised he was knocked about and bruised all over. But light was showing that was not yellow. It was a very diffused light, for it did not fall direct; it came down a slanted shaft that took a dozen different angles on its way up and was further broken by a dozen platforms. But it was daylight and safety for those who could see it. Now all that remained was climbing two hundred-odd feet up the ladders to find it.

II

Ross was at home when one of the Martin children came sputtering to tell him of the catastrophe. He dropped his pen and ran out of the house and up the hill towards the mine. Demelza, with two children to consider, questioned the boy more closely and then, leaving Jeremy and Clowance in Jane Gimlett's care with strict instruction that they were not to be allowed to follow her, she ran in Ross's wake.

By the time she got there Ross was already on his way down the main shaft. Unlike the other occasion when a whole cavern had subsided and smothered the excavations with dead ground, there had been no sound this time to alert those who were at grass level. First to give the alarm had been young Sid Bettrell, who had leaped up crying the news of disaster. Zacky Martin had been in charge, and his concern was to limit the flooding and the loss of life, so that it was not until the elder of the Curnow brothers sought instructions as to his pumping engine that anyone sent for Ross.

Zacky was on the way up and met Ross at the twenty-fathom level.

"Tes no use going further, Cap'n. They're coming up. We've cleared both main lodes. The few who're on the thirty level are in no danger."

"Loss of life," said Ross. "Are there some drowned?"

"Tis hard to be sure, but certain tis little or none. The alarm were given in time."

"God rot those Maiden workings!" said Ross. "We should never've gone for them."

"Who was to know? Mines is strange creatures. She was always known as dry. Your own father was constant in saying so. He used to say to me after Grace failed: pity we can't start Maiden 'gain—she was always as dry as a virgin. Begging your pardon, sur, twas what he used to say."

"Where did it break? Where Sam Carne and Hoskin were working? Are they safe?"

"Hoskin's up. Sam's down but coming up. According to what I d'hear tell, twas him going down through the water to the lower level that gave the main tributers time to get out. They say three minutes more— even one minute—would've been too late."

"Then who's lost? Anyone missing?"

"Two, I think. Sid Bunt in the sixty level, Tom Sparrock tried to climb but was washed away. They're bringing Bill Thomas up now. He's unconscious but we know no more. That's the lot as far as I d'know."

"Where's Henshawe?"

"He went over to Renfrew's about some gear. They've sent over to his house but he'll not be back yet."

Ross stayed on the twenty-fathom platform while the men filed up. They were all dripping water but for the most part none the worse. One had a gashed head. Another had sprained his foot. Mostly they were barefoot, having kicked off their boots to swim. They would be more in need of new boots than Jud.

Sam came up, tall and clumsy, and gaunt in the flickering light. Ross shook his hand and asked a question or two but did not detain him, for, in spite of the heat, he was shivering and almost blue. Ross stayed on, shaking each man by the hand, putting the odd question. As one after another familiar face showed up he began to feel reassured that casualties were as light as Zacky supposed. Work in the mine was abandoned for the day as the half dozen men prospecting in the upper levels heard the news and downed tools and came up. When the last of them was accounted for, Ross followed.

Dwight had been found at home and was attending to minor injuries in the changing shed beside the engine house. Demelza was helping him, as were Mrs. Zacky and three other women. But there was not so much to do as might have been expected. On the floor in a corner and covered with a blanket was Bill Thomas, only part conscious but slowly recovering. Demelza said to Ross: "Dwight did the most strangest of things: he put Bill Thomas on his face and squeezed water out of him—so much as you'd hardly believe—then he laid him on his back and put his mouth to *his* mouth and *blew* into him. Blew and blew and blew, and then after a long time the—the man's eyes flickered and he vomited more water, and *now* look at him. He looks as if he's going to come brave again. Dwight says he's going to come brave."

Ross squeezed her arm but did not speak.

"The lodes—both lodes . . . they're flooded?"

"Totally. But that can be seen to in time. Our old fire engine will have to work the harder. It will be a loss of weeks—perhaps months. But it's the lives I care about. . . . Where's Sam?"

"He had his arm dressed and he went home."

"They say we owe a lot to him."

"Yes, I heard it up here."

"I'll go thank him tomorrow."

"We'll both go," Demelza said.

III

Sam had got home. There was still an hour or two's daylight left, but he had no energy to turn to the garden. Nor for the moment could he think whether he had a class tonight. What day was it? Tuesday? No, Monday. He wasn't certain. Surely yesterday had been church day. So there *was* a class tonight, at the Meeting House on the hill, a house built of stones from the mine that had caused today's disaster. Since it was opened it had become known as Maiden Chapel. Monday at seven was Bible reading, and Sam usually had a dozen or more of the converted, who sat and listened and then asked questions and spoke about the effect on themselves of the passages he had read.

So he must be feeling better by then. Best, no doubt, after he had put on dry things, to make a dish of tea and cut himself a slice—then maybe an hour with his feet up. For once he must indulge himself—take a bit of leisure in the daytime.

He scraped flint and blew a spark until it lit the shavings and bits of driftwood he had in the fireplace, then he tipped some water from his pitcher into a pan and waited for it to boil. A pinch of tea in a cup and a spoonful of sugar. In about ten minutes he poured the water in the cup and stirred it. Scenes from this afternoon were vivid in his mind. He thanked God that so few lives had been lost, and he thanked the Divine Father that He had seen fit to spare his own so that His will might be humbly done on earth, and so that he, Sam Carne, might continue on the great and glorious road of salvation.

It was an uplifting and a wondrous thought that came upon him every morning when he opened his eyes. Here he was, a humble miner in a desolate corner of England, whom God had chosen as His unworthy instrument to further His divine purposes. Through him more and more sinful souls were finding mercy and entering into the liberty of perfect love. He should not sit here sipping tea and munching bread and jam just because his limbs were aching and bruised and his head a bit swimming and his stomach queasy from the foul water he had swallowed. He must conquer this weakness and soon be on his feet again and about his Father's business. There would be distress at the mine. There would be widows to be comforted. Tom Sparrock had almost certainly gone; he had seen it with his own eyes; Jane Sparrock was a scold—Tom had always been henpecked—but she would grieve all the same. Sid Bunt was from St. Ann's way and he hardly knew his wife. . . .

A knock at the door. A head came round. Beth Daniel, Paul's wife.

"Aw, I came to see 'ow you was, my dear. To see if I could bring ee a dish o' tay. But I see you've been ahead o' me!"

Beth Daniel, though not a Methodist of the most earnest persuasion, was always wanting to help others. Sam thanked her and said he was fine now, well and fine.

Beth said, fumbling in her apron: "I got a drop o' something stronger if you've the mind, you. Put 'n in your tay, my dear, twill flavour it a morsel and give ee extra kick an' sprawl."

Sam thanked her again but refused. "The tea'll do me well, Beth. Thank ee, just the same."

They talked about the disaster and how Dr. Enys

had brought Bill Thomas back to life by blowing air into his lungs. Then Beth said:

"Aw, while you was down today, Lobb come—brought the *Mercury* to Cap'n Poldark. In it it d'say there've been a great victory for England. Cap'n Poldark were that excited he give all his servants a rum toddy. Nile, be it?—someplace. Admiral Nelson've destroyed the French ships. Blowed 'n out o' the sea, he did! Twelve out o' thirteen, Cap'n Poldark say. Twelve out o' thirteen French battleships. Never know nothin' like it, Cap'n Poldark say—not since Armada times!"

"Pray it will end the war," said Sam.

"Aw, my dear, yes. Cap'n Poldark d'say all the bells be ringing London way. I expect they'll peal at Sawle so soon as they d'know."

"When did it happen, Beth?"

"Aw, weeks gone, I b'lave. August, I think he d'say." Beth broke off and clicked her fingers. *"Now,* then. I near forgot what I just come to tell ee. After he'd been Nampara, Lobb came over here and I seen 'im knock on your door, so I come over and say: 'Sam be down mine,' I say, 'you'll find no one 't home, you.' So he say to me, he say, 'I got a letter, this here letter, for Sam Carne,' so I say I'll hold 'n for ee, and this I done and yur tis, thas if I can find 'n in the deeps o' me pocket."

She proceeded to fish out the small medicine jar which contained the brandy, then a length of string, two clothes clips, and a stained rag. After this came the letter. Sam stared at the handwriting: it was poor and ill-formed and spelt his name without an "e." His heart began to thump.

Beth clearly expected him to open it in front of her and if possible give her some idea of the contents, for letters to people in their station of life were a rarity. So she stood there chatting, sometimes about the mine and sometimes about the victory, and occasionally her eye would stray unbidden to the letter in his hand. But he did not, could not, break the seal while she was there, and at length he took a step or two and put it down on the rough mantelpiece that Beth's brother-in-law had once made when he had built this cottage for his faithless moonflower wife. Then he turned and smiled at Beth, his sad attractive smile, so she knew she would receive no satisfaction and was presently edged towards the door, praising him for his work today and saying it was likely Paul owed his life to him (which was not true, for Paul had been on the north lode), and so left.

He stood at the door and saw her trudge back to her cottage at Mellin, just over the fold of the land; then he went in and picked up the letter. He felt he could not yet open it. He felt he must pray first. But pray for what? Not his own happiness; not even Emma's. He could only pray for her soul, and that he had done every night since she left. Could he add more now, any special or different plea?

He knelt at the foot of his bed for a few moments, saying nothing, thinking nothing, then rose and broke the seal.

Deer Sam [it said],

I am no writter as you well do knaw so I ave asked my good freind Mary to writ this for me.

Sam deer Sam deer Sam I ave asked my good freind Mary to say that to ee for I do meen it most truely. But Sam I be gwan to wed the secund footman. He is a kynd man ten year olderer than me but jolly an kynd an thortful of me an I blave he do truely love me. He be not a wyld man like Tom nor yet a good man like you but he have good ways an quiet ways an do wark onest and true an ard an I do like he and enjoy his company.

Mary say I giver er some awful ard wurds to spell but she arnt at the end of un yet for Sam I do want ee to knaw that if twer just so simpel as it did oughter be then you an me wud be wed and no other. But tedden so an never could be so for you be a man of God an I be no more an a jooly gurl. Sam tes worser an that. Youm such a good man that you dont knaw the wurld so well as me. Ef I wed you and come to chappel along of you the folks wud

*look athurt an point an say lookee at that thur braz-
zen ussie who do she think she be wed to our Sam
our preecher. Her what weve all seen in Sallys kiddley adrinkin wi the best an walkin arm in arm wi
alf the fellers an who do knaw whats gone on in the
mowhay. That we all do knaw an twas mercy she
wur never forceput. An she wed to our Sam our
preecher it edn fitty nor proper nor never shal be an
if Sam do think defferent he be mazed or not so holy
as he pertend.*

*Sam deer Sam deer Sam I watch my good freind
Mary writ it fur me an she say no more she will writ
no more but I give er a shillun for writtin this so she
must do some more lines wether or no. Ef ee do
think defferent ef ee do say the Bible do say defferent that bad wemen be redeamed that be true of
Bible days but no so naow. Im not bad an you do
knaw I be not nigh so bad a woman as many in the
Bible but is reppertation that do count on your folk
your prayin folk you may think they be as kynd as
you but that they wud never be. They wud not tak
me in as you wud tak me in an you wud be afightin
them for me. Then deer Sam what ef I went an took
a drink in Sallys kiddley an you did not knaw an
one of your prayin folk come up and telled ee.
Twould never do not in this wurld.*

*So good by my deer. I be some sad talkin this let-
ter to my good freind Mary an the tears be on my
face an on my ands fur tis sad to say good by to
your best love. But Ned Artnel do love me truely an
I surely like im an thas the way it must be. Wed
sum good woman thurs many about an forgit me.
Nay never forgit me fur Ill never forgit you but thur
cud be no appiness in our wedden together an one
day deer eart you will know I do speak God's truth.*
       Your every loving
      Emma. XXXXXXX

After he had finished it he read it carefully through
again. Then he folded it away and put it back on the
mantelshelf and went to the door and stared out over

the scene. Brown mellow stubble of harvested fields folding upon each other and merging into the scrubland that led to Hendrawna Beach. And England had won a great victory. The only other houses in sight were the empty Gatehouse up on the hill and a chimney or two of Mingoose House showing above the windswept trees. The sky was clear. The sea was at peace. Smoke from a Mellin cottage/chimney drifted across the sky. A cow was roaring in a dip in the valley. And England had won a great victory.

Then the scene was no longer clear and he began to blub through his hands. He cried noisily, like a boy, hurt and in pain. For a while he could not stop, gulping and jerking, and then he fetched up some of the foul water and the tea he had drunk.

After that he cried more quietly for a while and then took a rag from his pocket and tried to dry his eyes, his nose, his mouth. The water still kept oozing out of his eyes. He had never felt so much alone.

He went into the cottage and poured some water onto the tea leaves, but it was half cold.

He said: "The Lord is my strength and my Redeemer. Blessed is the name of the Lord."

He sat down and began to say out loud many of the great passages from the Prayer Book that he had learned by heart. "Oh, God, who art the author of peace and lover of concord, in knowledge of whom standeth our eternal life, whose service is perfect freedom. Defend us thy humble servants in all assaults of our enemies . . ."

It helped. Soon it would take over again. Soon. The heartbreaks of this temporal life were as nothing compared to the joys of the everlasting grace to come. Soon.

But this was a double heartbreak for Sam. He had wanted Emma for himself to have and to hold in sickness and in health so long as they both should live. But also he had wanted her as a soul won for God—hers was the most precious soul of all to him. Had he been able both to bring her to God and to wed her, then his cup would have been full. Now it was empty. And just for a while the eternal spirit of salvation ran low in him. It came to him to think that perhaps he should not have struggled and swum so hard this afternoon.

It was blasphemy and sacrilege to think so; he knew that. Perhaps he was among the worst of sinners even to have allowed the thought to settle for a moment. Evil thoughts were like evil birds: one could not prohibit their existence, one could only prevent them from settling in one's mind. With a cold heart he took up his Bible, drew a chair to his homemade desk, and began to read. When it grew dark he lit a candle and continued. He read right through the Gospel of St. John and then went on to some of the epistles.

Thus Ena Daniel found him—Beth's sister-in-law and one of the most faithful of his flock. Excuse her, she said, but they were all over to the Meeting House and had been waiting a fair while. They all knew he must be feeling some slight after the terrible, terrible time of this afternoon, and, though they didn't like to start without him, Jack Scawen would be glad to try and read for him if so be as they might borrow the Bible.

She was quite startled at the empty look Sam gave her—as if something had been washed away from him for ever in the flooded mine—but after a few moments he passed his hand across his eyes and made an effort to smile his old smile.

"Why, no, Ena. I'm fine and well now. Just—a little sore, as ye might say. Just a little sore. Wait till I change my shirt and I'll come."

BOOK TWO

Chapter One

Ross did not go back to London that year. The disaster at the mine occupied him for the better part of two months. He wrote a letter to Lord Falmouth explaining.

Demelza, always looking for the bright side, said it could have been so much worse; and, for once, Ross had to agree with her. Two lives lost—that was the tragedy; but miners were constantly in danger. Three had been killed at Wheal Kitty last year—all in trifling accidents. One or two a year had been a natural wastage when Grambler was working. The miracle here was that a major disaster had killed so few.

There had been some miraculous escapes. Micky Green had been on his own in the fifty level and had heard the water coming—it sounded, he said, like the burst of a boiler. He had run to a hummock of rising ground and climbed to a crosspiece of timber and clung there for two hours with the water surging and boiling round him. Then as the worst began to subside he had lowered himself and cautiously, still waist deep, made for the nearest shaft. One of the Carters, a boy of thirteen, had hung back behind Sam because he was unable to swim, and when they were gone he had made his way up the ladder—from which Sparrock had recently been swept to his death—and had somehow avoided the worst of the falling debris and came to the surface bruised all over and as grey as a rat.

Chief honour for the minimal loss of life fell on Sam Carne, but he was a difficult man to thank. He did not drink. He did not favour a party at which, inevitably, everyone else would get drunk. He shrugged off, smilingly, words of appreciation and usually tried to turn the conversation to the prospects of Another Life than this. He seemed sometimes even a little sadder about it all than he had any overt reason to be, and it took Demelza a while to discover the truth. Then she said: "Oh, Sam . . . Oh, Sam. I'm that sorry. Oh, Sam, I feel it is part my fault."

"No, no, sister, tes far from that. You did what you b'lieved to be best. And mebbe *twas* for the best. The eternal Jehovah have thought fit to put this temporal burden upon me and I must thank Him for the privilege of His mercy and forgiveness. If I have sinned, then I must seek to be cleansed. If dear Emma have sinned, then I do truly believe that in the goodness of time her spirit too will be cleansed and she will come to a new life in the spirit of Christ."

It was hard at times to feel total sympathy for a young man who embellished his personal feelings with the language of revivalism, but Demelza, who knew her brother fairly well, perceived that under his genuine, burning religious faith he was suffering just as acutely as any man who sees the girl he dearly loves lost to him forever. And sometimes, she saw, in the dark of the night he would wake and know —the earthy carnal side of him would know—that but for his religion he could have married her last year. Even maintaining his religion at a slightly less personal and intense level, he could still have married her. Demelza thought, too, that they would have been good for each other; Sam toning down Emma's vulgar high spirits, Emma charming and teasing Sam into a more homely approach to his faith.

But it was not to be; and Demelza felt unhappy for her part in it. Now Sam, hero of the whole community, found himself joyless, and it was joylessness which for a while at least would affect his attitude to God and his flock.

Work soon began again in the forty-fathom level of Wheal Grace, and much later in the fifty-fathom, but it was work of repair without ore being raised. The great flood had broken the pumping rods, and this was the first and most essential repair. Then in many places in the fifty level soft ore-bearing ground, which did not look likely to yield rich results, had been set aside in substantial piles while the better lodes were pursued; it was intended to be taken up whenever there was more time and less good work ahead. But the torrent of water had spread this around, along with whatever attle had been left, so that it had been sucked out of the caverns and blocked the tunnels. Men going down as the water was laboriously pumped out had found themselves knee deep in mud and unable to get through to the paying lodes until the mud and the rock had been dug out and wheeled back to the kibbal buckets and hauled to the surface.

The water had brought down falls of rock, and in places the timber supports had collapsed, making the roofs and sides dangerous. In an old book on mining Ross had read that "after fyre water be ye element most penetrating and destructive." So he found it. Since normal method of payment was invalid while the mine was in such a state, he introduced the old whip system, whereby the number of kibbals of mixed ore, attle, mud, and stones that were brought to the surface each day were counted and a payment made per kibbal, divided equally among every person working at the mine.

At first they had wondered whether the present fire engine would be able to cope with the vast amount of additional water. The forty-fathom level had soon cleared, but it was almost two weeks after the pump rods had been repaired that one saw a lowering of the water further down. Then it was inch by inch, day by day, and always the fear that autumnal rains would check the gain.

November came in wild and wet, but in the main the rain was fine stuff driven this way and that by the gales. At times the wind was so thunderous that it drowned the roar of the sea. There had not been many substantial wrecks on Hendrawna recently, but two came ashore in the middle of the month: a small schooner outward bound from Truro to Dublin, carrying serges and carpets and paper, and a larger brig, with coal out of Swansea.

The schooner drifted in stern first and broke up below Wheal Leisure: the crew of four were saved, but the contents of the vessel vanished like magic in the wild wind and the rain. Ross, once he knew the crew was safe, discreetly kept his house; he wanted no repetition of the charges of 1790. The brig came ashore far up the beach, almost under the Dark Cliffs, where no one lived at all, and seven of the nine crew were drowned. This wreck was of value to the district, and few poor people went short of coal that winter. For the next month and more the tawny sands of Hendrawna were black-edged like a mourning card.

Towards the end of November, Jeremy caught a cold, which develop'd into a cough, as usual, and he ran a fever. For the offspring of such healthy stock on both sides, he had a surprisingly weak chest. There was consumption enough in the villages, not only among forty-year-old miners, whose complaint was a natural consequence of the conditions in which they worked, but among the young, and there were special families where one after another of a handsome brood would cough and sicken and die. Sometimes a whole family of five children would be wiped out in five years, leaving behind two healthy parents without issue. Sometimes five or six out of eight would go. And this would be among children who had survived the perils of childhood and were just entering their teens. It ran in families, inexplicably, with the next-door house or cottage immune.

But Jeremy, who had been warm and cared for and never gone short in his life, was a chesty subject and therefore suspect. She mentioned this to Dwight, who reassured her that he could detect no symptoms of phthisis.

On the afternoon of the twenty-eighth she came downstairs after sitting with Jeremy for an hour, and found Ross had returned in her absence. He was reading a book, standing over it by the window where the light was best. Even now they scarcely used the new library except on special occasions. She saw the book was *Mineralogia Cornubiensis,* published twenty years before by a surgeon from Redruth, one William Pryce, and the pages of it were as often thumbed by Ross as the Bible's were by Sam.

She went to peer out at the other window. This afternoon the clouds matched the colour of the beach; sagging bags of coal moving over the valley with the swiftness of the turning world. The lilac tree beside the window bent and quivered; her garden looked derelict; the unknown plant left her by Hugh Armitage flattened its big green leaves against the library wall.

He said: "Another month should see us working the fifty level again. It will have meant about three months' loss of output—that is all—if you count it just as profit and loss."

"No one does that, Ross."

"I wonder sometimes. Listen to this: this is what Pryce says: 'In some places, especially where a new adit is brought home to an old mine which has not been wrought in the memory of man, they have holed unexpectedly to the house of water before they thought themselves near to it, and have instantly perished. Great precaution must therefore be taken, and a hole should be bored with an iron rod to the distance of a fathom or two so that before breaking the ground with a pick axe they may have timely notice of the bursting forth of the water. This advice however may not be relished by those who are impatient to be rich and value a little money more than the lives of their fellow creatures.' "

"What is that saying? When the damage is done everyone is wise?"

"Presumably I was impatient to be rich and valued a little money more than the lives of my fellow creatures."

Demelza pushed her hair back impatiently. "You

know that to be untrue, so why say it? Money was never the important thing in your mind. Not like the time when the mine fell in—then we were living from hand to mouth, and maybe a risk was something we *had* to take. So you could reproach yourself then. Not now."

Ross closed the book. "All the same, what Pryce says makes uncomfortable reading."

"Then don't read it."

Ross half smiled: "The more I hear of your reasoning, the more specious it sounds."

"I don't know what 'specious' means," Demelza said, picking at a small cut in her thumb.

"Well—nor I, to be exact. Plausible but devoid of inner truth—that's as near as I can get."

"That's near enough. Well, your specious wife thinks tis time you stopped plaguing your conscience with specious arguments as to why you are to blame for the errors of the whole specious world!"

"You'll make it sound like a swear word soon."

"That's what it is," said Demelza.

Ross laughed and picked up the book. "I'll take this back where it belongs. And my uneasy conscience too." He peered out through the same window as Demelza. "God, look at those clouds."

She said: "Did you go into the Maiden workings yesterday?"

"Yes. They're dry enough, for all the water has drained into Grace. They're dry, that is, except for the stinking mud. But the air's so bad we could hardly venture any distance. All the mud and attle tipped down the shafts, instead of preventing water accumulating, imprisoned it; and there's no air from the shafts at all."

"I don't like you going down," said Demelza. "I always think what happened to Francis."

"He went on his own. And would you have me shrink from the tasks I expect others to do?"

"No," she said, "I can bear you as you are. But I don't want to lose you as you are."

He put his hand on her arm. "Are you fretting about Jeremy?"

"No, no. I just wish the fever would abate."

From this window they could see a few lights beginning to wink up at the mine.

"Would you like Dwight to come again? I can send Benjy Carter."

"I thought not to bother him, Ross. Sarah is none too well, he says."

Ross looked up. "Sarah?"

Demelza raised her dark eyebrows at him. "Sarah. His own little girl. Why do you look so strange?"

"Do I? No. I could not think who you meant."

"She has caught a cold like Jeremy. There are so many about. Half the countryside is snorting and sniffing."

"Ah," said Ross. "Well, yes. I suppose." He patted her arm again and went through the dining room into the library.

She put coal on the fire, watched a spurt of smoke billow into the room as the uncertain wind eddied about the chimney. Then she went to the piano and began to play a piece she knew by heart, a simplified sonata by Scarlatti that Mrs. Kemp had taught her.

Ross came in again. "I had forgot," he said. "There is some unfinished business up at the mine. It will take me about an hour. It will be—well, I'll be back in good time for supper."

She nodded, hair over brow, tongue between teeth and lip, where it tended to go when she was playing. But presently she heard a clatter on the cobbles and she went out to the kitchens.

"Has Captain Poldark taken his horse?"

"Yes, ma'am. John have saddled it for 'n."

"To go up to the mine?"

"Dunno, ma'am. He just say to John, he say, I'm taking Sheridan."

II

The light was fading as he turned in at the gates of Killewarren. It was a featureless house: long, low, and built without benefit of architect. The drive and grounds were better kept than they had been in Ray Penvenen's day, but a branch of one of the old pine trees had come down in the gale and the arm of it, sweeping in the wind, startled Sheridan and made him sidestep. There were three or four lights.

When he knocked at the door Bone came. He had been Dwight's personal servant before he married and he had sailed with Ross on the French adventure. "Oh, good evening, sur; come in, sur; some wild, isn't it. Did you wish to see the master?"

"Either him or Mrs. Enys or both."

"Yes, sur. Please to come in here. I'll tell them you've called."

He was shown into the small parlour on the ground floor. Most of the better rooms were on the first floor and the big drawing room was above the stables.

Dwight came in. Although he was dressed and shaved and his hair neatly brushed, Ross was reminded of the emaciated wreck he had rescued from the Quimper prison. It was the look in his eyes.

He smiled. "Well, Ross. Is Jeremy none so brave?"

"Jeremy will do again. But Demelza told me Sarah was—ill."

"She has a cold."

"That is all?"

Dwight made a grimace. "It will be enough."

"Oh, God. Does Caroline know?"

"Yes . . . I felt now I had to tell her."

Ross hit his crop against his boot. "I'm no use to you. But I had to come."

"It's good of you."

"No . . . How is she taking it?"

"Very well," said a voice from the door.

Caroline, as always, the tall stalk of a flower, red-haired, green-eyed, freckled across the nose. The only difference was that her lips were without colour.

"Caroline . . ."

"Yes, Ross, it is all a trifle distressing, is it not. Had Dwight already told you?"

"He'd warned me it might happen."

"Confidences between men from which wives and mothers are excluded . . . Yes, it has been rather a shock, but Caroline is taking it well, with all the dignity and stoicism of a lady of breeding."

"Let me get you something, Ross," Dwight muttered.

". . . Caroline, I don't know what to say. I don't know why I've come; but I felt . . ." A glass of brandy was in his hand.

Caroline looked at the glass Dwight had given her. "My husband clearly wishes me to become a toper. Or is it that he thinks drink softens the edges of tragedy and converts it into some lighter form of grief? Or are we proposing a toast to something or someone?"

"Caroline," said Dwight. "You are deceiving no one. Sit down. Perhaps just sitting quiet for a while . . ."

She sipped her drink. "D'you know, Ross, I said I didn't want the wretched little creature—and that was true. I find animals vastly more grateful and rewarding. But, over the months, I have to confess she has wormed her way into my affections. Poor Horace has been quite put out that I have neglected him so. Well, well, Sarah Penvenen. *Ave atque vale.* How my uncle would have been annoyed that his grandniece was to have so short a stay."

Nothing was said for a while. Some light branch, torn away by the wind, was tapping at the window, like a bird trying to get in.

Ross said: "Is she? . . . How long?"

Dwight said: "Hours, I would suppose."

Ross said: "I should have brought Demelza."

"No, no," said Caroline, "that would have been the greatest of a mistake. You are two strong men and can support me. I am a hard woman and can fend for

myself. But Demelza—Demelza would not be so—
formal; she would not be so—controlled; she would
not be so—dignified. Demelza does not understand
dignity and—and all that it stands for . . ." Caroline
sipped her drink again. "I believe Demelza would cry
—and that, and that, I rather think—would—ruin us
all . . ."

Chapter Two

While the frail fair-haired waif born in 1798 and
baptised Sarah Caroline Anne departed this life in the
same year with scarcely a struggle, dying, as she
had lived, peaceably and without purpose, an old man
born as long ago as 1731 and baptised by his doting
parents Nathaniel Gustavus, refused altogether to go
when everything pointed to the suitability of his passing. His doctor predicted it, his vicar expected it, he
daily forecast it himself, and his Methody daughter
had three times supposed that he was gone. But Mr.
Pearce, Notary and Commissioner for Oaths, was
made of stout and enduring material. The door was
open but nothing could squeeze him through it. Lying
in bed he grew weekly more amorphous in bulk, and
though Dr. Behenna had twice tried to tap him for
dropsy, the bulk did not seem to be composed of
water. There he lay like a stranded whale, slightly
putrescent, mulberry-coloured of face and hands, constantly clutching his nightshirt beneath which
somewhere, very deep buried, his overburdened heart
continued its lonely labours.

His attack of conscience had passed—or perhaps it
had been submerged in the day-to-day struggle of
keeping alive. He no longer thought of the widows
and orphans he had cheated—indeed, there were no
widows and only two orphans among them—and he

welcomed the visits of his spiritual adviser with a new appreciation. Had he not had this latest manifestation of the Reverend Osborne Whitworth's concern, he would have called Ossie a selfish young man—and conceited too—conceited especially about his prowess at whist—but he had been touched and grateful at the regularity of Mr. Whitworth's visits. Every Thursday without fail. True, Ossie only stayed half an hour; and then took himself off with relish. But the regularity of the visits—when there was no longer any whist to attract, and the canary wine was probably no better than one could get elsewhere—these visits touched and impressed him. He had misjudged the stout young man.

Mr. Pearce, though aware that he caused Dr. Behenna some irritation by continuing to breathe when he no longer should have been able to, was quite unaware of that other frustration he was causing—and causing to no less a person than Cary Warleggan, who waited like a puppet master with all the strings ready to draw, but no one to play the introductory chorus. While Mr. Pearce survived, the puppets could not be made to dance.

In the meantime, that more distinguished member of the family, Mr. George Warleggan, continued to acquire interests in the parliamentary borough of St. Michael. Sir Christopher Hawkins had been persuaded to part with most of his property there—at a handsome price—but the Scawen interests were still strong, and George, never a man to do things by halves, was anxious to obtain a controlling interest over both seats.

The Scawens were an old Cornish family who for centuries had had property at St. Germans and elsewhere, and, though more recently, through marriage into the Russell family of Northants, they had made more of their extensive interests up-country. James Scawen, a tetchy bachelor, saw no reason to part with property in St. Michael which had been theirs for generations. It was going to require patience, persistence, and skill to make him change his mind. Not to mention money. In the meantime, on a visit to

London, George had contrived to make the acquaintance of both sitting members, and had taken particular note of Captain David Howell, who had been Sir
Christopher Hawkins's nominee. Captain Howell did
not appear to be a wealthy man—he was a Cornishman with a relatively poor estate near Lanreath—and
it did not seem likely that he would be unsusceptible
to financial inducements when the time came.

Following these manoeuvres at a distance, like a
non-participator at a fox hunt, but avidly interested
in the outcome, was the vicar of St. Margaret's, Truro.
He realised that if George should once become a
boroughmonger, his influence would be far greater
than any he had ever exercised as a mere M.P.

He said as much as this to George one evening when
they were supping together, but George was uncom-
municative. Even if Ossie had not used the word
"mere" he would have been lacking in encouragement.
But Ossie, undeterred, pointed out the various forms
of patronage that could be exercised when in such a
position—notable among them the furthering of the
prospects of younger relatives who had made the
Church a career.

"The Church," he said between mouthfuls, "the
Church as a career is a lottery. Everyone must agree
that, George. The Archbishop of Canterbury gets
twenty-five thousand pounds a year! The Bishop of
London twenty thousand pounds! But men such as
myself have to make do with three hundred pounds!
Some get less. Some get even less. And not bad fellows
neither! The revenues of the Church, the total revenues, if divided all round would probably not *come*
to more than three hundred pounds a year each. So
one enters the profession as one buys a ticket in a
sweepstake—hoping for one of the great prizes. If
gentlemen didn't have that hope, they wouldn't enter
the profession at all. You'd get men like Odgers—
unlearned, unwashed, doesn't know how to dress—or
sometimes how to spell!—uncouth—little better than
agricultural labourers. And then where would the
Church be?"

Nobody answered.

Ossie took another quaff of wine. "I've been looking at the living of Manaccan, George. It has just became vacant and would be a useful little addition to my stipend. The tithes are worth a good three hundred pounds a year, I'm told."

As he went on Elizabeth glanced at Morwenna, who sat quietly picking at her food, scarcely eating anything. Elizabeth and George were seeing less and less of the Whitworths as George jibbed at these family suppers. They had dropped off from one a week to one a month. Elizabeth made up for it by going to tea with Morwenna at St. Margaret's from time to time—usually when she knew Ossie would be absent. She could not make Morwenna out. She never made any complaint; but she was frequently strange—absent-minded, untidy, distraught. Her dark eyes seemed so often to be gazing at something her visitor could not see. And it was certainly something unpleasant. Sometimes her soft, gentle voice was quite harsh, and it was startling then in its strength. She did not answer when spoken to. (This usually passed off after Elizabeth had been there a few minutes.) She hardly ever wrote to her mother now, and the last time Mrs. Chynoweth had proposed to come on a visit she had made an excuse and said it was not convenient. She never spoke of Rowella, and if Rowella's name was mentioned the conversation dropped.

Yet she did not seem ill. She moved about with energy when she chose to move at all; and the house, though superficially untidy, was well run. She did many good works and was never unwilling to visit the sick and the dying. Superficially a vicar could hardly have had a more suitable wife. Nor had she lost her looks. But they were different looks, wilder, more unstable.

One thing that surprised Elizabeth on her visits now was that they never seemed to have a satisfactory nurse for young John Conan. The pleasant young girl they had employed for eighteen months had been discharged, and a succession of strange women took her place: strong, thick-legged, middle-aged, grim-faced, grey-faced, or warty, with sharp narrow eyes and smelling of starch and camphor balls, they varied between the obsequious and the insolent. Elizabeth would not have had one of them in her house and ventured to say to Morwenna that she would have thought a bright young girl more suitable: she knew of two she could recommend.

A grimace crossed Morwenna's face. "It is Ossie who chooses them, Elizabeth. And Ossie who discharges them. I believe he cannot find just the right person. Or so he tells me."

"To companion and care for a little boy? How strange."

"Osborne is a strange man, Elizabeth."

"I wonder you do not think of one of your other sisters. I think Garlanda might be glad of the opportunity, and it would be company for you."

Morwenna said: "I would never have a sister of mine here again."

II

On the tenth of December, a week after the pathetic little coffin had been put into the ground beside the ostentatious memorial Ray Penvenen had had erected for himself, Caroline Enys came into her husband's study after supper and stood a moment with her back to the door staring at his gaunt sensitive face and greying hair. He rose and pulled a chair forward so that they could sit near each other at the desk, but instead she walked over and warmed her hands at the fire. She was wearing a green pinafore over a white satin frock, as if there were still a child to be taken on her knee.

"Dwight," she said, "I think we are taking this far too much to heart."

"It's possible."

"Children die every day. We are agreed on the overpopulation of the world, are we not? There are far too many of us already. What does another matter? You told me last week of Mrs. Barnes who has lost nine in ten years. The fact that this one is ours and that we esteem it above the others only shows a doleful lack of proportion. We have lost a baby, that's all. I—if I were of a true motherly condition—I might be expected to take it a trifle hard—my very first and me already in my middle twenties! But *you*—you who spend all your life observing the feeble struggles of your patients to escape the inevitable end, you who tell me of this or that person who has a goitre or scrofulous eczema or scorbutic anaemia and can do nothing to help them, who can only try to alleviate and palliate the universal suffering that you see all round, why should you grieve that the product of our union should be excused and pardoned the pains of living and allowed to escape into an early grave? It puzzles me."

Dwight smiled slightly. "No, it does not. Because you are a human being, and so am I, and the penalty of this condition—and also the reward—is that we do not see each other as numbers on a board but as persons for whom love and emotional attachment is all. We can't escape the obligations of humanity. And one of those obligations is to grieve at the loss of those who are—are part of our love and part of our blood."

Caroline pursed her lips. "But you know, Dwight, I was never meant to be a mother."

"What nonsense! You have been one—and a good one—and I trust you'll be one again."

"No . . . Or not yet." She took two paces to come behind him and to put a hand on his shoulder. "Dwight, I want to leave you."

In the silence some gas blew in the coal, burning brilliant and blue until it was exhausted.

Dwight said: "What do you mean?"

"Oh, not permanent. Don't rejoice: you can't rid yourself of me as easy as that. . . . But I want to get away. I want to get away from Killewarren—and Sawle—and the people here. I feel I have failed you, have failed myself, everything—there's such a *weight* on me. I've never been able to cry about this—you know that—and I carry about in my breast such a weight of unshed tears that it seems it will burst me open. This is a terrible and humiliating confession that I would make to no one but you. But I feel—so long as I stay here, in this house, with its . . . furnishings, and Uncle Ray's silver, and the medicine bottles, and all the servants trying to be kind, and my—my horses, and Ruth Treneglos for company on a day's hunting, and—and your kind, hurt indulgence—I feel I shall not take any steps to mend."

Dwight got up, closed his book without seeing it, stared at his cuff on which there was some sort of an ink stain, and then looked up to meet the brilliance of his wife's eyes.

"What do you wish to do?"

"I don't know. Perhaps go to London, stay with my aunt for a month or two. I don't know."

"Do you wish me to come with you or do you want to go alone?"

"How can you go? There are fifty—a hundred—two hundred sick people who depend on you. How could I take you away from them? I am already—I already feel sufficiently selfish in saying that I want to get away. There is no such escape for you. And it is only three years since you were rescued like a skeleton from a French prison; it is barely a year since you appeared to recover from that ordeal. Now you are *rooted* here, *surrounded* by your bereavement, the loss of Sarah; and your useless brittle wife wishes to leave you to your own devices and to comfort herself by some sort of escape. I *can't* ask you to come with me, Dwight. I wouldn't. I could never ask you to be so selfish. Only I am entitled to be so selfish."

Dwight said: "A much kinder interpretation could be put upon it all."

"Don't bother to try, for I shall not believe it."

Dwight looked down at the title of the book. Unlike Ross's preoccupation, it had only just been published and was called *An Inquiry into the Causes and Effect of the Variolae Vaccinae,* by one Dr. Edward Jenner. One of the candles had a fault in it, the wax was dribbling down and congealing, like some stunted white dwarf, forming dewlaps: the drunken wick sent up hairy smoke.

He said: "If it were for a month only I could engage a *locum tenens*. There are always advertisements in *The British Critic*."

She shook her head. "I think it would be for longer, my dear. And—I think it would be better if we did separate—for a while. For three years I have—have tried to nurse you back to health, and I think I have almost succeeded? . . ." She waited until Dwight had nodded. "But sometimes, you must confess, my insistence on this and that, my veto on this and that, has been irksome to you. In the same way but with less reason and less good grace I have curbed some of my—my social impulses, knowing that they would involve you in activities that you did not enjoy. We had come to a compromise. And Sarah cemented the compromise. . . . Now she is gone, and I think—I believe that because of her having been, and now not being, we would find that compromise more trying to adhere to. It might lead to friction, or even quarrels . . . and whatever some fools say, marriages are never better for the quarrels that take place within them. So I think we both need a breathing space. And I think you too will be . . . the better for it."

Dwight said: "Allow me to decide what is best for me."

"My dear, that is just what I have not been able to do, and it is what I cannot do now. In three or four months, once the darkest days are over, then we can decide something more, and I trust agree it together."

"And you wish to go—right away?"

"Quite soon . . . Forgive me. Quite soon."

III

The great victory of the Nile invigorated and revived England as nothing else in the war, and following the illuminations, the bell ringings, the dancing in the streets, came other news which seemed to portend a turn in the long lonely struggle. General Buonaparte and his veteran army were bottled up in Egypt by British sea power, and the French grip of the Mediterranean was suddenly loosened and immobilised. Turkey, having disliked for some time the way in which the French had overrun their Egyptian province, now decided to declare war. India was safe, and smaller nations no longer went in such fear of the conqueror. On a more personal note, it seemed that General Buonaparte's wife had been deceiving him in his absence and he, having only just learned of her perfidy, wrote a fiercely furious letter to his brother which the British captured, and this was published in full in the London *Morning Chronicle*. It was the talk of the town, to set beside his opponent Admiral Nelson's scandalous dalliances with the wife of the British Ambassador in Naples.

Ross had recently talked to two émigrés newly escaped from France after the latest of the many abortive loyalist risings. They spoke of Paris as a city without order, filthy and decrepit, with refuse choking the streets and everyone dressing alike in shabby, nondescript clothes; though there was still wild gaiety and licentiousness in the salons and the theatres. But under the gloomy picture they naturally wished to paint, he detected a reluctant admission that conditions were not so severe for ordinary people as they had been. Metal coins had been introduced and had helped to check inflation; there had been a good harvest; there was food enough; bread, meat, butter, wine. And people under the directory were less afraid to speak their minds. The war was not over yet.

Dwight spent Christmas at Nampara. There was an inner iron to this rather delicate man that enabled him to sustain the misfortunes that life beset him with. Caroline had not come to say good-bye to the Poldarks: she said she was too full up; so Dwight had ridden to tell them after she was gone. There had been no hint of criticism in his tones when he gave them the news; there was none in theirs when they received it. Ross thought, however, of a time when there had been a break between these two people before and he had gone to London to fetch Caroline back. Perhaps it would come to that again. But then, he thought, he and Demelza were separating more often. Was it a good thing? At least he could not this time interfere in other people's lives with such conviction.

For Christmas Demelza had a party that for a time made her heart glad. The Blameys arrived from Falmouth—or Flushing, where they had now moved to: Andrew, very grey, but looking sturdy and well, still making the perilous Lisbon voyages but home for a month for repairs to his packet; Verity, plumper but prettier than she had been in her twenties, as if life and love, coming to her a little late, had brought a late bloom; Andrew, their five-year-old son; and also James Blamey, Verity's stepson, who had lost two fingers in a skirmish off Brest and part of one ear at St. Vincent, but was his noisy, jolly, swashbuckling self and determined to make the most of a brief leave. For the Christmas dinner Demelza had commanded both Sam and Drake to be present, and, since she seldom commanded anything of them, they both in some surprise came.

It was the sort of party she had not quite been able to assemble before. Sometimes she and Ross had been alone; once, the first of all, they had spent at Trenwith; once with the Blameys in Falmouth; once with Caroline here alone while Dwight was a prisoner in France. But this was the best so far. Three young children at the table, eight adults; and all people whom she loved and could talk with and understand; people who had no barriers between each other, at whom and with whom you could smile and be totally at ease. Sam and Drake were reserved to begin, feeling themselves as she had once felt; but they soon found the company too cordial to resist. They even drank a glass of wine each and listened and talked with the best.

James Blamey was the great success. While it was still daylight he played lions with the children, and when it was dark he told them stories of wild days of sea and storm and battle that held them goggle-eyed. His relationship with Verity was extraordinary; more like a lover than a stepson, but all so good-tempered that he made a joke of it. Demelza hoped Jeremy would grow up like that—though not to go to sea.

On the day after Christmas Day they gave a children's party, consisting of Jeremy's friends. Apart from three Tregnosses from Mingoose, these were offspring of the miners and farmers around. A dire consequence of prosperity was that the Poldarks could no longer release twenty-odd children in the newly rebuilt and redecorated library, so the old parlour was cleared of most of the furniture and they were given their head in that. Again James was worth his weight in gold; but both Demelza and Verity joined in everything. The two Carnes, of course, had only been visiting for the day, and Dwight had gone home after breakfast; so Ross and Andrew Blamey escaped for a long walk on the cliffs and talked of war and peace and ships and weather and the condition of the world.

Blamey had heard that General Suvarov had recently been reappointed head of the Russian army; he was the only one with the sort of dynamism that might yet match the French. There was, of course, no war between Russia and France, but if something was not intended, why was there now a Russian army as far west as Bavaria? The Congress of Rastatt was dragging on, but did anyone believe it would achieve anything? The French armies in Europe were wasting away. Very soon the old coalition against France, which had totally disintegrated two years ago, would begin to re-form.

And all because of Nelson's victory, said Blamey. Well might they make him Lord Nelson of the Nile and the Duke of Bronte. It was the importance of sea power demonstrated to perfection. Let us keep our armies out of Europe and tighten the stranglehold by sea.

In their walk they had now reached Trenwith land—Warleggan land, as it was today. A fence had been erected all round it, not quite blocking the cliff path but allowing a five-foot gap to the edge of the cliff. It was not yet a wall: George would get round to that in due course.

They stopped, and Ross put his hand on the fence.

"Enemy territory."

"Still, Ross? It's a pity."

"Demelza wanted to invite Geoffrey Charles to our party yesterday, but I knew we should only meet with a rebuff."

Blamey scanned the horizon with a professional gaze. Two sail only, hull down, over St. Ann's way. "We shall call in on the way home, Ross. Verity wants to see her nephew—and of course Elizabeth, and she thought it better to pay the visit as we were returning."

"Very proper. First things first."

The fence had been put up four years ago, and some of the wooden posts had been too green for their purpose. At this point, nearest the sea, the rain and the salt-laden wind had caused rot round the collar of the wood where it went into the ground. Ross noticed some play in the post he was holding. He moved it experimentally backwards and forwards a few times and then exerted his strength on it. The post cracked. Ross pulled it towards him, breaking the two side struts so that a gap appeared in the fence about six feet across. With raised eyebrows Andrew Blamey watched Ross go to the next post and try to treat it in the same way. This one was tougher, but by pulling with all his force he broke it. In a few minutes six of the posts were down, leaving an enormous gap in the enclosing fence. Sweating with the effort, Ross picked up the broken posts and crosspieces and threw them over the cliff. Gulls rose screaming.

He smiled grimly at Blamey. "I wonder no one has done this before."

"There are gamekeepers?"

"Oh, yes."

"Then I think we should go."

"Perhaps it would be wrong to provoke a disturbance." Ross threw a last piece of wood over the edge. "This being the season of goodwill."

Blamey looked at him and perceived where in Ross precisely the goodwill began and ended. Sometimes he was not a comfortable man to be with; and just now the pent-up rebelliousness in him was very near the surface. It came near but never quite went over the edge of unreason.

As they returned to Nampara the young were just leaving. James Blamey in his shirt sleeves had got some elastic and was using his part-fingered hand as a catapult. Demelza and Verity were tousle-haired and exhausted; Clowance was sucking a sweet-meat, her face smothered in grease; Jeremy had become too excited, and Jane Gimlett was taking him to bed. Ross felt ashamed. Was he too old to play his proper part? Blamey was fifty, that was a different matter. He went across to Demelza.

"Have you survived it, love?"

She looked at him in surprise. "Of course, Ross. Twas all lovely. It is all part of life—of having children—of growing up."

"I know," he said, "I should have helped more."

"You do your part. That's all that matters."

"Do I? Not always. Not always."

Clowance was clutching his legs and clamouring to be picked up. He hoisted her into his arms; she was still fat; and suddenly her enormous, hair-streaked, toffee-stained face was very close to his. She kissed him, leaving a great stain behind.

"Papa, you wasn't here."

"No, my dear, I was lazy. I'll take you both out tomorrow."

"Where, Papa, where?"

"I don't know. Somewhere."

"Even if it rains."

"It won't rain if I tell it not to."

"Ooh, that's a fib," said Clowance, opening her eyes wide at him.

"True enough. You're just like your mother; you see right through me."

"Ross, that's not true either," said Demelza.

"Well, halfway."

Verity said: "I agree: she sees through the dark part to the nice part."

IV

Before they left, Verity came on Ross alone in the library and said: "My dear, it's been such a lovely time. Thank you for having us. It has been—refreshing to be with you both again."

"For us too."

"Ross, you are happy in your new life?"

"My *new* life? Oh, you mean in Parliament . . . I'm not sure. I'm content to allow it to run for a year or two more. If I felt I was being of some value, either to the country or to the county, by being there, then I think I should be happy."

"And your own life—with Demelza?"

He met Verity's eyes and then glanced down at the books he had been arranging.

"What makes you ask?"

"My dear, for the usual reason, because I want to know."

"Did you suppose there should be some special reason for the question?"

"Not unless you tell me so. But we have often shared each other's troubles and perplexities in the past."

"So you think there is some trouble or—perplexity? Has Demelza said as much?"

"Of course not. She never would. But I detect—or fancy I detect—some element of—of strain. I *think* . . ." She patted his arm and turned over a book or two on the table herself. "For instance you, Ross. You are more—unquiet than I have seen you for many years. It's as if the old wildness that you used to show—as if some of it has come back. From the days before you even married Demelza."

He laughed. "Perhaps it is that the leopard cannot change his spots. Put him in a satin coat and knee breeches and he behaves with all the circumspection expected of him. But such behaviour does not last indefinite. Every now and again his nature rebels against it and he wants to go out killing lambs. Do leopards kill lambs? Well, you understand what I mean."

"Yes . . . oh, yes. I understand. If that is all, then I understand. But is that really to do with your life with Demelza? I should not have thought that at all contrary to Demelza's own spirit."

He said: "You probe too deep."

"Perhaps I'm the only one with the right."

"The right?"

She smiled at him. "Well, then, the only one who dares."

Ross said: "We should meet more often, Verity. It is monstrous that a mere eighteen miles should separate us so completely. Come again and bring young Andrew. He's a fine boy."

Verity said: "Seeking perfection, Ross . . . in life it's dangerous, for it makes the less than perfect seem less than enough. Time is not indefinite. This year I was forty . . ."

Ross put some books on a shelf. They were old books, and on the new shelf they looked shabby.

"Do you know when I was born, Verity?"

"You? Serious? I know roughly. Don't you?"

"No, I can find no record. I was christened late in January '60, but whether I was born in January 1760 or in December '59 I have no idea."

"I have always thought myself eighteen months older than you."

"You still look about twenty-four."

"Well, thank you. Sometimes, I confess I feel one, sometimes the other. But I make the utmost of all the good that comes. With both my men in danger . . ."

"My dear, I know that must be hard for you."

"I'm not talking of myself, Ross, but of you. The lack of compromise in many of the Poldarks. Really, it was Francis's downfall."

"And could be mine?"

She smiled again. "You know I don't mean that. You know very well what I mean."

"I know very well what you mean," said Ross. "But one or two things have happened, Verity. Oh, I know they are small things—small to set beside the great—and they are best forgot on both sides, and indeed many times *are* forgot. But now and then you do not have all the control of your feelings that you should have—and then thoughts and feelings surge up in you like—like an angry tide. And it is hard, sometimes it is hard to control the tide."

Chapter Three

In mid-January, Demelza received a letter from Caroline.

My dear,

I write weekly to my friend Dr. Enys, and trust he passes on my affectionate greetings to you both. I do not know quite what I have Achieved coming to London and isolating myself from most of the people I care for; but it has created a sort of break from the life I had been leading, which, like it or not, had become bound up with Sarah. The difficulty of marrying a Serious man and living among people of observable size, shape and volume, is that the frivolous life of a London society lady comes to lack one of the dimensions of Reality. Rising at eleven, breakfasting at noon, lounging and gossiping in loose gown or déshabillé until six, when dinner is taken, and then preparing for a night at the theatre or in the gaming rooms, seems to indicate an existence of considerable length, a small degree of breadth and no depth!

Yes, but there is another side to London. It is the

place where you come to find the best of so many and diverse Things. Art, Literature, Science, Medicine, pure Intellect: they are all here; and if the exponents were not born here they come here to live and work. I truly believe it is the Centre of the World. So, though my present life tends more towards the first aspect than the second, there are Compensations from time to time that cannot be ignored.

My dear, when is Ross coming to London? I assume he is not yet arrived, or he would have waited on me. I trust your Mine has moved from Convalescence to full and vigorous Health so that it may be left to be plundered of its mineral by other and lesser Mortals.

Demelza, why do you not come to London? I think you said you have never been, and it would be so splendid for me if I could meet you here and show you some of the Things there are to see. Tell Ross he should bring you. If you had come with him before, you might have been a little at a Loose End while he was preoccupied in Westminster. Not so now. I would be enchanted to tie up all the loose ends. Indeed, I sometimes think I need such a one as you to serve as a Touchstone so that nothing is exaggerated out of its proper importance.

Horace is very happy in my aunt's house, and has made friends with the two King Charles spaniels she owns. But I do believe—after all the early jealousy—that he now misses my friend, Dr. Enys—. .

As do I.

But the cure is not yet.

Affectionate kisses to you all.

Caroline

When Ross read it he said: "Well, why don't you?"

"Don't I what?"

"Come to London, of course. Caroline has a talent for pointing the obvious, when it is the obvious that others have missed."

Demelza picked up a bit of sealing wax which had fallen on the table. "When do you think to go?"

"I should have gone a month since, but I lack the urgency. This is my home. However . . . if I don't put in an appearance soon . . ."

"Then would you return at Easter, or stay?"

"Stay. Since I have missed the autumn sitting in its entirety, it would not become me to appear for a few weeks and then scuttle back to Cornwall."

Demelza considered all round it. Her brows were a straight line. "I couldn't stay so long, Ross. The children."

"You could come with me and return at Easter."

She considered again. The suggestion had really come from Caroline, not from him. If it had come from him it would have been different.

"Jeremy still has this cough. I know it's perhaps nothing important, but I want to keep an eye on him."

Ross said: "You run the risk of my having to turn some more harlots out of my lodgings."

"And you being called whatever it was you were called."

"Yes . . . You'd risk that?"

"Could I come maybe after the summer? I'd dearly like to see London. But in September or October, then the garden, the farm work, most of it is over. Then I could stay till Christmas."

"Caroline might not still be there then."

Demelza said: "I have a feeling she will."

II

Ross left for London on the twenty-eighth of January. He travelled by the same route as that by which he had come home in May, a coach as far as St. Blazey and then by ship from Fowey to Tilbury. With war in the Channel it was a more hazardous route, but if the wind were fair it was quicker, and he liked the motion of the sea better than the preposterous jolting of the stages.

The house when he had gone seemed, as usual, as empty as a tomb. In previous years he had been away a deal with the Volunteers; this summer and autumn, especially with the preoccupation of the mine, he had been much at home. Demelza more than once regretted her decision to stay in Cornwall; but she was so uncertain of his inner feelings on the matter that she thought it better it should be as it was. Never since Hugh Armitage's death had there been total ease between them. Love and laughter, she had discovered before this, could exist on a plane which was not at all superficial but which did not penetrate to the depths of one's being. It had been so five years ago; it was so again now. She longed more than anything for the total submersion in each other that had occurred at other times. Only when it was withdrawn did one observe the tremendous gap that existed between that and the next stage.

With him gone, she busied herself in the concerns of the countryside; and, Dwight being also bereft, she saw much of him. One day, having walked with Jeremy as far as Sawle Church to put flowers on the grave of Ross's parents and to inspect the newly raised stone to Aunt Agatha, she avoided the tight, stooping breeches of Jud Paynter shining like a decaying planet in the rays of the afternoon sun, and went as far as Pally's Shop to take tea with Drake.

Jeremy had no interest in the forge, which was a fascination for most children, but soon found his own interest in the geese that Drake kept in the yard behind.

"Going to be a farmer, is he?" said Drake.

"We don't keep geese, so they're new to him. He has no fear of any animal. And always he draws them. His paint book is full of cows and pigs and chickens and horses."

"Maybe he'll be a painter. Opie lived round here."

"You used to draw when you were a little boy, Drake. Do you remember? On the walls of the cottage with a crayon you had picked up."

"And got a rare cooting for it. I remember *that*. Will Cap'n Ross be back at Easter?"

"I don't know. I don't think so." Demelza began to

talk of the rest of her brothers, the family in Illuggan, widow Carne, their stepmother, Luke married and working in Saltash, John married with two young babies and no work at all. Bobbie recovered from his injuries, likely to wed soon.

Drake said: "And Sam's love have gone astray like mine."

"He's told you, then."

"Yes. He've told me."

They were sitting in the parlour, in honour of Demelza's visit. Demelza glanced cautiously round as she sipped her mug of tea. It was a tiny room, no bigger than a box room, and clearly unused by Drake. The place was clean, but the curtains she had given him hung down and needed a hem, the chair from Nampara still had horsehair sticking out of the arm, the candles leaned askew like three drunken guardsmen, the cloth covering the primitive table was wrong side out.

"So we're two of a kind," said Drake.

"Yes . . ."

"Yet now and again he sees fit to advance the cause of matrimony to me."

"Who with?"

"You have not spoken to him, then?"

"About you? No, Drake."

"With Rosina Hoblyn. Who else?"

Demelza said: "Have you been seeing something of her?"

"Twice more, that's all. I walked her home once from church, and once I was going down to the Guernseys and stopped by her door."

"She's a good girl. She'd do you well."

"Maybe . . . Oh, yes, I'm sure. I mean nothing against her."

Jeremy was shouting outside, and Demelza went to the foot-square window that looked over the back yard. But he was only exchanging some information with one of the young Trewinnards, who was bringing in a reluctant goat.

"Her father don't know what to make of me," said

Drake. "One moment he d'smile as if I'm an old friend, the next he d'glower as if he think I'd steal his daughter without the parson's aid."

"You must take no notice of Jacka, Drake. He's always had a curious temper. Ross knows how to handle him, but I truly believe he's a bully. For sure he bullies his womenfolk."

Drake refilled her mug and then his own. Demelza, who did not like goat's milk, accepted a little out of politeness.

"So you think I should wed her, sister . . ."

"I cannot tell you what you must do, Drake."

"But it has been in your mind ever since last May. Edn that true?"

She smiled. "Ross warns me I must not interfere in the lives of other folk. It is dangerous, he says."

"But if I wed Rosina it would pleasure you not a little?"

"How much do you like her?"

"I like her very much."

"And does she, you?"

"I think."

"But it isn't love."

"Not on my side it isn't love. Leastwise not what I recollect of love."

Demelza stared at him. "I know how that is, Drake. I know how that is. . . . But—that is lost. No one can bring it back in the way it was then. . . . I—just want you to be *happy*—not sitting here lonely and alone. Did you enjoy our Christmas dinner?"

He said: "Yes. Twas handsome."

"Well, then, for a little while then, especially after dinner with the children, you were gay. The way I remember you the first two years you were here. I'd like you to be that way more often, and tis unlikely to happen if you only have Aunt Nelly Trevail to see for you." She hastened on as he was about to speak. "I have a taking for Rosina, I must admit as much. She is—different from the other girls, bal girls and farm workers—more thoughtful—cleverer. She's pretty, she's quiet, she would move up with you in the fine business

173

you are making for yourself here. She would be a nice —sister-in-law."

Drake said: "Yes, I see all that."

"So now please think no more of it, Drake." She smiled as he looked up. "No man should marry a girl just because she's suitable, still less because she'd make someone a nice sister-in-law. It is your life, brother. And marriages, once undertaken, are not to be dissolved. Only . . . I want you to be happy, not lonely and alone. It would be good to have someone to work with and someone to work for. I don't want you to get set in loneliness. And sometimes—love grows."

He got up and went to the smaller window, peered out. "Did it with you, Demelza? I've often thought but never wished to ask."

The question brought a tightness to her breast. "No. It was with me always. But not with Ross. It grew with Ross—over the years. He did not love me when he married me. But it grew so over the years."

III

The cold set in soon after Ross had gone. Snowstorms swept England, and Demelza waited in anxiety for a letter telling her he had arrived safe. There was little snow in Cornwall but bitter frosts inland and even on some days on the coasts. The drier weather was a welcome help to the labouring engine of Wheal Grace. It was the nineteenth of February before she heard from Ross. His ship had berthed just ahead of the storms, but many roads he said were blocked and impassable, and London looked like a fairy city with the Thames frozen over and all the buildings encrusted in ice and snow.

Early in the month Mr. Odgers was taken ill with a severe chill and fainted twice, so there were no services at Sawle Church on the first three Sundays in Lent. On the third of these, which was the twenty-fourth of February, a sudden clearance of the weather and a mild open day brought out a fair congregation, who went in or stood about outside for a while chatting sociably in the unexpected sunshine like survivors after a disaster, and waited to see if the preacher would turn up.

The preacher did not turn up. Nor did Ossie, who had been informed of his curate's illness, so after twenty minutes or so the congregation began to disperse.

Among them was Drake Carne, and among them was Rosina Hoblyn, with her younger married sister, Parthesia, who was great with another child by her somewhat doltish husband, Art Mullet. Drake went across to Rosina, and they walked home together.

They stopped beside one of the ruined walls of Grambler. In the nine years since the big mine had ceased to be, wind and weather had taken toll of the subsidiary sheds, the casual buildings that grow around the heart of a bal; but the two main engine houses pointed their chimneys at the powder-blue sky with more arrogance and certainty of tenure than the spire of Sawle Church just over the hill. It was still a barren land here, there having been so much mineral waste brought up through the previous half century that only a little hardy grass yet sprouted among the rubble and the stones.

Drake said: "Rosina, I'd wish to tell you something. Have you the time—five, ten minutes to spare—twill take that long, to try t'explain."

Rosina said: "Yes, Drake." The reply was quite simple, unequivocal. If she knew what was coming she made no pretence of being reluctant to hear it.

He stood there, tall and pale, the old mischievous fun long gone from his expression, but some turn of lip and eye that suggested it was not in his nature to be sad. She was small beside him; wearing her best, her only best, the same yellow muslin dress and the black boots, but, it being winter, a snuff-brown cloak and a darker bonnet with yellow ribbons.

He said: "If I ask you to hark to me, Rosina, you must know why."

"Yes, Drake," she said again.

"Tis because I have a taking for ee that I wish t'explain what is deepest in my mind and—and in my heart . . ."

So he told her of Morwenna, when she was governess to Geoffrey Charles, of his first meeting with her when she and Geoffrey Charles had surprised him and Sam carrying the oak post through the wood on Warleggan land. Of the strange courtship, carried on always in the presence of the boy, unnoticed by him and almost, for a while, unnoticed by themselves, growing by slow and secret stages all through the summer and the dark quiet autumn of four and a half years ago, of the wild and bitter early months of '95, when Mr. and Mrs. Warleggan's plans had come between them, and of the final break of any hope at all, first by his false arrest for having stolen Geoffrey Charles's Bible, and then by the arranged marriage between Morwenna and the young vicar of St. Margaret's, Truro.

"Maybe," he ended, "twas ill-wished from the start. She was—a dean's daughter—she was educated, could read 'n write betterer'n I ever shall. Maybe she never were for me; but that could make no manner of difference at the time. Love her I did, and—and love her I always shall. Tis a hard thing to say to you, that I well d'know, but I can't a-bear to say what I wish to say next without first telling you all the truth, just as tis writ in my soul . . ."

"Yes, Drake," Rosina said for the third time. Briefly she had lowered her head, so that her bonnet hid her expression; but her voice told him that there was no doubt in her mind as to what he was going to say next and what she would reply.

"But Morwenna be lost to me for ever. We've never spoken, not for three and a half year, and I seen her but once. Tis over and done, and I have a life to live, and folk tell me—and I come to believe—that I d'need a wife. Now that you know it all, now that you know what I feel and what I don't feel—maybe never shall feel—yet liking you and wanting your company . . . a friend, a helpmeet, a wife, in due time perhaps a mother . . . I have a home, a trade . . . that's what I want you to think over . . . and in due time you'll give me your answer."

The wall had been broken here, many of the stones carried away to build two cottages. Rosina put her hand on the wall, a small, firm, capable hand.

"Drake, I'll give the answer now, if ee do not think tis forward of me to know my own mind so soon. I'll marry you and try to make you happy again. What you d'say—I knew some of it from gossip, but I'm glad to hear it from your own lips. You're a brave, honest man, Drake, and I respect you and love you, and I trust and b'lieve our—our lives will be good and true and honest, and I hope . . . I hope . . . oh, I can't find the words . . ."

He took her hand and held it for a few moments. There was a man tending cows in a field, and a group of old people talking in the distance, so he did not make any more explicit gesture. They had said all that was needed—indeed, by the standards of village life, where proposals and acceptances often scarcely exceeded a dozen words on either side, it was garrulous. But in this engagement there were things better not left unsaid. It was formal, a little stiff yet, and both were superficially calm.

Rosina said: "Twould be best, Drake, if you was to come down wi' me now and tell Mother and Father."

"Yes." said Drake. "I suspect that'd be for the best."

Only then, when they turned to move together towards Sawle, did Rosina give a little inadvertent skip which betrayed the excitement and pleasure she was feeling underneath.

IV

Jacka said: "Har! So that's how the land lies, eh?" and glared at Drake as if he'd discovered him in some disreputable circumstances.

Mrs. Hoblyn said: "There, now! There, now well, Rosie! Well, Drake! Dear of 'n!"

Art Mullet said: "Proper job. Proper job."

Parthesia said: "When's it to be? Oo, not yet! Not till I've 'ad this," and thumped her belly.

"What with Lent not half through," Drake said, "I thought Easter Sunday. Twill give good time for the banns to be called. But I've scarce give it a thought. Perhaps Rosina . . ."

"No," said Rosina. "That'd be well. That'd be fine and well."

"How long off's Easter Sunday?" said Jacka suspiciously, seeing some trap.

"The twenty-fourth March," said Drake. "Five weeks today."

"There, now!" said Mrs. Hoblyn. "Isn't that handsome, you. Twill give us fair time to prepare. Twill give Rosie time to make ready. She's so fitty wi' her hands, Drake, you'd not believe it. There, now, Jacka, have you not a good word to say?"

"So long as there's no *need* t' hurry," said Jacka.

"There, now, how could you!—"

"Well, knowing how twas with her sister—"

"Hey on!" said Art. "There's no call to be duffy 'bout that. One way with th'other, that's no way to talk."

Rosina smiled at Drake. "I'll walk back with ee, Drake. Just so far as the top o' the hill."

V

Very soon the weather turned foul again. The normally early Cornish spring showed nothing of itself, and the vegetable world was at a standstill. Demelza forced herself to take the children out walking every day whatever the conditions: it was a fad Dwight had that the open air was good for people and not deleterious and that unkind spring it seemed to be borne out. Scarlet fever was raging in the towns, and a number of cases turned up in Sawle.

As soon as she heard the news Demelza went across to see Drake, taking a protesting Jeremy again—it was still just too far for Clowance's fat legs—and kissed Drake and wished him well. He seemed gravely pleased at her pleasure, and happier in himself. The barrier against his friendship with another woman had been broken, and he talked freely with her of his plans. Sam, too, was happy, he said, and foresaw his brother's full return to the Society along with a wife who was half saved already. They both laughed at this joke, for half saved in the Cornish dialect meant weak in the head.

Two more letters from Ross, the second to say he had accepted a commission that August to train with a group of the militia, somewhere in Kent. It would mean his being away all the month, but because of that, in agreement with Lord Falmouth, he would not see the parliamentary session out and hoped to be home in April. He had seen Caroline, he said, as Dwight would no doubt have told her, and Caroline seemed superficially well but determined not to come home until she had shaken what she called "the demons" out of her. Ross added that at Caroline's he had met "that fellow whom I first met in the garden of Trenwith last summer, Monk Adderley by name. He tells me that George is hoping to be back into politics by the next session. Happily the Commons is the sort of place where the avoidance of one's friends is not difficult."

Ross was not the best letter writer in the world. His warmth, of which Demelza knew so much, came out in personal contact. When he was with you he could suddenly say the sort of things to melt any woman's heart—or on another occasion to freeze it. His letters by contrast were informative but detached. The physical distance between them was measurable.

He did not mention his suggestion that she should return with him to London in September.

Chapter Four

The nurse who came to look after John Conan Osborne Whitworth on the twelfth of February arrived with the highest recommendations. It was true she had not recently cared for a child, but she had been nurse to Mr. Gerald Van Hefflin, of Hefflin's Court, near Salcombe, and Mr. Van Hefflin for two years before he died had been subject to homicidal impulses. Except for a solitary occasion, when a servant was stabbed, she had always been able to prevent serious harm.

In appearance she was not the grim-faced woman some of the others had been. She was quite small, very neat, with a frail, obsequious voice that was studiously genteel. Only in the way she stood was there something both spinsterish and aggressive: legs apart, broad spare shoulders braced. Fortyish. Clean-looking. Miss Cane. Ossie had an interview with her and was gratified. She impressed him with her total command of the situation. If Mrs. Whitworth were subject to homicidal impulses solely towards her own son, the task was a simple one. John Conan must be guarded. John Conan *could* be guarded. To protect everyone meant watching Mrs. Whitworth as she had had to watch Mr. Van Hefflin. To protect John Conan it was only necessary to be constantly with him.

After two weeks Ossie was very satisfied indeed. It was natural, he believed, for a man like himself, head and shoulders above the herd, vigorous, young, intellectual, a man both of the world and of God, it was natural that he should have what he called bodily vigour; and for this the Church had designed the state of Holy Matrimony, whereby those natural needs might be fulfilled without fornication or other perverse sins.

This outlet, this usefully ordained channel for those who did not possess the gift of continency—recommended by Paul and sanctified by two thousand years of experience—had been denied him by his wicked and ungrateful wife; and so he had fallen into the sin of visiting her wanton sister every Thursday.

But once a week, Thursdays only, was itself a serious strain on his mental and physical self-control. If only he might return to his wife, perhaps Mondays and Fridays—he was willing to be restrained in his demands—his existence would settle into a less turbulent pattern. If that happened, and if Morwenna came to accept him with a good grace, as he felt more and more convinced she eventually would, once the natural process was resumed—then he might even consider breaking with Rowella altogether.

For his visits carried their continuing risk. Every Thursday his horse was left in the ostler's yard hard by Mr. Pearce's house for upwards of two hours. When the summer came it would again be impossible in the long light evenings. Also in the last few weeks Rowella had been in a more demanding mood. There had been a new carpet to buy, some new candlesticks, new shoes, a velvet gown. Of course it was not done blatantly, in any vulgar fashion such as he would have had to indulge in with the harlots by the river. But however discreetly done, the money still flowed out, and if by any chance he chose to withold it, he had no doubts at all but that little Rowella's exciting favours would be withdrawn.

So Miss Cane pleased him. And after three weeks he felt sufficiently encouraged to take the dread risk. Morwenna had retired early, pleading a headache, and he had been sitting in his study, carefully but unsuccessfully reading a book of sermons by the Reverend Anton Wylde. They did not impress him. They were banal and repetitive. They brought in the name of God too much and emphasised faith rather than works, spirituality above the practical routines of the Church. Ossie was a practical man and knew that on this earth at least it was the "external fitness" of formal, ordered religion that mattered most.

He put down the book. Possibly this evening even the best sermons of the age would have failed wholly to engage his attention. Because he was aware that upstairs was a young woman, desirably comely though resentful, to whom he was bound by the holy rights of the Church and of whom he had had no satisfaction for upwards of two years. He pictured her, soft and yielding, or hard and resisting, enclosed in her white woollen nightgown and preparing herself for sleep. There should not be sleep yet. There must not be sleep yet.

He would have her, as was his right. He would take her if necessary in despite of herself, as also was his right. Neither the law nor the Church recognised the sin of rape as committed by a husband upon his lawful wedded wife. And tomorrow, if by any vile chance, she really meant that she would retaliate upon him by attempting to injure his son—*their* son—Miss Cane, strong, watchful, patient, and indomitable, would see that she was thwarted. Then, if she did so act, the question of her being committed to a madhouse might be raised again.

He got up, straightened his waistcoat, took a last gulp of port, went upstairs. He knocked lightly and entered his wife's bedroom. Morwenna, as he had expected, was in bed and reading one of those obnoxious library books. She looked up, at first inquiringly, then startled, horribly alarmed when she saw the expression in his eye.

He shut the door and stood with his back to it, taking her in, making sure that he saw her aright, all his skin crawling at the sight of her lovely shape outlined in the bed. Then he took off his coat and waistcoat and began to unfasten his stock.

"Ossie!" Morwenna said. "Why are you here? Why have you come tonight? You know what I *said!* You know what I threatened!"

"Yes," said Ossie, quite gently for him. "But you are still my wife, and this *terrible* penance, this *dread-*

ful deprivation that you have callously imposed upon me—against all the marital vows that you took on our marriage—it must—it *must* come to an end. It is a long time, Wenna. It is high time, Wenna," he went on, as if confiding a secret to her that no one else must know. "You swore before God to be a wife to me. It is your holy duty. This time you must—*must,* please, give way to me. But first . . . first, let us say a little prayer . . ."

II

Mr. Arthur Solway, librarian of the County Library in Prince's Street, which now offered near five hundred books that might be borrowed or read on the premises, was a tall, thin, frail-looking young man, of a peaceable and nervous disposition. When he had first fallen in love with Rowella Chynoweth and discovered to his joy—almost consternation—that his affection was returned, he had been unable to sleep at nights for thinking of his wonderful fortune. The fact that she confessed she had been taken advantage of by some vile brute of a man—unspecified as to name and date—rubbed a little of the gilt off the gingerbread; but he was soon able to forget it in the appreciation of his future wife. Coming from the terrible slums in Water Street, where his family still lived, teaching himself to read and write every night after work by the light of a guttering ship's candle, being offered—as young as twenty-four—the librarianship of the new library, thanks to a recommendation from the Hon. Maria Agar, to whom his mother had at one time been a servant; slowly edging himself out of the pit of dire poverty to a state in which he could at least pay for a proper suit, eat a few sparse but nourishing meals, mix on terms with the cream of the town's literate society, help his family a little, and walk the streets of Truro feeling himself to be a respectable citizen—these were marks of an achievement he never ceased to thank God for. He was poor, he was hard-working, he was shortsighted, but he was supremely lucky.

His marriage to Rowella raised him in a single step higher than he had ever thought to go. She was so refined, so beautiful—to him—in a strange oblique way; she could read Latin and Greek; her mind was both sharper and deeper than his; they talked books often, and he soon knew, soon acknowledged, her superior intellect.

But in some ways she was less proud than he—she called his a false pride—and the memory of his meetings with her brother-in-law, the vicar of St. Margaret's, during which they had argued and wrangled almost to the point of physical combat as to the size of the dowry that the Reverend Mr. Whitworth was going to provide, such memories made him sweat even now to think of. Rowella had been at his back all through, giving him resolve, fortifying his weakness, salving his embarrassment, telling him that if he really wanted to marry her he must fight for a sufficient sum to set them up in the town in some small comfort.

So he had done battle, a most reluctant warrior, and somehow between them they had cajoled Mr. Whitworth into giving them five hundred pounds. With some of it they had bought and furnished this four-roomed cottage, the rest had gone into Consols and provided them with an income of thirty pounds a year. And true enough, just as Rowella had said, it made all the difference to their lives. They were in moderate circumstances but they were substantial.

In another field too his marriage had worked a miracle; for Rowella was a first cousin to Mrs. George Warleggan, now through her husband one of the most influential ladies in Cornwall. He had married, as it were, on the one hand into the old landed impoverished gentry and on the other into the new rich mercantile class. From an infinite nonentity he had become a small somebody.

Not that, as yet, his mother-in-law had ever visited him, and the Whitworths, after giving them the dowry and being present at the wedding, appeared to have totally cut them off. But Mrs. Elizabeth Warleggan had done them several kindnesses, and she was always particularly gracious to him when she came into the library. And it was early days yet. There was no need to rush. By the time he was thirty he would have learned better manners and how to speak better from Rowella, and gradually, he was sure, the family would accept him.

It was clear to him also now that Rowella had a little money of her own that she had not told him of. This last year she had spent small but noticeable amounts on amenities for the house. The new carpet in the bedroom must have cost quite a sum and was a tremendous improvement, for in the winter it stopped the cold draughts coming up through the floorboards. Sometimes too she had a half sovereign in her purse, which he could not imagine her having saved from her housekeeping—quite apart from the fact that he always gave her this in silver. But it was all part of the wonderful new life he was leading.

He worked most evenings at home until nine, but Thursday evenings he regularly spent with his family. Rowella was very good about this, always insisting on his going, wet or fine, so that he should not disappoint them. She would not come with him—she said she sometimes called in during the day—but she almost always had a little present to send them: a pot of jam, a few eggs, a twist of tobacco, or some sweetmeats for the children; she was very thoughtful.

On the second Thursday in March, Arthur Solway arrived home from the library about six-thirty, just as the sun was setting and throwing magenta and jade-green feathers across the sky. It was still very cold, so cold in fact that Rowella had lit a fire in their bedroom; but there was too much wind for a likelihood of severe frost. He ate a hasty snack with her and left at seven. The colours had faded but the sky was still high and light. She gave him a half pound of butter to take.

Water Street, which was a narrow slit of sheds and houses leading off the more respectable Quay Street, was not ten minutes' walk from their home, but the shortcut led through the even more derelict area bordering the wharves, where the lowest and poorest and least law-abiding lived. Arthur hunched his narrow shoulders as a woman called an invitation after him; he decided that, as there were two ships in, he would go home the long way tonight.

His father's home was one of a row of cottages belonging to the Corporation and let out at a rental of two guineas a year. It consisted of a front room, a scullery behind, and a small kitchen which Mr. Solway had turned into his workroom as a carpenter, and one room, about sixteen feet square under sloping eaves, where everyone slept. Arthur's visit was the red-letter day for his family, since his success was greater than any of them had ever dared to expect; and as a result of it he had been able to pay the arrears of rent, so that the Corporation had returned Mr. Solway's tools and he was able to scrape a bare living again. Unfortunately, though a hard worker, he was not really gifted with his hands and usually received only simple commissions. But he had his own simple dignity and his own pride, and in the bad days of a few years ago he had persistently refused to be turned out of his cottage and to allow his family to be accommodated in the Poor's House. Now, thanks to Arthur, those dangers were behind them.

As usual the librarian was welcomed, and was happy in his welcome. Surprisingly, every child Mrs. Solway had borne had survived—though one or two were of dubious health and intelligence—so that, with only two away in service, there were nine people living in the house, the eldest child after Arthur being twenty-two, the youngest not yet three.

Although he had already eaten something, Arthur had to share their supper, spartan though it was, and talk was of the weather and prices and scarlet fever and how Penrose's son had lost a leg on the Nile and was being sent home and how people were complaining the road was too wide to cross in safety now the Middle Row had been pulled down, and how Mr. Pearce the Notary of St. Clement Street who had been sick for so long had now had a further heart stroke, and how George Tabb had been so drunk he had fallen in the gutter and lain there in the freezing cold half the night till his wife found him.

Right at the end of supper Tabbie Solway, the eldest girl, suddenly said: "I'm goin'. 'Old me. 'Old me!" But it was too late. Mr. Royal, the apothecary they went to, had advised them to tie a handkerchief tight around each arm as soon as she felt a fit coming on, and sometimes this did seem to halt or subdue the attack. But this time the seizure occurred too sharply for any of them to act and in a minute she was lying on the floor, twitching and foaming at the mouth.

It was a horrid sight, but everyone was so used to it that even the baby did not cry. The mother and the next-eldest daughter saw to Tabbie, in so far as they could, putting damp cloths on her forehead and a stick in her mouth to save her tongue; the younger ones carried the plates and the mugs into the scullery; Arthur and his father drew near to the fire, and Mr. Solway lit his pipe. They watched the struggling girl on the floor and talked in low tones.

Presently her convulsions grew less and she began to breathe more easily as if going gently off to sleep. Sometimes this happened, and it would then be necessary to carry her up the creaking ladder to the room above. But just as everyone was relaxing another fit came on, and it was clear this was going to be one of her bad times.

The second fit lasted nearly as long as the first, and was succeeded by a third.

"I'd best go for Mr. Royal," said Arthur.

"Yes. He d'give her something betwixt one fit and the next, and it d'seem to soothe the poor maid."

"I'd like for you to have Dr. Behenna," said Arthur. "He's a more learned physical man and people speak high of him everywhere."

"Another time, maybe. But I doubt he'd come so late to the likes of we. And he's further away. Mr. Royal is but just up the hill beside you."

"I'll go fetch him," said Arthur, and put on his cloak and hat.

Braving the wharves again, he hurried to Mr. Royal's shop. It was not in fact much farther to Dr. Behenna's, but he understood his father's reluctance to summon so important a man.

While he had been indoors the northwest wind had blown up a heavy hailstorm, and it was only just over; the black belly of the cloud was still obscuring the young moon. There was a light over the shop and Mr. Royal, a tubby pockmarked man, answered the door himself and agreed to venture out to see his patient. He must, however, mix the medicine he wished to bring, since it was a volatile substance and could not be kept. Would Mr. Solway care to wait or would he return and tell them to expect him? Mr. Solway said he would return.

This he set out to do, and then the thought crossed his mind that he might warn Rowella he would be late. It was some time since he had seen one of Tabbie's turns; indeed it was the worst he'd witnessed and he thought it probably the worst she'd ever had. Tabbie was a simple soul but ineffably sweet; no ill thought had entered her mind since childhood, and Arthur was deeply attached to her. He felt he should stay at least until she was quiet, at least until the storm was over and she was safe in bed. And he would like a private word with Mr. Royal.

He stopped at the end of his street and went up it. Theirs was a four-roomed cottage and he was a little surprised to see no light downstairs. Their bedroom was at the back overlooking waste land. She was probably up in the bedroom. He tried the door. It was locked.

This was as arranged. Rowella had said to him that her only objection to Thursday nights was that she was nervous of being alone, so she now locked the door. But she was always waiting up for him when he returned at ten, and sometimes he joked about what would happen if she went to sleep and he was locked out all night. Surely she had not gone to bed so early. It was barely nine.

He hesitated whether to knock now. It might startle her, since she would wonder who it was. Perhaps he should not bother her now. If he were very late and she *had* gone to sleep he could easily shower a few pebbles at the bedroom window and wake her then.

But if she *hadn't* gone to sleep and he *didn't* return at ten she would be worried. She had probably let the fire out downstairs and was sitting upstairs for warmth.

He hesitated a second more, and as he did so the retreating clouds moved off the face of the moon and the moon lit up the shabby street. And as it happened he was looking down. His own footsteps were clearly marked in the half inch of hail that had fallen. And there were other footsteps, larger than his, heavier than his, part obscured by the hail, part outlined by it; so that it was plainly evident whoever had trodden this way had done so at the height of the hailstorm. And the footsteps appeared to go up to the door but not to return from it.

III

A terrible liquid feeling clutched at his guts, so that the more logical side of his mind found time to wonder if he had been suddenly taken with the flux that was so prevalent in the town. But his heart lurched and thumped as if it were coming to a stop, and he did not think he had heart trouble. And his mouth was dry so that he was incapable of moving his tongue. He had never, never been suspicious until this moment; but in the horrifying clarity of the moment it seemed to him that underlying his love and his trust had been some basic, animal sense that had told him all was not well.

And he had not listened. Not for a second had he listened. He had believed. He had trusted. He had never considered betrayal.

It need not be so now, his logical mind argued. Twenty explanations could exist. Twenty different ones, all utterly innocent. But one thing was certain: he could do nothing else, he could think nothing else, assuredly feel nothing else, until he knew the truth.

He stared at the locked door. Then he walked away and up to the end of the street. Then he climbed the broken railings and stumbled through the brambles and the gorse until he reached the back of his house. There was a light in the bedroom.

It was a low house and the chink of light showing through the cheap curtains was not five feet above his eye level. He stared around like a wild man, and saw a few yards away a homemade truck that the children in the next cottage used for play. It was really an old box on two wooden wheels, but it was longer than broad, and he pulled it across the glistening grass and through the dripping brambles to prop it end-up against the wall. Then, climbing on the sill of the lower window, he stepped up onto the rickety end of the truck, careless, as he would not ever ordinarily have been, of collapse and a sprained ankle. The chink of light came onto a level with his eyes, and he peered into his bedroom.

A sight met him which for a few seconds paralysed both his mind and his body. Rowella was lying on the bed—naked, totally and utterly naked and in a wanton posture that even he, her husband, had never seen her assume. And, horror of horrors, disgust of disgust, a big man, also totally naked, was kneeling over her and twisting her feet this way and that. And from the expression on his wife's face, she appeared actually to be enjoying it.

He never remembered climbing down, but he could not have fallen, for next day he found no injury upon himself; somehow too he must have had the presence of mind to pull the truck back into its old position. He remembered nothing of this at all. All he remembered was crouching against the hedge and being sick —over and over until there was nothing but bile to bring up.

And when at last the sickness ceased he began to

shiver, and then he pulled himself to his feet, and, crouching, hunched, low to the ground like a dog that has been fiercely thrashed for something it didn't do, he began to make his way back to his parents' home.

Chapter Five

Cary Warleggan called to see St. John Peter that same week. It was such an exceptional occurrence that the young man could hardly believe his eyes. Cary Warleggan, being now an old man of fifty-nine, scarcely moved from the office behind their bank in Truro, except to climb the stairs to the small apartment that he occupied above. He ate and slept there, and a hundred-yard stroll on a fine Sunday morning was as much as he normally ventured. Possibly this was more to do with preference than age, for, excepting his persisting bradypepsia, he ailed little.

But St. John Peter's estate was seven miles out of Truro, and although the day was fine the roads were foul. The gaunt old scarecrow arrived on an elderly brown mare, accompanied by one servant, who had difficulty in getting him down. St. John had been spending the morning with two stable boys and his thirty couple of foxhounds. Joan, his wife, Harris Pascoe's daughter, welcomed the old man and sent for her husband.

"God's flesh and blood, Cary! What brings you here in the ill of winter? Has Truro burned down? Joan, offer him a brandy and treacle. Twill help to keep the chill away."

"Ah," said Cary. "Ah, my boy. Glad to see you looking well. Mrs. Peter . . . We've scarce met before. Thank ee, no. A little rum and water will excellently suffice."

They made conversation for a few minutes. St. John

rolled down the sleeves of his shirt, pulled out the lace of the cuffs, crossed his booted legs and watched bits of dry mud fall on the polished oak floor. Joan Peter superintended the servant who brought drinks, her calm expression and unruffled demeanour belying the feeling of disquiet and aversion produced in her by the arrival of this old man at her front door. She knew, of course, and had done for years before she married, of the ill-will that existed between her father and the Warleggans, and of the rivalry between the banks; and since their marriage she had tried to persuade St. John to change his allegiance and bank at Pascoe's. But St. John, for reasons of his own, had refused to swap horses.

Joan was not quite sure how her husband handled her money, but she knew that most of it was still kept as fluid capital at her father's bank, and that St. John seemed to manage his extravagant living without touching more than the interest. She knew that he chose to use Warleggan's for his day-to-day accounts, and suspected that he was in debt to them, and that the debt was secured against her dowry. But that was all. Nevertheless she felt that the arrival of this black-draped, bony-shanked old man could bode nothing but ill.

And she was right. Seeing that what had to be imparted was not going to be imparted in her presence, she made an excuse and left them, and Cary, who had little finesse, and a minimum of small talk outside the subject of money, soon came to the heart of the matter. Because, he said, of certain failures of schemes that Warleggan's Bank had recently financed: a joint-stock company here, a land-drainage scheme there, the temporary abandonment of the building of the Portreath railroad because Basset's Bank had withdrawn its support, these and the sudden shortage of liquid funds which was affecting the whole country at this time, compelled them to call in a number of their short-term accommodation bills. The ledger accounts of all customers of the bank with such outstanding loans had been carefully scrutinised, and some twenty to thirty names had been selected for a shortening of their credit. St. John had to appreciate, Cary said, that although he, Cary, was a full partner in the bank, his brother Nicholas was the senior partner, and beside him was his nephew George. Between them these two had been adamant that Mr. St. John Peter's notes should not be renewed when they came due. He personally, Cary assured St. John, had done his utmost to alter their decision in his favour, pointing out the long association all the Peters had had with the bank and trying to replace his with some other name. But they had pointed out—and with perfect truth, he had to admit—that Mr. St. John Peter's was the largest unsecured personal loan that they carried and that it was a matter of pure business common sense, in this present emergency, to call it in.

"Unsecured, by God!" exclaimed St. John, whose back hairs had been rising throughout this explanation. "You have my guarantee of the capital I hold in Pascoe's Bank. That's free and fluid money, held in the best securities, by God, and you'd scarce obtain better if you was to scour the City of London! By God and all His angels!"

"Sir," said Cary, a little more formal now. "We appreciate that. *I* appreciate that. Apart from our friendship, our long friendship; which counted; be sure it counted; apart from that it was the *nature* of the security which encouraged me, which enabled me to discount for you so many bills of your own and to offer you ever-increasing credit. But you must see, my boy, that such fluidity is precisely what we now require. Had you offered us land as guarantee, we might now ask you to sell it to realise the money; and land is not an easily marketable commodity at this time; land is peculiar; land is very fickle; unreliable. It might fetch the amount of our loan made against it; it might not; but in either case there would be delay, the processes of auction, lawyers and the like; they take months. The money that your wife brought you—that, as you've told me often, is in ready cash or easily negotiable bonds. That is just what Warleggan's Bank *needs,* to tide it over the next three months. Indeed the next month, I would say."

"You mean—you are demanding—a repayment of . . ."

"Only as the notes fall due, Mr. Peter. Nothing more than that—"

"But all of them are due for renewal this month and next! You must know that. Indeed, you've seen to that by steadily shortening the dates each time I've signed 'em. By God, you can't mean to call in the whole of the amount I owe you!"

Cary pulled his coat around him like a raven folding its wings. He stared about the sparsely furnished but handsome room in which they were sitting.

"As a favour I ask you not to mention this to no one else—for that would be the worse for us all, see? We want no run. We want no loss of confidence. Warleggan's Bank stands solid as a rock. But . . . *you* know now. I know, that we have to draw in our horns . . ."

St. John Peter got up and walked to the door and back, plucking at his lower lip. "God's blood, I shall not be able to maintain my pack!"

"Hunting will be over soon," said Cary. "Who knows what next autumn will bring?"

"How d'you mean? What d'you mean?"

"This is temporary," said Cary. "See? We're far too big, far too widespread, to suffer for long. Warleggan's Bank? The biggest and soundest in the county! We've smelting works, tin mines, flour mills, schooners, rolling and pressing mills. We shall soon recover, see? It's temporary."

St. John Peter thrust his hands into his hip pockets, stared at the old man suspiciously. Hard, bitter words had been on his tongue; he'd been about to say things which would have been unforgivable by any of the Warleggans. Between friends he had always contemptuously referred to George Warleggan as "Smelter George." He could think of fine names, more offensive names, to apply to Cary, and had been about to apply them. To come here in this way, to enter a gentleman's house, not like a banker but like a common usurer, to *demand,* at such short notice, repayment of a *vast* sum of money, something he had always assured St. John he would never do except—if at all—in the most gradual manner—it was outrageous and required the reply that only a gentleman could give: Very well, I will pay you, but never crawl into this house dragging your slime after you again. Out, out by the back door, and in future use the servants' entrance, where you belong!

St. John Peter, who had more pride than sense, and too precise an idea of what a gentleman could and could not do, who had married for money and at his wedding had said to a friend: "I bring the blood, she brings the groats," who had all the pretensions of the aristocrat without the means to maintain them, needed at this moment the declaration of his utter contempt for this black-coated creature sitting before him, needed it above everything to maintain his self-respect, his self-conceit. But Cary's last words gave him pause in spite of himself. Temporary? How temporary?

It was a bitter pill to swallow, on top of the ignominy of knowing that this man could almost ruin him. "How temporary?" he said.

"Six months," said Cary, sitting back in his chair. "Six months at the most. I guarantee you, my boy: we'll advance you the same amount again, *and* at the same very low rate of interest, on the first September next. Just in time for your hunting. How will that do?"

St. John Peter went across and picked up his coat from the back of a chair, put it on. Cary observed it. It was of green velvet, a handsome cutaway, with basket buttons. He had never owned a coat like that in his life. Not that he wanted to. Not that he wanted to. There was far more pleasure to him in controlling the people who owned such elegant apparel.

II

Holy Week, Ossie thought, was an inconsiderate time to die. Not that he or many of the other clergy put themselves out too much for the onset of Easter, but generally there was more to do in the parish, particularly the tiresome rash of marriages that broke out on the Sunday. And although Mr. Odgers was sufficiently recovered to resume services in Sawle, his vicar had been planning a sudden descent, perhaps on the Good Friday, spending the one night at Trenwith, just to ginger up the little man and to comment on the neglect from which Sawle Church must now clearly be suffering.

But several people obviously weren't going to last out the week, and that meant a tiresome number of funerals too. Among them, and by far the most important, Mr. Nathaniel Pearce. Stabbed in the back, as it were, by an attack of influenza, his heart really had decided to give up the struggle at last. He lay now, an inanimate mountain, breathing in short painful gasps which certainly could not sustain that large body much longer. So he had been when Ossie called on him on the previous Thursday, and the clergyman expected every day to hear that he was gone. But as Easter approached no final message came, though his daughter on the Tuesday sent a note round to say it could now only be a matter of hours.

On the morning of Maundy Thursday, Ossie debated with himself whether he should follow his usual Thursday routine. Though not a man of deep spiritual commitment, he did realise his self-denials through Lent had not been extensive. Once or twice he had checked himself when about to open an extra bottle of Mountain. He had cancelled the delivery of porter to the house, which Morwenna, remembering Dr. Enys's advice, sometimes still drank. Each Sunday he took care to preach for ten minutes longer. He had cut down the consumption of butter by the servants. He said a prayer every morning when he rose, as well as every evening. And he came home earlier on the nights when he played whist.

But against that he had continued to visit Rowella, even though he had now been able to resume intercourse with his wife on two nights a week. He still lusted after Rowella, and lust, he knew, was not an admirable thing. It must stop, he told himself, thinking of his lust with pleasure. And this week was the proper week to stop it. Even if he gave up these visits just for a few weeks it would make Rowella less sure of him, less demanding of his little presents. And now that his wife was available again, he hadn't the excuse for this extramarital indulgence on the grounds of its being necessary for his health.

After the first forceful taking, Morwenna, he thought, had given in better than expected. True, she would now often speak to no one for hours on end, not even the servants, especially on Tuesday or Saturday mornings. And she had suddenly abandoned much of her parish work. But she accepted him when he came in to her and put up no resistance. She made no physical response to him at all, which was in sad contrast to her lascivious sister; but at least it was satisfaction of a sort. And the first night, before he left her, he had told her of Miss Cane's role—something he saw Morwenna already suspected—so there had been no attempt at all on Morwenna's part to carry out her threat. He saw it now as the wild menaces of a hysterical woman, which never should have been taken seriously. He could hardly believe that he had been timid enough all this time to take them seriously. He had flinched at a shadow.

But when Mr. Pearce died it would be much more difficult to arrange a regular Thursday meeting with Rowella. So perhaps this Thursday, if Mr. Pearce lived until tonight, he would stifle the stirrings of his better self and go for the last time. His better self told him that he had had a thoroughly enjoyable Lent.

He left at his usual time, having had his evening word with Miss Cane to warn her never to leave her charge unguarded—for however much the threat had

proved an empty one it never did to relax one's guard
—and rode to Mr. Pearce's and left his horse and was
let in by Miss Pearce, red-eyed and swollen-faced—
and led upstairs to where the lawyer lay, still gasping,
like a fish that had been put on a slab to die. There
was no other sign of life, except that his eyes were
half open. Ossie wondered how he was going to spend
a half hour in this close, unpleasant room.

"He is—unconscious, what? Gone, eh? All but?"

"I believe he recognises us," said Miss Pearce, gulping. "He can't move neither hand nor foot; but he still
understands. He understands by winking. That's all
that's left. Hullo, Papa, dear? Hear me, do you?"

The enormous face on the pillow slowly closed one
eye.

"Dear Papa," said Miss Pearce, tears squeezing
onto her cheeks. "Here's the vicar to see you. Do you
hear me?"

The eye closed again.

"Ah, well," said Ossie sonorously, and cleared his
throat. "So I'm glad to see you once again, my friend,
if it *is* for the last time. Let me try to comfort you. Let
me read you something." He took the handkerchief
away from his nose and sat on a chair a little way from
the bed. Then he opened the Bible. Miss Pearce discreetly withdrew. "Let me read you something out of
Psalm Seventy-three. 'Thou hast hold of me by Thy
right hand, Thou shalt guide me with Thy counsel,
and afterwards receive me in glory. Whom have I in
Heaven but Thee? My flesh and my heart faileth . . .' "

He stuck it for twenty minutes and then took out
his watch. There was still a smear of daylight in the
sky. A little early to climb the hill; but he could stroll
round the town, or even go into St. Mary's Church
for a while.

"I must leave you now," he said, closing his book.
"I trust the Lord will welcome you into the glorious
company of heaven. I must go now, for I have work
to do."

As he turned to leave, Mr. Pearce winked again,

and a twitch of a smile moved across his mottled features. The mulberry was almost ripe.

This smile, no doubt, was his way of expressing his appreciation for the attention Ossie had paid him all through this terrible year. It meant, good-bye, my boy, good-bye. But registering itself on that face it seemed to have a faintly cynical, almost sinister leer about it, as if Nat Pearce, at the threshold of death, whence comes all knowledge—or no knowledge—had seen through the subterfuge of Ossie's attentions and knew all about his trysts in the cottage up the hill.

III

Ossie stayed with Rowella a shorter time than usual. She had greeted him with the news that she had *almost* had to send back word; Arthur had been very strange and ill all week—with influenza or some sort of ague —which had laid him low, shivering and sometimes weeping in his bed, for five days, and he had only recovered, suddenly and completely, yesterday and gone off to the library as usual. Tonight he had seemed quite better and left at the same time to see his parents.

Osborne did not much like the sound of this: the idea of going into someone's bed who had only recently left it shivering with the ague or influenza did not appeal to him; but she, smiling her demure secretive smile, lip trembling, eyes downcast, perceived his hesitation and told him she had changed the sheets that morning. Still a little put off, he climbed the rickety stairs after her, and it took her all her wicked wiles to make him lose himself in the wantonness of passion.

Then for a while all was forgotten: his wife (easy), his cloth (not too difficult), Lent (scarcely more so), caution, lest she should ask for more money (quite thrown away: it was worth it); but concern in case he should pick up her miserable husband's infection (not far below the surface). So that in a pause of reflection and semi-exhaustion, while they both lay back staring at the rain-spotted ceiling, when she chanced to sneeze he was immediately on his guard again and made decent haste to be gone. Holy Week, he said, pronouncing it as if it belonged to him, was a time of tremendous pressure, as she must well know; it imposed stresses and strains upon the parson and demands on his time and energies perhaps the most exacting of the church year. He had a sermon to prepare, notes to make on a meeting with the wardens, all the usual services, not to mention the problems posed by Odgers's illness at Sawle. He must go a little early; and rose and began to dress.

She squatted on the bed, watching him out of her narrow, sandy-green eyes.

"Vicar . . ."

"Not now," he said, knowing with a conviction amounting to certainty that she was going to point out that during the storms of this week the roof had been leaking. "Not now, Rowella. I haven't time. Next week . . ."

"Next week . . ."

"Yes," he said, and bent and kissed her, an unusual act of affection, as distinct from passion, that made her open her eyes a little wider. It was, in fact, a kiss of betrayal, for he knew he would not come next week. He had intended tonight to tell her of his uncertainty about the future; but he had realised with a flash of inspiration that it was better to say nothing at all. With luck he would leave tonight having given her nothing but a promise of the usual visit. Let her wait for him. It would do her good and teach her not to be greedy. If he did not turn up it would only make her need him the more. (He flattered himself that she was now caught up in their passionate meetings nearly as much as he.) It would only make her more welcoming if and when he was able to visit her next.

He put on his waistcoat and bent to button his boots. Then, somewhat red in the face, he drew on his coat and cloak and fastened the high collar. He looked at her crouching there, pastel-coloured in the candlelight, naked, voluptuous, and the need for her crept up in him again. He quelled it, turning away from the sight of her.

She said: "Good-bye, Vicar," and sneezed again. "You need not think," she said, "that I have a rheum. But if I did, it would not be surprising the way our roof now leaks. While Arthur was so ill, I had to cover the bed at times with a tarpaulin to keep off the drips. It was the storm of Saturday particularly; I know we have lost some slates."

"Next week," said Ossie. "We will discuss it all next week. I will hear all you have to say next week, and you have my promise of help."

"Thank you, Osborne. I think you would be advised to come a little later if you can, for the evenings draw out, and there will then be less risk."

"I'll come later," said Ossie. "Wait for me. Good-bye."

He went downstairs, picked up his hat and crop, unlocked the door of the cottage, and looked out. The moon was due to rise in half an hour, so perhaps it was an extra-wise thing to have left early. Hunching himself into his cloak, he stepped out, shut the door, and walked down the dark cobbled street. There was no one about.

Even in the somewhat larger streets the town was empty of life. Stumbling here and there over a loose stone, splashing through a muddy puddle, ignoring the hands of the occasional beggar or drunk crouched in a doorway, he soon found himself back at the ostler's yard. A boy, yawning, though it was still not late, led out his bay horse and was given sixpence. The Reverend Mr. Osborne Whitworth climbed the mounting stone, swung his considerable bulk onto his horse, and clattered out of the town.

As he rode home he began to think of the reconciliation he had persuaded his wife to accept, and of her lack of violent response. It gratified him in a way few other events would have done. He hoped that with the ice now thoroughly broken—so to speak—a little reflection would bring Morwenna to a truer understanding of her foolishness, and perhaps even to a reluctant admiration for her husband's position, eminence, strength, virility, and manhood. Whatever the nervous complaint she thought she was suffering from, she was still the mother of his son, and it was far, far healthier for her—apart from himself—that a regular human and physical relationship should be re-established. Most women, he believed, admired him, and it greatly irked his self-esteem that he had been utterly refused by the one woman who had the distinction of bearing the name of Mrs. Osborne Whitworth. As master of his household, as captain of his ship, it had gone against the grain that there should be one rebel, one person in constant if silent mutiny. Now that mutiny was quelled, and he felt so much the better for it.

Indeed, all was going well for him. Although Luxulyan had not come his way, and although he had failed over Manaccan—the bishop had preferred some totally unsuitable fellow from Totnes; clearly it had been a political appointment—he was now interesting George in the idea of seeing if he could get him appointed rural dean for the district. It would be a useful move forward, and though George at the moment was not being too cooperative, he felt sure a little extra pressure would bring it into his hands. He had arranged recently to have his sermons privately printed, and these, as soon as they came in, he intended to circulate widely among church dignitaries.

The only tiny anxiety moving in him—scarcely so much as a worm in the bud, scarcely more than the stirrings of an embryonic worm—was a doubt as to exactly what might have been wrong with Arthur Solway. Weekly the man went back to the slums where his miserable family lived, and slums bred pestilence. Influenza was unpleasant but it was a temporary disease. Ague was worse. But typhus? . . . It was often occurring among these poor families. . . . Or even plague, which had not reached epidemic proportions in Cornwall for fifty-odd years. But a case or two here and there—not always identified, of course—tending to be hushed up for fear of panic—they occurred, he well knew. And then, it was usually death, and a very nasty death. Rowella had sneezed twice. Wasn't sneezing the first sign of the onset of plague?

Skin crinkling, he rode on, trying to put the thought out of his mind. The lane from the town of Truro out to St. Margaret's followed for part of the way—up the steep hill and down the other side—the main coaching road from St. Austell to Truro, the road Ross Poldark had continued on after *he* had alighted last May. But for the last half mile or so it was a sharp right turn and down a gentle declivity lined with trees before you got to the church and the vicarage.

By now the old moon was riding high, and at a broader clearing where two other lanes crossed he had no difficulty in seeing a tall thin man who rose suddenly in his path. His horse shied, and Ossie felt a twinge of apprehension, for one could never be sure that some solitary footpad might not be on the prowl.

"Mr. Whitworth," said a voice. "Is it Mr. Whitworth?"

Confidence returning, Ossie replied: "That is so. Who wants me?"

He could not see the face of the man, for he seemed to be wearing some sort of a muffler about his head. He also carried a stave in his hand.

"*This* is what I want!" said the man, and raised his stave and swung it at the clergyman's head.

But the aim was poor, inhibited by the tremulous grasp with which Arthur Solway held the stick, and misdirected by his feebly nervous excitement. The blow struck Ossie across the chest, part unseating him; but he quickly regained his balance and raised his crop. From the vantage point of his startled horse he was able to hit his attacker again and again about the head and shoulders, while Solway could only get in one more wild swing which missed Ossie and hit the bay, which reared. Ossie clung to the saddle, one stirrup lost, and decided quickly that much as this man deserved the beating he was receiving, he himself would be safer breaking off the engagement. He steadied his horse, recognising now the man attacking him and realising why.

He pulled at the reins and dug in his knees. Solway, stung about the head and seeing stars from a chance knock between the eyes, but aware of the total frustration of a revenge he had been planning for seven days, took a despairing leap forward and clutched at Ossie's cloak as it was disappearing past him.

He held on, and Ossie, one foot out of the stirrup, was off balance as his horse lurched forward. He came toppling off like a felled oak, but the one stirrup still held, and Arthur Solway, rolling on the ground with a piece of torn cloak still in his grasp, saw Mr. Whitworth dragged fifty yards by one foot. Then the well-trained bay came slowly to a halt and looked round at the figure of its master lying head down in the road.

Solway, sobbing for breath and for life, climbed slowly to his knees, to his feet, stood there swaying. His head was cut and his hair was sticky with blood. His shoulders were stinging with the blows and bruises he had received. And now there was silence. The clearing was silent, and so was the wood. The only sound in the distance was the discordant scream of a white owl, making his commentary on the night's affairs.

Arthur Solway was so unused to violence that the aftermath of it choked him; he thought he was going to die. It seemed minutes before the blood stopped thumping through his head and he was able to see, to breathe again. Then more time before he could persuade his legs to move, to take him step by slow limping step in the direction of his adversary.

Careful not to startle the bay, he circled round until he could approach Mr. Whitworth closely. The stirrup still held, but Mr. Whitworth's foot was at a peculiar angle. The moonlight showed up Ossie's face. It was as dark almost as the ground he was lying on. His mouth was open and his tongue was prominent. His eyes were open too. But they did not see the sky.

Arthur Solway had just enough strength to resist the waves of faintness coming over him. He turned and, staggering, fled from the field of battle.

Chapter Six

The vicar of St. Margaret's was found just after midnight by the faithful Harry and another servant, who, compelled to wait up until he returned, had at last gone out to look for him. Mr. Whitworth was still hanging by one foot from the stirrup. His horse, aware of some disability in his master, had scarcely strayed a yard. The grass within his reach was well cropped; grass only a few feet away was not touched.

The death of Mr. Whitworth in such dramatic circumstances was the sensation of the hour. Mr. Whitworth was known as an excellent horseman—did he not ride to hounds?—and his horse as a most reliable and docile beast, so foul play was at once suspected. Rogues and footpads were known to live in the woods and on the moors a mile or so away. But there was no actual evidence to suggest murder. The body had several cuts and bruises, but these were not out of keeping with such an accident as appeared to have occurred. A piece was torn off the cloak, but it might well have been caught on a passing tree. And a purse containing five sovereigns was still about the waist of the dead man. If he had not been robbed, what possible reason was there for his being killed?

And while the clergy as a whole drank as much as their neighbours, Osborne Whitworth was known to be moderate in this respect. A fox leaping across the road—or perhaps the bay had stepped on an adder—a moment's panic. Osborne, off his guard, might have lost a stirrup and then been hit by an overhanging branch. Lady Whitworth, his mother, at once ordered the horse to be destroyed.

The one suspicious feature was the presence in the clearing of a stout wooden stave, which might have been used as an offensive weapon. It was well fashioned and of such good chestnut that its owner would not be likely to have thrown it away. But no one came forward either to claim it or to say they had seen it before. Two parties went through the woods as soon as it was light and picked up an old man who was living in the shelter of a fallen tree. But he was of feeble intellect and in so poor a physical condition that it would have been hard to suspect him of killing a hare. There was a gypsy encampment at Tresillian, but they swore their innocence, and five guineas in a dead man's purse did more to convince the constables than all their indignant alibis.

There was always the possibility of some wandering highwayman who, happening upon the young clergyman, had struck him down and then fled without searching the body. But it scarcely carried conviction. When the coroner's inquest took place the verdict seemed certain to be death from misadventure.

Formal sorrow was widespread, for Osborne, though not a saintly man, had performed the duties expected of him and had done a good deal to build up the life of the Church. It was universally felt that he had been destined for higher things.

None more so than his mother, who at once came to stay at the vicarage and took charge of a disintegrating household. The vicar's widow was completely stunned and quite unable to deal with the problems and decisions that beset her. Although Lady Whitworth frequently jogged her attention and reminded her of her various duties, Morwenna remained in an impenetrable stupor. Her beautiful eyes had often, when she was not wearing her glasses, worn the dazed look of the shortsighted; now they were like windows over which a curtain had been drawn. It was the shock, Lady Whitworth explained to the many callers, but privately she had never had much opinion of her daughter-in-law and considered her lazy and her present attitude likely to be assumed to escape responsibility. Fortunately Ossie's servants were all very capable, and Miss Cane took charge not only of young John Conan but also of the two girls.

The body was in the house and upstairs, mountainous it seemed, swollen with death, tumescent, black, behind drawn curtains, with a candle at the head and the foot and one person always watching. A special silk-lined coffin had been ordered. The funeral would be on Easter Monday, when a very large turnout was expected. Lady Whitworth, carrying all sails like a first-rater going into battle, wrote urgent letters about the countryside, not only to her many friends, but to all the clergy she knew, telling them she expected them to be present.

Elizabeth came early on the Friday, apologised that George was busy, saw Morwenna, saw Lady Whitworth, sympathised with them both. Only she perhaps perceived the brimming emotion under Morwenna's dazed exterior, guessed that the girl was near to some sort of a breakdown, a crisis of nerves. She tried to get her alone, but always someone was calling or Lady Whitworth was bustling in and out.

The following morning Elizabeth happened to drop in to the library to change some books, and was startled at Arthur Solway's appearance. He explained that he had had a severe fever last week and had thought it gone, but now it had in part returned. He constantly wiped the sweat from his brow, his glasses steamed up as if he were poring over a boiling kettle; his hands trembled on the books. And it was the first time she had ever seen him in a wig.

Elizabeth said: "How is Rowella?"

"Oh . . . well, thank you, ma'am. She did not catch it. Indeed I—I—I doubt if it is the—the—the catching sort. She—she—she is well."

"This tragedy—Morwenna's husband—I know the sisters have been estranged for a time, but will you tell Rowella that I think she should go to see Morwenna now. It would be—the time for a reconciliation."

Arthur dropped three books and took a long time picking them up. When he did so he had to stop and rub the lenses of his spectacles again. "Oh, she can't do that, ma'am. She—she—she can't."

Elizabeth looked surprised. "Do you mean she will not want to? Perhaps if I called I could persuade her."

"No—no, you couldn't do that, ma'am. Rowella is —away." His hand jerked convulsively and almost knocked the books off the desk again.

"Away? Rowella. She didn't tell me. Where has she gone?"

"To—to—to . . ." He stopped and swallowed. "To her—to stay with her cousin, my cousin, I should say, in . . . in Penryn. When I was better, after I seemed better, she felt the need for a change. So she is there, will be there for a week or more. Over Easter, you understand, ma'am. Through Easter week. I thought she would enjoy the ch-change. My cousin is a farmer and has a nice farm looking—looking down the estuary. I thought it would be a—a change."

"Indeed, yes. I'm glad. But she didn't tell me. Please ask her to let me know when she returns. And I trust you will be better."

Arthur wiped his hand across his forehead and tried to smile. "Thank you, ma'am. Yes, ma'am. Indeed I'm r-r-recovering now. Tomorrow I shall stay in and rest and then I shall be well enough."

"Shall you come to the funeral? It is to be Monday."

Arthur's smile became even more ghastly. "Certainly I shall—shall try."

When Elizabeth's slim, white-clad beauty had moved out of his sight Arthur went rapidly into a corner and took a gulp of brandy. He had to stick it out today. He had to put in this appearance just in case anyone should suspect. It was unlikely anyone but Rowella *would* suspect, and Rowella already knew. He could not imagine what had got into him on Thursday night; for, returning in a ghastly state from his encounter with Ossie, his rage had gradually overmastered his weakness and had burst out all over again when he got home. So Rowella lay in bed with split lips, a black eye, and a swollen jaw; and her body was black and blue where he had beaten her.

It was a terrible thing to do, and he knew he was a terrible man, and at present he was in horror at himself and at the possible consequences. His nerves jangled and at every moment his tongue seemed about to betray him. But far, far in the future, if he survived undetected and one day could lay his head on the pillow without fear of the consequences of his act, there was going to come to him a little secret male satisfaction from this crime. Already the seeds were being sown. Each morning and each night he came to Rowella and, though she would not speak to him, he fussed over her, putting ointment on her bruises, salve on her lips. And each night when he returned home he brought with him a little bunch of flowers which he placed in a pot beside her bed.

II

The news reached Sawle on Friday night, and a tinker who plied regularly between St. Ann's and St. Michael tossed it in casually to Drake as he passed early on the Saturday morning. Drake went white to the lips, sat down, put his head in his hands. Yesterday Rosina had been over here with Parthesia and her two-year-old and two-week-old baby, and they had laughingly rearranged the bed and rehung the curtains and Rosina had brought some cushions she had worked and had said, blushing, that Art Mullet would carry over her box Sunday evening. In it were the small treasures of a lifetime. Clothes, of course; a cloam teapot, three good spoons, two pewter tankards, a pretty case decorated with shells, a bead necklace, a book on needlework, a length of silk given her by Jacka from the wreck of 1789, embroidered slippers, a bonnet or two, a Prayer Book, a lucky charm.

These would come Sunday evening after the wedding. There would be laughter, some coarse jokes, a bit of horseplay, and then they would be alone. After the wedding.

Drake got up and went to the forge. It was still early and the Trewinnard twins had not yet come. It was only by chance that he had been up and near the gate when the tinker passed. He clenched his hands and cried to God. God did not seem to hear him. Nothing changed. He was standing at the entrance to Pally's Shop—which someday soon people might begin to call Drake's Shop—and looking over the steep declivity of the lane to where it began to rise towards St. Ann's. In the distance a mine chimney smoked. A Warleggan chimney. Sea gulls screamed in the upper air. Wind blew across the rough grass, ruffling his hair. And he was betrothed and sworn to a sweet, intelligent girl whom he did not love, but might learn to love.

And nine miles away the object of his real love, his consuming love over the whole of his adult life, a tall young woman in black, a mother, a vicar's wife, an unsuitably well connected and genteel person who since she married had taken on a totally new personality, was suddenly, arbitrarily, become a widow. What did it mean? What did it mean for any of them? How could this indissoluble but insane fact be in some way absorbed into the more or less sane world?

The first thing was to be sure. Rumours in Cornwall flew quicker than crows, and sometimes as thick. Drake ran across to the field where his pony was grazing. The pony did not wish to be caught, but Drake's need was the greater, and in a few minutes he was riding bareback up the hill towards the low ill-kept cottage that passed for a vicarage.

He found Mr. Odgers crouched in a dressing gown and a blanket over a small coal fire trying to write a letter between fits of coughing. Mr. Odgers did not like Drake, for he was the brother of the leader of the renegade Wesleyan set who had gained—or regained—such a hold in the neighbouring villages. Also, although this was unknown to Drake, Mr. Odgers had been the first person to tell Mr. George Warleggan of

Morwenna's unsuitable attachment and so had precipitated what followed. Nevertheless the young man looked in such distress that he answered the questions put to him.

"What? Yes? Oh, he's dead for sure. And I am summoned to the funeral. It is all very well, you know, for a fit young man; but I am no longer young and far from well—this bronchitis keeps me awake *every* night, every night without fair—and nine miles on a hired nag in the depths of this wicked winter may well cause me to follow him within the month! And who would be the gainer from that? Not Mr. Osborne Whitworth, who has already gone to make one of the blest above. His mother and his widow, no doubt, and other clergy living nearer, would benefit by my presence . . ." He stopped and coughed long and almost lovingly into his handkerchief. "The wind whistles under that door and has done throughout this month and last. And we have no *heat* in our bedroom. At night we pile things upon the bed, and then I find the weight oppressive to my cough and cast them off, and so the freezing cold creeps into my bones day and night, day and night."

The marble clock on the mantelshelf struck eight. Mr. Odgers pulled his blanket closer.

"I am writing this moment to the bishop, explaining my situation, my plight . . . What? Well, there is no suggestion in the letter of foul play. Just fell from his horse. Fell from his horse. Broke his neck. Was found at midnight with one foot still in a stirrup. Broke his neck." The slightest suggestion of unchristian relish had crept into the little curate's tones. While Mr. Webb had been vicar Mr. Odgers had at least been left undisturbed in his poverty. Life under Ossie had been a bed of nails.

"No, no," said Mr. Odgers, "I know nothing more." He stared at Drake, for the first time allowing his self-absorption to slip and suspicion to creep in. "What is it to you, boy? What is it all to you? I am to marry you tomorrow, isn't it, to one of the village girls. Mary Coade? No, Rosina Hoblyn, that's it. There will be six couples to marry. I trust I shall be able to get through the ceremony."

"Thank ee," said Drake. "Thank ee, Parson."

"Why are you asking?" Odgers said. "Why are you asking?" he called after the closing door. But Drake was gone and only the draught of his going remained.

Drake rode on as far as the higher ground by Maiden Meeting House, and from there he could see both the roof of his brother's house and the chimneys of Nampara. But to talk to his brother about this would not help, for he knew already everything that Sam would say. He could not have been more certain. Demelza was much better—she would understand, might understand the agony of mind in which he now found himself. But this wedding with Rosina was partly of her making; there could be no doubt about that. She would listen to him and be truly sympathetic—for when was Demelza anything less?—but she could not but advise him in the same way as Sam. There was no one, no one from whom he could get an unbiassed answer. There was no one to trust but himself.

He rode down to Nampara and across the bit of rough ground to the stile leading to Hendrawna Beach. There he looped the pony's reins over a post and left him, left him to walk on the beach alone.

It was not a suitable day for the beach, but the weather matched his mood. A watery sun was out at present; the wind kept blowing the clouds into smoke; they drifted in streaks before the washed sky, then reformed in masses with the swiftness of moving scenery. It was half tide, and the surf made a noise like another wind, hissing and roaring. Icebergs of froth slid about in the surf, twisting and turning as they did so.

He walked for an hour, the wind blowing and shaking him and unsteadying his steps. He passed the Holy Well where—long, long years ago, it seemed—he and Geoffrey Charles and Morwenna had traced three crosses on the surface of the water, put in their hands, said a prayer and made a wish. He could hardly, he thought, none of them could hardly have done worse if they had prayed to the Devil.

He reached the foot of the Dark Cliffs, where the gaunt skeleton of the wrecked brig was just clear of the present tide and surrounded by a lake of water that was still black and grainy. He turned and began to walk back. The sand was very soft and his feet in places sank so deep it was like walking through thick snow. The tide was making rapidly. Tongues of water came rushing over the sand at him, bubbling and sliding, receding again, leaving fringes of froth behind and the new-wet sand swelling and sinking. Foam detached itself and trundled across the beach, hurtling as far as the cliffs before it disintegrated. The tide would beat him to the Wheal Leisure cliffs—by the time he got there it would be suicide to try to reach the next piece of beach. Perhaps it would solve everything if he did so try. But solve what? Only solve everything for him, and that was the coward's way out.

"Oh, God," he said, "oh, Lord . . ." and stopped. "The Lord is my shepherd," he said, "therefore can I lack nothing. He shall feed me in a green pasture, and lead me forth beside the waters of comfort . . ." He stared at the raging sea and wondered what comfort his present walk had brought him. Had his mind been working at all on this long slogging tramp?

Perhaps. Some thoughts, some decisions were formulating, though they owed more to feeling than logic. It was as if the news this morning had shaken his soul into such a violence that for a time he could not know himself at all; now the news, the shock were sedimenting and giving his mind its first stability back again. He began to mount the cliffs and presently passed the abandoned sheds and stone buildings of Wheal Leisure.

He knew what he must do first. He must see Rosina.

III

The news that Drake had gone from his forge reached Demelza early Easter Sunday morning. Sam brought it.

She stared at her brother. "But—he is to marry today! We are all to be at the wedding. . . . What d'you mean, Sam, gone? Where has he gone? . . ." She put her hand to her mouth. "Oh, Judas God!"

Sam nodded. "Tes true, I fear. Though I've prayed it might be different."

"Did he *know* of Mr. Whitworth's death? Yes, I suppose. But what . . . Are you *sure?* He *couldn't,* Sam. He's pledged to Rosina! He couldn't leave her just like this on her wedding day! It would be too cruel!"

Sam shuffled his feet. "Drake have very strong feelings, sister. Very strong—loyalties, even if they be wrong directed. Oft there was trouble in his early days when he was seeking God. At times he wrought mightily and failed to end his estrangement—"

"But this!" Demelza interrupted him. "This is not *religion* . . . Forgive me, Sam, I don't wish to offend, but we do not all see these matters in their—their true importance, and to me—just at this moment—and to most folk, indeed, it is his worldly behaviour that seems of the greater import. Has Rosina . . . been told?"

"He told her himself," Sam said, "yester eve. He told her and they talked for ten minutes, she d'say, and then he left."

"Left?"

"Just left. It seem that afore ever he proposed marriage to Rosina he told her all 'bout the trouble he'd had and how he'd loved this young woman and how this had been the love of his life and no other, and because that was over, would Rosina take him as he was? And she did so. But now yester eve he come to her cottage, all of a sudden, haggard and wild, praise be while Jacka was at the kiddley, and told her of the news that his young woman was widowed and in dire distress and he must go to her, go to her whether or no, to see her, to see how he could help, to be at her side at this time. And Rosina . . ."

"Yes?"

"She could not stop him. She is trying to understand."

"Judas God," said Demelza again. It was not often now she used her old expletive. "So there's to be no wedding today . . ."

"It 'pears not. There cannot be without Drake."

Demelza took a pace or two up and down the room, biting her thumb. "So I should not have interfered."

"Please?"

"You know, Sam, as well as I do, that we half persuaded him into this marriage, thinking twas for his own good."

"So twas. So twas. Rosina would have made him a proper little wife. They'd have grown happy and served Christ together."

"Maybe. But not now. Unless . . ."

"Unless?"

She made a despairing gesture. "There is no hope now, I suppose? How is Rosina taking it?"

"Nobly."

"Poor girl. But others will not take it so nobly, Sam."

"No . . . Jacka would barely allow me in the house. Purple, he was. Half the blame were mine for being his brother."

Demelza put her clenched fist to her head. "Oh, God, Sam, is this not the greatest of a mess? I so wish Ross were here! I do wish he were not *always* away. What can we do?"

"Naught. Except wait, I reckon."

". . . It will not be only Jacka. Folk in the villages . . . It is not good to promise to marry a girl and then go off and leave her! You and he are still foreigners to some folk. Illuggan's a long way. *You're* popular. So's he been. But for a foreigner to promise as he's gone and then leave the girl the day before, when everything is arranged, when it is all set, all prepared, down to the last detail. There's Art Mullet too. Parthesia is sure to be angry and to egg him on. Drake may not even be safe when he returns—if he returns."

"No," said Sam. "Tis easy to see the dangers. If he returns. Especially if he bring the young woman with him."

"That could hardly be," said Demelza.

Chapter Seven

The funeral of the Reverend Osborne Whitworth, B. A., vicar of St. Margaret's, Truro, and St. Sawle-with-Grambler, took place at eleven A.M. on Easter Monday. The funeral of Mr. Nathaniel Pearce, who did not die until the Saturday, was postponed until Tuesday. (Possibly there was some premonitory knowledge in deaf old Mr. Pearce's parting wink and leer. Ossie, after all, was to be there before him.)

It was a big funeral, conducted by the elderly Dr. Halse and attended by most of the important figures of the town. The widow and her mother-in-law were attired in long black dresses and the heavy veils that custom dictated to hide their expressions from the common gaze, though at one stage Lady Whitworth threw back her veil and glared round at the company with her underpouched piercing eyes as if the better to see that all who should have been were there. (Mr. Odgers was a notable absentee, and the fact would be noted against him.) Mr. Arthur Solway came, though not Mrs. Solway, which was strange, for Mrs. Chynoweth had come from Bodmin accompanied by her daughter Garlanda. It was later understood Mrs. Solway was away.

There were some strangers, though not many in a town and district where almost everyone who was anyone knew everyone else worth knowing. But one tall

dark rough-clad young man was in the back of the
church and at the back of the throng surrounding the
grave. Morwenna did not see him, for she was so near
breakdown that she could not raise her eyes to anyone; but Elizabeth, on George's arm, saw and recognised. She said nothing to George, but she thought to
speak to the young man if the opportunity presented
itself. However, she looked around at the end of the
committal, and it appeared that he was gone.

After the funeral there was a discreet tea, with cakes
and scones and jams and jellies and tarts. Over the last
few years there had been a reaction in Cornwall, particularly among the upper classes, against the massive
funeral celebrations of the last decade or so, with one
family vying against another, until some men of property had begun to leave instructions in their wills that
they were to be buried at night to prevent such extravagances. Lady Whitworth, totally in command of everything, and grieving for her son, if she grieved at all,
so privately that no one noticed, had decreed a morning funeral and a well-furnished but simple tea.

This lasted until two, by which time nearly all had
gone, and one by one the relatives congregated in the
parlour for a discussion about the future. Present were
Mr. Pardow, the family solicitor from St. Austell;
Morwenna—with the sturdy Garlanda beside her,
ready to help her sister in any physical or moral way
she could; Lady Whitworth, square-jawed and square-
shouldered and rasping of voice; Mrs. Amelia Chynoweth, Morwenna's mother, still as pretty as ever in a
yielding fragile way—one wondered why she had not
remarried; Elizabeth Warleggan, Morwenna's cousin;
and Mr. George Warleggan, who had been persuaded,
greatly against his personal wishes, to stay.

The conversation beat backwards and forwards over
the problems that had to be faced. How much money
had Mr. Whitworth left, how long would Morwenna
and the three children be allowed to stay on in the
vicarage, was Lady Whitworth prepared to continue
her allowance—it was the first Morwenna had heard
of it—might Morwenna, if pressed for time, live with

Lady Whitworth or Mrs. Chynoweth until a suitable place could be found? There was a cottage on her property near Goran, Lady Whitworth grudgingly admitted, where a rascally shepherd now lived who had let it fall to ruin, but he could be turned out and with a pound or two spent it might be made into a cosy little home. Unfortunately there was no well water nearer than the main house, and John Conan could not be expected to drink whatever fell into the rain tub. It became fairly clear in the course of the conversation that Lady W. had her priorities firmly fixed. First came John Conan; second, but a poor second, Ossie's two daughters by his first wife; and third, but so far third as to be hardly noticeable, Morwenna.

Every time Amelia Chynoweth said anything Lady Whitworth talked her down; they had met only once before—at Trenwith immediately prior to and during the wedding—and her ladyship had a poor opinion of all the Chynoweth family, particularly Amelia, whose voice, she thought, was like fudge and whose opinions had as much backbone in them. The young woman her son had married was a faceless nonentity who'd been no good to anybody, except that by some fortunate chance she had produced a handsome vigorous lusty son to carry on the name.

And that faceless nonentity, that wild-eyed, downcast young woman about whom all this talk swirled and eddied without her ever contributing a useful comment, she was thinking: how Ossie would have enjoyed this meeting; what a pity he can't be here to join in. But he's dead. Why am *I* alive, why am *I* here? What is *my* purpose? I would be far better dead and buried like him—only in some distant corner of the graveyard as far from his resting place as it is possible ever to get. He tried to prove me insane—he hoped to put me away somewhere. In those days I was as sane as he was. But not so now. In a moment—any moment—my head will burst open and I shall tear my hair and my clothes and *scream* to God and high heaven! They are *talking* about me as if I were a parcel; as if I didn't exist. And really it's true. I *don't* exist any longer. Nothing of me—it's all gone—mind, body —soul, even; I am an envelope, a useless sack of clothes from which has been squeezed all feeling, all reason, all sentiment, all goodness, all faith. I don't *need* to be buried, for I am dead already, there is nothing *left:* ashes, dust, sand, dirt, blood, semen, urine, pus, excrement, ordure—

"Excuse me, Mama," Garlanda said. "But Morwenna is feeling faint. If I might take her to her room . . ."

"Of course."

The limping, staggering girl was led out, and a brief silence fell as they heard her retching in the hall.

"And what do *you* think, Mr. Warleggan?" asked Lady Whitworth. He was the only person in sight to whom she was prepared to defer.

George stared at her unemotionally, taking in the coarse, heavily powdered skin, the button eyes, the dewlaps. "My interest, Lady Whitworth, is purely a contingent one, deriving as you know from my wife's cousinship. Clearly we shall want to have more details of your son's debts before we can be sure what is left for his widow and children to live on."

"Debts?" said Lady Whitworth, bristling. "I doubt if Osborne was a man to incur debts."

"He had a number of substantial ones when his marriage with Morwenna was arranged."

A little wrangle broke out, with Mr. Pardow and Amelia Chynoweth involved.

George thought: Elizabeth is looking older this year; her hair is losing some of its lustre; yet those few extra lines at the side of the eyes have an attraction, give her face more strength and character; she'll still be beautiful even in ten more years. It's for her that I sit in this stuffy untidy parlour listening to this hard-faced old sow grunting about her lost, dead piglet. As if I cared for any of them. What I care about is that James Scawen has at last been persuaded to sell me enough of his property in the borough of St. Michael, and in measurable months I shall own a controlling interest in the borough. Two parliamentary seats. I shall get rid of Howell at once and take his seat next autumn; I shall buy Wilbraham out too, install someone who will do my bidding—who?—must look about me—here or in London—someone like Monk Adderley who cares nothing for how his vote shall go so long as he has a seat and enjoys the privileges. Pity the Warleggan family has bred so sparsely. Sanson is dead and his son a drunkard. Cary's never married. All Cary will ever marry is an accommodation bill.

Garlanda returned with news that Morwenna was lying down and the children's nurse was with her. She'd go up in a few minutes again. George caught sight of his servant in the doorway and flicked his fingers at him.

"We must go, my dear," he said to Elizabeth, and rose. "I have business to attend to."

The meeting broke up with general expressions of concern and affection. Amelia Chynoweth looked with alarm on the imminent departure of the Warleggans, for she saw herself spending the rest of her time here dominated and almost eaten up by Lady Whitworth. Only George's presence had maintained a sort of balance.

But there was no stopping them. Off they went, clattering on their fine horses up the hill towards the main road, followed by their groom.

At the small road crossing and clearing Elizabeth reined in her horse and looked about. "This is where it happened, I believe. There *are* overhanging branches, but it is strange that so reliable a horse should take fright. I cannot help but feel there was something exceptional."

George grunted. "For once in his life, perhaps, he was drunk."

"Where had he been? To see old Mr. Pearce?"

"Miss Pearce said he stayed with the old man but twenty minutes. None of the inns or brandy shops had seen him. But does it matter? You were never attached to him. And of late nor was I."

"It is just—very strange," said Elizabeth. "I have

thought much about it. . . . But certainly it was an unhappy marriage . . ."

"Of my arranging," said George.

"Well . . . you could not have known."

As they went on George thought that one of the great virtues of Elizabeth as a wife was that she never reproached him. She would always close ranks behind him, even if in private she had argued the wisdom of the course he was taking. He had come more and more to appreciate how unlikely his suspicions had been of her association with Ross Poldark. The poisoned barb inserted by Aunt Agatha with her dying breaths had at last worked its way out. Or almost. Certainly this was a happier marriage than he had ever believed possible two years ago. He had not told her of all his ambitions yet. But he knew she would welcome the return to London, and he knew this time that his ambitions were such as would please her. It might be the sort of prize—if and when achieved—to offer a woman on her birthday . . .

As they clattered through the streets of Truro they passed near St. Clement Street, and Elizabeth made some remark about "poor Mr. Pearce." George did not reply. Now that Nat Pearce was finally dead Cary would be on the move. Cary on the move was not a pretty sight. Elizabeth had never got on with George's uncle. They each thought the other "a bad influence" on George. George knew that Elizabeth would disapprove of Cary's manoeuvrings, and wondered whether to put a stop to them before it was too late. If he could, which was doubtful. Cary had a lot of money of his own in the bank and would be a hard man to turn off course. George and his father might just *together;* but was it worth the row to prevent Cary from doing, in a not too respectable way, what all three of them would like to do in their hearts—bring down Pascoe and clip Ross Poldark's wings at the same time?

His manoeuvrings, Cary's manoeuvrings, had nearly achieved the first of these objectives in the nationwide crisis of two years ago. Then it had been partly with George's approval, and it had come to nothing because of last-minute support of Pascoe's Bank from Basset, Rogers & Co., the other Truro bank, and as a result of that, of the alienation caused by that, the growing cooperation between Basset's and Warleggan's had come to a sharp stop, and the discord between George Warleggan and Lord de Dunstanville had begun, setting in motion events which had lost George his seat in Parliament to Ross Poldark.

A long and tortuous chain of cause and effect. But it showed that Cary's behaviour could be harmful to the Warleggan good name, and even to Warleggan ambitions. The point was, in this case, would Cary's manipulations come to light? If they did, they would bring the Warleggan name into some disrepute. Need that happen? Could not all the blame be pinned on Mr. Pearce and his misappropriations? It was necessary to be sure of this. George resolved to see his uncle that evening. It was shortsighted for a man of his, George's, position and eminence to allow himself to be seen to be connected with the exercise of dubious financial pressures upon a rival bank.

They reached the Great House and were handed down by liveried servants who came running out. George followed Elizabeth into the house, watching her kid shoes under the grey velvet skirt, with the occasional lick of white underskirt showing. He turned before he went in and looked out at the leaning walls and crooked roofs of this small town in which he had made his career and begun his fortune. Life was good.

II

Jacka Hoblyn had been drinking steadily for two days.

There had been a terrible scene in his house on Sunday morning when he was told. He had thumped his wife and hit Rosina across the head, as if they were to blame; then he had rampaged off to find Drake and beat the skin off him with his belt. But Drake was nowhere to be found, the blacksmith's shop empty, the fire in the forge glimmering low, and only one scared young boy of twelve to answer his bellowing questions. Smith Carne had gone. Didn't know when he'd be back. No one did. No one home. Brother'd been a-searching for him. But smith Carne had went off last night and not been seen since.

In his frustration Jacka had kicked over a couple of pails and left, to be met halfway home by Art Mullet also seeking Drake. They had turned into Sally Tregothnan's kiddley and spent the rest of the day drinking there. Like Jacka, Art was for doing something to punish the skunk who had let Rosina down, but how punish him when he was not there? True, his Bible-thumping brother was still about, but even their gin-fuddled sense of justice could not rationalise the beating up of one man for another's sins on the strength of a blood relationship.

Also, they were annoyed to discover a mixed reaction to the news at Sally Chill-Off's. Everyone agreed that Drake had behaved bad, and though one or two reckoned he'd gone off to sniff round that wench in Truro who'd just been newly widowed, others thought he'd changed his mind about Rosina at the last moment and cleared off for a few days while the fuss died away. It was a crying pity it had to be Rosina, who had been so bad let down a few years ago by Charlie Kempthorne: a nicer purtier girl than Rosina never breathed, and she deserved better of life than to have her heart broke twice, poor maid—not that she ever cared for Charlie Kempthorne, they shouldn't wonder—but . . . but, though she'd been left at the church—or as near as made no difference—no one claimed that Drake had took any *advantage* of her; which was something to be said these days. All right, Jacka, we know what you d'mean—but there's advantage *and* advantage; and though he may have broke his word, no one's accusing him of having soiled the goods afore he bought them, no one's accusing him of having a finger in the pie afore it were put on the table. You got to say something for them Carne brothers, they be open and aboveboard in all that they do do.

" 'Boveboard!" said Jacka. "I'll splinter him like a board if so be as I ever lay hands 'pon him!"

There were some, of course, who took Jacka's side more openly, but it was not at all unanimous. Demelza's fear that her brothers were regarded as strangers was true enough, and they would be till they died—five miles was the absolute outside radius of "belonging"—but that they were her brothers and therefore Ross Poldark's brothers-in-law carried much weight. If they had been unpleasant, grasping, contentious characters this would have been quite a different matter: Poldark or no Poldark they would have been soon shut out. But no one in his right mind could accuse them of any of these things. It so happened unfortunately that one of them had just let a nice good girl down. The tendency of the majority was to mutter and shrug and say, well, well, twas all a great, great pity.

By Monday Art Mullet's anger had also lost its edge. He had his goats to tend and his nets to see to. Couldn't spend all day and every day breathing threats over a gin. But Jacka's resentment was fed by his drink, which again needed more drink to appease it. As night came on he went into a kiddley at the top of Sawle Combe, known as Doctor's, and found in there Tom Harry and Dick Kent, both gamekeepers from Trenwith. The Warleggan men were generally unpopular, Tom Harry and Harry Harry being particularly disliked, and none of them ever ventured into Sally Chill-Off's, where their reception would not have been kindly. Doctor's, however, run by a mouse-faced man called Warne, was not so particular, and over the last few years it had become the drinking place for the Trenwith men when they had time off.

Jacka Hoblyn had now reached the stage beyond ordinary drunkenness where he had become sober again, waveringly, grimly, soakingly sober; and he took no notice of the company and retreated with his drink to a stool in the corner. Tom Harry nudged Dick Kent and went over to Jacka, sat down on the next bench, and began to talk. Kent was beckoned to join them.

Here at last Jacka found a full and understanding sympathy. He didn't normally like these men any better than his friends did; but he realised he had misjudged them. They saw Drake as he saw him; as a coward, a liar, a deceiver and as a casual breaker of innocent hearts. A man who cared nothing for his promises, a stinking fitcher, a cheating finaiging villain, a worm not worthy to be left to crawl on the earth, a disgrace to the name of Sawle. A disgrace to the name of Hoblyn.

"If I had my way," said Jacka, wiping his mouth with the back of his hand, "I'd beat the life out of him. With a whip. With a horsewhip. I'd do him, I can tell ee that, and that's for certain!"

" 'E's back," said Tom Harry.

"Back? When? Where? I never seen him! Where's he to?"

"Back at his forge, I 'eard tell," said Tom. "Not's I've *seen* 'im, mind. But I 'eard tell. Edn that so, Dick?"

"Well . . . I dunno," said Kent. "Did ee hear that, Tom? Ah .. .Well, mebbe . . . Ais, I reckon."

Presently the three men left the kiddley and tramped off towards Pally's Shop. It was a long, steep descent, with one or two lights winking in St. Ann's on the other hill. No light at Drake's. As they got down Tom Harry went up to the door and hammered on it. No reply.

Jacka spat. "Forge's out. There's no one here."

"Reckon I 'eard tell he were. Maybe 'e's skulkin' indoors afeared to show 'is face. Eh, Jacka? Eh, Jacka? Let's go 'n see."

The door to the house was locked, but it was a flimsy lock and burst at their third shove. They lumbered in, Jacka first, stumbling over a chair and cursing.

"Gor damme, tes black as a tinker's sack. If I had my way—"

"Are ee thur?" shouted Tom Harry. "Come out, Drake Carne! We want t'ave word with ee! Come out, you."

They stumbled in the dark again, and then Dick

Kent struck flint on tinder and they lit a candle. The simple kitchen showed up, some bread on the table; a leg of rabbit beginning to mould. A jug of water, a tin mug full of tea. Harry gave the table a kick, overturning it with a mighty clatter.

" 'Ere, 'ere," said Kent nervously. "Folk'll think there's a war."

"So there be," said Jacka, glowering round like a bull goaded by flags and not sure which way to charge. "But the damned skunk bain't here to fight."

"Well, we can spoil 'is love nest! said Tom Harry, shouting from the tiny parlour a few steps up. " 'And me that candle, Dick!"

" 'Ere, 'ere, take care what you'm doing! Tes dangerous wi' that flame!"

"I'd burn un to ground," said Jacka through his broken teeth, swaying. "By God, I'd burn un to ground, so I would."

"Les do 'im," said Tom Harry. "Tes no sort of trouble 'tall. Les do 'im, then. Come on, Jacka, you be the one to think on it. Les see if your bite's so good as your bark!"

The candle wavered and guttered as it was put into Jacka's hand. He cursed as the hot grease ran over his fingers. Shadows ducked and dipped about the room, and then he thrust the candle at one of the cheap curtains. It caught quickly, went out, caught again.

" 'Ere, I'm 'avin' none o' this!" said Kent. "Ye can leave me out o' this. Tedn going to be none o' my business!" He stumbled out of the house.

Jacka was staring at the licking flame, half scared, half defiant.

"Now, then," said Tom Harry. "Make a job of 'im. Finish 'im off. Down wi' skunks and cheats and liars. Eh, Jacka? Eh?" He thrust a cloth at the other man, and when the candle nearly fell he steadied it with his other hand until the cloth had caught alight. Then he carried it up to the small parlour and laid it where it would lick the planking below the thatch.

They stayed another couple of minutes, making sure it caught. Dick Kent had already gone. Then they stumbled out after him and climbed the hill towards Sawle. At the top of the hill they sat down, panting for breath. Looking back, they could see that Pally's Shop was no longer quite in darkness. A yellow glow was rising and falling in one of the windows. They thought it better not to stop and watch for more.

III

Morwenna first saw Drake on the Tuesday afternoon. She had been ill all night, living with and trying to escape from monstrous nightmares. Ossie was constantly beside her bed in his winding sheet. "Let us first say a little prayer," he kept urging her. "Let us sow in corruption, let us be as the beasts of Ephesus, let us indulge in evil communication; the first man Adam was made a living soul, the last man Adam was made a quickening spirit; but let *us* quicken the flesh by the *indulgence* of flesh! Come, Morwenna, let us say a little prayer, and then you shall show me your *feet . . .*" Twice she had found herself out of bed and trying to find a door that did not exist in a wall that bricked her in with the living corpse of Ossie. Twice she was sick with the fright and the fear. As day came Garlanda had crept in from her own room and shared her bed. It was Garlanda who finally prevailed on her to get up and face the intolerable day.

Drake came in through the French doors that had blown ajar, dripping out of the rain.

"Drake!" she said, her voice breaking.

"Morwenna!"

She stared at him, wide-eyed, scared, scared of him, scared of what he stood for. After a moment he made a move towards her. She shrank back.

"Don't . . ."

"Morwenna. I been here—here and around ever since Sunday. I tried to see ee but there was always folk about—"

"Drake," she said. "Don't . . ."

"Don't what?" He picked the wet hair off his forehead.

"Touch me. Come near me. I—I can't bear it!"

"My dear, I know how ee must feel—"

"Do you?" She laughed harshly. "No, you don't! Nobody does. Nobody does. All I know is that what has happened to me has con-con-contaminated me. I'm not for you. Nor for anyone. Ever again."

"My dear—"

"Keep *away!*" She shrank as he made another half movement. "And please *go!*"

He stared at her, and she looked back at him wildly, with wild hostility in her eyes. He could not believe what he saw. She was a stranger and she was looking at him as if he were an enemy.

"I came," he said, stumbling now with his words, cold dread in his heart where minutes ago there had been nothing but high hope. "I came so soon as ever I heard. A—a man told me Saturday morning. I went to see Mr. Odgers to see if twas the truth. I'm sorry—was sorry that it happened; but when I knew you—when I knew you must be on your own I dropped everything and came." He put a hand again to his hair, trying to straighten it. "I—been sleeping rough, Morwenna, so you'll—I beg ee to excuse how I d'look. I've tried to see ee alone every day but there's been so many folk . . . I thought I—could help. Perhaps—later—if so be as you're still too upset . . . I can come back."

She took a breath that stifled the vomit in her throat. *"Never* come back, Drake. *Never* come back . . . if what you want is . . . Drake, it ended years ago. It can never begin again. I'm sick, sick, sick. It's over. It's *over,* finished, *done* with! Go away and forget me! Leave me, leave me, leave me *alone!"*

His hands began to tremble, and to control them he clenched them; half turned back towards the window and then stopped again.

"Morwenna, we can't part like this—"

The door opened and an ugly, powerful old woman with pouched eyes and a tight mouth came into the room.

"Who?" she said, and stopped. "Who are you? Morwenna, who is this person?"

Morwenna put a hand up to her eyes. "Someone—someone I used to know. He's—just going. Will you—will you get someone to show him *out*."

Chapter Eight

The burning of Pally's Shop created a greater scandal than Drake's disappearance. Breach of promise might be a wicked thing, but arson was serious crime. If it *was* arson, and nobody knew, but everyone believed so. The forge fire had been allowed to go out on Saturday. There was nothing to cause an untoward spark forty-eight hours later.

Sam came to tell Demelza early on Tuesday morning, and she had Judith saddled, lent Sam another pony. There was a small crowd around the smouldering shell. The cob walls survived, but the roof had gone and most of the furniture. They went in, picking their way through the wreckage.

"So it gets worse and worse," said Demelza, "one thing leading to another. Oh, God I don't know *what* to do!"

"There's little to do, sister," said Sam, "except pray for the forgiveness of sins and sinners."

"Do we sin by looking for happiness—by seeking happiness for others? This has happened—the way it has happened—it's as if fate has been working against us! Do human beings, can human beings deserve even less than they are given?"

"We do not sin by seeking happiness for others," Sam said slowly. "Maybe we err in supposing in our ignorance that we d'know what is best for others—or best for ourselves. Only our merciful Father know that."

229

"Sometimes it seems . . ."

"What, sister?"

"Oh, no matter."

"It is best to say it."

"Sometimes it seems as if our Father is not concerned with human happiness at all."

"He may not always be concerned with *earthly* happiness," said Sam, looking into his own heart. "But if you give yourself to Him you will find a greater happiness in looking towards the—the summits of eternity."

There was silence for a while. Demelza stirred a tin plate with her foot.

"D'you think he will come back, Sam?"

"Drake? He must sometime—surely, sister."

"He could hardly come back with—with Mrs. Whitworth, as a new widow. If something—if they still want to be together, then maybe it would be better if they went right away from this district."

Sam was feeling the walls, which were still warm. "Twould not cost so much to rebuild if twas done gradual. Timber and thatch, that's all tis. And thongs and nails and a few sticks of furniture. Drake have money in the bank, sister. And this is a proper little trade, regular and good. If God wills, he would do best to stick it out."

"With her?"

"Ah . . . that I don't rightly know. I never met her. Did you?"

"Two or three times, but only to say a word. I have no idea . . ."

A small figure limped in behind them.

"Rosina . . ."

"I had to come see, ma'am. Isn't it some awful. What a wicked thing t'happen."

"Wicked indeed," said Demelza. "I do not see how it could have been an accident."

Rosina's colour rose. "No, ma'am, nor me. But I do not think, I cann't think nor suppose twas on account o' me. Reely, I cann't."

"I seen the constable, Vage," said Sam, "but twould need the justices to move afore he could. And where do he look? It would be fruitless to search the villages, for whoso was so far gone in iniquity as to fire the house would be little moved by remorse to admit of it."

Rosina was looking at Demelza: "Ma'am, I truly do not b'lieve twas my father, nor none of his friends. My father were in the greatest of a passion and swore to beat Drake black and blue, but there be a power of difference twixt that and burning down his house."

Demelza said: "Did Drake give any idea of what he planned to do?"

"I do believe he had no plans. He came to me looking so ill I could have cried for him, and he said, he told me what had happened and said he had to go because of what he called his—his 'prior love.' ''

"Rosina, I am *that* sorry—that sorry for you."

"Tis funny, ma'am. I dearly cared for Drake, and had built up—all sorts o' dreams about our life together. Tis funny to see it all snatched away in a single day. By now, if this had not happened, we should have been wed. Even if it had happened but one week later we should still have been wed. And then Drake would *never* 've left me, I know that.'"

II

When Demelza got home, which was much later, for she looked in at the mine, Sir Hugh Bodrugan had called. It was not a propitious time, for she was feeling lonely and worried and very upset, and the thought of putting on a bright front to entertain this lecherous old roué did not appeal. But, in spite of herself, she had come to have a mild affection for Sir Hugh, as one does for almost any nuisance if it persists long enough. They had known each other upwards of ten years: he had lusted after her through thick and thin, as you might say, and had never yet had more than a brief kiss and a squeeze when he had manoeuvred her into some inescapable corner. Once or twice he *had* been useful to her and done her good turns, and always she had meanly refused to repay him in the only currency he was interested in. And there was a certain good temper about his lust; if the hand on her knee or the fingers trying to slip the blouse off her shoulder were evaded or rebuffed, he seemed to bear no ill-will but simply shifted his dispositions ready for the next move.

She went in and found him sprawling stertorously in their best chair, with a present for her in the shape of a large bunch of broom which had been forced into early flower in his conservatory. She thanked him gratefully—nothing pleased her, as he knew, more than winter flowers—and perched on a chair a fair distance from him, whereupon he did not return to the big chair but took one nearer to her.

They talked in a friendly but peripatetic fashion for a while. He commented on the latest moves in the war —not that he seemed very interested in them—that that fellow Buonaparte had now invaded Syria and was fighting the Turks there—appalling cruelties on both sides—there was talk of him trying to seize Acre, where a Turkish garrison was supported by a small English force. No holding him. A new chap called Wesley—nothing to do with that preacher fellow—was doing well in India, fighting the Frenchie's allies in Mysore. Demelza answered, yes, and no, and made the excuse of arranging the broom in two vases when it was necessary to keep him at a respectable distance, so that little yellow flakes decorated the carpet—the bunch had been half shaken to pieces on Sir Hugh's saddle in a strong wind.

Sir Hugh said Mrs. Fitzherbert was living openly with the Prince of Wales again, and there was talk that the Pope was going to recognise their marriage. . . .

Sir Hugh made a short sharp move and slid his arms round her.

"Got you!" he said, with a trumpet of satisfaction in his voice.

Demelza looked up at him, and tried to get an arm free to push the hair out of her eyes. He kissed her neck.

"Now, Sir Hugh," she said. "It is not good for the digestion in the forenoon."

"Nor is it ever for you, little madam," he said, as she gave a preliminary wriggle. "Don't I know how you tempt and tease me, eh? Got a face and figure as saucy as a doxy, but you behave as if there were some dangerous ill to be caught from a little lively pleasuring from time to time. Your better half's away, ma'am, and you've seen no sight nor sound of him for weeks. You don't need to stick so close to your marriage vows as if you was a piece of sealing wax!"

"That's a compliment," said Demelza. "A rare compliment. Light me at one end and I congeal upon a piece of paper. You're too kind."

"Of course I'm too kind."

"Any moment, I should warn you, someone will come in."

"Let 'em. They do it among themselves."

"We should set an example. That's what I was taught."

"You was taught wrong." He became aware that any moment her not inconsiderable strength would be exerted to break the clinch. "I'll make a bargain with you, m'dear. Give me a kiss—a proper one—no chicken picking at a morsel of grain—a proper kiss and I'll tell you a secret."

"What about, Sir Hugh?"

"What about, Sir Hugh? Don't it sound pretty on your lips. Well . . . it is something I came to tell you —to *warn* you of—but damn me, I'll go away with my confidences locked away unless you agree to unlock 'em."

"Afterwards, maybe. After you've told me. If I think it's important."

"Ah, no—you've cheated me often enough that way, madame minx. It is cash on the counter today."

She looked at him. His big coarse face was much too close. The hair in his nostrils and his plumy eyebrows were still black in spite of his age.

"It is to do with your husband, Captain Poldark."

"In what way?"

"A hint. A warning. Something I heard."

"He isn't here."

"Never mind. You can write and tell him. Maybe you should act on his behalf."

"How act on his behalf?"

"Because it may be necessary."

She hesitated. Sir Hugh was one of those men who often "heard" things—he had the capacity some people have for picking up information ahead of the rest.

"Well . . ." she said.

He needed no further invitation but fastened his big mouth on hers. She endured it for a few moments, and then as his intentions became more aggressive she freed herself, turning away to hide a shiver of distaste.

"Damn *me!*" he said, licking his lips. "Damn me! That's as good as I've tasted for many a day. Well, well. Damn *me*. Twas not dislikeable, mistress, I swear it wasn't to you. Tell me it wasn't."

She smiled at him through her hair and went to look out of the window.

"Damn me!" he said.

She said: "When you have damned yourself often enough, Sir Hugh, tell me what I am buying."

"Ah"—he sat down in the big chair again and stretched his legs—"ah, yes, well, I suppose I must inform you now . . ."

"I think you must."

"Well then . . . well, I was in Truro yesterday on business to do with the bench. I don't know why I bother with the bench, nor why anyone does. Hang a half dozen sturdy rogues at Bargus every week, and there'd be little need of justices and all that hot air. Just see 'em dandle—it has a salutary effect on the rest!"

"It's not having a salutary effect on me, Sir Hugh."

"Madame minx. By God, you taste good."

"Not of sealing wax?"

"You will have your joke. So, well, I was in Truro yesterday and there was much whispering going on. Among 'em as *knew,* as you might put it. In the know, as it were. You remember old Nat Pearce?"

234

"The notary? Ross's solicitor? Yes?"

"Did ye know he'd just gone around land? Died? Well, he has: And there's much talk that he has left his affairs in a serious bad state. Peculations. That's the word. Many people affected in Truro. Poldark have any recent dealings with him?"

"Not that I know."

"Lucky for that. There's going to be a crash. People taken in this way and the other. And they say—and this is what I came to tell ye of—they say Pascoe's Bank's involved."

Demelza turned from the window. "How? Why?"

"Don't ask me, m'dear; I'm no financier. I know little of how these things work. But there was much whispering yesterday—and among those who *know,* mark you—that Pascoe's may no longer be a safe place to keep your money, nor will his notes be worth their value neither. Doesn't Poldark bank at Pascoe's?"

"Yes."

"Well, then. I'm a good neighbour, ye see, as well as being your old suitor. I thought it was only fair to warn you."

Demelza's stomach was rather cold. "I can do nothing without Ross."

"Yes, you can. You can withdraw your balances. It is the safest thing to do. Bring the money home or spend it among the other banks. You've nothing to lose by doing that, have you? Better to be safe than sorry."

III

Drake stayed in the neighbourhood of St. Margaret's vicarage for the rest of Tuesday and for the whole of Wednesday, living rough, sleeping under a hedge in the bitter cold, buying a little food from an old woman in a cottage by the river. He could not bring himself to leave. He hung about the graveyard, within sight of the house, hoping to catch a glimpse of Morwenna again. He simply could not believe that it was all over, that she had changed so utterly from the girl he had known and loved. He appreciated that his arrival so soon after Osborne's death and the nervous tensions of the funeral must have startled her; he should have waited longer, perhaps have written first, anything to ease the shock. His coming upon her in the way he had, still surrounded as she was by relatives, perhaps— who knew?—still grieving in some perverse way for the solid comfort of her lost husband . . . might she not impulsively have rejected him, while an hour or two, a day's reflection, would bring a different feeling to her heart?

But there had been such fear, such open hostility in her gaze. Whence had come that? How did you excuse or explain that? Or the cold, trembling disgust in her voice. He might have been someone who had once done her a mortal hurt, instead of being someone she had once loved.

Yet, he hung on, still hoping, hardly able to admit to himself that now *everything* was dust and ashes. Twice he almost went to the house again, but felt he could not risk being turned away. So all through Wednesday.

On the Thursday morning, which was dry and less cold, he saw her come out of the house with two little girls—presumably her stepdaughters—and walk slowly towards the river. She was wearing her veil but it was thrown back from her face. She walked so slowly that she might have been ill. He hesitated, afraid now that the opportunity was on him to put it to the test.

He decided he must not come on her by surprise. He skirted round the edge of the garden, got down to the river, and by splashing through the muddy shallows was able to appear among the trees that she was approaching. He stood there, plainly to be seen.

One of the little girls saw him first and said something to Morwenna. Then she saw him and stopped dead. He saw her face. She stood quite still for perhaps five seconds, then she swung on her heel and walked swiftly back into the house . . .

After that he knew it was the end. He turned blindly

away and stumbled out of the garden, across the churchyard, and began to walk up the hill.

He walked all day, not quite knowing what he was doing but gradually making for home. His stomach was empty but he couldn't eat, his mouth dry but he couldn't swallow the water he scooped up in his hands.

About halfway home he realised he had lost his way and had come round in a circle. He sat for a while, wondering what to do. Then he set off again. Then he was very tired and went to sleep in a clump of pine trees. It was dark when he woke, and he was shivering, but his mind was clearer and he knew where he had gone astray. He began to walk again.

The night was clear and cold, moonless but lit with stars. The wind had dropped and there would be a touch of hoarfrost before morning. In some of the dips fog had collected, and here and there it was so shallow that he waded through it, his feet scarcely visible but his head clear. On some of the fields it lay like white smoke. Goats and sheep stirred among it, ghosts of themselves.

He came at last to St. Ann's and through it, the little church town sleeping; only one light glimmered for a sick man; and a solitary cat blinked its slit eyes at the stars. Then down the hill to his own shop. It took a time for him to see that something was wrong. The light was just enough to show up the gaunt walls, a frame of roof standing, but his senses did not at first take it in. He leaned against the gate, under the bell, took a breath, stared again. Then he walked into the yard, stumbling over the debris.

His front door gaped wide, hanging by one hinge. He tried to go in, but a charred fallen rafter barred his way. He tried to force it back but seemed to have no strength in his arms. He leaned his head against the drunken door, unable to go on.

Someone touched his arm. It was Sam, who had been sleeping in an outhouse each night, for just such a contingency as his brother's return.

"Well, Drake, well, Drake. How are ee? Come home at last, have ee."

Drake swallowed and licked his lips. "What—is it? This . . ."

"An accident," said Sam. It happened while you was away. There's no cause 'tall to worry. We'll have him fixed in no time."

"Sam," Drake said. "She wouldn't . . . She's changed . . ." He sagged at the knees.

"Come along, old love." Sam said, supporting him. "We'm going home to Reath Cottage. Just for a while, just while things be straightened out; you and me got two ponies in back—Demelza lended them—so twill take no time at all to get home. Come along, my old love. I'll give ee a helping hand."

IV

The following afternoon a constable with an assistant called at Reath Cottage. As soon as Drake left the vicarage Lady Whitworth had sent a servant to report that a suspicious person had forced his way into the house and had attempted to engage her daughter-in-law in loose conversation. Her daughter-in-law refused any knowledge of his name, but by urgent inquiry Lady Whitworth had succeeded in identifying him, and the constable was despatched to discover what culpability he might have in her son's death.

Fortunately Sam was home, for Drake seemed barely capable of answering questions or even wanting to; and if Sam had been absent Drake was likely to have been taken off to Truro to stand before the magistrates without protest. Sam pointed out that his brother *must* be innocent of any part in it, as he had been at his shop throughout the day and evening when Mr. Whitworth met his death. To this the constable asked what proof Sam had of this. Sam then patiently questioned his brother in front of the men and elicited the fact that Arthur and Parthesia Mullet had been with Drake until eight in the evening, and then he had gone up at nine to Mr. Maule the tailor to have his new jacket fitted, and had not left him until ten.

The constable appeared not altogether satisfied with this, for, he said, Drake had no proof that he hadn't rid in to Truro after this. Sam said, what time was Parson found? Well, then, short of flying, twould be hard to leave the tailor at St. Ann's at ten o'clock of the night and be in Truro in time to attack a man who'd been found dead shortly after midnight. Wouldn't it now.

Presently the men went off, professing themselves still unsatisfied, but, after calling on Mr. Maule to hear what he had to say, they rode back to Truro with their report. No more was heard of them.

Chapter Nine

Ross had written that he expected to be home during the week following Easter; but he had not arrived by the Friday, when Demelza had to make a decision for him. Friday was the twenty-ninth, so Saturday was payday at the mine.

It was customary for Zacky or Henshawe to ride in to Truro, accompanied by Paul Daniel or Will Nanfan, draw the money from Pascoe's Bank, and return the same day. Whoever went as second man carried with him an old two-barrelled pistol. Whether it would fire if you pulled the trigger no one was quite sure, but its presence was a useful deterrent if there were a thief who had designs on the bags of money. Apart, of course, from the fact that both Daniel and Nanfan were very big men.

They normally left at eight, and she walked to the mine just before seven-thirty and found Zacky Martin there, with Will Nanfan. Luckily Captain Henshawe came in a moment or two later, so she was able to put the situation to them all.

After she had finished there was silence for a few seconds while they each waited for someone else to speak.

"Reckon tis only a rumour," said Zacky uneasily.

"Tis not a rumour about Mr. Pearce," said Henshawe. "I heard that Wednesday. Some manner of trust that Mrs. Jacqueline Aukett made for her grandsons and Pascoe's Bank was guaranteeing . . ."

Zacky said: "But even if it is more than rumour, tis unlikely that we shann't get our money. I've known Mr. Pascoe, man and boy, all my life, though ever at a distance, like, him being a banking man and me just a miner. There'll never be a straighter."

"It is not the money that worries me," said Demelza; "it is drawing it out, if there are many other of the same mind, it will look bad, even though it is what we always do at this time every month. Tell me, Will, what money do we have here?"

"Here?" Henshawe looked startled. "In the mine, like? Twenty guineas, twenty-five maybe. Just the loose cash for the odds and ends we d'buy from time to time. There's always less at the end of the month."

"How much do we need? What do you reckon to bring home?"

"We thought to draw four hundred and seventy. We need four twenty for the wages, minimum."

She frowned her perplexity at the heavy day showing through the dirty window, layer upon layer of cloud glooming down to the sea. "We have perhaps a hundred in the house. Ross always likes to keep something hid for emergencies. But it is not enough, is it? It is not enough."

"Pardon me, missus," said Will Nanfan. "It is scarce to do wi' me at all, since I be only part-time and helping out here and there, but might it not be best if you was to come with us today? See Mr. Pascoe yourself? See for yourself if there be trouble or not. It would be what Cap'n Poldark would do."

"Captain Poldark," said Demelza, "knows all about money. And I do not."

"All same," said Will Nanfan, "I reckon you got a good instinct for it. I reckon you got a good instinct for most things."

II

They left at eight-fifteen, Henshawe coming with them at Demelza's request, making a quartet. There might be some decision to make in Truro which was of vital importance, and four heads, she felt, would be better than three, in spite of their somewhat pathetic belief in her capabilities.

They were in Truro before ten-thirty, and made a detour to ride past Pascoe's Bank. They soon saw that rumour had not exaggerated the effect of rumour. There was no disorderliness, no rush, no panic—yet —but there were dismounted horses in the street, one red-wheeled tandem cart, a farmer's gig, some pack asses, and groups of people standing about talking, so that the four riders had difficulty in getting through.

"I'll dismount here," Demelza said when they came to the corner. "It would not do for us all to go in. You go on to the Red Lion, but you, Zacky, come back when you've stabled the horses and wait for me at this corner."

"Yes, mistress. That I will do."

She walked back, not pushing through the crowd but taking her time, avoiding people and sidestepping round them. They did not know who she was, but her good clothes, her leggy slimness, her startling dark eyes all drew attention and a degree of respect. People made way for her. It was not at all a question of putting on airs, but a dozen years of being Mrs. Ross Poldark had left their mark.

She remembered that down the slit of an alley beside the bank was a side door through which they had entered on the night of Caroline's wedding, so she decided to try that. A scared-looking maid answered the bell. Yes, Mr. Pascoe was in, but was engaged. Could she have the name? Oh, Mrs. Poldark, of course, she should've remembered, beg pardon. She'd tell Mr. Pascoe, if Mrs. Poldark'd care to wait.

Mrs. Poldark would wait, and was shown into a little box of a room adjoining the bank parlour. She sat on a blue plush chair and moistened her lips and was wondering precisely what she should say, when it came to her notice that she could hear the conversation in the next room through the door that the wind of her entry had caused to come ajar.

"It's a big sum," said a voice. "I know that. But ye see, Mr. Pascoe, the money's not all mine. I cannot afford to take the slightest risk . . ."

"What leads you to suppose there is a risk?" Pascoe's voice.

"Well, tis all over the town. People saying old Nat Pearce has been embezzling funds and some of those funds carry your guarantee. If that be so—"

"Mr. Lukey, my old friend Nathaniel Pearce has, alas, used funds that were not his own for stupid sp-speculation in India and elsewhere. In order to do this he has written and issued and signed statements which would surely see him committed to prison if he were still alive. Some of these funds which he has misappropriated carry our guarantee, and, though the way in which he has taken this money gives me the opportunity to r-repudiate these guarantees, I have every intention of honouring them in full. That does not mean that the stability of the bank is threatened. Unless . . ."

"Unless?"

"Unless every one of my old clients proceeds to do as you do and suddenly demand in full deposits which have lain with us for years."

"Ah, yes . . . Yes, well. That may be." There was the clink of a glass. "But you can meet this cheque now if I present it?"

"Of course."

"Then I think I must, Mr. Pascoe, I think I must. Ye see, as I've said before, all this is not my own personal money. Over the years there's been this steady growth of investment in my little businesses, and should I not be able to repay it in full . . ."

"Very well . . ." There was the "ting" of a bell.

"No hard feelings, I'm sure, Mr. Pascoe? None on my side."

"No hard f-feelings," said Harris Pascoe. "Except that in times of temporary stringency one comes to know one's friends."

"Well, sir—"

"Oh, Kingsley, will you take this slip and pay Mr. Lukey the amount on it. I trust, Mr. Lukey, you do not want it all in gold?"

"Well, sir . . ."

"Bills on Basset's Bank are still I b-believe worth their face value?"

"Why, certainly. I'm sorry ye take it this way."

"I'm sorry that I have to. Half in coin, Kingsley; the rest in bills."

The door was heard to close and there was silence for a while except for the rustling of paper. Demelza thought she might have been forgotten; but then the door opened some extra inches and Harris Pascoe looked round it.

"Mrs. Poldark. Alice said . . . This is a pleasure. Will you come in now." His face was thin and drawn, the indented lines dark furrows. "Is Ross not here?"

"No . . . We're expecting him any day. I—hope he comes soon." Demelza sat on the edge of a chair. "I came because I thought he would want me to. I hear there is—a sort of trouble."

"Indeed. Perhaps you heard that c-conversation. Ah, yes, you did. Well, Lukey is one of my largest and oldest depositors but he has allowed himself to be infected by the general fear—and fear, once it begins, is like a forest fire. It is no respecter of persons. He, I would have thought, m-might have kept a cool head. But money rules all . . . Perhaps as a banker I should not be surprised that money rules all—yet I confess at times to a slender feeling of disappointment."

"Mr. Pascoe," said Demelza, "I do very much wish Ross was here. I—am not well versed in these money matters you speak of. Is it possible for you to explain a little—simply?"

"Nothing easier. Mr. Pearce must in his last years have suffered some softening of the moral fibre that I was unaware of. He became enamoured of various financial bubbles that promised him a fortune in quick time—and they all burst. He has, I would estimate, r-robbed his clients of some fifteen thousand pound. For about half of this we stand as guarantors. I trusted him, and in that am at fault, and so will bear the loss. Seven th-thousand odd will not sink this bank nor sink me. But if the crude public who make up the population of the town and country round lose their confidence in Pascoe's Bank, then I do not know whether we can keep our heads above water. I think there has been ill-will."

"Ill-will?"

"Well, this." Pascoe handed her a letter. "Mr. Henry Prynne Andrew is our oldest client, and one of our most substantial. He received this, put under his door this morning."

Demelza's eyes went rapidly over it. "Honoured Sir, It has come to the notice of Well Wisher that you continue to entrust your savings to Pascoe's Bank in Truro. I have to inform you on the highest authority —that of a member of the staff of that bank—that it is now on the verge of insolvency. Monies made over to Mr. Pascoe's daughter on her marriage a few years ago have been helping to support a larger notes issue than any sagacious Banker would sanction. It so happens that this money has now been withdrawn, and the event coincides with the revelation of the criminal activities of Mr. Nathaniel Pearce, Mr. Pascoe's old crony and confidant; and the threadbare nature of the cover that this bank offers by way of guarantee of the value of its notes is painfully revealed . . ."

It went on in such a vein for another half page and was signed "A Well Wisher."

"How did it come about—who wrote this?"

Mr. Pascoe shrugged. "It has been written. And if, as I suspect, many people have received a similar letter, there are some among them who will b-believe what it says; and even those who do not altogether believe will wonder if their money is *quite* safe . . ."

"It is wicked—monstrous. But you can—meet the demands?"

Again he shrugged. "The basis of banking, the way it has developed, explores the very nature of credit. If a thousand pounds is paid into a bank, a prudent banker will keep perhaps two hundred of it in his safes and will lend out the other eight hundred—on good security, of course—at a higher rate of interest than that he is paying the d-depositor. So credit expands, and instead of having enormous reserves behind the counters he is concerned in land, in mines, in mills, in shops, in India Stock, in bonds, anything which bears with safety the higher rates of interest. If one depositor comes in of a sudden and demands his thousand pounds to be repaid at once, that is nothing: it is all in a banker's day. If ten such come in he will still be able to meet it. But if m-more come to the counters and clamour, he must first sell his stock and his bonds before he can pay them, often at a substantial loss; and after that it is a question of what short-term loans he can call in. If they are not due for two months, four months, six months, they are out of his reach. The money is safe but not today, not tomorrow. And if the clamour continues he will be unable to meet his obligations and must close his shutters."

They could hear the murmur of voices from inside the bank. The clerk put his head round the door.

"Mr. Buller to see ee, sur."

"Tell him I will see him in five minutes."

The head withdrew. Pascoe said: "Apart from this, there is the note issue. All Truro banks have been issuing notes of late years. We have been the most restrained, but even so, once mistrust begins . . . Yesterday I l-learned that people with Pascoe notes were being advised to spend them while they still had value. And some shops are already refusing to change them —on the pretext that they are short of silver."

"How long has this been going on?"

"Since Wednesday. Yesterday, we paid out near nine thousand pounds. Today, thanks to Mr. Lukey, we have already paid six." Harris Pascoe got up. "But in my preoccupations I am forgetting my m-manners. A glass of port, my dear?"

"Thank you, no. As you know, Mr. Pascoe, this is the end of the month, and it is our custom—our usual custom . . ."

"To draw money," he helped with a smile. "Of course. For wages. What is the usual amount? About five hundred? There will be no difficulty. I will instruct my clerk."

"No," said Demelza, "but I've been thinking, if you are in this trouble . . ."

Pascoe stared at the glass of port he had poured for himself. "You may wish to safeguard yourself by taking more? It is natural. Your husband has just over two thousand to his credit at this time. Less than usual because of the accident to your mine. B-but I should esteem it a favour if you did not draw it all— at least not for the next two weeks. By then we shall, I hope, have weathered the storm."

There was another silence. Demelza said: "Mr. Pascoe, you must not think all your friends are like Mr. Lukey."

III

In his porticoed mansion overlooking the river Fal, Mr. Ralph-Allen Daniell was writing letters when a servant came to tell him he had a visitor. He walked out and found the lady standing in her velvet riding suit beside one of the broad windows that offered a view of young chestnut trees and a group of Devon yearlings.

"Mrs. Poldark. This is a pleasure, ma'am. Captain Poldark is not with you? Do sit down."

It was the second time this morning that a grave, elderly man had bowed over her gloved hand, and almost with the same words. There was little to choose between them in sobriety; this one the stouter in build and by a few years younger and verging on the Quaker in style of dress.

"Mr. Daniell, it is very good of you to receive me. Mrs. Daniell is well? I came—Ross is still at Westminster, and I came to ask your urgent advice . . . and help."

He insisted on having canary wine brought for her, and while it was being brought she speculated on whether she might not have crossed the river instead in the hope that Lord Falmouth had returned to Cornwall.

"Mr. Daniell, you will have heard, I suspect, that there is trouble in Truro and pressure on Pascoe's Bank?"

"I have not been in this week, but my steward told me of it. A pity. But I think it will blow over."

"It depends," Demelza said, "on what support he gets from his friends."

"Well, yes. But he weathered the national bank crisis of '97. This is only a temporary crisis of confidence, surely; and this time the other banks will not themselves be under stress and will lend a hand."

"Warleggan's will not."

"Well, Basset's, where I bank . . ."

"Mr. Daniell," Demelza said, "you'll forgive me because I don't understand these things, and I dearly wish that Ross were here and then he could do what he thinks is best. But while he is not I must—must try to think for him. . . . It is the end of the month and the wages are due on our mine. I came to draw this money to take home tonight for the payday tomorrow. But I find I cannot . . ."

"You mean"—Daniell's brows contracted—"that Pascoe's can't pay you? Why, I would have thought—"

"I mean," she said, "that I cannot draw it."

"I don't understand."

"In the years when Ross was struggling, so near to a debtor's prison that even now sometimes I wake in the night—Mr. Pascoe helped us again and again. He has been Ross's personal friend—certainly his closest in Truro—for twenty years. This is the time for us to put money *into* his bank, not draw it out!"

He had been watching her interestedly. "The sentiment does you credit, ma'am. Though there are times when sentiment is a bad business adviser. You have a considerable deposit in the bank, more than you need?"

"Oh, yes. Much more."

"Then you should not hesitate to take this lesser amount. . . . Oh, I see your dilemma, and I applaud you for your feelings. It would be a sad world if we were all like the Warleggans. But . . ." He got up to refill her glass and she smiled her assent. "If you have come for my advice, then—"

"More than advice, Mr. Daniell. Your help."

She had seen that cautious look come into men's eyes before. How warmly they looked at you until you mentioned money! But Mr. Daniell was known for his philanthropy, his generous business ethics.

"How can I help?"

"Ross has an interest in your reverbatory furnaces. I do not know the extent of it, but he tells me it is profitable."

"It's on a sound footing, yes. We're all pleased with the way it has developed. And it has an assured future."

She took a breath. "Then will you buy his interest in it and pay me the money?"

His glass tinkled as he put it down, and he took out a handkerchief to dab a spot on the table.

"My dear Mrs. Poldark . . ."

It was a very peaceful scene. You could not hear the wind in this sheltered valley; the only sound was the crackling of the wood fire.

"That is out of the question."

". . . I'm sorry."

"You do not have the authority. Nor could I possibly, under any conditions, take this as his considered decision without his signature."

"At present he is likely to be at sea—on his way

home. His signature cannot help Mr. Pascoe if it comes in a week's time."

He laughed, though more in embarrassment than amusement. "Well, it's out of the question. I am more than sorry." He stared at her. The last man ever to be influenced by a pretty face, he could still observe the appearance of this young woman with appreciation. And the directness of her mind. She made no bones . . .

"How much do you need to meet your wages?"

"Two thousand pounds."

He blinked. "A moment ago, ma'am, I was admiring you for your candour. That remark, alas, disillusions me."

"Well . . . a thousand at least."

He smiled. "How many men do you employ in total?"

"I can't remember."

"I would guess that seven hundred pounds would more than cover all your possible needs."

"I have a hundred at home," Demelza said. "With that, perhaps about eight hundred would do."

He got up and took a turn about the room. She watched his slow pacing out of the corner of her eye.

He said: "What I could do—the most I could do— would be to advance you seven hundred and fifty pounds. This would be writ off against Captain Poldark's share of the future profits in the furnaces—and I would warn you that that would more than absorb anything he could hope to draw in the next twelve months. Even this I could do only by breaking my legal obligation to him. If he challenges me as to why I have done this, I shall have no excuse."

"He won't, Mr. Daniell."

"So you say. And so I believe, or I would not do it. But I know his quixotic temperament, and his wife's, it seems, matches it. Pascoe is lucky in his friends."

"Some of them, Mr. Daniell."

"Yes . . . There has been a good deal of malice in Truro over the last years. It is too much in so small a town. Happily I have kept out of it."

"I don't think it is of Mr. Pascoe's seeking."

"No. . . . It wants barely an hour to dinner now. Will you stay? I know my wife would much like it."

"I'm afraid I can't. You see . . . if you are to give me a draft . . . I must have time."

"Of course. I quite understand. Will you wait here? . . ."

He was gone five minutes. She admired the Reynolds portrait of Ralph-Allen Daniell's forebear, Ralph Allen, the son of an innkeeper, who had revolutionised the postal system of England and made half a million pounds for himself thereby, later to become one of the great philanthropists of his time. She stared at the fluted ceiling of the room, the Adam mantelshelf, the Zoffany paintings. This was what money brought, just as it had brought them their beautiful new library at Nampara. Money could bring beauty and elegance and taste, just as it could bring—or the lack of it or the fear of losing it could bring—the ugly scenes that were developing in Truro as she left.

He returned with a piece of paper. "Here is a draft on Basset's Bank for eight hundred pounds. It is the most I can do for you."

"I'm that grateful, Mr. Daniell. I know Ross will be."

"Yes, yes." Having parted with the draft, he eyed it uneasily as she put it into her purse, as if there were second thoughts hovering. "My dear . . . may I call you that? . . . you're so young . . ."

"Of course . . ."

"A last word of advice. This money is for you and for your mine. It is not to try to support a shaky bank in Truro. And if you have quixotic thoughts in that direction may I point out that eight hundred pounds will neither sink nor save it. If it is going to crash—which I doubt—not eight hundred pounds nor the two thousand you first asked for is likely to be a sufficient raft for it to cling to to keep its head above water; and if it survives—as I believe it will—then it will survive without your having to deprive any of your miners of their monthly wage. Draw this money, take it home, keep it safe. There is a surplus here over and above your immediate needs—I am not deceived—so that will be useful to you both *if* by any mischance the rest of your deposit in Pascoe's Bank should be lost or temporarily frozen. I admire your loyalty, Mrs. Poldark. And your generosity. But I do not suppose you deficient in common sense, and I would remind you not to allow your emotions to blind you."

Demelza smiled at him and then dropped her eyes. "Thank you, Mr. Daniell. I do appreciate your kindness and consideration to me."

He went to the door with her. "Are you unaccompanied? Is that wise?"

"No. I have the mine manager waiting by the gates."

"I'm relieved," said Mr. Daniell, and she thought he meant it in a double sense.

IV

Not only the mine manager but her other two companions were waiting for her, one smoking, another sitting in the grass chewing a leaf of chucky-cheese he had picked from the hedge. In this sheltered part the blighting effects of the cold spring were not so plain.

As soon as they saw her they scrambled onto their ponies. They looked at her expectantly.

She said: "I have a draft for eight hundred pounds. It is not as much as I hoped but it is better than I feared."

"It d'seem a mint of money to me," said Zacky Martin.

The horses were snorting and trying to get their heads together, so that conversation was not easy.

"And now?" said Henshawe, watching her very closely.

"Now," she said, "you and I, Captain Henshawe, will go into Basset's and change this draft—and as little of it for notes and as much of it for coins as we can persuade them to give us. Perhaps all coin. I do not think they can refuse us if we demand it all in gold and silver."

Henshawe gave his horse an admonitory flick. "And then?"

"Then we go into a back room of the Red Lion and divide the money into—roughly into three parts. One part you will take, Will Nanfan, one you, Zacky, and one you, Will Henshawe. And then, one at a time, with a suitable interval in between, you will go, each one of you, back to Pascoe's Bank, push your way through those noisy, sweating, ugly folk, and fight your way to the counter and then empty your bags on the counter and pay the money into the Poldark account. Make as much noise as you can. Clatter the coins. Let everyone see and know that you are paying the money *in*."

There was no sound then but the snorting of the horses and the occasional creak of leather.

"*All* the money?" asked Zacky.

"All," said Demelza.

Chapter Ten

It was two weeks more before Ross got home. He was furious. On several occasions he had taken the sea route, finding it easier, smoother, quicker. This time they had left the Pool of London on Easter Monday without incident or delay, sailing on a full tide. But they had called at Chatham and there been embayed eight days with the wind dead in the port and no hope of stirring. When they finally left it had been the wildest voyage of his considerable experience. They had lost a mast off the Goodwins and nearly gone aground. With a jury rig they had been blown down-Channel and put in to the Solent for repair. Out again, they had encountered high seas and contrary winds, and finally limped into Fowey as battered and exhausted as if they had been attempting Cape Horn.

So April was well advanced and spring was imposing

itself on the countryside in spite of all discouragement. Anxious to be back, and not savouring the thought of another chance encounter with Osborne Whitworth or some other sturdy citizen in the flea-infested stage-coach, he bought a young mare in Fowey and rode her straight home. It was late, and light was fleeing from the sky as he reached his own land. He looped his reins over the old lilac tree and opened his own front door. There was a light in the parlour but it was empty.

Jane Gimlett came up behind him and uttered a little squeak. "Cap'n *Ross!* Oh, *sur!* At last! We was all expecting of ee—we all thought t'expect ee last week. Well, sur! I'll go get John!"

"No hurry. But when you go, tell him I've a new mare and she's gone a thought lame. I think it is nothing but an ill-fitting shoe." (God, did life never tire of repeating itself? Darkie had been so affected fifteen years ago.) "Where's your mistress?"

"Out visiting, I b'lave, sur."

"Visiting?"

"Her brothers, sur. That's where I d'think she be."

"Which brother? They are widely separated."

"No, sur. Not just now, sur. They'm both over to Reath Cottage."

"Ah," said Ross, and waited for an explanation, but none came. "How are the children?"

"Brave an' well. Both asleep. God's little messengers. Shall I wake 'em?"

"No, no. Let them sleep for a while. I'd like some food, Jane. What do you have?"

"There's half a leg o' pork, just fresh—"

"Not Ebb or Flow slaughtered yet?"

"No, sur. And there's part of a capon. And . . . But tes all cold . . ."

"No matter. Just bring anything you think I'll fancy . . ."

The fire was low and his hands were cold. He threw his gauntlet gloves on a chair and tipped some more coal on, then struggled with his boots.

"Let me do that, sur!" Jane said, returning.

"No, I've managed. Thank you."

"Will ee eat here, sur, or in the dining room? I b'lave the fire have gone out in there . . ."

"Here, then. Is all well with your mistress?"

"Oh, yes, brave and fine, sur."

"And the rest of you?"

"Yes, yes. Betsy Maria have had a carbuncle but he have gone down now and be nearly mended. What wine shall I bring?"

"What has your mistress been drinking?"

"Just ale with meals. And port for after."

"Ah, port," said Ross. "Yes, port . . . Well, ale will suit me very well."

He wandered round the room for a minute or two, remembering old things, recognising new, while the food was brought. A few letters for him, but he opened only three, first two of which were begging letters, the second being from Clarence Odgers asking him if he would use his influence to obtain for him at last the living of Sawle. What the devil did that mean? The third invited him to a ceremony in Truro at which Baron de Dunstanville of Tehidy would open the new Cornwall General Infirmary which had been built on the outskirts of the town. This would be followed by a service in St. Mary's Church and a dinner at the Red Lion Inn, to which all governors and principal subscribers were invited. The date for this was still two weeks hence.

He had almost finished his meal when Demelza came in. The collar of her cloak was up and her hair was blown by the wind. She looked young and doubtful and startled and almost *sulky*—a word he would never in his life have chosen to describe her before.

"Ross!"

"My dear." He got up and kissed her on her cold sweet-smelling cheek. (Had she slightly turned her mouth away?) "They say a bad penny always returns."

"Not before its time," she said, one hand on each of his arms. "We have been that *worried*."

"For me? I wrote you from Chatham."

"But that was two weeks ago! I pictured you captured by the French!"

"Oh, in wild weather there is small risk of that."

"You could have been blown into one of their ports! You could have been—*drowned!*"

"But am not. As you see. Only glad to be home. But I shall think twice before travelling by the sea route again."

She looked at him. "You—smell different. You're thinner."

He laughed. "Different may be the genteel term. I came straight from the brig as soon as we docked. If I smell like an old tarpaulin that can be corrected. And as for thinness; you've interrupted me in my first attempts to redress the balance."

"Please, you must go on! What has Jane got for you? Oh, we could have cooked something quickly!" She continued in this way for a moment or two, and then he said:

"No. It was a joke. I've really finished; really. The edge has gone and the rest can wait till tomorrow. Let me look at you. Sit down. This coal is not burning well. Sit and tell me all your news."

Talking lightly between themselves, exchanging casual superficial information that kept the silences away, they took seats on either side of the fire. She had dropped her cloak, straightened her blouse, flipping up the lace at throat and breast, found slippers for them both, joking that it was a wonder his were not mildewed, run fingers about her hair so that it surprisingly fell into the half-ordered density of curl and spring and turn that he liked best, jabbed at the fire with a skilful vigour that he lacked so that flame leapt up the chimney, brought a glass of port for herself and a brandy for him; and in the course of it all the turn of her mouth had changed to a shape he better recognised, and her eyes come to have a light that sparked a light in him.

He told her of London and work there and his visits to Caroline and a further meeting with Geoffrey Charles, and the frequent frustrations and occasional pleasures of the House, and that Caroline, he thought, was returning to Cornwall next month to rejoin Dwight for the summer, and of his commission to help train raw militia in Kent throughout the month of August, and of his landlady's expectation that at the next session in the autumn he would bring his wife with him, and of the progress and successes and failures of the war.

To all this she listened without any straying interest, and put numerous questions; but after he had been talking for a quarter of an hour he stopped and said:

"And what has gone wrong here?"

"Why do you suppose something has gone wrong?"

"Because I have never before seen you look the way you did when you came in just now. I think something is gravely wrong, and that you feel I am in some measure responsible."

"Did I look like that? You misread me! Something is wrong, much has gone wrong in the last few weeks, but I hold no one responsible. How could I? I wished —I have wished that much that you could have been here. But that is not the same as—as what you said."

"Tell me."

"From the beginning? It will take a long time."

"From the beginning."

So she told him first of Osborne Whitworth's strange death, of Rosina's broken marriage, of Drake's disappearance and return, of the burning of Pally's Shop.

"My God," he said. "Is it a total loss?"

"The walls are blackened but sound enough. The roof has gone—and the floor—and the furniture."

"And no one is responsible, eh? No one saw anyone at all."

"No one saw anyone at all. Or will not say."

"I must see Jacka. It's the sort of evil-tempered thing he might essay. And yet . . . and yet . . . Now Drake is with Sam?"

"Yes. We can't persuade him to go back and try to begin a repair."

"And Morwenna Whitworth? What does he say about her?"

"Nothing. Not a word. He will not utter. But clearly she does not want him."

Ross grunted. "What a wry, ugly mess! It could hardly have been worse for them all. And Rosina?"

"Is amazing. So strong in her quiet way. And it is the second time she has been let down."

"Do you think she would take him now?"

"Who, Drake? Oh, Ross, I don't know—or if he would take her. I can't do any more. Already I feel part to blame."

"Well, I can understand how it has upset you. I'll go over in the morning and see what can be done about the house. We could help with the cost of the repair."

"Maybe."

Ross took his pipe from the shelf and then changed his mind, put it back. "There is more? Something wrong at the mine?"

"No . . . Not at the mine. Did you not come through Truro, Ross?"

"No. Direct. Through St. Stephen's and St. Michael. Why?"

"Pascoe's Bank has closed its doors."

"*What!*"

She blinked at his tone. "It has gone bankrupt and failed to meet its creditors. And with it have gone our savings. And Drake's savings. So perhaps we shall not have any money yet awhile to build his new roof."

Ross was staring at her as if he totally failed to understand what she said. "You're telling me that—that —Pascoe's Bank . . . It's—impossible! Since you last wrote . . . In—in three weeks? *Pascoe?*"

"I'll tell you," she said, "how it happened, how I first heard of it."

So she began the harder part of her tale: her visit to Truro, her decision to see Ralph-Allen Daniell, her return to Truro—putting the money in.

"It was—horrible," she said. "I—didn't go right into the bank again; but folk were six deep, clamouring for their money. Of course the two clerks were taking their time, paying out as slow as they could. But some of the folk were noisy, getting rough. I thought they might climb the counter. Our three went in, at intervals—made a great show of paying the money in—it was a big pile each time on the counter—and each time they went in it—it quieted the crowd. Some of them jeered when they saw money being paid in, but it quieted them—they were more orderly, more willing to wait. After all, some of them only had thirty or forty pounds to draw—some just a few notes to change. When they saw the money it—helped to restore their confidence."

"But not enough."

"Not enough. It was the big depositors who broke him. A few stood firm—like us—like Henry Prynne Andrew—like Mr. Buller—like Mr. Hitchens. But the others—did not."

"But you say Pearce—old Nat Pearce had been embezzling money . . . That's hard to credit! The poor old fool must have been *senile*. What in God's name! But it shouldn't have broken Pascoe?" He got up. "There was clearly the old malice at work."

"Yes, Ross." She got up too, went to a drawer, handed him the anonymous letter. "About fifty of these were written, so Joan Peter told me, delivered by hand to the most important people in the town, especially customers of Pascoe's Bank."

He dropped the letter on the table, where it curled like a snake beside the slice of cheese he had been eating. "Joan Peter. You saw her? Where is Harris now?"

"I went in last Monday, Ross. Just to see. See if I could help. The bank was shuttered, the door nailed, a notice on it stating that because of inability to meet its creditors Pascoe's Bank had closed and would not reopen. I was turning away, but Joan saw me, called me to the side door. Harris was not there: he's staying with his sister in Calenick."

"And what in the Devil's name was Joan doing there? It says in this paper that *her* monies were withdrawn. Is it some fool behaviour of that God-damned cousin of mine?"

"Yes, Ross. He was in debt and his bills were called in—"

"To the Warleggans, I suppose."

"I think so."

He picked the letter up again. It uncurled reluctantly in his fingers, and he stared at it as if it were unclean.

"So this is George's doing. If so—"

Demelza said: "George and Elizabeth left Truro the day after the Whitworth funeral. They went to stay with some cousins of hers in Salcombe. That was before the crisis started."

"He would wish to keep his fingers clean while others did the work. . . . It would not be Nicholas: I give him credit for a modicum of ethics. It was Cary, I suppose."

"The uncle? I think so from something Joan said. Ross."

"Yes?"

"Cary Warleggan called in his loans to St. John. That's all we know. We may suspect, but that's all we *know*. He couldn't have been responsible for Mr. Pearce, for other things. He may have used the opportunity. But I don't want you—at war with George again."

"Must I stand being kicked in the face all day and all night and return a simper and a smirk? My dear, you cannot admire being married to a worm. You must give it permission to turn once in a while."

"I would want it to turn, Ross, but not with violence. If you broke the law, did something destructive, knocked George down, broke his jaw, as I'd love for you to do, twould exactly suit the Warleggans. He'd nurse his jaw with satisfaction if he could have you up in court for it. You—a—a reformed renegade—with a long record of violences. He'd like nothing better than to see you forced to resign your seat in the House."

"My dear, I think you overrate the delicacy of those men who sit on the benches at St. Stephen's. I've seen some rough dealings from time to time." He refilled his glass, brought the port decanter to her without asking her, without looking at her. She raised her eyebrows at him as he came back. He let out a slow breath and slumped in his chair. "As God is my judge, I still can't believe it! Pascoe had *friends! And* his three partners!"

"Men of straw, Harris called them."

"And Basset's. Warleggan's I know he could not appeal to, but Basset, Rogers & Co. stepped in two years ago."

"Joan told me: she said Pascoe's paid out over nine thousand on Thursday, nine thousand on Friday, eleven thousand on Saturday. They'd two thousand left, and needed at least eight more to see them safe. Harris went to see Mr. King of Basset's on Sunday afternoon, but Mr. King said Lord de Dunstanville was in London and Mr. Rogers in Scotland, and he couldn't commit himself without their authority."

There was a tap on the door and Jane Gimlett put her head round. "Is it convenient to clear, ma'am?"

"Yes, do." Demelza thought the breathing space a good thing, to give them a few moments to reflect. Ross began to fill his pipe furiously. So furiously that the bole snapped from the stem.

Demelza got up quickly. "There's another in the cupboard." She went across and rummaged, handed another pipe to him, took the broken pieces. With an effort he smiled.

"Thank you."

By the time Jane had finished, the next pipe was going.

When the door closed Demelza said: "Was I right to do that, Ross? To go to Mr. Daniell and borrow money from him?"

He didn't answer, frowning into the fire.

"I did consider trying to see Lord Falmouth, but was afraid he might be in London."

"He was. You didn't think of Dwight?"

"Dwight? How could he? . . . Oh, you mean——"

"He is now in control of Caroline's money."

"But you know he will not touch it."

"I know. He might just possibly have taken a risk for this. For a bank to fail only for eight thousand pounds . . ."

"No, I didn't—it never occurred to me. I'm sorry."

Silence fell. The pipe was not drawing properly. He took it out and looked at it. Then he threw it violently on the fire. In a charged voice he said: "But if you paid *all* the money you borrowed from Ralph-Allen Daniell into Pascoe's Bank, how did you meet the wages here next morning?"

"I didn't."

"You . . ."

She said: "We had a hundred and ten pounds in the house. You know what we always keep, Ross. I went to the mine in the morning and spoke to them all in groups. I said Pascoe's Bank was in trouble and it was necessary that we should help. I said if it had not been for Pascoe's Bank the mine would not be in existence at all. That was right, wasn't it?"

"You might say that," said Ross.

"So I said I—we could not pay them in full but that I—we would pay them a quarter of what was their due, and that you would make up the rest when you returned."

"Ah," said Ross.

The stem of the pipe had fallen in the hearth and he picked it up with the tongs and put it back into the flames.

"In fact," said Ross, "it has so happened that I paid ten guineas in Fowey today for this two-year-old mare. Therefore in my purse at the moment is one guinea, a seven-shilling gold piece, and five pennies. That is my total wealth. I thought to replenish it when I got home."

There was silence again.

He said: "I suppose none of the bills have been paid either, for the timber, coal, and other supplies delivered to the mine in February and March?"

"No, Ross."

"Do we still owe Jonas for flour, and Renfrew for tackle, and those other bills to the Truro tradesmen?"

"Yes, Ross."

He said: "I think there's another pipe in the drawer

beside the desk. I might as well break them all." He got up and went to the desk.

She said: "Did I do right or wrong, Ross? I have to know. I had to—to make the choice."

As he passed her he put his hand briefly on her shoulder.

"You're worth all Westminster," he said.

Chapter Eleven

Harris Pascoe said: "My dear Ross, it has been a very miserable business, and I agree that if more of my friends had been on hand we might just have w-weathered the storm. But in some circumstances life does not admit of grades of success or failure. If I were captain of a ship that had been wrecked it could be argued that two more lights at the harbour mouth would have enabled me to avoid the rocks. But if the ship is lost, it is lost and the captain bears the responsibility."

"For treachery? For false lights? For desertions of the crew?"

"You carry the analogy too far. In fact I am getting on in years and shall not feel a lessening of responsibility altogether unwelcome. Money? Yes, I have lost it all, but my sister is unmarried and has a c-competence. I regret most the loss of reputation. One does not *want* to take one's *exeat* after thirty years in a town with a cloud on one's good n-name."

Ross tapped his boot. "You sit there in such apparent calm. It doesn't become you. If you don't think of yourself, what of your clients?—all those who have relied on you for judgment and advice: they don't disappear overnight."

"Basset, Rogers & Co. will take over the business, and the accounts will be automatically transferred unless a client expressly wishes different. They are also taking over the liabilities—though I think these, apart from my own losses, will be negligible. It is a little early to be sure yet—much good stock was thrown on the market at a loss—and we had to discount bills at fifteen percent—of course liquidations are expensive in many ways—but I would have thought all debts could eventually be met in full. Eventually. So I don't think your money—even the last eight hundred pounds, which your wife with such noble generosity paid into the bank on the Friday—will ultimately be lost. It may be a few months—"

"Then for God's sake, why cannot the bank be reconstituted as before? Harris, that must be possible!"

Pascoe narrowed his eyes. "With what capital? *I* have no capital now. A bank—and the partners in that bank—must possess a large sum of money of their own before they begin to accept the responsibility of lending and borrowing other p-people's. There *must* be a—a large nucleus, free of encumbrance, as it were. It is from that nucleus that the whole system of credit springs. It may be wrong. In my case, as you have observed, it has proved disastrous. But that is the way it has all grown up. There is not a bank in the country, I venture to believe, that could meet all its creditors at the same time. But they do not need to, for their creditors have sufficient faith in them."

Ross glowered at Miss Pascoe's ginger cat, which was performing genuflections round a table leg and asking for his attention.

"In any case," said Pascoe, "my experience of banking, such as it is, may not altogether be lost, for Mr. King has offered me the post of ch-chief clerk in the office of Basset, Rogers & Co."

Ross tried to say something, but all that came out was a slight spray such as a bad actor produces when declaiming.

Pascoe smiled wryly. "I have not decided yet whether to accept."

"Then I will refuse for you," said Ross.

Pascoe shrugged. "The salary is not to be sneezed at."

"No, it is to be spat at, *spat* out, as is the offer! If I cannot do something better than that for you, you may drop me in the mud of the river!"

"Don't attempt too much, Ross, for you will be disappointed. Money is tight in the county. You may find a lot of well-wishers but not many well-doers. Above all and especially it will be realised that it is n-not a good thing to be fighting with the Warleggans. It is not impossible that some extra obloquy will settle on their name from this. (Although nothing can be proven, many will guess.) But the success of their manoeuvre, while it may darken their reputation, will also strengthen it. Fewer voices will be raised against a family who have the power to do what they have done."

"I've not feared them in the past, so I'm not going to fear them now."

"Not fear them, no. But n-not to be—hotheaded about them. Circumspection is all."

Ross smiled grimly. "You'd like me to deny my own nature."

"Well, may I say if you quarrel with them it must not be on my behalf. And another thing," Harris Pascoe said, as Ross rose to go. "Do not quarrel with your *friends* on my behalf neither. Oh, it can easily happen. You will w-want them to do more than they are prepared to do. An impatient word can turn quickly to an angry one."

"Not if they are true friends."

"Well . . . I have said my say. And remember, just at the moment your own financial position is very far from secure."

II

From Calenick, Ross went to see Mr. Henry Prynne Andrew. Mr. Andrew was not a personal friend, but he had supported Pascoe right through and must be feeling sore. The next visit was to Mr. Hector Spry,

Pascoe's Quaker partner. Throughout the crisis Mr. Spry had not visited the bank but had spent all the time, he said, in prayer, feeling that this was the most effective help he could offer. Then Ross called on Lord Devoran, who was out. So he rode down the hill to see Ralph-Allen Daniell. An hour later he was back in Truro and had a bite to eat in the Fighting Cocks Inn, which was crowded, it being market day. The street outside was full of bleating lambs and stolid cattle and men in smocks and the smell of fresh animal dung.

After this snack he crossed the river to Tregothnan, but as he expected Lord Falmouth was still in town. Mrs. Gower invited him to tea, which he politely declined; but before leaving he had a word with Mr. Curgenven, who was full of quiet self-satisfaction that (unspoken) thanks to his attentive stewardship, his lordship would lose nothing from the Pearce peculations. Mr. Curgenven was also at pains to point out that Viscount Falmouth was quite uninvolved in any Cornish banking house and, by implication, was unlikely to wish to be. This Ross already knew.

On his way north he called in to see Mr. Alfred Barbary, one of his old partners in the Carnmore Copper venture, and made his final call of the day on Sir John Trevaunance. He had not much hope here. Sir John was a warm man and kept what he might have called his petty cash in Pascoe's Bank, but in such investments as he had made in Cornwall he had always tended to lose money, so the glaze that came over his eyes whenever financial matters were mentioned grew to be of extra opaquity if the subject involved investment in the county. So it proved now. They drank a brandy and talked of parliamentary matters, and Ross left.

It had been a hard day and he was tired. This was not at all how he had expected to spend his first day home. He had seen nothing of his children, nothing of the mine, on which in effect his future prosperity still depended. He carried in his saddlebag eight pounds' weight of gold coin, twelve of silver, and one of copper, having confessed to Ralph-Allen Daniell his wife's use for the former cash and his need of another draft to meet the as-yet-unpaid miners. He had asked for it as a plain loan, not an advance against profits on the furnaces.

He was annoyed at the way he had been paid the money at Basset, Rogers & Co., but they said they could do no other. Small change was the bugbear throughout the county, and barter widespread. Harris Pascoe had always saved up for him an abundance of copper for his monthly payday. If the miners got paid in coin too large they would take a four-shilling piece —or even a half sovereign—to a kiddley, the owner of the kiddley would be unable or unwilling to change it and would accept the coin and mark the man's credit on a slate. So the man would be encouraged to drink it all away instead of giving it to his wife.

He was passing Doctor's kiddley as he reflected on this, and just then the half door swung open and three men came out—not drunk but having had their share. It was half light, when night was coming to the land but the sky reflected the shining sea. He glanced at them and rode by. A hundred yards on he came to a decision and turned Sheridan down the steep cobbly lane, known locally as Stippy-Stappy, leading to the inlet of Sawle.

His horse did not like the descent, so he dismounted and led him down. He looped his reins over a post a dozen yards beyond the cottage he needed, took the saddlebag with him as a precaution, and went to the door.

Rosina opened it. "Oh, sir! Cap'n Poldark! Do ee come in. We—was not expecting . . ."

"Is your father in?" Knowing he was not.

"No sir. I thought twas his footfall. Mother, Cap'n Poldark be here!"

"No, no," said Ross, stooping in the low room. "I wanted a word with you. By then perhaps Jacka will be in."

She seated herself nervously, and he sat too, refusing her offer of drink. If he had taken all the drink he had been offered today, he thought, he would be in no fit state to ride home.

"Perhaps you don't wish to speak of what has happened since I went away, Rosina. Perhaps it is better that we shouldn't speak of it. But I would like to say I am very sorry."

"*You* sir? Why, twas naught to do with you. Nor Mrs. Poldark. It was betwixt me and Drake Carne, and what has gone amiss is no one's fault nor failure."

He looked at her, so respectable in this near hovel; muslin cap, dimity frock, tidy, clean, pretty little face; she deserved a good man.

"I think my brother-in-law failed of his duty, and shall tell him so when I meet him. I have been home little more than four and twenty hours and have scarce seen anyone yet."

Her head came up. "I don't think, sir, if you'll pardon the liberty, that I d'want Drake Carne nor no other man to wed me out of a sense of duty. That is not what marriage ought to be."

"I agree. But if a promise is made in all truth of heart, then it should not be broken for an impulsive whim."

"Twas not a whim," she said. "He loved she afore ever he saw me, and when she became a widow he felt he must go. I respect him. I don't respect *her!*"

"She was forced into the marriage. Oh, you mean, now—now she has turned him away?"

"So I've heard tell."

"You haven't seen him since?"

"*No!*"

Her eyes were filling with tears. Just then a heavy tread outside the window announced the arrival of Jacka.

The door shivered as he came in, flush-faced, heavy-browed, belligerent. Because the horse was further down, he had not expected his visitor, and his face registered the shock.

"Cap'n . . ."

"Want a word with you, Jacka. And I want it alone."

"Why, what's amiss? I didn' knaw ee were home. What's amiss, Rosina?"

"Nothing to do with her," said Ross. "I want a quiet word."

Rosina gathered her sewing. "I'll go see where Mother's to."

While she was leaving Ross stared at Jacka, returning the heavy half-drunken glare until the miner blinked and looked away.

"A bad business, this, Jacka. Drake Carne leaving Rosina like this. A very bad business."

Jacka growled in his throat.

"Have you seen Drake Carne since he returned?"

"Seen him? I'd break his bones if I did!"

"Always one for violence, eh? Well, one day you'll have to see him if you both go on living round here."

"He wouldn't dare come back to his forge!"

"I haven't seen him. It is likely he'll not want to; but if he does you shall not stop him."

Jacka wiped a hand across his mouth.

"Not," said Ross, "that I like what he did. Nor never shall. I don't defend him. But I don't like what happened after, either."

"What? What happened?"

"Pally's Shop is a ruin. It will cost a deal of money to repair. Did you burn it down?"

Jacka gulped. "Me? . . . Why, *no!* Me. Not *me,* Cap'n!"

"Was it your new friends?"

"Wha' friends?"

"The two Warleggan men I saw you with a half hour gone. One was Tom Harry. The name of the other escapes me."

"Ah? . . ." said Jacka, sweating. "Oh, Harry and th'other un? Nay, I was but coming out o' kiddley same time. Passing time o' day, as ee might say."

"You're a bad liar, Jacka."

"Me? Here on. There's no cause nor excuse t'say I be a liar. We'm old friends but—"

"Old friends and old shipmates in one good adventure in France. But don't count on it too far. Arson's a hanging matter, did you know?"

"Arson?"

"Setting fire to a house. That's arson. You hang for it. By the neck. Outside Bodmin gaol. On the hill overlooking the gaol. They drive you on a cart, put the rope round your neck, and then drive the cart away. It takes a little time to die."

There was a silence. The solitary candle flickered in the draught of Jacka's breathing.

"So it was your two friends, eh?"

"*Wha'*? Two friends? They edn friends of mine! I don't know what they do and don't do! Tes not my consarn."

"But it *was* the night Pally's Shop was burned, wasn't it. Were you there? Did you see it? Did you agree to help?"

Jacka half got up and then sat again, wiping away the stale beer that had come to his lips. "I swear on the Book I know naught 'bout un! Twas not me nor nothing to do wi' me, and tes no manner o' good accusing me, Cap'n. I sw-swear on the Book, Cap'n! Honest to G-god I do truly!"

Ross looked at him for a long time. He wondered if he persisted with a flow of questions whether he could trap the man into inconsistencies and contradictions. It might be so. But if he did that tonight, Jacka would deny everything again in the morning. And how to catch those evil bullies he had seen him with tonight? Proof, proof, proof: there was nothing. And the trail was near a month old. You could act on suspicion, *retaliate* on suspicion, that was all. Or do nothing. Except instil a healthy fear.

He got up. "I'll see you again tomorrow. There is a lot more I want to know of it. But let me say this. You are keeping bad company. Get out of it. If they burned down the house and you helped them, *they* will not spare you if they are charged. You'll stand in the dock with them, be sure. And if my brother-in-law comes back to live there, to try to rebuild, he shall come back *unmolested*. Understand?"

Jacka grunted and belched.

Ross went to the door. "I accused you of being a violent man just now. Well, that's a case of the pot calling the kettle. So let's end this first meeting—and it *is* only the first, Jacka—with my promise that if you molest Drake Carne in any way, or are a party to his molestation, I'll not wait for Bodmin but see you strung up at Bargus for the crows to pick. It is a nasty threat to issue to an old shipmate, but I am sure you know I mean it. Say good night to Rosina and Mrs. Hoblyn for me."

III

He liked riding in the dark. Grambler village was near asleep, though it was barely nine. A light flickered, surprisingly, in Jud's cottage. He wondered if people had got tired yet of calling the old man Jud Pilchard. Someday, he thought, he would have a track made cutting through the rough gorse and heather and the little ravines so that it was not necessary to make this half circle on the way to Nampara.

As he climbed the rising ground towards Wheal Maiden a badger ran across the road and Sheridan sidestepped in alarm. The saddlebag clinked. Jacka's eyes had strayed to it, lying on the table between them, before Ross's accusations had driven everything else out of his head. A lot of money to be carrying through the night—a splendid haul for some cutpurse if he but knew.

A patter of feet beside him and Sheridan sidestepped again. Ross gripped his whip, but it was two young people he had disturbed lying in the gorse; they were off, hurrying, not to be recognised.

How could Ossie's horse have thrown him? Give the man his due, he was more at home in the saddle than in his pulpit. A man dead in the road, hanging by one stirrup. A house burned down. A bank and an honourable man broken. All this had happened while he was beating about in the English Channel on his way home. Now he had to try to repair the unrepairable. All the king's horses and all the king's men . . .

Past the mine which had temporarily destroyed his own mine and which did not yet show any promise of making up for it. Life was such a gamble, and the safest, sturdiest man existed on such a tightrope of circumstance that the merest vibration could throw him. We lived, belonged, felt solidly based, important in the world—and then, flick, and we were nothing.

Lights in Nampara tonight. Demelza was waiting by the parlour door. She looked at him and he smiled and threw his hat and cloak down. She helped him pull his boots off. But she didn't ask anything.

"I've waited supper," she said. "It's hot, so give me five minutes."

"Of course." But when it came he did not eat much.

"Not hungry?" she said.

"Just tired. Tired of talking, tired of arguing, tired of inquiring, tired of riding."

"Eat a bit more."

"No," he said, "I think I just want you."

IV

To acknowledge his appreciation of their work and their cooperation Ross gave the mine folk a day's holiday on the Thursday. A flag—an old one of dubious derivation once belonging to Joshua Poldark—was hoisted to the top of the headgear, and at midday those miners who were underground came up and no more went down. They joined the queue outside the office, where Captain Henshawe kept the accounts. Ross stood beside Henshawe and spoke to each man as he was paid and gave him an extra two shillings "for his patience." He told them that Pascoe's Bank had closed its doors but might reopen, and that in any event the mine was safe. It would mean "hand to mouth" for the next few months, but there was no cause for alarm. So long as everyone pulled together.

The holiday took the miners by surprise, but they soon got into their stride. A mass of sixpences was collected and two men sent off in a cart to buy a barrel of beer from Sally Tregothnan; since the day was fine it seemed more fitty that everyone should carouse together at Nampara than disperse to various beer shops. A few men broke up some old pit props—of which there were a lot lying about since the accident, too sodden to be trusted again below but dried out now in the winter air—and built a huge bonfire, which crackled and spat dispiritedly for a time but presently caught and roared up into the sky. Some of the tributers started making fireworks out of the gunpowder, and blew up old kegs and boxes. It was not a safe exercise, but Ross did not interfere: these men were all old hands in the use of explosives, and if they could be trusted with their own lives below, they could be trusted now. It greatly amused the women and children, who shrieked with terror and laughter, as splinters of wood fell in flakes and strips around them. Later they had a feast, roasted a pig on the fire and potatoes in the embers.

While this was going on the sun came out and splashed the scene with colour: dotted blues and greens and browns on a slope of the valley about the flame and smoke of the fire; coarse, hard-working faces, young ones yet unscarred, greasy hands, raised mugs, banter and laughter, the flirtings of youth and the croak of old age; a rare companionate time.

Ross said: "Our combe is badly scarred. Rubble and refuse and pits and sheds. Every month more of the vegetation is going."

Demelza said: "We can none of us live without it."

"Neither of your brothers is here."

"No. Sam went home to fetch Drake but has not come back."

"I can understand Drake not wanting to mix, yet."

"Perhaps I should go to see him."

"No. Leave him be. Sam's the one to deal with it.

I think Drake has to work this out for himself. And it will take time."

"Will you be away again tomorrow?"

"Yes. There's a half dozen more people I must see. Then it must wait on Basset's return."

"Do you know when?"

"They expect him Saturday."

"What hope do you have, Ross?"

"Not the greatest."

Chapter Twelve

As Ross rode up to the gates of Tehidy on the following Monday he thought: sometimes before I have tried my tact and other persuasions, and not often with success. Once before magistrates, trying to save a young miner from prison and—as it turned out—death. Complete failure, due to ignorance both of tactics and of tact. Once I pleaded for my own life—much against my own wishes, having been bullied into it by my counsel, Mr. Clymer—and, presumably, succeeded. Once I went to see my dear friend George Warleggan on behalf of this same Drake Carne who is always getting into trouble, and by a fair mixture of persuasion and threat—chiefly threat—succeeded in getting him to drop a charge of theft. Once—and not so long ago—I came to see the man I am now about to visit, Francis Basset, Baron de Dunstanville of Tehidy, and suggested he should help to commute the death sentence on a rioting miner to transportation— and signally failed to move him.

Since then his relations with Basset had been noticeably cool. They had not been assisted either by his having turned down Bassets' invitation to stand as his nominee for Parliament, and then, little more than a year later, accepted Viscount Falmouth's nomination for precisely the same seat. It suggested, quite wrongly, that Ross did not care for the thought of having the newly created lord, de Dunstanville, as his patron and preferred the senior peer, Lord Falmouth. It might even suggest a personal antipathy. Which was not the case either. But Ross had gagged at the thought of trying to explain his own infinitely complicated motives to another man, especially one to whom such an explanation might look like an excuse and an apology.

In any case, how could you state one of the principal ingredients, the simple fact that one year you were happy with your wife and contented in Cornwall; the next you were not?

As the great Palladian mansion came into view with its noble porticoed front and its four sentinel pavilions, he decided that if for any reason Basset should be busy or seem preoccupied with other things he would pay his respects, make an appointment, and ride away. What was to be discussed was too important to everyone to be aired at the wrong time. But his lordship was in: his lordship could see him: his lordship had caught a slight cold on the journey and seemed not unwilling to have a visitor to pass an idle hour.

They discussed the unseasonal weather, the backwardness of all vegetables and crops, the pleasure with which, these first few days of May, one at last felt a balmy touch in the air. They talked of the seige of Acre and wondered if Sydney Smith would inspire the Turks to hold out; whether, with the balance of power in Europe at last beginning to swing against France, that man Buonaparte would be content to remain bottled up in Egypt or whether, if he failed at Acre, he would try to slip through the blockade and return to France.

There seemed to be no particular signs of coldness or disaccord on Basset's part. Perhaps he was a big enough man to disregard small slights. He told Ross in friendly fashion of a lawsuit he was in with the Hon. C. B. Agar over mining rights, and another suit likely to come up with Lord Devoran on the rights of a watercourse. He was always involved in some minor litigation or other. He also said money was now available for the reopening of the great Dolcoath Mine, which would not only profit him as mineral lord but also give work to eight or nine hundred miners. The project had been almost cancelled in March with the price of copper threatening to fall below a hundred pounds a ton, but now that it had rallied the great day could not be far off. By the bye, would Captain Poldark be present next week when the opening ceremony for the new Cornwall General Infirmary took place?

Ross said he would have that pleasure, and added that it was an agreeable change to be able to talk of happenings in the world, both near and distant, in a modestly optimistic tone. The war. Conditions in the country. Summer on the way. He had, however, been deeply disturbed on his return to Cornwall to discover that Pascoe's Bank in Truro has failed.

Lord de Dunstanville sneezed. "Unfortunately, yes. You were not here either, then? Unfortunate. But I'm told on good authority that the depositors will lose little in the end. I presume you are quite substantially involved, Poldark?"

"Yes. But it is not for that that I am so much concerned. It is rather that Harris Pascoe is ruined, and, unless he can be re-established, Truro will lose one of its most prominent and upright citizens, and one of the major influences for good in the town."

"Re-established? Is there any possibility of that? I'm afraid I'm a little out of touch with local affairs; but Tresidder King called to see me yesterday, and I had the impression that our bank was taking over the assets and making itself responsible for the liabilities of Pascoe's Bank, and therefore any attempt to revive that bank had long since failed."

"So far as I can tell, no attempt was made."

"Then I don't see what prospect there is of its being re-established now, after several weeks have passed."

"A number of its old clients would greatly favour that, my lord."

"Sufficient to provide finance?"

"That I don't yet know."

Basset dabbed his nose. "I should greatly doubt if the money could be found at this time. In any event—in any event, the day of the small bank, the personal bank, is coming to its close. I appreciate that Pascoe is a man of great integrity, but for years—you know for years—his bank has been insufficiently financed. It has wavered more than once. If it had not been for the help we gave it two years ago it would have fallen then."

"And why would it have fallen then?"

"Why?"

"You must know, my lord."

For the first time Basset began to look a little irritated. I must be careful, Ross thought.

He said: "Two years ago the banking system of England stood in danger and Pascoe's was only one of many in trouble. It would have survived well enough if it had not been for pressure exerted on it by Warleggan's Bank at the wrong moment, throwing all Pascoe notes on the market, cutting off normal credit cooperation, ceasing to discount bills that were to come through Pascoe's hands, etc. You, my lord, I believe, returned from London just in time to save the situation."

The little man nodded. "Yes, that is so."

"On that occasion a credit of six thousand pounds saved Pascoe's. This time about the same sum would have saved it again."

"This is rather my point, Poldark. One cannot—or one should not have to—go on supporting another bank in this way. It should—"

"Even when the pressures are false ones."

"False? Well, I don't know about that! This man Pearce, whom personally I only knew by sight, had got himself deeply into trouble and had involved Pascoe in it. That doesn't seem—"

"Pearce was an honest man most of his life, but ran into debt late on by incautious speculation. What impulses moved in him we shall never know now. . . . He took money from trusts: in some cases he was the only trustee surviving, in other cases Pascoe, a very old friend, relied on him too far. But Pascoe could meet all the claims, and wished to. The total was less than eight thousand. There was no need for the general public to take alarm. And would not have done, I believe, but for these, my lord."

He took the anonymous letter out of his pocket and handed it over. Basset put on a very small pair of spectacles, the lenses of which were smaller than his eyes. Outside blackbirds and thrushes were fluting. They had had little to call about yet, and so were carrying it on into the middle of the day.

Basset said: "Monstrous. How many—"

"Fifty," said Ross. Careful, I must not interrupt him so much.

"Um . . ." Basset scratched at his greying hair. "And this business about his daughter?"

"Warleggan's closed suddenly upon her husband, who, to my shame, is a relative of mine and should be kicked from here to Plymouth."

"Yes, well . . . yes, well."

"I'm told, my lord, that you have held the Warleggans in poor favour ever since you returned from London two years ago and found them on the point of forcing Pascoe out of business."

"Who told you that?"

"I can't remember."

"Or don't wish to. Well, yes, there's some truth in that. We all have our ethics in business, and I have little fancy for sharp practices."

"Still less so now then, I hope."

There was a long silence. Basset sniffed and blew his nose. "Where I slept on Thursday night last was infernally draughty. It's very difficult at times. If one stays at an inn one has no hesitation about complaining of the poor quality of the bed curtains. But when spending the night with a friend . . ."

"Yes, my lord, it's difficult. But it's better than the trip I had by sea."

"Tell me of it."

Ross told him of it. Basset invited him to dinner. Ross accepted. The other man seemed disinclined to discuss the matter of Pascoe's Bank further at this stage. It was clear that he wanted time to think. Ross almost suggested that he might come back another day, but decided not. To let Basset have too long to think might give him an opportunity of having Mr. Tresidder King to see him again, and although Ross had never met the gentleman he distrusted him. Of course, there might still be the dusty answer, the "I must consult my partners" escape. But it was worth waiting.

Dinner was with the ladies: his wife, his daughter, his two sisters, no one else. Ross was thankful he had a son. Small talk was pleasant and not taxing, but Lord de Dunstanville did not join in it. In spite of having been received in a more friendly fashion than he had expected, Ross did not allow himself to be too hopeful. Francis Basset, among many other attributes, was a businessman. The wealthiest man in Cornwall —so far as actual money went—did not willingly throw away opportunities of becoming wealthier. And his bank in Truro had just swallowed a rival. Was he going to make it regurgitate its meal on a point of principle? Was he going to re-create a situation in which those of his clients who happened to be dissatisfied with the accommodation they were being offered at Basset's could turn round and say, "Very well, then. I'll go to Pascoe's"? Was it common sense to expect it? Basset disliked the Warleggans, and this event would make him distrust and dislike them more. But he had no deep-rooted, long-standing enmity such as Ross had. He had none of that personal conviction to sustain him.

Yet, from his many visits to friends and old Pascoe clients over the last few days, Ross knew it must all depend on Basset. They wished Pascoe well, as Harris had predicted, but where was the money coming from to set him up again? Humpty-Dumpty had had a great fall. If Basset, Rogers & Co. were prepared to back him there would be no shortage of clients willing to return. But the money that Pascoe had personally lost was lost. The nucleus, as Harris had called it. The foundation on which everything else was built.

The ladies left the table early: the day was so mild that they were off to pick bluebells and wild orchids in the woods. The two men were left at the strewn table.

De Dunstanville said: "My steward has had this Somerset cheese sent him. It weighs twenty pounds, and he feels it will not endure long enough for him to eat it all, so I am obliging him. Pray help yourself."

"Thank you."

"And port? How is Mrs. Poldark? I do remember her preference for port."

"She's well, thank you. You have a good memory, my lord."

"I found her a very taking person, with a wit as sharp as a knife and a warm sense of humour."

"Thank you. I trust you will come to visit us again."

"No, you must come here first—if we can get this banking matter out of the way without quarrelling."

"I should be most grateful if we could."

"You mean you would be most grateful if you got your own way. Well . . . that is difficult. Tell me first whom you have seen and what help they promise."

Ross had been afraid of this question. It was the destructive one—yet he must not answer it too evasively. He gave a list of the names: Lord Devoran, Ralph-Allen Daniell, Henry Prynne Andrew, Henry Trefusis, Alfred Barbary, Sir John Trevaunance, Hector Spry, etc.

"Not your patron?" The question was asked with a hint of quiet malice.

"No, he is still in London."

"You'll get no help from him. . . . Well, and what was the outcome?"

A reluctance, a great reluctance, Ross said, to see Pascoe's Bank go under.

"Yes, yes, a reluctance no doubt, but what offer to practical help?"

Ross said: "The practical help of their complete trust in Harris Pascoe, their willingness to allow balances still in abeyance to remain in his hands, and an eagerness to see him trading again and to entrust him with their deposits."

Lord de Dunstanville chewed slowly. He was a moderate man in everything and had only allowed himself four glasses of wine.

"It's all very well, Captain Poldark. I appreciate precisely your wishes and the wishes of your friends. What they are saying is, put the bank back where it was, set Mr. Pascoe in charge of it, open the doors, and we shall be happy to trade with it as usual. Exactly. They want a restoration of the *status quo ante bellum*. They want the clock put back. But who is going to pay for the clock being put back, who is to finance this restoration? They are not."

"I have had some offers. They are not enough, but with your cooperation . . ."

"With our *finance,* and it would cost a mortal lot. The eggs have been scrambled. No doubt we could advance a large loan, and this Pascoe, over a number of years, might be able to repay. It has always been a good little bank. But Pascoe is not a young man, and he has no son ready to succeed him. We could advance a large loan—perhaps twenty thousand pounds —but we could make much better use of the money in *other* ways. No . . . I'm sorry, Poldark, I know how you must feel, but it seems to me that the amalgamation that is already in process of being achieved is the only common-sense, the only practical solution. But it could be worse. I understand Tresidder King has already offered Mr. Pascoe a position in our bank—"

"As a clerk!"

"As chief clerk. I appreciate that that is not quite the style to which Mr. Pascoe is accustomed, but it would be something. Possibly we shall be able to offer him something better at a short remove. King is a young man, but there could be some other situation available."

Ross drew breath. It looked as if he were to be defeated in his primary objective. Should he try any further, or now abandon that and go for the secondary one? A difficult decision. So far the interview had been surprisingly equable. It might not remain so if he pressed it the more. And how could you press a man if he were not willing? To make it a challenge to his honour might well be something that Basset would resent as well as reject, and then all would be lost. You could no more *demand* a reprieve from this man for Harris Pascoe than you could for "Wildcat" Hoskin. Only negotiation, only diplomacy was left.

"You spoke of amalgamation, my lord."

"Yes. Amalgamation and absorption."

"You did use the former word first. And if you are willing to give it that name, then surely the proprietor of the second and smaller bank might be offered a partnership in the new concern?"

Basset raised his eyebrows. "More cheese? If we were to do that, Mr. Pascoe would bring with him the aura of misjudgment and failure that many people will remember."

"Most people will remember—all men of goodwill will remember—that his only real misjudgment was to cross swords with the Warleggans."

"Shall we go into the drawing room? It faces west and the sun is such a shy visitor . . ."

Ross followed his host, who paused to sneeze and dab his nose. Three spaniels who had been sleeping rose to greet him and fell about his feet as he sat down.

Ross said: "Not many men of goodwill, with the interests of the whole community at heart, can view with complacency the idea of the Warleggans completely dominating the commercial affairs of the county."

"We are a long way from that situation yet."

"Well . . . again, I hate to bring the matter too much to a point of principle, but every victory they gain over a smaller man makes the next small man less willing to fight. They—it is in their nature to eat up what they can and destroy what they can't. Beginning of course with their enemies. But moving on. And constantly making new enemies as they go."

"D'you take snuff? No . . . I'll give what you say consideration. But it's only fair to point out to you that, though I am senior partner in the bank, Captain Poldark, I have three partners. There is my brother-in-law, Mr. John Rogers, and there is Mr. Mackworth Praed and Mr. Edward Eliot. They must be consulted on all significant points. I cannot take arbitrary decisions without their consent."

"Am I to understand, my lord, that your Mr. Tresidder King, who is not a partner, was able to take arbitrary decisions without *your* consent?"

He thought he had gone too far. Basset flushed and glanced at him with a flicker of anger.

"King has authority to act as he thinks best when we are not present. May I make a suggestion to you, Poldark? It is a mistake to press too hard from a position of weakness."

"That is precisely what I was thinking myself, my lord."

Basset looked at him and then laughed. "At least you're candid."

"It's all I can be. But," Ross said, "if I may continue in the same vein, although my position is weak, it is not entirely without a negotiating basis. If Mr. Pascoe joins your bank as a full partner he will bring all his clients with him. If he does not, then some, many indeed, will be tempted to look elsewhere."

"Elsewhere? To Warleggan's?" Again the malice.

"No . . . but there is Carne & Co. of Falmouth. To many people I spoke to Falmouth is little less convenient than Truro. Lord Devoran, Mr. Daniell, Mr. Trefusis. Even I would go there if Carne & Co. became Carne & Pascoe."

"Ah . . . you have been canvassing."

"Only opinion. But I think, if I may say so, that if Basset, Rogers became Basset, Rogers & Pascoe it would be a move which would greatly enhance the popularity and prestige of those who made it possible."

"Well, that is quite out of the question—the name, I mean. And I don't like being blackmailed, sir."

"Nothing was further from my thoughts. I can only appeal to you and to your generosity."

A long silence.

"Have Carne's invited Pascoe to join them?"

"They will do so if I offer them the clients that I can."

"And you say that is not blackmail?"

"No, my lord. Only business. And really I am a beginner at it. I only attempt this on behalf of an old friend."

"You have a certain aptitude for your new role. Or does that insult you?"

"I'm greatly flattered."

Lord de Dunstanville bent to one of his spaniels. "Poor Trix has a canker in her ear. I must ask your wife sometime. She has a reputation with animals. Now look you here, Poldark, I can do nothing, I can promise nothing, nothing at all. I'll think about it, think it all over. I'll consult with John, my brother-in-law. I'll consult with the others. Can I keep this—this letter? There'll be a meeting sometime next week. If it takes place before the hospital opening, and if there is anything useful I can pass on to you, I'll do so at the ceremony."

"I'm greatly obliged, my lord."

"Don't be greatly obliged at all. I have promised you nothing."

Chapter Thirteen

It was on the day of the opening ceremony that Elizabeth Warleggan knew she was with child again. She had wondered yesterday and had not been certain. Now, together with the failure of her period, the sudden faintness, the nausea. For a woman of superficially delicate health she had a strong constitution, and she had only felt like this twice before in her life: early in 1784 and in the midsummer of '93. After her first child was born she had been subject to fainting fits for a while, but while they might have been similar in appearance they were entirely different to the person suffering them.

She was startled, a little shocked at first, apprehensive, and then pleased. So, if all went well, she would now have three children. When this one was born Geoffrey Charles would be almost grown up, Valentine nearly six. Another boy? She would dearly like a girl. Another child when she was thirty-five, rising thirty-six. His (its) birthday would be likely to be the same month as Valentine's.

One person who would most certainly be delighted would be George. She knew how much he still prized her, and nowadays it was more as a husband should, not as an object he had unexpectedly won. He confided his plans—some of them—aware that she was his friend. She felt she deserved this. It had been a hard five years.

So, this new child was likely to put the final seal on their marriage as nothing else would. She would tell him this evening. Or perhaps wait a little while until she was even more sure.

But wait a little while? How long? And with what purpose? Suppose this were another boy? . . .

In that terrible time following Aunt Agatha's death, when George's suspicions—that Valentine was not a seven- or eight-month baby and therefore not his— had reached explosion point, her oath on the Bible had convinced him—or nearly convinced him. But even then, even after that, his jealous thoughts had taken months to die. Supposing this were another boy? This one *must* be his. Would any of that old lingering suspicion lead him gradually to withdraw his favor from Valentine and give it more and more to his new son? There would always be more likelihood of an alienation between Valentine and George if there were a younger and undisputed child to take the father's affections.

Elizabeth was a woman with very strong maternal instincts—her obsessive love for Geoffrey Charles had produced the first breach between herself and Francis long ago—and though Valentine, for various reasons, had taken longer to establish his position in her heart, he was there now, and she was deeply concerned for his future. It was more for his sake than her own that she had fought George and bested him.

She thought about this all morning while she was dressing for the "occasion." So long as George was convinced that Valentine was a premature child the danger could be contained. Ross, in the one strained, emotional meeting she had had with him outside Trenwith three years ago, had suggested something which now might make sense. He had said: if your marriage to George means something to you—or even if not, then for your son's sake—should you ever give George another child try to contrive a mistake in the month of conception. Let your confusion be deliberate and unconfessed. It shouldn't be difficult. Another premature child would convince George as nothing else would.

Was it difficult? Hardly, at this time. Nothing was lost by her withholding her news until next month, or even the month after. This faintness usually passed quickly enough, and she was hardly ever sick in the mornings. Nor, as the months progressed, did she ever get very big, in spite of her slight frame. She carried her children high, and was agile to the last. It would be easy to deceive George. She would tell him she was expecting a child in April. Then if she had it in February, as before . . .

Nor should the doctor be an unsurmountable difficulty. She would call him in on some trifling ailment in July, and in the course of his visit tell him she believed herself pregnant. Her last period, she would say, had been in June. He would have no reason to disbelieve her, for she had nothing to gain. George would accept her statement for the same reason. When the child was born in February, it might look like a full-term child—as Valentine had—but they would both be likely to jump to the conclusion that this was a repetition of the peculiarity of last time. And in no way to be questioned.

The hospital was due to be opened at ten. George, to please her, had subscribed a hundred guineas in her name, so she would be one of the few women present. At nine forty-five the Warleggan coach arrived outside the house, rattling over the cobbles, with four greys tossing their small heads and the postilions looking spruce and fresh in their yellow jackets. It was a very short distance to go, but George had insisted they should ride. Elizabeth was wearing a full white satin skirt with a pad at the back to expand it and make the waist look smaller, a tight bodice of azure satin and a paler blue toque. George, elegant in a new black coat much cut away, with wide reveres on both coat and waistcoat and two rows of silver buttons, handed her into the coach, and they lurched up the hill to where many other carriages were arriving.

The Cornwall General Infirmary was an oblong building of a grey stone well suited to the exposed position it occupied. As guests arrived they were shown over it; the two long wards, one above the other, each containing ten beds placed end to end parallel with the walls, the lower ward for men, the upper for women; the small side rooms leading off, for the occupancy of the nurses; the dispensary, the mortuary, the kitchen, the living rooms for the house surgeon and his wife. Friends greeted each other as they walked around, for many of the best of the county were here: The Earl of Mount Edgcumbe, Lord and Lady de Dunstanville, Mr. Ralph-Allen Daniell, Mr. and Mrs. George Warleggan, Mr. Trefusis, Mr. Andrew, Mr. Mackworth Praed, Mr. Rogers, Captain Poldark, Mr. Molesworth, Mr. Stackhouse. Dr. Enys was there, reluctantly representing his wife, who was a notable subscriber but unavoidably absent; Dr. Bull, the house surgeon, a youngster of twenty-nine, who had been brought down from London to take up this position; Dr. Behenna, who had been appointed a visiting physician; the Reverend Dr. Halse. There were eight ladies to thirty-odd men.

It was not quite a large enough gathering to be able to avoid those one wished to avoid, and Elizabeth's heart thumped as she twice came near enough to Ross Poldark to speak to him. Of course she did not, and of course he did not, since George was not far away. Happy with the discovery she had made about herself, Elizabeth had no wish at all to mar the day. George, though ignorant of her news, was also well satisfied with the way things were going—especially with the complete success of Uncle Cary's schemes, since the objective seemed to have been attained without loss of reputation on their side—and he had no desire to cross swords with his rival in public. As for Ross, his feelings were so explosive that if something started he had no idea where it would end. But he was still playing for high stakes, and his cause with Francis Basset would not be advanced if he became involved in a brawl—even of words—at the official opening of Basset's hospital.

So the meeting was held, addressed by the Earl of Mount Edgcumbe, by Lord de Dunstanville, and by Dr. Hector Bull, and the infirmary was declared open. That done, they all trooped out into the warm sunshine and got into their carriages to rattle down the hill again for the service at St. Mary's Church. It was a brightly coloured group, and the townsfolk stood agape to watch them pass.

Dwight said cheerfully to Ross: "Well, it's a beginning. We could do with a hundred beds, but twenty is better than nothing. Dr. Bull seems a likely man. I hope admission will be by need and not by patronage . . ."

He was looking much older, Ross thought. He had suffered in fact two losses—of his child and his wife; and though the latter might be temporary it hit him nearly as hard. He was a dedicated man, one not given to wearing his heart on his sleeve; but his sympathy for the plight of others did not detract from his personal affections, and Ross wondered if Caroline realised what her leaving him so long was doing to him.

By the time they had stabled their horses St. Mary's Church was nearly full, for the ordinary populace were allowed in at the back, but they found two seats together and knelt in prayer. Ross wondered if either of them was really saying anything: Dwight, he thought, had perhaps more faith than he had, but neither of them had much room for orthodoxy, particularly in the person of the Reverend Dr. Halse, who who was to preach the sermon. Ross knew plenty of clerics who were admirable men, but the two who had occupied the Truro livings were two of his aversions. Even this hard-visaged, ambitious man was to be preferred to the late vicar of St. Margaret's. Ross wondered if there were pluralities in heaven; if so Ossie had by now no doubt put in an application.

Dr. Halse chose as his text Job, Chapter 7, verse 13: "My bed shall comfort me, my couch shall ease my complaint," and proceeded to wring the withers of his audience by describing the conditions that the new hospital was designed to alleviate.

"It is beyond the power of language," he went on, "to describe a more afflicting scene of human misery than that which too often presents itself in the wretched hand of some indigent creature who lies languishing on the hard and uneasy pallet of sickness and drags out his wearisome life, either wasted by slow and intermittent fevers or racked by excruciating pains, or writhing under the anguish of festering wounds —devoid of all medical skill and assistance, wanting even the necessaries of life, much more the comforts; unfriended, unaided, unpitied; they feel the pinching gripe of poverty under its most frightful form, and at last expire with the heartrending reflection that a wife and helpless children, now robbed of their only prop, are left heirs to this misery, destined in due time for a similar fate! And will justice, will gratitude, will any consideration that ought to influence social beings, suffer us to be careless spectators of such pitiable distress?"

It was splendid powerful stuff, and Ross, who disliked the old man for his harshness at other times, acknowledged that on occasion he could pull out the right stops. It was the sort of thing that would go well in the House.

But, he wondered, *were* these exactly the right stops? To be good to the poor, to be benevolent to the poor, to be generous to the poor, to build them a fine new hospital where they might be treated free under the most modern conditions: all these were admirable aims and deserving of high commendation. Now abideth Faith, Hope, and Charity, and the greatest of these is Charity. But what about Hope? All these people gathered here today were kindly people bent on alleviating distress. But how many thought of trying to *prevent* the distress? Not to give money to the poor but to create conditions in which the poor could earn money for themselves. Was that asking something altogether different?

In the congregation, listening to this powerful sermon, it so happened that there were three Chynoweths, though all now bore different names, and for other and more personal reasons they sat in different parts of the church. Elizabeth Warleggan was in the front row with her husband. On the left side of the main aisle, towards the back, Rowella Solway also sat beside her husband. Her bruised and beaten face and body had now quite healed, and except for a missing tooth which only showed when she smiled broadly—a rare occurrence—she looked as good as new. Hers was always a difficult face to read, and had been more so of late; but Arthur's discovery of her perfidy, and his utterly violent reaction, seemed to have cowed her, to have made her realise the error of her ways. Indeed, once she had finally decided to speak to him again, once she had forgiven him for the terrible assault upon her inviolate body, she had assumed her old intellectual supremacy—without claiming as yet a return to a moral one. Once in the night—two weeks after that terrible night—when there had been the first shift towards a reconciliation between them, she had explained to him the evil way in which Mr. Whitworth had first seduced her while she was living at the vicarage and had drawn a graphic picture of the way in which he had since pestered her—almost blackmailed her—into resuming their association. All the same, Rowella had ardently declared, it was only Arthur's neglect of her, his *physical* neglect of her, his failure to be a husband to her in the most absolute sense, that had finally driven her to give way. Arthur was flabbergasted, angry over again, and as ardent in his own declaration that, far from lacking in the physical and sensuous virtues, he had often restrained himself out of consideration for her. Since then he had done much better. Sometimes these days, he had to admit, he found the long hours at the library more tiring; but recently he had been taking a medicine called "Balsamic Corroborant or Restorer of Nature," and it had benefited him a great deal.

Neither of them after that time ever referred to Osborne Whitworth or to his untimely death. The carved stave found beside the clergyman's body might, Rowella thought, be not dissimilar to the one that had disappeared from their kitchen; but she did not ask to see it, nor to see the constables who were conducting the inquiry. Although she thought her husband's brutality towards her was perfectly outrageous, she appreciated that it was not altogether without provocation, and, once in a while, as the incidents receded and became part of the past, she allowed herself to warm towards him for the unexpected violence of which he had found himself capable. He was after all a man of passion, carefully though he generally hid it.

The third Chynoweth, who had been widowed by that same carved stave, was in church on the other side with her pachydermatous mother-in-law. She was equally inscrutable, but whereas no one had ever known precisely what Rowella was thinking since she was old enough to think at all, Morwenna in her teens had been as open as the day, warm in immediate re-

sponse, ingenuous and impulsive; and only life since
her marriage had altered her nature. Now her eyes
were no mirror of her soul; they were filmed, vacant,
uninterested. The quicksilver had come off the back
of the mirror. Since Mr. Whitworth's death she had
become completely dominated by her mother-in-law.
She did what she was told, listlessly but obediently, as
she had come to this service today. It mattered not.
Only one thing mattered. Mr. Whitworth's return to
her room that last month had not been without result.
She was again with child. Another little Ossie was on
the way.

II

After the service was over, the general congregation dispersed, but the governors and subscribers were
to attend a dinner at the Red Lion Inn, which was to
begin at three-thirty. Dwight said he could not stay,
and Ross was for going too, but Basset had so far
given him no indication of any banking decision and
he felt he must remain. So Dwight changed his mind
and stayed with his friend. It was fortunate he did,
for he was placed next to Elizabeth, with Ross opposite but one place down, and George on Elizabeth's
right, almost within speaking distance. Ross had Miss
Cathleen Basset, Lord de Dunstanville's sister, on one
side and a man called Robert Gwatkin on the other.
However, in doing justice to all the dishes served, and
in having to talk above the hubbub of voices, there
was little time for enmity or constraint, and the meal
passed well enough. The difficulty came at half past
five when the ladies—what there were of them—retired, leaving gaps, which here and there men moved
to fill, and the port and brandy went round and now
and then brief silences fell as the wine circulated and
was poured, and repletion halted talk.

In one of these pauses Gwatkin said: "I hear you're
returning to politics, Mr. Warleggan." It was difficult

to tell, in the present company, whether the remark was mischievous or innocent.

George turned his head an inch or so. "I shall represent St. Michael when Parliament reassembles."

"Has Wilbraham resigned, then?"

"No, Howell."

"I hadn't heard."

"It has not occurred yet."

Gwatkin circled his brandy in the glass. "It's good to know more local gentry are to represent us. Too often folk are nominated and sit in our name when they know nothing of Cornish needs."

"I believe these pocket boroughs are very expensive to maintain," said the man on Gwatkin's other side. "Tisn't just the expense of buying 'em, sir; the voters band themselves together and demand this, that, and the other before they'll elect your man. Then, bi God, if you're not careful there's an appeal to the Commons and you have your election made void because of bribery!"

"—What Burke said," a voice came across the table, cutting their exchange. "What Burke said, sir! He said that republicanism in France will be killed by a popular general's sword! And it may not be long afore that happens. Now Buonaparte's failed at Acre he'll not be content to stay long in Egypt. There's matters in France he'll want to attend to!"

"To say nothing of attending to Josephine," came the reply. There was a general laugh.

"—But the Presbyterians are all in Belfast," came another fragment. "And they're republicans to a man. And the reason they keep the Catholics down is not because the latter are heretics but because they support despotism!"

"The Ulster men are not republican in a French way—"

"I never said that—I never said that. But they don't like being under the English heel and they don't like corruption in politics. No taxation without representation is their cry. And we know where *that* came from!"

Gwatkin said: "And you, Captain Poldark, how have you enjoyed your first year at Westminster?"

"Enjoyed," Ross said slowly. "That is not an appropriate word. I think I have learned a little. Yawned a little. Thought I was of use and then thought again."

"Do you find it corrupt?"

"What is not?"

"Oh, dear! This cynicism, sir!"

"Politics are of their nature unclean," said the other man.

Ross drained his glass, dabbed his lips. "I don't know that there is much to choose between politics and other forms of power. Westminster has everything, from the highest ideals to the lowest. What has this town got except the same? In lesser quantity but not in lesser degree."

"Well, sir, if you refer to politics here—"

"Politics or business. I was thinking then of business."

"—three million of 'em," said a voice. "I tell you, sir, there are three million Catholics in Ireland, or nigh on that, and all but a small favoured minority, all reduced lower than the beasts in the field!"

"Heretics to a man!"

"Oh, yes, agreed; but I tell you there's not a Negro in the West Indies who has not more to eat in a day than some of those people in a week."

"That could be said of English labourers. You don't need to go overseas." This was Ralph-Allen Daniell. "The war has brought the extremest poverty, so that many a man has to choose between crime and starvation."

"Oh, dear," said the first man, "now I do not know whether we speak sedition or patriotism!"

Gwatkin said to Ross: "You talk of business in the town, sir? Do you suppose it to be corrupt? And if so, in what way?"

Ross hesitated, accepted the port decanter as it was passed round, helped himself and handed it on to Dwight. "This bank failure which has occurred. It was not a failure caused by any improvidence on the bank's part but was induced from outside by corrupt power, corruptly employed. Creatures usually hidden under stones emerged to bring this about. Venom is attributed to snakes; but human venom when evidenced in this way makes the rattlesnake seem as blameless as a blind worm."

Ross felt the warning pressure of Dwight's foot as Dwight handed the port across the empty space to George. Gwatkin was looking startled.

"I live a little out of town and therefore am perhaps out of touch. But I don't understand. Whom are you referring to?"

"—But he was murdered!" said a voice. "Quite clearly, in my opinion! A sedate and sober young cleric like Whitworth! He could never have come off his horse unaided! And a stick in the clearing and a torn cloak! . . . All the same I'm not sure I agree with you, Daniell, on the causes for the increase in crime. I believe much of it would cease if more of the rogues were strung up!"

"I feel sorry for the young widow. She's pretty enough, but I doubt she'll find a husband again with three children to rear and little money to recommend her."

"There's money in the family—*his* family—though I imagine tis well tied up."

With an effort Ross said: "I refer to those amongst us on whom the obloquy rests. If you do not know their names, Mr. Gwatkin, I suggest you ask among the traders of this town; and they will tell you—unless they should be too afraid, lest lying anonymous letters may be circulated about *them*." . .

George Warleggan said: "Egad, it all seems to me very much a storm in a teacup. This trying to find scapegoats for a perfectly normal business failure. I appreciate your loyalty to a friend, Ross; but as often happens with you, it has blinded you to the facts." He yawned, putting a hand back to his mouth. "And the facts are Harris Pascoe was a silly old man who had no business to have charge of large sums of money belonging to others. If he had ever been

capable of it he was long past it, for he allowed Nat
Pearce to embezzle large sums of trust money that—"

"You lie," said Ross.

There was a moment's pause. Fortunately few had
heard, for other talk was still proceeding. But before
George could reply or Ross could say more a manservant coughed—and coughed again—behind them.

"Begging your pardon, sirs. Dr. Enys, sir. Begging
your pardon, Mr. Warleggan."

George whirled round and stared at him. "What is
it?"

"Begging your pardon, sir. It's Mrs. Warleggan.
She's fainted."

III

A month passed. Summer light flowed in the sky,
and the hay at last was got in. Here and there a few
fields still stood and waited, cut and stooked round
the edges but not yet to the centre, so that they
looked like embroidered handkerchiefs. Sea gulls
called, standing on gateposts, or walked in the fields
like ungainly aldermen, the wind ruffling their tail-
coats. Summer clouds drifted like bruises across the
sky.

The French were reeling back everywhere. The
Austrians, with a reconstituted army, had defeated
them at Magnano, and now came word that the Russians, under the brilliant, eccentric Suvarov, had
swept the French before them and entered Milan.
The population greeted him with acclaim: a deliverer
to save them from their deliverers. A Russo-Turkish
fleet had recaptured Corfu. The French abandoned
Naples and began a slow retreat north. All Buonaparte's great conquests were at hazard.

Men's thoughts were turning full circle—from the
prospect of a French invasion of England to the
prospect of an English invasion of France—or one
of her subjugated allies. Few if any more armies were
to be sent to garrison the West Indies and to die in

their thousands of the tropical plagues—Negro regiments were to be raised for that, with emancipation as the ultimate reward for recruits: this in the teeth of bitter opposition from the planters. The young British army was to train and stay at home, ready for more local and more important adventures.

Elizabeth's fainting fit had been unfortunate for her plan. But worse was to follow, for she developed regular morning sickness; and although she had lied to Dwight when he asked her the obvious question, she could not conceal her sicknesses from George, who had Behenna in daily until, to save further examinations and inquiries, she confessed her condition. George of course was as delighted as she thought he would be. He too wanted a girl (which comforted her, for it showed he had finally accepted Valentine). More than ever she became the prized possession, to be looked after, to be guarded, for she carried the sacred seed.

Her disappointment at not being able to cheat him over dates was not long-lived, for George was so completely at ease with the situation that she forgot her doubts and fears. Indeed he accepted her being with child as a natural bloom upon his present good estate. David Howell had applied for the stewardship of the Chiltern Hundreds and a new member would have to be found for one of the seats at St. Michael. Mr. George Warleggan had so presented himself, and the writs would soon be cried. Almost certainly he would be returned without the necessity of an election. George had already taken a house in King Street, Mayfair, for the winter months. Elizabeth might even have her child in London.

Only one occurrence in late June clouded his horizon.

IV

It had been a long time coming, and it had only come as a result of delicate negotiation and an almost endless weighing of the advantages and disadvantages. Twice Ross had been called to Tehidy, on the last occasion when the rest of the banking partners were present. Twice he had visited Basset uninvited. In the intervals he had ridden about the county a great deal, assembling his own forces, gauging their weight—or lack of it—careful never to bluff —swallowing the occasional snub or rejection in a manner quite foreign to his nature, tenaciously refusing to accept defeat when defeat seemed most likely, taking obstacles as they came and taking time to overcome them. Demelza had never seen him so determined or so resolute.

On the last Friday in June the *Mercury* carried an announcement which was later repeated in a series of handbills circulated throughout the business community of central Cornwall. It was to the effect that as from July 1, 1799, Basset, Rogers & Co., Bankers, of Truro, incorporating Pascoe's Bank, of the same town, would change its name to the Cornish Bank and would trade as before. Partners in the new bank were listed as Baron de Dunstanville of Tehidy, Mr. John Rogers, Mr. H. Mackworth Praed, Mr. Henry Stackhouse, Mr. Harris Pascoe, and Captain R. Poldark.

The final name had been added virtually at the last minute, but, since the suggestion came from Lord de Dunstanville, nobody disagreed. Even Ross, to whom it came as much of a surprise as anybody and who certainly had his doubts, did not voice them. As John Rogers said to Mr. Stackhouse, who had not been at the very last meeting:

"Of course he'll bring no *money*. Nor never *will*. He's not the type to—accumulate. But it's a good name to have. And he's becoming a personality in the county. One never knows quite why this happens, eh? Not so much what a man does. More a matter of character."

BOOK THREE

Chapter One

Caroline came back to Cornwall in early July, and
they had a reunion party. She was better in spirits
and less flippant than usual; but she said she must
return to London in October for a while, as her
aunt planned some grand reception for the reopening of Parliament and she had promised to help. Dwight
also, she said, had promised to be present. Could
she count on Ross and Demelza? Before there could
be any hesitation Ross said of course. Demelza raised
her eyebrows and smiled, but commented nothing.

"Mind you," Ross added. "Your aunt is a Foxite,
isn't she?"

"If you mean she's at present much taken with
the member for Bedfordshire, yes. But I don't think
she allows politics to influence her social fancies. My
aunt," said Caroline in a pained voice to Demelza,
"is a widow, and not yet very old. She is not without
her men friends. The present one is staunchly opposed to the government. Ross is being peverse."

"That's not unusual," said Demelza.

"The reception, the ball, whatever it is going to
be," Caroline said, "will not take place at my aunt's
house, but at that of a great friend of hers, another
wealthy widow, Mrs. Tracey, who lives in Portland
Place, and whose present friend is Lord Onslow, so
I don't think it can be looked on as an opposition
lobby."

"Shall you engage a locum?" Ross asked Dwight.

"I'm getting Clotworthy, the druggist. He knows
little but he's not obsessed with theory, and uses his

common sense. I shall only be gone about a month, and I hope it will serve."

Caroline's eyes went over her husband. "When Dwight comes back I hope he will engage Clotworthy as his permanent assistant."

Dwight smiled at Demelza. "And while you are away, whom will *you* engage as a locum?"

"You mean? . . . Well, I haven't thought—"

Ross said: "Mrs. Kemp can look after the children. She'll be happy to live in for the winter months."

"Oh, I can't be absent all the winter months, Ross!"

"We'll see. Until Christmas, then."

As they rode home afterwards Demelza said: "Do you *really* want me to come with you? You're not just—being polite?"

"Polite?" said Ross. "Am I ever—polite?"

"Well, not in that way, perhaps. I just wanted to be sure."

"Well, you can surely be sure . . . That's if you wish to come."

"I very much wish to come. I wish to be with you anywhere. But the thought of London makes me a small matter anxious."

"Why?"

"I don't know. Just anxious."

"D'you mean for the children?"

"No, no. For all that London means. For myself, Ross."

"Don't be. You've taken every other hurdle in your stride. Even to entertaining the de Dunstanvilles to dinner."

"It's different."

"Every hurdle is different. This will be much easier. It's not so personal a thing. London swallows everything."

"I hope it won't spit me out," said Demelza.

Ross laughed. "Not if it likes the taste."

"When are you leaving for Canterbury?"

"About the twenty-first. They want me by the

end of the month. But it's only for four weeks. I hope to spend all September at home."

"Leaving the children will mean a lot of preparations."

"Well, make the preparations."

Before he left for Canterbury, Ross called to see Drake. They had met once or twice briefly but not for any conversation.

He found him digging in the garden of Reath Cottage, digging over, it seemed, ground already effectively turned, as if he could find nothing better to do. Sam was down at the mine.

Drake looked up and pushed back the lock of black hair which always to Ross was disconcertingly like Demelza's. They wished each other good morning, and talked briefly about the pilchard catch that had come in yesterday.

Ross said: "I'm off tomorrow and shall not be back till mid-September. When are you returning to your forge?"

"Well, that I don't rightly know, sur."

"D'you remember, many years ago I asked you to call me Ross and you said you'd do so after your twenty-first birthday? Well, that's long past."

Drake smiled slowly. "So tis . . . Cap'n—er—Ross."

Ross kicked a lump of the sandy soil with his foot. "I know since you came to live here you've had one miserable stroke of luck after another. Don't think I don't sympathise. It has all stemmed from one unfortunate love affair, but that makes it no easier to accept, nor to tolerate. I'm very . . . sorry."

"Why, thank ee, sur—Cap'n Ross, I mean. But you must not grieve for me. Tes no one's doing but my own."

"Ah, well . . . I don't think I would agree with that. But I think it's time you returned to the shop. It's nearly three months. You are losing custom. People are becoming used to going elsewhere."

"Yes . . . That I d'know."

"The framework of the roof has been rebuilt and part of the thatching is already done."

"Sam told me. Tis handsome of ee, but I can never repay you."

"Yes, you can. You have money in the bank."

"Tis all lost."

"It is all there. The deposit that you had in Pascoe's Bank will soon be available to you at the Cornish Bank. It will likely not be enough, but you can repay the rest over the years."

"Ah, I didn' know that."

"There is much to do at Pally's Shop still. It will take you all winter. The walls need interior repair. And whitewashing. You'll need to knock together some furniture until you can afford money to buy it or leisure to make it. But the place is habitable now. And while the weather is dry . . ."

Drake straightened up and shook some earth off his spade. "To tell the truth, Cap'n Ross, I don't b'lieve I've the heart to try."

"In that case you'll not be worthy of your sister."

Drake blinked. "How do ye mean that?"

"Do you think she would give up? Or your brother for the matter of that."

Drake flushed. "I don't know. But it is as if the centre of my heart . . . be destroyed."

Ross looked at him. "Do you wish to sell the place? It is yours to sell."

"I dunno. Maybe twould be for the best."

"What does Sam say?"

"He want for me to go back."

"We all do."

Ross looked across at the chimney of Wheal Grace, the top of which was visible over the hill. It had just been re-coaled, and the chimney was sending up cauliflowers of smoke into the still sky.

He said: "Sam has been hard hit too."

"Yes, I d'know."

"But he hasn't given up."

"Sam's religious . . . But maybe that don't make all that manner of difference. Seeing as twas his religion as . . ."

"Quite so . . . None of us can know what another feels."

"Sometimes I think he like me here for comp'ny."

"But he wants you to go."

"Oh, yes. He want me to go. But Sam's always thinking of what'd be best for the other man."

Ross said: "I'll tell you what *is* best for the other man, *always,* and that's work. Work is a challenge. I've told you—I tried to drink myself out of my misery once. It didn't succeed. Only work did. It's the solvent to so much. Build yourself a wall, even if there's hell in your heart, and when it's done—even at the end of the first day—you feel better. That's why you should go back to the shop. Even if you don't know quite what you're working for."

"That's *it!*" cried Drake. "That's it! What am I working *for?*"

"Your own salvation," said Ross. "Not Sam's type at all—though that may come along after: I know nothing about that—but *physical* salvation, on this earth. You worked once to forget Morwenna. And it helped. You worked night and day. Then do it again."

Drake hung his head. He looked a sick man. "Maybe you're right . . ."

"Then when are you going back?"

"I'll—think it over—Ross."

"The time is past to think it over. Three months is too long to think it over. Will you go tomorrow?"

"I—cann't say."

"Why not?"

"I . . . look, I just cann't say."

"Yes, you can. Next week, then."

Drake took a deep breath. "All right. I'll try."

"That's a promise?"

"Yes."

"Your hand on it then."

They clasped hands.

Drake said: "I'm sorry. You think me a fool, mourning all the time for all that's lost."

"I think nothing," Ross said, "except that I have satisfied myself—and Demelza—and Sam. And I hope you, in the end. You're too capable to mope your life away. It should not be possible—nobody should be able to destroy a man like that."

II

Towards the end of the month Demelza went to spend a few days with Verity, who was alone except for young Andrew. Verity had seen the announcement about the Cornish Bank in the *Sherborne Mercury* and was all excitement to know what it meant.

Demelza said: "Ross is very tiresome about it and pretends not to know, pretends that it means little. Of a certainty, if you know him, it was not of his contriving! It seems Lord de Dunstanville proposed it at the last minute, after Harris Pascoe's name had been agreed and all, so I suspect he must have had a secret appreciation for the way in which Ross worked so— so tenacious to gain his ends."

"And Wheal Grace?"

"Yielding again, but I think Ross and the others see the end of the kindliest lodes. All the trouble with Wheal Maiden, the disaster, has brought nothing in return. She seems, they say, a dead mine. But who knows? We are assured for the time of an income and work for all. And you cannot tell me . . . But perhaps you can. You are wiser than I am, Verity."

"What were you going to say?"

"I was going to say that if I have a husband who starts a small mine on his own property and, after many failures, it begins to yield big profits, that is one thing. Isn't it? But if you have that, and your husband comes to have an interest in a shipyard and in rolling mills and becomes a member of Parliament and then —a *banker;* that's another, isn't it? Even if four-fifths of his income still comes from the mine, there is a different feeling, Verity. I have a different feeling."

"You are quite right, my dear. And I believe there are other advantages."

Demelza smiled at her and waited. Verity adjusted her cap.

"Of course there are the financial advantages that must come to a man in his position. Knowing Ross, I know he is likely to reject any such advances that may directly come to him because of his position. But they will still come, and one here and there will be likely to slip under his guard because he will feel they will advantage other people as well. So if all goes favourable he should prosper now, whether or no. But I was thinking—when I spoke first I was thinking of more immediate, personal advantages—this year particularly."

"Of what sort?"

"Last time he was in, Andrew told me there was a big concentration of troops between Deal and Canterbury—where Ross has gone. There is talk of an invasion of France. It is four years since any British soldier set foot in Europe. Everyone is very enthusiastic. Ross might be. The more responsibilities he has to hold him in England, the better it will be for us all."

"Yes," said Demelza. "I hadn't thought of that."

And then Verity wished she had not spoken.

During her stay Demelza thought more than once of trying to talk about her own relationship with Ross. On her last visit Verity had seen that all was not well, but her questions had been too tactful and tentative to produce frank discussion. More than anything Demelza wanted a frank discussion; and Verity had such sympathy and understanding. Sometimes Demelza took out Hugh Armitage's poems and read them over. Had *she* inspired such passion? An educated young man, a lieutenant in the navy, who claimed he had known many women in his short life and loved only one . . . Well, that was gone for ever, and she did not want it back, with its pulling at her heart strings, the agony of divided loyalties. But so much waste, to die so young. She had heard people say they didn't want a future life, didn't want to live again. This she could not understand. So far she had done so little, seen so little.

She wanted an age, an aeon of life to plumb it and savour it to the last drop.

But she found she could not say anything of this to Verity. Verity knew nothing of Hugh Armitage; she had never met him and therefore would be unable to understand or even guess at his terrible attraction. Whatever her perception and sympathy she could bring no understanding to this. Only Caroline knew and, Demelza thought, understood a little of what had happened.

Chapter Two

In late August an English army landed at the Helder, at the tip of the Zuider Zee, and soon after an English fleet captured the entire Dutch fleet at anchor and without firing a shot: seven ships of the line and eighteen smaller ships with six thousand seamen who at once hauled down the Republican flag and offered themselves to fight for the House of Orange. Hopes for victory ran high everywhere.

Contrary to Demelza's fears Ross returned safely from Barham Downs on the sixth of September, looking fit and bronzed but with the news that, because of these victories, and in order to rush a militia bill through Parliament, the House was to reassemble on the twenty-fourth of that month, so they must be away in nine or ten days.

Everything then was bustle and haste. Caroline was leaving almost immediately, Dwight a day or two after the Poldarks. Demelza was uneasy that her absence from Cornwall was going to coincide with his and that her two children, if ill, would be left to the fumbling mercies of John Zebedee Clotworthy. Ross would have joked her out of it if it had not been for the loss of Julia.

Dwight brought Clotworthy over one day before they left. He was a pimply, down-at-heel, earnest man of about forty who had come originally from St. Erth and set up in opposition to Mr. Irby, the druggist in St. Ann's; and Dwight, who had had various passages with Mr. Irby for selling him adulterated drugs, had transferred his custom to the new man and had had honest if uninspired service ever since. Honest and uninspired would be his treatment of all Dwight's ailing patients, but at least anything he attempted would come from his own observation and not from some pet theory. Dwight was dead against theory. The followers of William Cullen had had too long a run. The great Boerhaave, who taught that empirical treatment was all and that one must help body to defeat its own enemies, had been everywhere despised, and the patient treated with ever more violent purging, more bloodletting, more sweat causers, and more powerful drugs. Dwight wondered sometimes if even he did not prescribe too much—often to please the patient—and thought he would be neither surprised nor offended if some of his patients had improved, when he returned, from being treated by someone who had never heard of Boerhaave or William Cullen—or perhaps even Hippocrates.

Ross and Demelza left on the fourteenth. Their coach left Falmouth at six A.M. and they were due to pick it up in Truro at eight-thirty. It meant rising in the dark, last-minute, hasty arrangements and rearrangements, a talkative, absentminded breakfast, then kissing the children good-bye—Clowance not minding because she didn't realise how long a month was, but Jeremy a bit tremble-lipped though putting a good face on it. Then both of them racing off up the hill with Jane Gimlett in vain pursuit, so that when Ross and Demelza reached Wheal Maiden they were there to wave good-bye and to stand in the dawn light waving and waving and gradually becoming smaller and smaller until they were little pin figures and so merged into the background of the pines.

"Oh dear," said Demelza, "I believe I am a small matter distraught."

"Try to forget them," Ross said. "Remember that in twenty years they will be likely to ride away and forget you."

Demelza looked at Ross. "You must've been keeping some bad company."

"Why?"

"To say a thing like that."

He laughed. "It was half in jest, half in earnest. I mean nothing derogatory."

"What a big word for a mean thought."

He laughed again. "Then I take it back."

"Thank you, Ross."

They jogged on a few minutes. He said: "But it is partly true. We have to lead our own lives. We have to give freedom to those we love."

Gimlett was catching them up. He was coming on a third horse to bring theirs back.

"Between husband and wife also?" Demelza asked.

"That depends on the *sort* of freedom," Ross said.

II

They left Truro ten minutes late because the coachman made difficulty about the amount of luggage they brought, but arrived at St. Austell in time for dinner at the King's Arms, took tea at the London Inn, Lostwithiel, and supped and slept at the White Horse, Liskeard. Including their ride in, they had covered the first forty-five miles of their long journey.

Over supper Demelza said: "I've been thinking, Ross, what you said about the children. I suppose in a way you're right—but does it matter? Isn't it what you give in this world that's important, not what you get back?"

"I'm sure you're right."

"No, don't agree so easy. I mean even if you look at it in the most selfish way: isn't there more actual *pleasure* in giving than in getting back?"

"All right," he said. "Yes. But I just wished you to keep a sense of proportion. So long as you're aware of that—that the giving is all. It's easy to say, but hard to carry out."

"Maybe."

"I thought if I reminded you of the way human nature operates, it might help you to grieve less now at the parting."

"No," she said, "it won't."

"Well, I'm sorry I spoke."

"No matter. I've stopped grieving already, Ross, and am just getting excited. After just one day. And I don't think that's a nice way for human nature to operate either!"

They broke their fast early next morning, crossed the Tamar by the ferry at Torpoint and dined in Plymouth. Tea was at Ivybridge and they slept at Ashburton, having covered almost exactly the same mileage as the day before, though this all by coach. Everybody was very tired, and Demelza could hardly keep awake over supper.

"You see why I travel sometimes by sea," Ross said. "But it improves a little from now on. The roads are better and the hills fewer."

The coach held eight inside. Sometimes it was uncomfortably crowded, sometimes half empty, as passengers left and joined. The only others making the full trip to London were a Mr. and Mrs. Carne from Falmouth, he being that banker Ross had threatened to go to with his friends if the Basset, Rogers bank would not accommodate Harris Pascoe. Mr. Carne had heard of Ross's becoming himself a partner and talked banking a good deal of the time, most of it over Ross's head. To divert him, Ross told him that his wife's name had been Carne before she married; but they seemed to be unable to establish any relationship.

The third night they slept at Bridgwater, having dined at Cullompton and taken tea at Taunton. Demelza realised now what Caroline meant when she said that Cornwall was a barren land. Here there were great trees, great belts of woodland everywhere, trees that made even the wooded parts of south Cornwall look puny and dwarf. The fields were so rich, the colorations of the soil always changing but always lush. There were more birds, more butterflies, more bees. And unfortunately more flies and wasps. She had never seen so many. It was a warm September, and apart from the jogging of the coach the heat was oppressive, for if a window were lowered somebody always complained of the draught. To make matters worse, one of the horses went lame on a stage on the fourth day and they were very late arriving in Marlborough.

The fifth day had to be a dawn start nevertheless, for they were due in London that evening. The road now was the best they had been on, the day was cooler but bright and sunny, and they reached Maidenhead for dinner after a spanking run. The food was good here: a neck of boiled veal and a roast fowl, and a rather heavy but seductive wine; Demelza dozed away the afternoon and traversed the dreaded Hounslow Heath without even noticing it. Ross told her that the only highwaymen to be seen were the unsuccessful ones hanging from the gibbets as a warning to the rest.

Great bustle in Hounslow—the hub of the western exits from London: the innkeeper told them that five hundred coaches passed through daily and that upwards of eight hundred horses were regularly maintained here. Ross had never heard this before. As always he learned more on a journey with Demelza than when travelling alone.

So the last ten miles to the city of which recently she had heard and thought so much. The last afternoon before leaving she had paid one of her regular visits to the Paynters to give Prudie a little money for herself, and Prudie had been appalled at the thought of such a journey and of what waited at the other end. "They d'say tis much bigger'n Truro," she'd muttered.

The first thing to be seen of the town bigger than Truro was the smoke: It lay low down on the horizon like a dirty fog.

"Don't worry," said Ross. "That's only the lime kilns and the brick works. It will be better beyond."

The coach entered an area as desolate as any mining district in Cornwall. Amid the smoking brick fields thin sheep browsed and pigs rooted, trying to find something green among the poisoned vegetation. Enormous dumps of refuse bordered the road, some of them also smouldering like half-extinct volcanoes, others sprawling in miniature foothills, where the waste and the refuse were being picked over by beggars and ragged children with scrofulous faces.

Houses met them and closed round them, sprawling, jumbled, leaning as if about to fall down. Some had, and men were at work rebuilding them. More fields, then a broader, cleaner part, with a few good buildings merging into older, more harshly cobbled streets, with dives and alleys leading off, in which children and slatternly women and mangy cats roamed. By now dusk was coming on, but the evening was very warm and in one street women were sitting out of doors on stools in their linsey-woolsey petticoats and worsted stockings, their leather stays half laced and black with dirt. Some were occupied stitching coarse cloth, but many did nothing but sit and yawn. They shouted obscenely as the coach passed and aimed bad oranges at the coachman. Bundles, supposedly human, lay drunk or dead, and children ran after the coach screaming. At last they reached a well-paved area, but this had higher paved ridges traversing the streets where pedestrians might cross, so that the coach bumped and lurched as it went over them.

So to the Thames. The windows of the coach, which had been tight closed to keep out the smells, were opened to let in better air. The river seemed to have a thousand small boats on it. People being ferried here and there. Ten-oared barges. Sailing ships tacked and lugged, in some amazing fashion not colliding with each other. A forest of masts further down, and a great dome. "St. Paul's," Ross said.

As they crossed a bridge the lights were going on. Link boys were rushing around lighting the three- and

four-branched lamps which hung from posts in the
streets. It became a sudden fairyland. All the squalor
and the dirt and the stenches were swallowed up by
the evening dark and the opaque light cast on the
streets from these crystal globes. The coach bumped
and rattled through fine streets now, but hardly able to
get along for the press of traffic. They jolted briefly
between a coffin on an open cart and a gilded carriage
in which sat a solitary woman with an ostrich-
feathered headdress. A brewer's dray, with great barrels swaying and a half dozen ragged boys clinging,
followed soldiers marching, while a group of extrava-
gantly dressed riders tried to edge their mounts
through the throng.

The coach stopped for a long time to allow Mr.
and Mrs. Carne to alight. There were polite expressions of gratification on all sides at the pleasure experienced in each other's company over five days, the
Carnes' bags were unloaded and at last the coach was
off again, edging its way slowly on to a wide street
called the Strand. They came once more to a creaking
stop.

"We are here," said Ross. "At last. Just down this
street, if you can walk after so long a-sitting. The
coachman will bring our bags down."

III

The rooms were nice and spacious, better than Demelza had expected after the cramped inns in which
they had slept, and Mrs. Parkins, a handsome, be-
spectacled woman, did everything to oblige.

They had done seventy-five miles on the last day
and in spite of their abounding good health they were
ready for bed and slept late next morning. Used to the
boisterous arrival of her children each day soon after
dawn, Demelza was startled and appalled to raise her
head off the pillow and to see by the marble clock on
the mantelshelf that it was nearly ten. Ross was part
dressed and washing.

"Judas! Why didn't you wake me, Ross?"

He smiled. "Don't alarm yourself. Mrs. Parkins is used to serving breakfast at ten. I seldom rise early myself in London."

"No wonder you look tired when you come home."

"Tired for sleeping late?"

"And bedding late, I suspect. It is the wrong hours to sleep."

"Do you want your nightdress?"

"Please."

"Come and fetch it, then."

"No."

He began to shave.

"What is that, Ross?"

"What? Oh, this. It is an improved washstand. Did you not see one at Tehidy? But this one has compartments for soap balls and razors. You will be able to admire it when you get up."

"Does Mrs. Parkins bring the water?"

"A maid does. There is a tap in the house."

"A tap? You mean like a barrel?"

"Yes. But water runs through wooden pipes from cisterns higher in the town, so you can draw what you will."

"Can you drink it?"

"I have done, and come to no harm. No doubt you found last night that there is always a bucket of water too in the Jericho down the passage. As well as one of sand. It's the best indoor system I have come across."

"Last night I was too tired to take much notice of anything."

"When I undressed you," he said, "you felt like a long-legged, cool kitten, slightly damp with sweat."

"It sounds some awful."

"Well, it wasn't, if you can recollect that much."

"I can recollect that much."

There was a pause while she yawned and ran fingers through her hair.

"A gentleman would fetch my nightdress," she said.

"It depends on the gentleman."

314

"I told you before. You've been keeping bad company in London."

"Not till last night."

He finished shaving in silence and tipped his water away into the other bucket. She was sitting up now, a sheet under her arms.

"It's not nice in the mornings, Ross."

"What isn't?"

"Nakedness."

"Opinions differ."

"No, you don't look nice in the daylight . . ."

"I don't?"

"No, I mean *I* don't. We don't. *One* doesn't."

"Well, make up your mind." He was putting on his shirt now.

"One doesn't look nice in the daylight," Demelza said. "At least, not as nice as *one* hopes *one* looks at night, by candle."

"I think two look better than one," Ross said. "Always have."

A knife grinder outside was shouting and ringing his bell, and someone was ringing a competing bell and offering to repair broken chairs.

"I thought this was a quiet street," Demelza said.

"So it is compared to most. You'll be late for breakfast if you don't bestir yourself. Not that it's much to miss. Milky tea with thick bread and butter. I intended to have brought some jam."

Cautiously she eased herself out of bed, pulling at the sheet so that it came with her. Out of the corner of his eye he saw her and advanced on her with mischief in mind as part of her back and legs became exposed. She dodged quickly but one corner of the sheet held firm and tripped her. She went to the floor with a thump. He knelt beside her as she rolled herself defiantly into a cocoon, the sheet ripping as he did so. He caught her and held her, laughing.

"No, Ross! Don't!"

"I'm m-married to a m-m-mummy," he said, laughing uncontrollably. "An Eg-egyptian mummy. They

315

look—look just like you, only they haven't got so much h-h-hair! . . ."

She glared at him from among her mane. She was so tight-wrapped around that she could not even get a hand free to hit him. Her hair lay in a tangle about her face. Then she saw the funny side and began to laugh too. She laughed up at him with all her heart and soul. He lay on top of her and laughed and laughed. Their bodies shook the floor.

Presently it had to come to an end and they lay exhausted. He put up a weak hand to clear her hair away from her face. His tears were on her cheeks. Then he kissed her. Then the strength came back to his hands and he began to unwind her.

At this point there was a knock on the door. Ross got up and opened it.

"Please, sir"; it was one of the maids. "If you please, sir, Mrs. Parkins says to say breakfast be ready and waiting."

"Tell Mrs. Parkins," said Ross, "that we shall be down in an hour."

Chapter Three

A first five days in London of unalloyed happiness. The city was a treasure trove into which Demelza dipped unceasingly, not put off by the squalid and the degrading, though often offended by it. At the bottom of George Street was one of the many landing stages marked by twin striped poles where you could get a ferryman in red and blue breeches and a red cap to take you anywhere. It was sixpence each to Westminster and the same to St. Paul's, where the great church seemed more monstrous in size and more impressive even than the Abbey, though it was disfigured by the conglomerate of sordid, tumbledown houses girdling it, by butchers' shops where stinking offal was thrown into the street, and by the omnipresent stench of the Fleet Ditch.

The weather was still fine and sunny, and one day they took chairs to Paddington and then walked east towards Islington, with the hills to the north and all the city straggling southward. They went to Vauxhall Gardens and to Ranelagh, and called on Caroline at her aunt's house in Hatton Garden. Dwight was expected on the morrow, and Caroline was full of the reception that was to be held at Mrs. Tracey's on the evening of the twenty-fourth. Seeing her so engaged, Ross wondered whether she would *ever* altogether settle as the wife of a remote country doctor. Yet he remembered coming to this house years ago, when Caroline and Dwight had apparently broken up for ever, and how wan and listless she had been. And there was the time of Dwight's imprisonment when she had seemed only to live from day to day. She needed Dwight, there seemed no doubt. But she also needed a stimulus in her life, a social round, or a mission of some sort.

For her evenings out Demelza had brought the evening gown that she had had made for her in those early days of her married life, and the other frock she had bought for Caroline's own wedding three years ago, and which she had scarcely worn. Caroline gently shook her head. It might be the perfect thing for Cornwall still, but it wouldn't do for the London season in 1799. Fashions had changed. Everything was of the simplest, finest, slightest. ("So I notice," Demelza said.) Waists were high, almost under the armpit, both for day and for evening. Neck and bust were much exposed but could be hidden or part hidden in a veil of chiffon. Ostrich feathers in the hair, or a few pearls. Demelza said, how interesting, and why do so many people wear spectacles in London? Perhaps they live more in artificial light, said Caroline; but then of course it is rather the fashion. I think, Demelza said, folk would walk on crutches in London if someone said it was the fashion. I have no doubt you're right, said

Caroline. In any case, said Demelza, there would be no time for anything to be made for me by tomorrow evening; but aside from that we could not afford, I should not wish to afford, London prices.

"I'll take you to my shop, Phillips & ffossick. Mrs. Phillips has a number of gowns half made that can be altered and finished in four and twenty hours. As for payment, it can go on my account. I pay yearly, and you can reimburse me if and when you have the fancy."

"It seems to cost even to breathe in London," Demelza said.

"Well, what is money for but to spend? We'll ask Ross, but only after we've spent it."

"I hope I can understand what your Mrs. Phillips says," said Demelza, weakening. "I often don't follow what the ordinary people say. It is almost like a foreign language."

"Oh, don't worry. You'll find Mrs. Phillips excessively genteel."

"That also," Demelza said. "I do not so much fancy."

But she went, like the moth to the flame. Shades of long ago when Verity had first taken her into Mistress Trelask's . . . The homely little seamstress's shop in Truro with a bell that tinged when you entered and you nearly fell down the two dark steps. This was a *salon,* though not large; just well-bred and discreet. You sat in a place like a drawing room, with silk drapes and lawn curtains and lush gilt chairs; and a woman who looked like a countess who had fallen on hard times brought out a succession of gowns, each one presented and considered separately before being hidden away again before the drawing room could begin to look untidy.

After rejecting three on the grounds of indecency she took to one of a fetching peach-coloured satin, which not only happened to be an opaque material but of a fractionally more discreet design. Before price could be discussed it was arranged that the gown should be finished and delivered to No. 6 George

Street "at this hour tomorrow," and that the account should in due course be presented to Mrs. Enys.

"I feel like a wanton," Demelza said as they came out into the noisy street.

"That's just what you must try to look like," said Caroline. "It's the ambition of all respectable women."

"And the wantons try to look respectable?"

"Well, not that always neither. Now I must fly, for there's much still to do, and Dwight should be with me this evening. Get this chair . . . I'll see you into it and then we'll meet tomorrow in the forenoon."

The twenty-fourth of September was a Tuesday, and day broke with a light rain falling. Demelza looked out to see umbrellas passing up and down the street below and to see the patten woman bringing back the shoes she had been cleaning overnight. But by eleven the clouds had split open and a hazy sun, much obscured by drifting smoke, peered through. The cobbles were soon drying. Caroline and Dwight and Demelza saw the royal procession from seats in Whitehall, the gold coaches, the bands, the regiments, the prancing life guards. Because of the successes of both the army and the navy a new wave of patriotism was sweeping Britain, and the old King was cheered the length of the street.

The reception at Portland Place was to start at nine, and there was some talk that the Prince of Wales himself might be there. Ross had ordered a coach for nine-fifteen, which to Demelza's idea was far too late but he would not alter it. She began getting ready at eight, and eventually slipped into her new gown at quarter before nine.

When Ross turned round saw it he said: "That is very pretty. But where is the gown?"

"This is it! This is what I have bought!"

"That's a petticoat."

"Oh, Ross, you *are* provoking! You know well it is nothing of the sort."

"Would you wish me to go in my shirt and under-breeches?"

"No, no, you must not tease! I need confidence, not—not . . ."

"Port will give you that."

She grimaced at him. "And this is for my hair," she said, showing him the feather.

"Well, I don't know what your father would say if he could see you."

"It is the fashion, Ross. Caroline insisted."

"I know just how women insist. And you, I'm sure, were protesting loudly and saying, no, no, no!"

"Well, I did protest, truly. And this is much the most respectable of the gowns I was shown. Some women, Caroline says, damp their frocks when they put them on so that they will cling more."

"You damp anything, my dear, and I'll smack you."

She paused while he tied his stock. "But, Ross, you do like it, don't you? I still have time to change."

"And you'd wear an old frock to please me?"

"Of course."

"And be miserable all night?"

"I wouldn't be miserable. I'm so happy."

"Yes . . . you look it, I'll say that. Why are you happy?"

"Because of you, of course. Because of *us*. Need I say?"

"No," he said, "perhaps not . . ."

Somewhere a clock was striking nine.

He said: "The vexing thing is, good-looking women look good in almost anything. Or should I say almost nothing? Well . . ." He stared at her. "On longer inspection I like the frock. I think it has a touch of elegance. I am only a little reluctant that so many men should see so much of you."

"They will have many other women to look at. Women who have spent their lives being beautiful."

"And men too. These confounded buttons are hard to fasten."

"Let me." She came up and busied herself at his wrists.

"I think," he said, looking down at her brushed and

combed and tidy hair, "I think I'll go in my night-gown. It might provoke a new fashion."

II

Portland Place was one of the broadest and best-lit streets in London, and a line of carriages and chairs waited their turn before a porticoed door with a royal blue carpet laid under a crimson awning. Gowned and beautiful creatures were passing up the steps followed by men scarcely less brilliant. When it came to their turn two white-wigged footmen were there to open the carriage door and to hand Demelza out. It seemed for a moment that they were at the centre of a circle of brilliant light from the periphery of which a sea of faces peered at them greedily as the hundreds of ragged onlookers stared at and assessed them. Then they had passed inside, to leave their cloaks in the care of more footmen, and to climb a short flight of stairs while a man with a rich tenor voice shouted: "Captain and Mrs. Poldark."

Caroline greeted them, brilliant in pale green, with jewels at her breast that were never seen in Cornwall, and introduced them to their two hostesses: Mrs. Pelham, her aunt, whose escort was a tall man called the Hon. St. Andrew St. John (the member for Bedfordshire, presumably), and Mrs. Tracey, with Lord Onslow. And then there was Dwight in a new suit of black velvet, and presently they moved on and were given glasses of wine and reached an enormous reception room already more than half full of people chatting and drinking and seated and exchanging greetings.

As they went in Dwight had drawn aside and said to Ross: "A word of warning. The Warleggans are likely to be here. Mrs. Tracey invited them. But they should be easy to avoid." Ross had smiled grimly and said: "Never fear. We'll avoid 'em."

In fact George and Elizabeth arrived soon after them in the company of Monk Adderley and a girl called Andromeda Page, a yawning, semi-nude beauty of seventeen, whom Monk was temporarily escorting round the town. They spotted the Poldarks quickly enough but moved to the opposite side of the room and were soon lost sight of.

The Warleggans had arrived in London only two days before and taken up residence at No. 14 King Street, just near Grosvenor Gate, having brought Valentine with them, since scarlet fever was so rife in Truro that he was unlikely to be at greater hazard in London with the fresh fields of Hyde Park on his doorstep. Theirs had been something of a royal procession from Cornwall, travelling as they did in their own coach and taking twelve days on the journey. In his year as a member of Parliament, George had been an assiduous collector of useful friends, and this stood him in good stead. He had written well ahead to various people telling them he would like to call, and few of the country gentry wished to offend a very rich man with a pretty and well-connected wife. As a result, they had only had to spend two nights in inns all the way.

George was in the best of spirits tonight, Monk having just told him of his election to White's, one of the most exclusive clubs in London. He had also had a conversation with Roger Wilbraham that morning. Wilbraham, unlike Captain Howell, was neither a Cornishman nor in need of money, and his first response to the suggestion that he might resign his seat at St. Michael had been unhelpful. Gladly he'd accept money to resign, he said, laughing loudly, if George would provide him with another seat. Not otherwise, since it would cost him as much to procure another seat for himself as he was likely to receive from George, so how did it profit him? An impasse had been prevented by Wilbraham adding: "But look, old fellow, I've stood for Scawen interests until now. I've no strong convictions. I can just as easy be your man as his. You can count on me." It seemed the easy way out, and George had accepted the suggestion. If Wilbraham should prove troublesome, there were ways of forcing him out later. The important thing was that, so far as the government was concerned, George now had two seats to bargain with.

Elizabeth, though slightly plumper in face, had not thickened in figure yet, and tonight looked at her most dignified and beautiful, having spent most of the day receiving the attentions of a hairdresser who had brightened up the faded fairness until it shone like a crown. As usual she wore white, this time in a Grecian style, light loose drapery over a tight tunic, decorated with gold chains, sandaled feet and flesh-coloured stockings with toes like gloves, fan in gold belt and tiny gold bag containing scent and a handkerchief. "My dear," Monk Adderley said, "you look like Helen of Troy."

She smiled at him warmly and looked at the growing company. "One day, when the war is over, I hope to travel, if I can persuade George to do so. I should like to see Greece and all the islands. I should like to see Rome . . ."

"Do take care," said Adderley, "I cannot bear to hear you say you wish to look at the scenery."

"Why ever not?" Elizabeth smiled. "Who is that man over there?"

"The fat one? The gross one? You don't know him? That is Dr. Franz Anselm, who, my dear, makes *more money* out of ladies than any other physician in London. Do you wish to conceive? He will see to it. Do you wish *not* to conceive, or to lose that which you *have* conceived? He will see to that also. Should you wish to stay young and to fascinate your husband— or someone else's husband—a valuable nostrum is prescribed. Do you have disagreeable warts? He will take them off you. Have you not heard of Dr. Anselm's Balsamic Cordial for Ladies in Nature's Decay?"

"A charlatan?"

"God, who in the physical profession is not? They all have their cure-alls. But his, I believe, are more effective than most."

"A pity he cannot prescribe to make himself a

thought prettier. Why do you say I should not look at the scenery?"

"Well, not to *admire* it. Some of these poets nowadays, my dear, offend me to distraction. They have a *romantic* view of life. It is so low-class, so mediocre. What are mountains and lakes, to be stared at as if they were of *interest?* Personally, when I go through the Alps I always draw the blinds of my coach."

"And who is that coming in now?" Elizabeth asked. "Like Dr. Anselm somewhat, but smaller."

"That, my dear, is another man of some import in the world, though no doubt as a high Tory you must disapprove of him—as I do. I could spit him on a sword for his wrong assumptions about the war. The Hon. Charles James Fox. And that's his wife, the former Mrs. Armistead, whom he married a mere four years ago."

The big Dr. Anselm waddled past. He had eyebrows like black slugs, mottled black hair which he did not deign to cover with a wig, and a stomach which spread from his chest and preceded him as he walked. Mr. and Mrs. Fox turned the other way.

"Ah," said Monk, "this one, this tall feller, is Lord Walsingham, who's chairman of the committees in the House of Lords. And behind him, the younger one, is George Canning, who's secretary for foreign affairs. I'm glad to see a few of the government turning up, else we should be swamped with the dissidents. Instruct me, where does George get his shoes?"

"My George? I don't know."

"Well, it is not the right place. Tell him to go to Rymer's. Outstanding, my dear. And Wagner's for hats. One can never afford to have anything but the best."

"I'm sure George would entirely agree," Elizabeth said with a touch of irony, and, to be polite, spoke to Miss Page. So the group re-formed.

Ross and Demelza were talking to a Mr. and Mrs. John Bullock. Bullock was the member for Essex, an elderly man and in confirmed opposition to Pitt, but he and Ross liked and respected each other. They were joined by the Baron Duff of Fife and his daughter, who was wearing a startling necklace that seemed to set fire to her throat.

When they had gone Demelza said: "There is so much wealth in London! Did you see that—those diamonds! And yet there's so little."

"Little what?"

"Wealth. Those faces as we came in! They would fight for a sixpence. Sometimes I think—what little I've seen, Ross—it's as if London's half at war with itself."

"Explain yourself, my love."

"Well, isn't it? All the crime. It's like a—a volcano. In the streets—those gangs at corners waiting for a victim. All the drunkenness and the quarrelling. The thieves and the prostitutes and the beggars. The stone throwing. The fighting with clubs. The starvation. And then this. All this luxury. Is this how it was in France?"

"Yes. And worse."

"I see how you must feel sometimes."

"I'm glad you feel it too. But don't let it spoil your evening."

"Oh, no. Oh, no."

He looked at her. "Sometimes I think we have as much control of events as straws in a stream."

A few moments later the Warleggans came into view on the other side of the room.

Demelza said: "Is Elizabeth going to have another child?"

"What?" Ross stared. "How do you know?"

"I don't. It's just a look she has."

"You could very well be right," he said after a moment. "She was indisposed the day of the opening of the hospital. Fortunately for me, she was taken with a fainting fit, or I should have had violent words with George, if not worse, and then I'm sure Francis Basset would not have thought me a suitable partner for his banking concerns."

"Straws in a stream," said Demelza. "How lucky we were!"

On the other side of the room Adderley said to George: "Did you actually *go and listen* to the speech from the throne, my dear?"

"Yes," said George.

"All this nonsense about militia? I could not bear it. I spent my time at Boodles. You're down, you know. The election's in November. I can arrange the necessary support."

"I'm obliged, Monk. I see Poldark's here."

"The noble captain. Yes. You don't like him, do you."

"No."

"You Cornishmen take yourselves so serious. What's in a feud? Who's that with him?"

"His wife. He married his kitchenmaid."

"Well, she's a good looker."

"Some men have thought so."

"With success?"

"Probably," said George, old malice stirring.

Adderley put up his glass to look across the room. "Her hair's provincial. Pity. The rest is good."

"Oh, no doubt she's been dressed in London."

"So she should be *un*dressed in London, don't you think? I cannot bear virtuous countrywomen."

"They are fewer than you think."

"Oh, yes, I know, my dear. Is there in truth one such in the land? Well, you know my claim."

"What's that?"

"I've never turned a woman empty away."

"You should try your luck."

"I'll test the water. Drommie!"

"Yes?" said the girl.

"Come with me. There's a feller I wish you to meet."

III

"This is Adderley coming across to us now," Ross said in an undertone.

"Who is he?"

"Friend of George's. He was down at Trenwith last summer. A member of Parliament. Ex-captain in a foot regiment, like me. A wild man."

"Wilder than you?"

"Different."

"With his wife?"

"I doubt it."

Demelza eyed the man as he came towards them, erect, thin as a pole, pale-faced. He was dressed in a dark olive-green spotted silk coat and breeches, the suit embossed with silver.

"My dear Poldark, I didn't see you at the opening today! May I present Miss Drommie Page? Captain Poldark. And *Mrs*. Poldark, I presume? *Enchanté*. I suppose the King didn't actually *read* his speech, did he?"

"No, it was read for him. Were you not there?"

"No, my dear, that's why I didn't see you. How drab it is to be recalled to London so early merely to pass some flatulent bill to do with the militia. The stinks haven't subsided yet. Do you live distant, Mrs. Poldark?"

"In Cornwall."

"But of course. Your husband not only sits in the Boscawen interest but *lives* there! Greater love hath no man!"

They talked for a few minutes, Adderley's snake-grey eyes travelling assessingly over Demelza's face and figure, Demelza smiling up at him from time to time and then glancing away, taking in the colour and the lights and the strolling, chatting figures and the palm trees and the music from a further room.

"Rot me," said Monk, dabbing his nose with a lace handkerchief, "I'm as hungry as a cannibal. Shall we go in to supper, Mistress Poldark?"

"Rot me too," said Demelza, and took a further look around the room.

"Well, then?"

"I'm sorry, sir, but I am engaged."

"By whom?"

"My husband."

"Your husband! My dear, it is simply not done! It is not permitted for married people to eat together! Not in London society."

"I'm sorry. I thought it was . . . But if you feel like a cannibal, might you not mistake what you were eating?"

Adderley's eyes crinkled. "That I might, ma'am. You, for instance. I have a catholic taste. Look . . . Poldark is busy with Drommie. He can lead her in. I promise we'll sit at the same table."

Swift thoughts: this man George's friend: Ross doesn't like him: but this an evening out: how to refuse? . . . needless offence . . .

She said: "Then let us all go in together! Ross . . . Captain Adderley is becoming ferocious for food. Shall we all eat now?"

She saw a mild glint on Ross's face when he turned, though it would have been imperceptible to anyone less attuned to his feelings.

He said: "By all means," though the words lacked enthusiasm.

On Adderley's arm Demelza walked to the supper room, followed by Ross and Andromeda.

"So you find me ferocious," Monk said. "I would not have thought you a woman easily intimidated, Mistress Poldark."

"Oh, very easily, Captain Adderley."

"Is it my reputation that frightens you?"

"I don't know your reputation, sir."

"Two things I like best of all: to fight and to make love."

"With the same person?"

"No, but on the same day. One whets the appetite for the other, ma'am."

In the next room a great table was heavy with food prepared in the most extravagant and artistic fashion. According to your tastes a white-hatted servant behind the table would cut you a piece of Windsor Castle, Buckingham House, St. Paul's, Westminster Abbey; or a whale, a giant dormouse, a horse, or a crocodile. Since they were early on the scene most of these wonders were unscathed, and everyone who entered the room gasped at the artistic ingenuity they must help to ruin.

"It looks," said George, "as if we have lost our friends."

"Yes," Elizabeth said; "I am somewhat surprised at Monk's taste."

"Oh, I set him after them. There's nothing Monk rises to so quickly as a challenge."

"I didn't mean the Poldarks," Elizabeth replied a little acidly. "I meant the young lady he had chosen to bring with him."

"Oh, Miss Page. They say she's the natural daughter of Lord Keppel. Pretty but penniless and vicious: it's a common tale. Oh, your lordship . . ."

"Sir?"

"Warleggan. You remember, at Ranelagh? May I introduce you to my wife. Viscount Calthorp; Elizabeth."

In the outer hall nearly all the guests had arrived. The Prince of Wales had sent a late message regretting that he would be unable to be present.

"Well," said Caroline to her husband, "the worst is nearly over. I trust you're not wishing yourself back with your patients."

"No," said Dwight, smiling. In fact he had that moment been reflecting that Mrs. Coad, in extremis when he last called, would be dead before the end of the month. And Char Nanfan struck with an inexplicable sickness. And Ed Bartle's children, three down with a pulmonary infection following the scarlet fever . . .

"Come, let us go and eat," Caroline said, linking her arm in his. "Some of the tabbies up here have been doubting that I really *have* a husband. I must display you all I can!"

"Where are Ross and Demelza?"

"I don't know. I saw them just now . . . Oh, with Monk Adderley and his pretty piece! That *is* a surprise. Well, then, we must eat with someone else."

"I imagine they must have been invited, for I don't believe they would ever have chosen that company," said Dwight. "Was that Lord Falmouth who came in just now? With the old lady?"

"Yes. His mother. We're honoured, since he is very little more sociable in London than in Cornwall."

They moved back into the reception room, where servants were discreetly rearranging the chairs so that later in the evening there would be room to dance.

Monk Adderley had steered Demelza into a corner seat while Ross and the girl were still choosing their food.

"Those are handsome buttons," Demelza said, pointing to the large ones he wore on each sleeve.

"Yes? You notice the lock of hair preserved in each?"

"That's what I thought it was. How nicely worked. Do they—does the hair belong to Miss Page?"

"No, to a Lieutenant Farmfield. He was the last man I killed."

For the first time Demelza noticed the scar on the side of his head, half hidden by his stiff, curled hair.

"The last?"

"Well, two is all. And another maimed."

"Do you not get put in prison for murder? Or even hanged?"

"Fair fight is not murder. Of course there is sometimes a trial. The first time I pleaded benefit of clergy."

"Are you a clergyman?"

Adderley's eyes crinkled again. It seemed to be the nearest he ever came to laughing. "A cleric, my dear. A clerk. I can write. I was excused on those grounds and sentenced only to be branded."

"Branded?"

"Yes . . . with a cold iron. Let me show you the mark." He extended his long thin hand in which the bones and veins delicately showed. She repressed a shiver.

"There is no mark . . . Oh, I see."

"The second time I was found guilty of manslaughter and sentenced to ten days in prison."

"And the third time you really *will* be hanged?" she asked politely.

"Who knows? Who cares? Ah, here's Poldark with my little girl. I feel sorry for Drommie."

"Why sorry? Ross is good company—if he likes his company."

"Which he appears not altogether to be doing at this moment. No, my dear, I meant on other counts. Drommie has a beautiful body. I should know. I have investigated it thoroughly. I could commend her to any sculptor. But as to her mind, I do not think there will ever be anything more important in it than a hairpin."

The lady being so discussed said to Ross: "Are you *strong?* You look *very* strong." Her voice and eyes were full of a bored innuendo.

"Very," he said, looking her over.

"How interesting." She yawned. "How vastly interesting."

"But I'd warn you. I have one weak leg."

She looked down. "Which one?"

"They take it in turns."

After an appreciable moment she tapped him on the shoulder with her fan. "Captain Poldark, you're making merry with me."

"I wouldn't presume on such short acquaintance. Has Captain Adderley never told you the old infantryman's adage?"

"What is that?"

"It's one leg of an elephant saying to another: 'Damn your eyes, move a little quicker.' "

"I call that quaint." She yawned again.

"Is it past your bedtime, Miss Page?"

"No . . . I've only just got up."

"My daughter's just like that."

"How old is she?"

"Nearly five."

"Now you're jesting again."

"I swear it's the truth."

"*No* . . . I mean by comparing *me!* Is Monk a friend of yours?"

"It would seem so."

"And of your wife's?"

"That remains to be seen."

"Of course. She's vastly attractive."

"I think so."

"And me?"

He looked at her. "You?"

"Yes . . . what do you think of me?"

He considered. "I think it *is* past your bedtime."

"That could be considered an insult, Captain Poldark."

"Oh, *no!*"

"Or—as a compliment . . ."

He smiled at her. "Oh, yes," he said.

People sat at tables of varying size, and wine and bread and knives and forks were rapidly put before them. Adderley had chosen a table for four, which made them somewhat isolated from the rest. Ross bore the company he did not want with great good humour, and only occasionally rose to bait that was put before him. As when Adderley began to speak of the expenses of the last election and how it had cost Lord Mandeville and Thomas Fellowes upwards of £13,000 between them to get in, of which he'd been told, by God, that nearly £7,000 had gone in innkeepers' bills. And how lucky he and Ross were to be the tame lapdogs of an indulgent peer.

"I think our 'indulgent peer' is here tonight," Demelza put in as she saw Ross about to speak. "I haven't seen him for upwards of two years, Ross, and I must ask him how Mrs. Gower is."

And, said Adderley, how old Reynolds was known in the House as the Dinner Gong, because whenever he got up to speak a hundred and forty members would walk out. And how on one occasion two years ago, a distinguished lady sitting in the strangers' gallery, caught up in a long debate, had been unable to contain herself, so that what she spilled fell upon the head of old John Luttrell, thereby ruining both his hat and his coat. "And twas lucky it did not blind him, by God!" said Adderley.

Miss Page went off into little muffled screeches of laughter. "How deliciously vulgar of you, Monk! I call that entertaining!"

"Don't tell me," said Monk to the others, "that you do not appreciate the anecdote! Walpole always encouraged vulgar conversation on the grounds that it was the only talk all could enjoy."

"Not at all," said Ross. "For are we not all vulgars ourselves?"

No one spoke for a moment.

"In what way?"

"Of a common or usual kind. You cannot suppose there is a uniqueness in human beings that puts one or an other above the rest—*surely!* Common, customary, or familiar. We all share the same hungers and the same functions: the young and the old, the lord and the beggar. Only the perverse fail to laugh and cry at the same things. That's common sense. Vulgar common sense."

The uneasy supper went on to its end, and presently broke up, and the ladies retired and the men also, and when they came down dancing had begun; and an hour passed pleasantly. Monk danced once with Demelza, and then not again, for Dwight took her away, and then Ross, and then other men intervened. She was not sure of the most fashionable steps, but what she knew seemed to suffice.

It was not until there was a brief interval at one o'clock that Monk, noticing her briefly alone, came across to her.

"When may I see you again, Mrs. Poldark?"

"But you are seeing me now, Captain Adderley."

"Is this your very first visit to London?"

"You know it is."

"Well, if I may say so, ma'am, I see you as a person of great undeveloped potentiality. My dear, you've scarce lived yet, believe me!"

"I've lived very well, thank you, Captain Adderley."

"You have not tasted the sophisticated pleasures."

"I always think they are only for folk who have tired of the simple ones."

"I'll wait upon you. When will your husband be out?"

"When I am."

"Then I'll wait upon you when he is in."

"You're most kind."

"I hope you will be also." His eyes went up along the lines of her peach-coloured gown, noting where it clung, to her bare arms and shoulders and low neck, the pale olive swelling of her breasts; at last up to her face and eyes, and his expression conveyed exactly what he would like to do to her. She found herself flushing, an unusual occurrence for her at any time.

Then she felt a hand put into her gloved hand. It was Ross, come up behind her.

"Adderley, you must return to your Miss Page. She is greatly lacking your attentions."

"Do you know, Poldark," Monk said gently, "there is only one person I ever take instructions from, and that is myself."

Demelza squeezed Ross's hand to stop his reply.

"Ross," she said, "Captain Adderley has paid us the compliment of saying he would wait upon us. While that would be—quite delightful, I was suggesting instead that we should all meet at the play on Thursday. You were telling me that we should go, Captain Adderley."

She could sense the hesitation on both sides. Since Adderley had told her nothing of the sort, it represented to him a small deception of her husband and therefore progress along the road he wished to pursue. Ross had indeed talked of going to the play, and a blank refusal at this point could only have been seen as an affront.

Adderley said: "That would be amusing, my dear. The play I have seen twice and it's tedious. But the women are interesting."

And so it was settled.

Chapter Four

By three in the morning people were beginning to depart. Caroline had seen what had been happening to Demelza, and took Monk Adderley off on her own and away from the danger zone.

Later she said to Demelza: "Sometimes I think him a little crazed. *Not* because he has taken a fancy to you! But because he is at times so . . . ungoverned in his behaviour. Treat it lightly—as a joke."

"That's all very well, but—"

"I know. But *explain* to Ross . . . I'll suggest to Dwight that we also go on Thursday. And in the meantime I will see what else there is in the pool of young women who might be dandled in front of Monk's nose to divert him."

. . . As they were waiting for their carriages to draw up George said:

"So you burned your fingers, Monk."

"Not at all, my dear. *Rome n'a été bâti tout en un jour.* One had to make the preliminary—clearances."

"And you have made those? I don't believe it! She is a virtuous woman!"

"You told me not."

"Well, who knows about any one of us? I said she was probably not. Perhaps later you will be able to inform me for sure."

"Of course. I can inform you now. Within a month she will not be a virtuous woman—if by virtue you mean faithfulness to her husband. I shall consider her virtuous if she is faithful to me, for as long as I want her."

"It's a big claim. I would be tempted to wager on it."

"My dear, by all means. Nothing would give me greater satisfaction. What odds will you offer?"

George licked his lips, and glanced across to see that Elizabeth was not within hearing. "A hundred guineas to ten. I am not prepared to make longer odds than that, for, after all, if you win you get all the fun."

"No," said Monk, looking at his friend with his cold eyes. "I perceive that if I win you will be more satisfied than I."

The Poldark coach was called soon after, and Demelza was handed in, and they moved creakingly away. There was silence for a while and then Ross said:

"Monk Adderley is a freakish fellow."

"Freakish . . . yes. I am a little scared at him."

"It did not seem so. You asked him to join us at supper and have invited him to the theatre on Thursday."

Demelza struggled with the difficulty of explaining. "In the first instance he had just asked me to go into supper with him *alone*. I'm not sure of the courtesies in London, but I thought it might be insulting to refuse. So I suggested we should all go together."

"And in the second instance?"

"I thought he and you were going to start growling at each other like a couple of tomcats, so I said the first thing that came into my head to stop it."

They were crossing Oxford Road, and even at this late hour there were people about, drunks lying in the shelter of overhanging houses, drays and butchers' carts rattling over the cobbles on late or early errands, beggars picking over the refuse and the droppings.

Ross said: "It's strange that people who affect to find life endlessly tedious are themselves so tedious to know. Well, I suppose we must endure him on Thursday."

"Ross." Demelza turned her head and the light from a passing link boy showed up her intent expression. "Caroline had a word with me about him during the evening. She told us not to take him serious. Not me. Not you. Especially not you. She said you must always treat him as a joke."

Ross pursed his lips. "Adderley. Yes. He is a joke. But I think we must watch him lest the joke turn sour."

II

They took a box at Drury Lane, which cost Ross twenty shillings and held four seats, and there saw Mr. John Kemble, Mr. William Barrymore, and Mrs. Powell in *The Revenge,* a tragedy in five acts by Edward Young. Demelza had not seen a play since the one performed in their library more than ten years ago, and that was a mere charade compared to this. She forgot the pale man, taut as a wire, in the chair beside her, who took what opportunities he could to put his face against hers to whisper comments and to touch her bare forearm with his thin cool fingers. She was far more annoyed by the noise from the pit; the scrambles that took place, the flying oranges, the shouts at the actors if something was displeasing. The light from the three hundred flickering tallow candles was so disposed behind the scenes that the stage was clearly but subtly lit. The brilliance of the costumes and the scenery, the resonance and drama of the actors' voices, all cast a spell on her. Between the acts there was music to keep the audience entertained, and when *The Revenge* was over in a welter of blood and tragedy, two more short pieces were staged, as comic as the main piece had been sad. A wonderful evening.

Dwight and Caroline were in the next box, and in one interval Dwight was able to say to Ross:

"I met Dr. Jenner today."

Ross looked vague. He had been more than a little preoccupied with angers that were swirling up in him and then dispersing in waves of self-mockery.

"Jenner? Oh? This book you were reading . . ."

"I believe it may be one of the great discoveries of our time. Of course there have been inoculations against the smallpox for some years, but this is different. There has not yet, in my view, been sufficient experiment. But I am hoping to see him again before I leave."

"You are off home?"

Dwight smiled. "Not yet."

Half joking, Ross said: "Perhaps I shall have to take Demelza home soon. She is not going to be safe here."

"I believe she's safe, Ross. She can look to herself."

"That," said Ross, "was what I used to think."

The last short play was nothing but a musical lampoon, a satire on the new fashions, all of them grossly exaggerated on the stage. The song that caught the public fancy was sung by a Miss Fanny Thompson and went:

> *Shepherd, I have lost my waist*
> *Have you seen my body?*
> *Sacrificed to modern taste,*
> *I'm quite a Hoddy-Doddy.*
> *Tis gone, and I have not the nook*
> *For cheese cake, tart or jelly.*
> *For fashion I that part forsook*
> *Where sages place the belly!*

Everyone joined in the second and third choruses. It became a great roar of sound.

As the two thousand people were streaming out of the theatre Monk Adderley said: "Will you visit Vauxhall with me on Monday next, Mrs. Poldark? I believe there is likely to be a late sitting of the House."

"Should you not be present, then?"

"God forbid. But your husband will."

"Tell me," she said. "Why did they call you Monk? It seems—not apt."

The eyes crinkled again. In a less sinister face it would have been attractive. "Not apt, as you observe, my dear. My father was so called and so liked his name that he has given it to all my brothers, to make sure it should be perpetuated."

She raised her eyebrows. "Dear life! Do you mean

there are several more Monk Adderleys walking the streets of London?"

"No, ma'am. Two died in infancy. One had his throat cut in India. One is in Bristol still with my parents, but he is a tedious provincial boy who will grow up into a country squire. . . . But tell me of your name. What does it mean in that bizarre Celtic language you have?"

"I don't know," said Demelza, knowing well, but feeling it was a bad thing to give him a further lead.

"Well, it is a passably provoking name. Ecod it is . . . Demelza . . . Demelza . . . It needs to be peeled off—like a cloak, like clothes, like a skin . . ."

"Like a banana?" she suggested.

"Listen, satin arms," he said, "I will take so much from you and no more. You have a sharp tongue, which I shall find very entertaining in due course. And shall know what to do with. On Monday, then. At nine."

Before Demelza could speak Caroline said: "There's room for two in our coach. We'll take you home. Can you find a chair. Monk?"

Adderley said: "I shall go to White's for an hour. Would you care to accompany me, Poldark? You can go in as my guest."

Ross hesitated, and then said amiably: "Thank you, no, I think not. I'm not rich enough to be able to lose money nor poor enough to wish to gain it."

"What a tedious thought," said Adderley. "The importance of money is that it should always be treated as of no importance."

III

Later that night, just as Demelza was dozing off to sleep, Ross said:

"D'you know for once I believe Adderley was right."

"What? What about? What d'you mean?"

"That money should always be looked on as unimportant. Now that I run a tin mine and have interests in rolling mills and the rest I am becoming too attached to the stuff."

"I have never been *un*attached to the stuff," she said. "Maybe it's because I was born a miner's daughter. Maybe it's because I've never had so very much. All I know is that having coins in my purse makes me happy, and having no coins makes me sad. I can't work it out different."

"All the same," Ross said, "Adderley may be right in that, but he is wrong in all else. Wrong especially if he supposes I shall stand by and watch him attempting to cuckold me."

"And do you serious think he has the slightest chance?"

Ross did not answer.

Demelza sat sharply up in bed, wide awake now.

"Ross, what are you *thinking* of? You are not serious in supposing . . . Because—because *once* something happened, because once I felt deeply about another man; do you think, do you suppose I am like to do that again—with the first such who comes along? Am I condemned—because of—of Hugh Armitage—to be suspected of feeling the same for every man who pays me some special attention?" When he still didn't speak she said: *"Ross!"*

"No," he said judicially.

"It could not happen again—certainly not with a man like Captain Adderley."

"Then you should make it clearer to me that it can't."

"How?"

"By not encouraging him."

"I do *not* encourage him! I have to be polite!"

"Why?"

She made a despairing gesture. "Sometimes, Ross, you try me hard. You really do. I am—I am in London for the first time. It is a new society. I am your wife—truly, truly in more than name again, in more than mere *act* again, after so long. I am *happy,* excited, living in a new way. A man comes up to me and starts paying me compliments. He is a—he is educated, well-bred, a member of Parliament. Do I turn my back on him to please you? Do I smack his face to satisfy you? Do I sit in a corner and refuse to answer him? Better that I should never have come!"

"Better that you should never have come than that he should contrive to paw you. He must know every bone in your left arm from wrist to shoulder."

There was silence.

"Then tell me what I must do," Demelza said. "Do you wish me to go home?"

"Of course not!"

"Tell me how I must behave then."

"You know very well how to behave."

"That's not fair! Anyway," Demelza said mutinously, "he won't take no for an answer. He says he is coming to take me to Vauxhall next Monday when you are in the House."

"And shall you go?"

"Certainly not! I shall be out—or unwell. A fever might be most likely to cool his ardour . . . Perhaps I could paint some spots on my face and squint through the window at him . . . Ross, do not let this spoil our time here . . ."

"No," he said, "no," and put an arm about her shoulder, "but one cannot always contain or order one's feelings, and when I see you in the company of another man—being touched and pressed by him—my mind—or something in me—turns up old feelings, old thoughts, old resentments. Which aren't so very old."

She lay against him, saying nothing for a long time, but not so sleepy now.

IV

A basket of flowers came next morning. Ross was for throwing it out, but Demelza could not tolerate this. Flowers to her were objects of interest and pleasure, no matter where they came from; and there were some in this bunch that she had never seen before.

They spent the Sunday with Dwight and Caroline riding beyond the village of Hampstead, and dined and supped with them. On the Monday morning more flowers. On Monday at five-thirty Caroline came for her and they went to the other royal theatre, in the Covent Garden. It was over at nine and Demelza, feeling she was eating too much, declined an invitation to go back to Hatton Garden to sup and said she would eat lightly at home. Caroline left her there and she went up, to see lights in their sitting room. She burst in, supposing that Ross was back, and found Monk Adderley reclining in a chair.

He was in an eggshell-blue suit of the finest silk, and his shirt was ornate with amber buttons.

"Oh, welcome," he said, getting up slowly. "You have kept me waiting, but no matter. The pleasure is the greater."

"How did you get in?"

"By the front door and up the stairs, ma'am. It was not difficult." He bowed over her hand, and she saw the scar in his hair.

"Did—Mrs. Parkins let you in?"

"Yes. I said I was your brother. A simple device." He peeled back her glove and put his lips to the back of her wrist. "I always believe in simplicity first. Mind, there was an occasion last year when I wanted to enter a young lady's apartment, and an old dragon of a mother was downstairs and inspected everyone who went up. So I borrowed the clothes of a seamstress and the old dragon passed me without a second glance! I made a tolerably good girl."

"I'm sorry," Demelza said, "I must ask you to leave, Captain Adderley."

"*Leave?* Do I offend you? How prettily you have arranged my flowers!"

"It was kind of you to send them to me." She knelt and poked at the fire, put on two pieces of coal, giving herself time to think. "But it does not entitle you to— to . . ."

"To enter your apartments by a stratagem? Oh, come. I had no other way of discovering you alone."

"Why do you wish to?"

"Look in the glass, my dear."

"I—am married, Captain Adderley."

"Oh, yes. That I do know." A hint of amusement in his voice.

"And my husband would not like to find you here."

"Nor shall he. I have a man outside who will delay him long enough in the street to enable me to slip away by the back entrance. But that is unlikely to be for two hours yet. They are droning on about the militia."

"Please go. I don't wish to send for Mrs. Parkins."

"I would not wish you to. But can we not at least talk a little while?"

"What about?"

"Any subject under the sun you choose. Life. Love. Letters. Let me tell you of the men I've killed."

"Next time we meet."

He went across to a vase. "Look at these. Do you see these? Do you know what these flowers are called?"

"No."

"They are called dahlias. D-a-h-l-i-a-s. They have been imported into England for use by the poor in place of the potato. But the saucy poor do not like the flavour; so now they are selling not the root but the flower."

He had come up to her again as he was speaking but she moved away.

"You will notice that they have no scent."

"I've noticed that."

"Let me relieve you of your cloak."

"When you have gone," she said.

His eyes were very narrow. "Are you afraid of me?"

"Not a bit."

"Do you dislike me?"

"No-o."

"You sound a little uncertain. Are you afraid of what I might do to you? Have you never had a man but your husband? Don't you want to understand any of the finer complexities of love?"

"Are you talking about love at all, Captain Adderley?"

He shrugged. "Call it what you will. I can instruct you most delicately in it all."

There was a moment's pause. He put his fingers gently on her breast; they lay there as light as a paw; then she as quietly moved away again.

He said: "You see?"

She turned: "What do I see?"

"How quickly you respond."

"You flatter yourself."

"Do I? Let me prove it."

She shook her head.

"I am—deeply enamoured," he said. "Don't suppose this is some trivial fancy. You are a very enchanting woman."

"I am—deeply flattered," she said. "But—"

"Let us sit down and I will tell you of your enchantment."

"I'm sorry."

"Why are you so harsh?"

"Harsh? Not at all! I just happen not to feel as you wish me to feel."

"It could be altered, I assure you. I have a sovereign remedy, which I will explain to you—"

"Not now. Another time, sir."

They stared at each other.

He said: "You have a strange voice, ecod. It's West Country, I suppose."

"I come from the West Country."

"Well, I like it. Do you cry out when a man takes you?"

She drew a deep breath. "In a moment—in a moment I think you will call me a prude, so perhaps I should say it now to save you the bother—"

"Ma'am, you put words into my mouth that I—"

"Are you a gentleman?"

He flushed. "I trust so." It was the first time she had ever seen colour in his face.

"Then—forgive me, as you rightly say I am from the far west and don't understand London manners—

but is it not a gentleman's duty to withdraw when a lady ask him?"

His eyes crinkled. "Only when the gentleman has already been in."

That settled it. She went to the bell rope. "I find that —remark a little . . . offensive. Will you please go."

He considered her a moment more, weighing up the probabilities. He took out his handkerchief and dabbed each nostril in turn.

"Perhaps I may wait upon you some other time."

"Please do."

He gave a little sniggering laugh. "Ecod!" he said. "I know what it is. It is not me you're terrified of, it's your husband! Does he beat you?"

"Yes, often."

"When his arm gets tired," Monk Adderley said, "tell him to send for me. Good night, Mrs. Poldark."

V

The Poldarks' second week was not as pleasant as the first. Demelza had told Ross of Adderley's visit, though she had glossed over the details. It was better that he should know from her than find out by accident and suppose she was deceiving him. He reprimanded Mrs. Parkins: in future no one must be admitted to their rooms while they were out, whatever the pretext. But their relationship did not settle down to what it had been before. A cloud of non-explanation and misunderstanding lay around them and could give rise to forked lightning at any time.

They visited the Royal Academy and the British Museum, and at the beginning of the third week they supped with the Boscawens at their house in Audley Street. This was not as much of an ordeal as Demelza had feared, since the Viscount's mother, the widow of the great admiral, was a vivacious old lady and made up for the absence of Mrs. Gower.

When the ladies retired the two men discussed the invasion of Holland, which, after the first successes, was becoming bogged down with problems of supply and by generals and admirals hesitant to take further risks. Lord Falmouth observed dryly that he had heard Captain Poldark had become something of a banker, and Ross explained what had occurred.

"I trust you don't feel this conflicts in any way with my ôbligation to you as a member of Parliament."

"No . . . Nor would I suppose you would take much heed of me if I said it did."

"There you do me an injustice, my lord. I would take heed of anything you say. Though obviously . . ."

"Yes, quite."

"But I hope that nowadays there are fewer areas of disagreement between yourself and Lord de Dunstanville . . ."

Lord Falmouth sniffed. "Basset's a pusher, and always has been. He's too *active* about the county. In some cases worthily enough, but most often serving his own ends. However, I believe his peerage has somewhat quieted him down. . . . Now I gather it is *Hawkins* who is befriending the Warleggans. If I know Sir Christopher, it will have been at a price."

"And George Warleggan would be willing to pay it."

"It is interesting," said Falmouth, dusting away the snuff, "if all you say about the Warleggans is true, they have, by putting such pressure on Pascoe's Bank, only succeeded in establishing Pascoe in a stronger position and made the other object of their feud—yourself—into his partner!"

Ross said: "I think Harris Pascoe would greatly prefer his own bank to this new arrangement, but it is true their success was limited. As for me, I don't look on mine as a serious appointment—but, yes, it is diverting, the way it has occurred."

"I would support it," said Lord Falmouth, "were there no other reason than that."

The following Monday there was to be a debate in the House on the new Treaty of Alliance with Russia. It was not something Ross felt deeply involved in, but some of the most famous speakers were likely to take part; Lord Holland was to move an amendment, and

Pitt and Fox were likely to take part. So he went at three to get a good seat for the debate, which would open at four.

But in the ordinary course of business of the House, a few smaller bills were in process of debate or amendment beforehand, and in one of these, relating to the treatment and succour of disabled soldiers and sailors, there was a call for a division, instead of for the customary show of hands, and Ross was sufficiently concerned to vote for the bill.

When such a division took place only one side was called to go out; and they were then counted as they came in again. The other side remained in their seats. It was the Speaker's responsibility to nominate which side should have to go, but normally he chose the side proposing and supporting a new bill. So it was in this case, and perhaps Ross should have known better than to move.

In a house which would barely seat 300 when the total numbers were 558 there was likely to be pressure for seats before an important debate; and it was the custom of the House that any member who vacated his seat to vote was liable to forfeit it. For this reason members often failed to vote for a bill they supported so that they should not lose their seats, and sometimes it was a tactic to call for a division, knowing that fewer people would walk out to support than would have called "Aye!"

In this case the bill was carried on its first reading by a majority of thirteen but when Ross returned he found his seat occupied by Captain Monk Adderley.

"Ah . . ." said Ross.

Adderley looked up at him through half-closed lids. "Lost something, Poldark?"

"Yes . . . my seat."

"That you cannot have, my dear. There is no such thing as *my* seat in this house, as you well know. You'll have to go and stand at the back, won't you."

A fat little man next to Monk chuckled but kept his eyes down.

"Is there such a thing as *my* gloves?" Ross asked.

"*Your* gloves? You should know, Poldark. Why should I?"

"Because I left them in this place. It occurred to me you might be sitting on them."

"I?" said Adderley, and yawned. "Not at all, my dear. I would not touch them. You see, I'm no longer interested in any of your . . . your worn possessions."

So many people were still walking about—others returning were trying to squeeze into seats—a man was on his feet speaking, or trying to speak, on some other bill—that only a dozen witnessed the sharp movement —scuffle—that broke out on the back benches. Ross's hand had flown out and clutched Adderley by the cravat; Adderley was hauled to his feet; with his other hand Ross picked up his gloves; Adderley was dropped back with a thump.

"Order! Order!" some members shouted.

"I beg your pardon, Adderley," Ross said, and handed him his hat, which had fallen off. "I felt sure my gloves were here. I beg your pardon, sir," he said, bowing to the Speaker, and left the Chamber.

VI

About two hours later a Mr. John Craven arrived at George Street and delivered a letter. It said:

Dear Poldark,

The Insult you paid me in the House was of a nature that brooks no apology. I know you to be an infamous braggart, and believe all your display of courage to be the mask for a cowardly disposition. I therefore desire to give you the opportunity of showing me whether this epithet is rightly applied or not.

I desire that you meet me in Hyde Park on Wednesday at 6 A.M. with a brace of pistols each, to determine our differences. My second, Mr. John Craven, carries this letter and I desire you to tell him whom you will appoint to represent you.

*I desire that this Meeting be kept a dead secret,
for reasons which must be plain to you.
I am, Sir, your humble servant,
Monk Adderley*

Chapter Five

Demelza was out when the letter came. He said nothing to her when she came back. That evening he walked round and had a talk with Dwight.

Dwight said: "But this is monstrous! A brief scuffle in the House? They're always happening! The man's *mad!* That injury to his head. I should ignore the whole thing."

"I have already written accepting."

Dwight stared at Ross as if unable to believe what he heard. "You have what? . . ."

"I have accepted."

"But, Ross! You should *not* have done! The whole thing must be stopped at once!"

"It can't be."

"But—but there's nothing at *stake!* The merest storm in a teacup . . . In any event, the fellow's a noted duellist. He's killed two or three men!"

"So have I."

"In duels?"

"Well, no. But I'm accustomed to using a gun. As the rooks know when they raid my crops."

"That's not a pistol, Ross! How long since you used one of those?"

"I'll take some practice tomorrow. You know why I came here? To ask you to be my second. Indeed, presuming on our friendship, I've already given your name."

Dwight bit at his glove. They were pacing the street

outside Caroline's house, and it was beginning to rain.

"Well?" said Ross.

"Yes, I'll be your second," Dwight said abruptly, "because then I have the right to interfere and see what may be done to have the whole scandalous nonsense called off."

"Small chance of that. Also—it is of advantage that you should be there, because in the event of either of us being wounded we shall need to look no further for a surgeon."

Dwight frowned at the letter by the yellow light of one of the street lamps. "What is the meaning of this emphasis on secrecy? I know of course—"

"John Craven explained it. If Adderley should be—accurate with his ball it is essential that it should not be known that he is responsible. If he stood a *third* trial he would be likely to go to prison for some years."

"As he deserves anyhow. But good God, he is the *challenger!* Are we to accept *his* conditions? I never heard of anything more outrageous!"

"It will suit me well," Ross said. "If I should kill Adderley it will not suit me to stand a trial either. Once is enough."

Dwight looked at his friend's dark face. "It will get about. This sort of thing can never be altogether hushed up."

"Well, that is something we shall both have to risk."

They stopped where a cellar trapdoor was open and two men like black dwarfs were unloading casks of ale from a dray. Beside it someone had tipped a load of bricks, making passage along the uneven pavement impossible.

"Does Demelza know aught of this?"

"No, and must not! Nor Caroline. Fortunately there is only a day to wait. Remember this, Dwight; you are sworn to secrecy. *No one* must be told."

"And are you proposing that we should go to Strawberry Hill tomorrow as arranged?"

"Of course. Otherwise they will guess something is in the wind."

Dwight shook his head in despair.

"And when will you get your pistol practice?"

"First thing. We don't leave until ten."

"So I must also be about early on my efforts at a reconciliation. Ross, what are the grounds on which you would agree to withdraw?"

"I have nothing to withdraw, Dwight. I have only accepted the challenge."

Dwight gestured irritably. "To say that you meant no offence in the House?"

"I apologised to him at the time."

"Did he hear it?"

"He should have done."

"Did you mean it?"

"No."

They turned back, towards the top of the Garden and the better houses.

"So . . . I never thought when I came to London that I should be involved in such a childish, *wicked* affair as this. Because it is *both,* Ross. When there is so much suffering and pain in the world already . . . And when we are at war. There is enough killing to be done without fighting among ourselves."

"You must tell Adderley that. If he wishes to withdraw his challenge on those grounds—or on any other honourable grounds—I'll be willing to let the matter drop."

Dwight said: "You speak as if you would not *really* be willing."

After a moment Ross said: "You know me too well, Dwight. Anyway, I leave it in your hands."

II

At ten next morning the quartet set out for Strawberry Hill. The house, built by the great Sir Horace Walpole, was one of the sights Caroline had planned they should see. It was fine again, after the cold rain of yesterday, with balustrades, of white cloud arranging themselves in the west; a good day to clear the smells of London; a good day for riding; and the distance little more than ten miles.

In a few minutes alone before they left Dwight was able to gesture his disgust and say: "If it were possible, he is more intransigeant than you. But while perhaps he has some excuse, being unstable, you have none."

"What would you have me do?" Ross asked. "Go to his lodgings and knock on his door and when he comes kneel and offer him an abject apology? An apology that I became annoyed at his insult to my wife?"

"Are you sure it was intended as such?"

"Of course. Nothing else."

"In any event a challenge like this is not important coming from such as him. I would suggest you go to see him this evening and tell him you have no interest in his false heroics. You are a veteran of the American war. If he calls you a coward people will only laugh—at him."

Ross smiled but did not reply.

They reached Twickenham at midday. Walpole had now been dead a couple of years, but the Hon. Mrs. Damer, the daughter of Walpole's great friend General Conway, was in residence and was maintaining the tradition of allowing only four people to visit the house daily.

Demelza found the gardens inspiring. Flowers she had never seen, trees and shrubs she had not imagined. "And, Ross, if we could have a *lawn* like this— or just a little like this—at Nampara. It is so smooth, so *green*." More indulgent towards her than he had been of late, Ross explained that grass would never grow so lush in the sandy soil of the north coast, and that this was all scythed to an inch in height by apprentices learning to be gardeners. Well, Demelza said, when she got home she would do *something*. She could have a lawn of a *sort*, not just tufts of grass pitted with rabbit scratchings and Garrick diggings. Think how much better her hollyhocks would look if you saw them across an expanse of neat, tidy, green lawn! And she saw a shrub like the one Hugh Armitage had given her, and it was called a magnolia. As soon as she saw the name she remembered it.

There was much of interest, too, in the eccentric house with its differing styles; and inside it was a treasure trove: one complete room full of Italian cameos, another with snuffboxes and miniatures. There were water colours and oil paintings and rosaries and bronzes and French glass and Brussels lace and porcelain figures from Dresden and Chinese masks and Turkish swords, and ivory figurines, and fans and clocks, and in a library so many books that it was impossible to guess at the number.

After dinner, on the way home, Demelza suggested that perhaps sometimes it was possible to be *too* rich and so accumulate too much of everything. Nothing, she thought, could be more exciting than to have a passion for something, whether it was fans, or ivory or glass, and then, if you could afford it, to build up a collection, precious piece by precious piece, so that you could put it on your shelves and take pleasure in it every time you saw it. But Sir Horatio, even though he had lived to be old, must have made some of his collections in great *quantities* at the same *time*. How, then, could you find the same pleasure? Six lovely things would always be six lovely things. Six thousand and you'd lose appreciation.

"It's like wives," said Ross. "Enough is enough."

"That cuts both ways," said Caroline. "Though I'm told there is a maharajah in India who lives in his palace, the only man among a thousand women."

"From what I hear," Dwight said, "women were one of the few treasures Walpole did not collect. But I agree with Demelza; a man of the most exquisite taste can still lack taste if he indulges it too freely."

"Like a man of courage?"

"Exactly."

As they drew near London, Caroline said: "Why don't you two sup with us? My aunt always has more on her table than she knows what to do with."

"I had thought," Ross said, "of visiting the theatre

again. There is a change of programme. It is a comic play by Goldsmith."

They all looked at him in surprise.

"We'll scarcely be back in time," Caroline said. "We should have no time to change."

"Then go as we are," said Ross. "Or miss the first act. It will be easy to pick up the story."

"Let's go as we are," said Demelza immediately. "What is the hour now? Oh yes, we could do that. And then, perhaps, we could sup afterwards."

So it was agreed. They stabled their horses at an ostler's in Stanhope Street and found seats in a box only five minutes after the curtain had gone up.

Thereafter for two hours they were brilliantly amused by the play. Sometimes Dwight glanced across at Ross. He knew that neither Ross's nor his own enjoyment could be anything but assumed. It was a remarkable effort of controlled behaviour on Ross's part, and Dwight now and then wondered if the other man, in one of his moods of dark fatalism, had almost totally accepted whatever the future had to bring.

They did not stay for the later plays, but just remained long enough to hear the orchestra in: "Shepherd, I have lost my waist, Have you seen my body? Sacrificed to modern taste, I'm quite a Hoddy-Doddy." Demelza humming it in her slightly husky sweet voice, they were at Hatton Garden by nine o'clock.

Mrs. Pelham was out, so they supped alone. It had just been announced that both houses of Parliament would adjourn early and would not be likely to reassemble before the third week in January; so this set Demelza off—in high spirits after the play—with thoughts of Christmas. Last year had been such a success that she wished exactly to repeat it. Caroline said it was always a mistake to attempt to repeat anything, and anyway Demelza could not, for she, Caroline, intended to spend Christmas in Cornwall this year, and that would break the pattern. Demelza said it would only improve the pattern, whereupon

Caroline replied, not at all so, and if fact, although personally she would look on it with some misgiving, she intended to command an attendance at Killewarren of *all* the Poldarks she could muster, not excluding the Blameys, however many of them happened to be not afloat at that particular season. She had heard what a ravishing young man James Blamey was, and she hoped to see for herself. And as for the children, well, she said, Killewarren's bigger than Nampara, so let us hear *some* little feet pattering about it, even if they are not Sarah's.

In a half-wry, half-jolly wrangling way, supper proceeded, until Mrs. Pelham arrived back with three guests, the first being that tall dark man of forty, the Hon. St. Andrew St. John, who was at present her "special friend." This devoted adherent of Fox was a bachelor, a landowner and a barrister, and had been undersecretary of state for foreign affairs under Fox when only twenty-four. Since then he had been in the wilderness with him; but he enjoyed London social life and most of all, it seemed, Mrs. Pelham. The second was Mr. Edward Coke of Longford, Derbyshire, a man of about the same age, who had made no mark in the House but had much to say out of it, another adherent of Fox; and the third, a rich, sour, sardonic old bachelor called Jeremiah Crutchley, who was member for St. Mawes and had been a friend of Samuel Johnson.

More seats were drawn up round the table, servants scurried with napkins and glasses and wine and dishes of food, and general chatter began. Presently Ross heard St. Andrew St. John mutter something in an undertone to Dwight, and he immediately said:

"May I ask you to repeat that, sir?"

St. John said: "Supper, I think, is a time for *bavarderie,* not serious talk. But I mentioned to your friend that it is reported General Buonaparte has given the blockading squadrons the slip and reached France."

"When? . . ."

"Early this month," Coke put in. "They say the great man was at sea six weeks and scarcely escaped capture! He landed at Fréjus with a bare half dozen of an escort, and was greeted like a king. Fox was thinking of sending him a message of congratulation."

There was silence. Ross held his tongue.

Presently he said: "Certainly, since Hoche died, Buonaparte stands alone. The French armies no doubt will look on him as their saviour."

"Which it's doubtful if he can be," said Crutchley, who, like Ross, supported Pitt and the war effort. "While he's been bottled up in Egypt, all his conquests in Europe have been lost. Now we have a firm foothold in Holland it will be no time before Russia joins us there. Nearly all the French possessions overseas are in our hands: Ceylon, all of southern India, the Cape of Good Hope, Minorca, Trinidad. The best that their 'saviour' can do is rally the defeated armies and sue for peace."

"There's been a great bungling of our efforts in the Helder," said Coke, with some satisfaction. "More determination would have given us the whole of Holland by now."

"If Abercrombie had not been forced to use his raw militia last week—"

"Gentlemen," Caroline said. "Mr. St. John is right. The supper table is for light talk, however weighty the platters we put on it. This *soirée* you have been to: was it an interesting evening?"

III

They stayed late, drinking and laughing and talking. It had been a long day in the open air and Demelza's eyes were pricking with sleep long before they finally said good night and took two hackney chairs home. Ross had been slow to leave, and she could not know that it was a part of his design that she should be tired and sleep late in the morning.

When she lay in bed at last she talked for a moment or two about the Strawberry Hill garden and all the fascinating things there were in it. No one in Cornwall, it seemed to her, had begun to lay out a garden like this. There was a small formal garden at Tregothnan, and splendid landscaping had been done at places like Tehidy and Trelissick. But this was *small* landscaping, within the compass of a few acres; superbly arranged trees of all shapes, sizes, and colours; golden bushes, blue pyramids, grey towering sentinels, with all the profusion of flowering plants set between and showing them off. Where did you *get* such trees and shrubs: where did you *buy* them; did you have to order them from the Indies and Australia and America? Ross answered yes, and no, and I have little idea, and perhaps we can inquire. He should, he knew, have warned her again that not a quarter of the plants she coveted would stand the sandy soil and salt-laden winds of the north Cornish coast; but for the moment he had not the heart. He waited until she had fallen asleep, and then he quietly undressed and slid into bed beside her and lay for a long time, hands behind head, staring up at the ceiling.

He had arranged to be wakened at five; and he rose and by the light of a shaded candle washed and shaved and brushed and combed his hair. It was still pitch dark outside, and was likely still to be so at six. He supposed that by the time the preliminaries had been gone through dawn would be breaking. One presumably had to be able to *see* one's opponent.

He had never himself fought a duel before, but he had been second to a brother officer in New York when he had quarrelled with a lieutenant in another regiment, and they had fought it out in the fields behind the encampment. Both had been severely wounded. Even then, when he was himself only twenty-two and more romantically inclined, he had thought the whole procedure an exaggerated and outdated way of settling differences. In the camp at that time there was an average of one duel every week, and frequently good men killed; and he knew that although decrees had been issued by both the civilian and the military authorities, the frequency of such affrays had scarcely dropped since then.

Often the dispute was of the lightest, some joke misinterpreted. Dwight was wrong in supposing his disagreement with Adderley too trivial for such a resolution. Only last March when he was in London there had been a quarrel in Stephenson's Hotel in Bond Street. Viscount Falkland had been drinking there with some friends, among them a Mr. Powell, and Falkland had merely said: "What, drunk again, Pogey?" whereupon Powell had made a sharp reply and Falkland had hit him with a cane. In the resultant duel Falkland, a man of forty-one, had been shot dead. So it went on, and so it would go on. But he had not supposed that he himself would ever be involved in such an affray.

Long years ago he had made a will, and it was deposited with Mr. Pearce—and would now presumably have been passed on among all the other boxes of legal documents to whoever was taking over the remnants of Mr. Pearce's devastated practice—but that had been done before the children were born, when he had been about to be tried for his life in Bodmin. He supposed he should have made some later attempt to set his affairs in order. He knew one or two Cornishmen who made a fresh will whenever they set out for London.

Well, it was too late now. In less than an hour the matter would be decided. At five forty-five he heard the clop of hooves. Most of the lamps in the narrow sloping street had gone out for lack of fish oil, but the few left showed that Dwight, for all his angry protests, was not late for his appointment.

Ross glanced at the sleeping figure of his wife. Her face was half hidden and he decided not to make any attempt to touch her, for she was quick to wake. He put on his cloak and hat, tiptoed to the door, which creaked maddeningly, and then, guttering candle in hand, went down the stairs. At the outer door he blew out the candle put it on a ledge, and stepped into the street.

The air was cold, and a light drizzle was falling. Ross mounted the other horse that Dwight had brought, and stared at his friend.

"Did you have any difficulty? . . ."

Dwight said: "Only the difficulty of believing that so rational a man as yourself, and my best and oldest friend, should indulge in such madness and pursue it to the bitter end."

Ross said: "Unless the sky lightens soon there will be more danger to the birds in the trees. Or do we hold a torch in our left hand?"

Dwight said: "Even by the absurd standards of today, this meeting is ridiculously irregular. As challenger Adderley must give you choice of weapons. Yet before you even consult me you accept all his terms."

"Because they suit me. I have never used a sword except in practice with the regiment seventeen years ago. At least with a pistol I have a very good idea what happens when the trigger is pulled."

"*Did* you take some practice yesterday morning?"

"Yes, with a sergeant at the Savoy. His chief advice however, seemed to be 'Watch how you load the pistol, sir: too much gunpowder destroys the equilibrium, too much velocity affects the precision of the ball. If anything, sir, it is better to undercharge.' Since you will be in command of the pistols and not I, I can only pass on this gem of wisdom for your attention."

They turned and began to move up the hill. They rode along the Strand and up Cockspur Street and the Hay Market to Piccadilly, thence to Hyde Park Corner. There were a few shadowy figures still skulking about, seeking whom or what they might pick up or rob. As their horses turned up Tyburn Lane the watch was ringing his bell and calling: "Past six o'clock and all's well." It was his last call before he went home. In the Park although there was no wind the leaves were falling regularly like

359

some too conventional stage set. The rain had just stopped. In the dim light there seemed no one about when they reached the ring, and, for the five minutes they sat there while their horses' nostrils steamed in the still morning, Dwight had time to hope that Adderley had thought better of his challenge. But presently there was the clop of a hoof and the snort of a restive horse, and two figures loomed up in the semi-dark.

"As God is my judge," said Monk, erect as a lancer. "I thought you'd run home to Cornwall."

"As God is my judge," said Ross, "I thought you were going to plead benefit of clergy."

It was not a good beginning on which to base a move of reconciliation, but as they rode further into the trees Dwight drew Craven aside, and after they had dismounted there was a further conference. In the meantime Ross paced slowly across the clearing they had chosen, hands behind back, taking deep breaths of the fresh morning, listening to the occasional sleepy chirrup of a waking bird. Adderley stood quite still, like one of those thin pencil trees Demelza had so admired yesterday.

There was now a faint glimmer of light showing from over in the direction of the city. The air was fresh here, with none of the town smells to pollute it. The leaves squelched under Ross's feet. Dwight came across. His face looked thin.

"I've agreed with Craven that the light will be good enough in twenty minutes. We have that time still to come to some accommodation."

"I want no accommodation," said Ross.

"God curse it!" Dwight said, and it was rare for him to swear; "have *neither* of you any sense? The bloodletting will solve nothing!"

"Let us walk," Ross said. "The morning air is chill, and warm blood makes for a steady hand."

They began to walk through the trees, a hundred yards this way, a hundred back again.

Ross said: "Let us not dramatise the situation, Dwight; but if by chance his aim is better than mine, you and Caroline, as our close friends, will bear a responsibility for the future of those in Nampara."

"Of course."

"There is nothing writ. It will all have to be understood."

"It is understood."

Time passed slowly. Ross remembered a story he had heard somewhere of two men who had challenged each other to a duel, and they happened to be dining together at one of their houses in a great company of society. Having dined and spent the evening and supped, they left at one, and each rode to the rendezvous in his own coach and sat there in the dark, till six, when they got out and shot each other to death.

Trees at last were assuming definition; and in the distance the shape of buildings could be seen. Fortunately with the end of the rain had come a break in the clouds, so that as sunrise neared the day broke suddenly.

Dwight said: "Come, it is time."

Chapter Six

They came together and while the pistols were examined and loaded Dwight made one more effort.

"Captain Adderley, I think it is acknowledged even by you that at the time of this disagreement in the House Captain Poldark apologised for his brief loss of temper. That is the act of a gentleman and it would equally be the act of a gentleman if you were now to accept it. Why do you not both shake hands and go home to a hearty breakfast? No one knows of this encounter except yourselves. At your request it has been kept secret. Therefore there is no honour to be maintained in the face of other people. There is nothing to lose and everything to gain by looking on this as a superficial quarrel not worthy of bloodshed."

Adderley's macabre face looked as if it had spent all its time in the dark. "If Captain Poldark will apologise again now, and undertake to send me a written apology couched in suitable terms, I might consider it. Though I should think ill of him if I did so."

Dwight looked at Ross.

Ross said: "My only regret was that I apologised in the first place."

Dwight made a gesture of despair, and Craven said: "Come, gentlemen, we are wasting time. It should all be over before sunup."

"One thing," Adderley said. "I take it that your second has given to mine the letter of challenge that I wrote you."

"Yes. You asked for it."

"And mine has given to yours your reply. So there is no evidence as to the occurrence of this duel, except for the presence of these two men, who are sworn to secrecy. The noise of the pistols may attract attention even at this early hour, so I should kill you or wound you I shall waste no time in inquiring into your injuries but shall mount and ride away as quick as I can. If by mischance you should injure me instead you have my full permission to do the same. And the injured party has been set upon by a highwayman."

"Agreed," Ross said.

"I would hate," Adderley said, "to languish in gaol for shedding *your* blood, my dear."

So they stood back to back. They were both tall men, and much of a height, but Ross the bigger-boned. Pistols in hand, one in each hand, loaded and primed. Too much gunpowder destroys the equilibrium, sir. If anything, sir, it is better to undercharge. Too much velocity affects the precision of the shell. Was this fear one felt? Not quite. A keyed-up will for violence, to destroy something that was half in the other man, half in oneself. To fire. To fire. Imagination stopped. So did apprehension. Flesh and its frailty was not as important as will and its integrity. One put all one's future on the table for the throw of a die. Heart pounding but hands calm, eyes clear, senses over-acute, smell of wood smoke, sound of a distant bell.

"Fourteen paces," said Craven. "I will count. *Now*. One, two, three."

The paces were slow as his count was slow.

". . . Thirteen, fourteen. Attend. Present. Fire!"

They both fired simultaneously and it seemed both missed. The light was still not too good. Ross had heard the ball go past.

"That will do!" Dwight said, moving forward.

Adderley dropped the empty pistol and changed hands, raised the other. As he saw this Ross did the same. Just as he fired the pistol was knocked out of his hand and he felt a searing pain in his forearm. To his surprise the force of the ball had swung him round. He half doubled, clutching his arm, and then through the smoke saw Adderley on the ground.

Blood was oozing through his fingers in great thick gushes. Dwight was beside him, was trying to tear the rest of the torn sleeve away.

"Adderley," Ross said. "You'd best go and see—"

"In a moment. You must get that—"

"Dr. Enys!" Craven was plucking at his coat. "Captain Adderley is serious wounded."

"Go on," said Ross, as Dwight hesitated.

Dwight said: "Get something round your upper arm quick as you can—else you'll bleed to death."

Ross sat down on a stone and tried to tear a piece of his shirt; it wouldn't give; eventually a piece of lace came away, and though it was thin it was strong. He wound this below his biceps with his left hand and then, unable to tie it, just twisted and twisted till it grew very tight. Then he could only hold it there. His forearm was a mess. Could not see if the ball had smashed the bone, but he had lost the use of his fingers. The trees were moving in an odd way, and it was all he could do not to keel over onto the damp, sere leaves.

The three men were over there in a group—could

not be more than thirty paces away—clearly. Had he hit with his first or his second shot? And if so, how good (or bad) had been his aim? He gritted his teeth, got up. Arm was still bleeding but it was not *gushing* out. More blood than he'd ever lost from his two wounds in America. He began to walk.

Just like pacing out for the duel, only twice as far. Long way. Twenty-eight paces. Adderley was stirring. That was good thing. Not dead. Not dead. As he came up John Craven suddenly left the group, went running off through the trees towards the gate of the park.

Dwight had his bag and had cut away Adderley's coat and shirt and waistcoat, was holding a pad of gauze. It seemed to be at the base of the stomach, or the top of the right leg. Ross swayed up to them.

Adderley's eyes fluttered. "Damned pistols," he muttered. "Not . . . accurate. Damn near missed you altogether . . . my dear."

Ross said: "Where's Craven gone?"

"To get a chair," Dwight said.

"Didn't . . . ride . . ."

"He thought it quicker. There's usually chairs by the toll gate. Look, sit down here. Then if you can hold this pad on Adderley's thigh with your left hand I can tie your arm."

"Hold the pad myself," Adderley said. "You get off, Poldark. While the going's good. That's—what we agreed."

"I'll stay till the chair comes," Ross said.

"Damn fool," said Adderley. "I knew it. Wish I'd *killed* you. No room for damned fools."

Ross squatted on the grass and held the pad over Monk's stomach, while Dwight tied up his arm. It was done with much speed and efficiency, and after a few minutes Dwight was able to slacken the tourniquet he had first put on.

"Can you ride home?" he asked.

"I—suspect so."

"Then go. Adderley's right. Craven might come back with a couple of the watch."

"Shoot him if he does," said Adderley.

"He might have no choice."

"I'll stay till the chair comes," Ross said obstinately.

Shafts of early sunlight were touching the tops of the trees. The faded leaves, still damp, were lit up with brass spears. Monk was only half conscious now. Ross looked at Dwight inquiringly. Dwight made a non-committal gesture.

They waited.

Leaves continued to fall, making eccentric landings on the trio of silent men. Running feet, and Craven came into view followed by a hackney chair. Panting, the chairmen set the chair down, and with great difficulty Monk Adderley was lifted into it. He seemed at this stage to have fainted altogether.

Dwight said: "Mr. Craven, I'll go with this chair. Do you help Captain Poldark to mount and then bring the other horses."

Ross said: "I think I'll come with you."

"No," said Craven. "Fair's fair, and the conditions have been properly observed. So observe the rest. I advise you to go home and send for another physician."

While the chair moved off, Craven somehow pushed Ross up onto his horse, and with his bad arm held in a temporary sling, Ross gathered the reins and turned his horse quietly round to begin what was going to be an interminable journey to George Street.

II

By nine Dwight was round. He found Ross in bed but unattended, since he had refused to see any other physician. Demelza was doing what she could for him. She was looking more sick than Dwight had ever seen her since she had had the morbid sore throat.

"Well," said Ross. "What of Adderley?" and gritted his teeth while Dwight cut away the bandage.

"I've extracted the ball, which had lodged almost in the groin. Lead is sterile and I have taken what precautions I can."

There was silence while he examined the wound. "Well?"

"It could be worse. The ball has split a splinter off the radius. I'll have to take that piece of bone out. The ulna is sound."

"Damned if I know whether I hit him with the first or the second shot."

"The second. The blow on your arm deflected your aim fractionally down. Demelza, have you a bowl?"

"Here."

"A bigger one. And brandy. This will be more painful than it should be, Ross, because if it had been done at once the shocked arm would still have been partly insensitive."

"I don't want brandy," Ross said. "Just do what you have to do."

So Dwight did what he had to do, and there was a lot of blood, and a moment when he had to saw the edge of the splintered bone. And sweat ran down Ross's face and he gripped the bed with his good hand until the rail bent, and there were sweat and tears on Demelza's face, and then presently the bandages were going back, and Demelza, anxious to keep everything as secret as possible, was carrying the bloody bowls out herself, and Dwight was closing his bag. And then they all sat and did drink brandy. And there was a long silence between them. The few words that were dropped into the silence did not keep it at bay. They had all retreated into their own thoughts: wry, bitter, anxious, recollective. Outside, London was fully awake, and the customary noises in the street were temporarily joined by the lowing of a cow. Upstairs two maids were busy: you could hear their footsteps on the floor.

At length Dwight tried to break the sour spell.

"Have you ever heard of a man called Davy?"

Ross looked up. "Who?"

"Davy. Humphrey Davy, I think he's called."

"No." He made an effort. "Who is he?"

"A Cornish youth working in some laboratory in Bristol. He claims to have discovered—or invented—

some new gas called nitrous oxide which he says induces insensibility when the fumes are breathed. The man is not yet twenty-one, but has already published his findings. He claims that, as the gas is capable of destroying pain, it may probably be used to advantage in surgical operations. I could have wished for some now."

"So could I have," said Ross.

Dwight got up.

"No doubt even if his claims be true it will be years before my profession puts it to the test. We are nothing if not conservative in our ideas."

There was a further oppressive silence.

"Is the pain easier?" Demelza asked.

"A little," said Ross. "Do you know, I have been considering. However much Adderley may have wished to keep this secret, it seems very likely to come out, now we are both in this condition."

Demelza looked at Ross, his drawn face, the blood already seeping through the new bandage. And she thought: I shall never forgive him for this.

III

And she thought it all the following days. To her it seemed like a blasphemy against life, to risk so much for so little. It showed a newer, darker side of Ross than even she had ever known. But also it showed a person bound by a foolish tradition of his class that he of all people should have been clear-sighted enough to disavow.

He was so introspective, and anyway so ill for a few days, that she could not bring herself to say anything to him, and the only person she could unburden herself to was Caroline.

Caroline said: "I was surprised myself—and yet, looking at it now, I am not so surprised. It was always —on the cards."

"I don't know what you mean."

Caroline steered away from explaining. "Monk

Adderley's a fighter. He will be all his days. It was just misfortune that he chose Ross."

Demelza's dark eyebrows wrinkled and contracted painfully. "That is not what you meant at all, Caroline. And it is not what I mean. They speak of honour. Honour having to be satisfied. What is honour?"

"A code of conduct. A long tradition. Ross would have lost respect if he had not fought."

"Respect? Whose respect? Not mine. And what else might he not have lost which is a small matter more important? His life? His health? We don't know even yet if those are safe. His wife, his children, his home, his career? What are those compared to respect?"

"Men are like that."

"I don't want men who are like that! Four years ago, Caroline, Ross risked all this before—to recover Dwight from Quimper prison in France. *That* is what I call honour. This I call dishonour!"

Caroline looked at her friend. "Go kindly with him, Demelza. You know him better than I; but if I read him right he will not escape his own self-criticism over this affair."

"So he should not! . . . But, Caroline, I feel so much of it is my fault."

"Your fault!"

"Well, my responsibility, like. It was over me. The quarrel was *really* over me. You know that, don't you."

"I know it was *partly* over you. But I do not believe it would have got so far on that alone. Ross and Monk detested each other from the moment they laid eyes on each other, and that is something in the blood, not a matter of behaviour."

Demelza got up. *"Was* my behaviour at fault?"

"None that I saw."

"You see, I was—happy. Ross and I were happier together than we had been since—since before Hugh; and I was excited, *enjoying* myself in a new society. Perhaps I was freer with Monk Adderley than I ought to have been. Maybe I'm too *free* for London society. Maybe men—anywhere—take too much encouragement from my manner, even in Cornwall. But it's the way I was *born*. Of course in all these years I've learned a lot, but maybe I haven't learned enough. Ross should never have brought me!"

"My dear, you can't make a general principal out of a single mishap. You could have come to London twenty times without this happening! Take heart that it's no worse. One or both of them might have been dead."

Demelza said: "That's what I think every minute of the day."

And then Monk Adderley died.

IV

Ross's fever was abating by the third day, and he was just making plans to get up, much against Demelza's wishes, to call on his adversary when John Craven arrived with the news.

Ross stared at him in grey silence, lying back on the pillows from which he had just part risen. Demelza, by the window, bit the back of her hand.

Craven said: "His own doctor was with him two hours before, and Dr. Enys visited him last eve, but there was nothing to be done. There appeared, Dr. Enys said, to have been some blockage in a blood vessel."

"When? . . ."

"This forenoon." John Craven brushed a hand across the arm of his tidy jacket, glanced at Demelza and then away. "I came to tell you because that was what he wished. And to warn you."

"Yes. I see that."

"He has given it out that he was practising with his pistols in the Park, when one of them was accidentally discharged into his stomach. This I will confirm."

"Thank you, Mr. Craven."

"Don't thank me, Captain Poldark. It comes distasteful in me to condone a lie and indeed to call in question my own honour in so doing."

"Then do not do it."

"Dr. Enys and myself were both sworn to this before the duel began. As it turned out, it may be necessary to go further than we had ever expected; but that is not your fault but the fault of the undertaking."

"Then I'll release you from it."

"Ross—"

Mr. Craven looked again at Demelza. "Have no fear, ma'am. I don't think he can release us from it, even if he so chooses. The man who could do that is dead."

No one spoke.

Craven said: "Captain Adderley also told me to tell you—and here I simply pass on his message, sir—that you were a damned fool to stay in the Park until the chairmen came; so there could be two witnesses that another man, also wounded, was in the vicinity. You are obviously, sir, in no position yet to hide your own wound. However, Captain Adderley instructed me to pay each of the chairmen five guineas to stop his mouth, and I think this will be sufficient."

Ross swallowed and licked his lips. "I was this moment about to come and see him. I wished to go yesterday but Dr. Enys said I must not move for another day. Now . . ."

Craven coughed. "Captain Adderley said I must point out to you that you now owed him ten guineas."

Ross stared. "Well, of course; do you wish me to—"

"He said it was not to go into his estate but requested that it be paid to Mr. George Warleggan in settlement of a wager."

Demelza turned sharply from the window, but decided to say nothing.

Ross said: "A wager in which I was involved?"

"Not necessarily, sir. I have no idea what the subject of the wager was."

Two women were screaming at each other in the street outside, and further down hand bells were being rung by a variety of hawkers.

Ross said: "I take it Captain Adderley had no dependants, Mr. Craven?"

370

"None. He left a one-line will in which he said he left everything he owned to Miss Adromeda Page."

Ross grimaced as he moved his bad arm.

"I'm much indebted to you, Mr. Craven. Can we offer you a brandy? There's little else."

"Thank you, no. I must be on my way. I have to tell Dr. Enys. There will be an inquest tomorrow."

"Of course I will be present."

"Of course you must not. That would defeat the whole object of the conditions for the duel laid down by Captain Adderley from the beginning. As I have said, I do not fancy any part in this affair—certainly not my own."

"The fact that I did not see him before he died, to make this matter up, is something I shall regret for the rest of my life."

Craven shrugged. "Well, Captain Poldark, it was a fair fight, fairly conducted. I can vouch for that. You have nothing to reproach yourself with. Monk Adderley was a strange man, given to excess. I have to tell you that though he bore you not the slightest ill-will for the mortal wound you inflicted on him, one of his last remarks to me was 'I wish I'd killed that man.' "

V

The coroner's inquest was held in the upper room of the Star Garter Inn, Pall Mall. Demelza had wanted to go and listen but Dwight said no. The less sign of any connection with Captain Adderley, the better it would be. So she stayed with Ross at home and waited to be told what happened.

It took about an hour. The first witness was a Mrs. Osmonde, Adderley's landlady, who testified to his arrival home at seven-thirty one morning with a severe wound in the groin. He was brought in by two chairmen and was accompanied by Mr. Craven and Dr. Enys. Captain Adderley then retired to his bed, she said, having told her that he had shot himself accidentally while practising with his pistol in Hyde Park. He had also made a sworn statement to this effect and she had been one of the witnesses to his signature. Mr. Craven was then called to the witness box and said that he had been out riding in the early morning and had heard a shot. He had ridden in the direction of the sound and found his friend Captain Adderley lying on the ground bleeding from a body wound. He had at once gone for two chairmen, and on the way had met Dr. Enys, who had come back with him to the injured man, and had given him temporary treatment until they could get him home. He confirmed Mrs. Osmonde's further testimony, and had been the other witness to Adderley's statement. Answering the coroner, he agreed that Captain Adderley was a noted duellist but denied that he knew of any assignation that morning. Further questioned, he stated that there was no one else but Adderley on the scene when he arrived.

Dr. Enys was then called, and testified that he had been brought into Hyde Park by Mr. Craven and had attended on the wounded man on the spot, and later at his lodgings until the time of his death. "Was there no one else about when you arrived to attend to the wounded man?" the coroner asked. Dr. Enys hesitated fractionally, licked his lips, and then said: "No, sir." Dr. Corcoran followed him into the box and confirmed Dr. Enys's report that Captain Adderley had died from the effects of a pistol ball which had wounded him in the groin and later caused a seizure of the blood vessels and cardiac failure. "Could this wound have been self-inflicted?" the coroner asked, a question he had failed to put to Dwight. Dr. Corcoran said he considered it unlikely but not impossible. Dr. Enys was then recalled and asked the same question. Dr. Enys said he thought it was possible.

The coroner then asked if the two chairmen had been traced; but they had not; indeed, it seemed that they had vanished, and none knew their names. The jury retired and were out ten minutes. They brought in a verdict of "Death by Misadventure."

Yet almost by the time the inquest was taking place it had become common knowledge in parliamentary and social circles as to what had happened. No one knew how it had leaked out. There was of course the brief fracas in the House. Perhaps Adderley had said something to Andromeda Page. It then just remained a moot point as to whether the authorities would decide to move against the survivor—whether if they did there was any sort of proof more substantial than "common" knowledge. Ross was determined to go to Adderley's funeral, and it took Dwight's brute force to prevent him. To go to the funeral might invite an insult or an outburst from one of Monk's friends; it would in any event certainly invite comment.

Fortunately, from this point of view, he was still very unwell, and only sat up in his chamber for an hour or two each day. His wounds in America, while in a way more serious, had scarcely incommoded him more. Dwight watched the arm with anxiety. It was refusing to heal.

Demelza forced herself to catechise Ross on what his attitude would be if a constable or some other representative of the law called on them. At first he had said that he could only answer the questions. When she had asked him if he would answer truthfully or untruthfully he had replied that it depended on what he was asked. This did not satisfy her, and she put question after question to him to see what he would say. It wasn't very satisfactory until she asked him what was the point of two honourable men perjuring themselves on his behalf if at the end of it he was going to despise their help?

So one day slowly followed another, and they both sat indoors waiting for the official knock.

Chapter Seven

In his own twisted way Adderley had played the game with his opponent until the very end, so that George Warleggan did not even hear of his wound until the Thursday. He went round to Adderley's lodgings on the Friday morning, to find the curtains already drawn and a landlady going on with her work while she waited for the boy to come back with Dr. Corcoran to pronounce life extinct. Even then it took time to elicit the facts. He went along to the inquest, still not sure of them, but suspecting what might have happened. Whispered gossip confirmed his suspicions during the next few days, and he was furious to feel that Adderley's adversary might escape the law.

On the Monday following he called on Mr. Henry Bull, K.C., at his office in Westminster. Nine years ago Mr. Bull had been concerned as leader for the Crown in a case in Cornwall where a man had been on trial for his life on a charge of riot, inciting others to riot and to wreck, and for assault on a customs officer. At that time George had got to know Mr. Bull, and since then had kept in touch with him as he watched his rise to a position of influence. He was now King's Advocate, which meant he was the principal law officer of the Crown in the admiralty and ecclesiastical courts.

He seemed to George the most suitable person to approach—the most suitable whom he knew, that was—and Mr. Bull, aware of Mr. Warleggan's growing power and influence, was careful to welcome him with a due display of courtesy and attention. With courtesy and attention he heard Mr. Warleggan state his complaint.

"Well, yes," he said. "Of course I remember Poldark well. Stiff-necked fellow. He should have hanged then if justice had been done, but your Cornish juries are too sentimental to their own. But this case, sir, this case—even if everything that's whispered be true, where's your evidence? Eh? Eh? The inquest's been held, the verdict's Death by Misadventure. To overset that we should need some fresh evidence to corroborate all this talk."

"Poldark has been wounded and is confined to his apartment. That is common knowledge."

"Yes. True enough. But it's only an inference that there is a connection. People may be jumping to conclusions."

"At least he should be interrogated."

"He could be. But I'm not certain on what grounds, eh? No one has actually *accused* him of anything. Adderley's dead. No one saw Poldark in Hyde Park that morning. Or if they did they've lied to save his skin. Looks to me there must have been some sort of pact. All very irregular, but y'know Adderley's been in more trouble than Poldark—at least so far as duelling is concerned—I would suppose they agreed to fight it out between themselves without seconds, nobody there at all, devil take the one who fell. Most irregular, I must say: not the way gentlemen should behave. But they're two army men; infantry at that; both mad as Ajax; what can you expect?"

"To me," said George, "it is outrageous to suppose that his great friend Craven should 'just have been passing' at the time of the shot. Also that Dr. Enys should be out in that area so early in the morning. No attempt—virtually no attempt—has been made to trace the chairmen who bore Adderley home. Nor any attempt to find any other witnesses to the scene. The whole thing stinks of contrivance, sir!"

"May be. May be." Mr. Bull pursed his thick lips and stared at the papers in front of him. "Well, Mr. Warleggan, happy as I should be to help—though it's not really my territory—there's little *official* action I can suggest at this stage. If unofficial inquiries should uncover some promising information I shall be glad to hear it and to forward it to the correct quarters."

With that George had to be content for the time being, but on his regular attendances at White's, where he had been careful to go three times a week since his election, he had noticed that Sir John Mitford, the Attorney General, was a member. George knew him by sight but no more; but he had already spotted a member who knew everyone and who was short of money and keen to befriend those who had much of it, so one evening he laid in wait, and after seeing Sir John go into the smoking room after dinner, he called on his new friend to contrive an introduction.

Presently it was done. Mitford accepted the introduction with a good grace, and after a few moments of casual talk the third man faded out.

So George was able to run the conversation tactfully in the direction he wanted, and remarked how much the club must be feeling the loss of one of its most popular members. Who was that? asked Mitford; ah, yes, and his eyebrows came together, ah, yes, young Adderley, something of a pity, though the fellow could never play a fair hand of whist without turning it into an outrageous gamble. George said he particularly regretted the loss because Monk Adderley in fact had been his proposer in the club, and was an old and valued friend. After a few more such remarks the word "murder" got itself inserted into the conversation. Murder? said Sir John, who says so? The verdict was Misadventure. George smiled and said, oh, yes, sir, but nobody believes that.

"Ah," said Mitford, "you mean this story of a duel? It's current, I know. What is the name of the fellow who's name is linked with all this? Pol-something. Don't know that I've ever met him or know anything about him."

George gave a brief, loaded summary of Ross's career, with some detail of the charges brought against him in Bodmin and the general agreement that he was guilty of the indictment but had been freed by a prejudiced jury.

"Ah," said Mitford. "He sounds a bit of a rake-helly. But then so was Adderley. Little to choose between 'em, I should say. Pity they didn't kill each other."

"Well, Sir John, but they did *not*," said George. "If I may venture to say so, should Poldark now go free, without even being *charged*, it would be a grave miscarriage of justice."

Mitford looked at the other man from under his eyebrows. "My dear Mr. Warlesson, I am not, as you will appreciate, able to keep an eye on all the day-to-day mishaps that occur in this metropolis. Nor is anyone else. The city is gravely underpoliced, as you must know. In the whole district of Kensington, for instance, there are only three constables and three head boroughs to police an area of fifteen square miles. What can you expect from that?" Sir John cleared his throat noisily. "But then, looking at it all the way round, who is to say Adderley did not take his own life deliberate? We know how hard drove he was for money. There's some in this club will never see the colour of their gold again. But even if it was as you say . . ."

"Yes? . . ."

"Adderley was not shot in the back, was he? No one's saying this fellow Pol-something didn't shoot him in fair fight?"

"Duelling is illegal in the eye of the law, Sir John. All the great authorities—Coke, Bacon, and the rest —have stated that it differs nothing from ordinary murder. And this is worse, being a secretive assignation."

Sir John got up. "I have a business appointment, so I trust you'll excuse me, sir. As to the law of the land, it so happens that I am acquainted with it. If a man is killed in a duel, his opponent shall be indicted for murder. The law of the land, however, I would remind you, demands evidence as to fact. Gossip and suspicion are noticeably unreliable witnesses when they go into the box. When you have something more concrete to go on than the tittle-tattle of the drawing rooms, pray let me know."

On the way out to the gaming rooms Sir John looked at the list of new members posted in the hall to ascertain that Mr. Warlesson was on it.

So George paid two men to make further inquiries, and Ross continued to nurse his wound while Demelza waited.

II

They had a fair number of visitors. The fiction that he had shot himself while priming his pistol was elaborately maintained, and talk was of the failure, after all the high hopes, of the campaign in Holland, of the bitterness and suspicion between the Russians and the English as an outcome, of the fact that the Russians who had landed at Yarmouth were drinking the oil out of the street lamps, of the acclaim with which General Buonaparte was being greeted in France, of the hopes of peace and of the weariness of the eight-year war. Or they talked of the latest play, the latest scandal, or the latest rumours as to the King's health. Nothing more personal at all.

And through it all, in the back of Demelza's mind, jingling now with a peculiar malevolence, ran the ditty whose tune she could not forget:

> *Shepherd, I have lost my waist,*
> *Have you seen my body?*
> *Sacrificed to modern taste,*
> *I'm quite a Hoddy-Doddy ...*

There was one surprise visitor. When Mrs. Parkins gave in his name Demelza went to the door to make sure she had heard aright. It was Geoffrey Charles Poldark.

"Well, well, Aunt Demelza—looking so anxious! Do you suppose I am a ghost? May I be permitted to see my respected uncle?"

Pale and thin, he came in. Ross was sitting in a chair in a morning gown, his arm still throbbing, but feeling better in health. He smiled at the young man, and offered his left hand, but Geoffrey Charles bent and kissed him on the cheek. Then he kissed Demelza. He was dressed in a blue and brown striped silk cloth coat and breeches with a white silk waistcoat.

"Blister my tripes!" he said. "Uncle Ross, what is this I hear, that you have been shooting off your own hand? As God's my life I should never have guessed you could be anything so careless! And how is it? Part mended, I hope? Near as good as new? Are you going to try your foot next, because I should advise against it. Feet are more painful."

Ross said: "I'd warn you it is hazardous to jest with an invalid. My temper is very short. But what are you doing here—playing truant from your studies to become a fop?"

"What am I doing here? There's gratitude for you! I'm visiting a sick relative, that is what. Excuse enough to absent myself from any studies, ain't it?"

"We'll pass it this time," said Ross. "Demelza, could you pull the bell. The boy will be hungry."

"I find it very diverting," Geoffrey Charles said, "at my age, that everyone assumes, as it were takes for granted, that I am always hungry."

"And aren't you?"

"Yes."

They all laughed.

"Serious, though," said Ross, when tea and crumpets and buttered scones had been ordered.

"Serious, now that Ma-ma and Uncle George are living in King Street, it is really no distance for me to come down, so I often take an afternoon off and spend it with them—or at least with Ma-ma and Valentine, Uncle George being frequently out and about his businesses. So I thought, learning of your mishap, I would take the opportunity of calling upon you instead."

They chatted for a while, agreeably, a sudden lightness in the air for the first time since the duel.

Ross said: "I had intended bringing your aunt to see you, or inviting you, as now, to come and see us; but you'll appreciate that as your uncle George and I . . . well, I hesitate to make any move that might upset—your mother."

"Ah," said Geoffrey Charles. *"Dicenda tacenda locutus.* Do you know, Aunt Demelza, one spends hours learning stupid languages solely to enable one to appear superior to those who have never been able to afford time. I would much rather be with Drake learning to make a wheel."

Demelza gave him one of her brilliant smiles.

"They do not know you are here, then?" Ross said.

"No. Nor shall they. Though in a short time I shall not give a tinker's curse what Uncle George thinks. In less than two years I shall be at Magdalen College, and then I shall feel pretty much my own master."

Ross moved his arm to ease the throbbing. "Geoffrey, you cannot come in for Trenwith for at least another three years. Then there is only property, no money. Without your uncle George to finance you the place would go to ruin—as it was going before your mother married him. So on all counts I'd advise you to exercise some discretion—not merely for your mother's sake but for your own. If when you are older —say in four or five years—you find it necessary for your own good health to break with Mr. Warleggan and to claim your inheritance absolutely, I shall have —by then I shall hope to have—enough money from the mine, and from other sources, to see you come into your inheritance not entirely penniless. But that is in the future. At present . . ."

Geoffrey Charles leaned back in his chair and frowned. "Thank you, Uncle. That's very handsomely said. I hope I shall not need your help. Though God knows, my tastes already outrun my allowance. What a degrading subject money is! And how disagreeable that Stepfather George has so much of it! Can we not change the subject to something more savoury? Would

you care, indeed—if it's not too delicate a subject—
to tell me a little more of how you came to be shot in
the hand?"

There was a pause. "No," said Ross.

"Ah. So that is not more savoury neither. . . . Aunt,
you look nice enough to eat. On the whole London
girls are prettier than Cornish girls. But just once in a
while, you see one in our county that really takes the
biscuit."

"Talking of biscuits," said Demelza, smiling at him
again, "I think this is tea."

III

He left about seven, scorning Demelza's concern
about his being safe in the streets of London. He had
been given permission to spend the night at Grosvenor
Gate, so there was no hurry. He walked up the street
as far as the Strand, pushing his way through a group
of prostitutes who plucked at his clothes and his body
as he went past, and soon found a hackney chair.

When he reached home he found a pleasant family
scene. George was home, and turning over a book—
it looked like an accounts book—in front of a bright
fire. Elizabeth was sitting on the other side looking as
beautiful as ever, though Geoffrey Charles thought she
was putting on weight. They had not told him yet. In a
corner of the room Valentine Warleggan, not quite
six years old, dark-haired, sallow-complexioned but
good-looking in a thin angular way, was playing with
his rocking horse. Elizabeth asked him how he had
enjoyed the Zoo, and surely he had stayed too late?
He replied that reptiles only wakened when night fell,
and he had spent the last hour in the snake house.
Lies came easily to him, he found, since he went to
Harrow.

George welcomed him with amiability. To give
George his due, he had always tried to treat his stepson with consideration. It was his stepson who refused
to unbend. It was his stepson who refused to let by-

gones be bygones. Their relationship now was as good as it had ever been: a sort of polite toleration existed between them, which was about as much as Elizabeth dared to hope for.

In spite of the half-meant, half-malicious wager with Monk Adderley which had gone so badly awry, George was in a fair mood tonight. True, the men he had set to make inquiries had turned up yesterday with two chairmen who claimed to have been the men who bore the wounded Adderley to his lodgings; but a little close questioning of them soon proved they were lying and had only come forward to gain the reward George was offering: any lawyer in a court would have split them open in five minutes. So they had been sent about their business, and George's men too, with instructions to be more careful as to the quality of the fish they netted.

George was philosophical about it. With the death of Monk he had lost one of his most valuable social assets; but Monk while he was alive had been a heavy financial liability. He had had no care for money at all, and, since he became intimate with George, had tended to look on George as an inexhaustible supplier. One loan had followed another. Sometimes he had repaid a little, and then had borrowed all over again. So, though it was sad to lose him, it was not all loss. George fancied he could get along quite well enough on his own.

And even if the guilt for the killing were never laid firmly on Ross Poldark's shoulders, the result was still a fair one. Ross was at present laid up with a wound that they said would likely result in the loss of an arm; and in any event such an affray could do his career considerable disservice. The Boscawens, if George judged them aright, were law-abiding above everything else, and they certainly would not want to be represented in Parliament by a firebrand who killed another member clandestinely, in a common duel, fought without even the proper formalities. As for the newly founded bank; news of the affray would travel swiftly to Cornwall; bankers too lived close within the law; it would likely damage him there also.

George's own affairs in other ways were prospering. Mr. Tankard, his personal lawyer and factor, had arrived in London yesterday with numerous documents and legal information. Now that he virtually owned the borough of St. Michael, George sought ways to render its possession less expensive.

There were in the borough about forty householders with sufficient of a dwelling to pay the poor rate. The fact that some of these dwellings were in such a bad state that they were almost falling down over their occupiers' heads did not prevent the householders from thus possessing a vote and capitalising on it. Such men would vote for whomever they were told, provided they received enough favours from the landlord. George was now the landlord. And he had found that the voters, though servile to a degree, were not easily satisfied with their requests. Getting oneself elected was of course the most expensive procedure, but it was by no means the only time at which they expected to benefit.

The scheme was simply to pull down some of the oldest and most derelict of the houses. It would take time, and perhaps a degree of firmness, but it could be done. For instance, the loss of ten houses would reduce his future costs by a quarter. Of course the inhabitants would vehemently object, but he had already bought a row of derelict cottages near a dead mine about two miles away and was having them repaired. No one could accuse him of inhumanity. The creatures he was moving were so indigent, and the houses he was moving them from were so poor, that he could even claim to be improving their lot. The only difference was that they would no longer be ratepayers in the parliamentary borough of St. Michael, and therefore their main livelihood would be gone. They might, George thought, even have to *work*.

He was at present examining the book that Tankard had given him, which gave in detail the nature of the properties to be pulled down, the occupiers, their ages, and the dates by which each one, with his family or dependants, might be expected to get out.

Elizabeth said: "Valentine, it is time for your supper. I think Mrs. Wantage has forgotten you."

"Yes, Ma-ma. In two or three minutes, Ma-ma." Valentine was riding his rocking horse, whip in hand, a dark lock of hair hanging over his face. He was clearly engaged on some dangerous mission that must not be interrupted.

Geoffrey Charles was amused at him. "Ecod, I think Valentine's going to fight a duel."

"Thomas Trevethan, shoemaker," George read to himself. "Aged fifty-seven lives with widowed sister, Susan Hicks, fifty-nine." Already Trevethan had had a note sent to George asking for his patronage in the matter of boots and shoes. He would be well rid of. "Tom Oliver. Dairyman, aged forty, wife and four children." Dairyman for whom? No doubt he kept one emaciated cow. "Arthur Pearson, maltster." What professions these parasites thought of!

Geoffrey Charles was laughing aloud. He laughed his high half-broken laugh, so that Elizabeth, smiling, lowered her needlepoint and George his book. Even Valentine lost his concentration and his horse began to rock less violently.

"What is it?" Elizabeth said. "What is it, Geoffrey Charles? What is amusing you so?"

"It's—it's Valentine!" Geoffrey Charles choked with amusement. "Just look at him! Ecod! Is he not the very spit and living image of Uncle Ross!"

Chapter Eight

On the ninth of November, Dwight gingerly un-
wrapped the bandages again, sniffing at them as they
came away. They revealed an arm still inflamed, but
only around the area of the wound. The swelling had
gone down.

He said: "You're more lucky than you know,
Ross."

"How so?"

"Three days ago I thought to amputate the arm
above the elbow. There is a stage, as I'm sure you
know, when the blood poisoning travels fast. Then it's
a question of losing a limb to save your life."

"Don't tell Demelza."

"She already knows. I could not take the gamble
without her permission."

Ross looked at his arm. "And now?"

Dwight was folding the bandage. "It must have
been dye from the sleeve that was carried in . . . Now?
Oh, it should be good enough for most purposes in a
month or so. Demelza will have to cut up your meat
a while yet."

"I can scarce move my fingers."

"Don't try too hard. A little gentle exercise each
morning. Ross, I'm returning to Cornwall next week.
I only stayed this long because of you."

"Caroline is going with you?"

"No . . . There are some events she wishes to attend at the end of this month. She will return in early
December."

"For longer this time, I hope."

Dwight put the bandage away and shut his bag. The
morning light showed up his face as unexpectedly
youthful under the greying hair.

"I think so. She says so."

Ross said: "At least, whatever value your visit has been to Caroline, it has very near saved my life."

"Your own body saved your life, Ross, because it was strong enough in the end to reject the infection."

"Stronger at least than my mind, which could not resist the infection of Monk Adderley."

"It's over and done with, Ross; all that. You must think of the future, not of the past."

"I'm not so sure it's all over yet. An act like that carries its own consequences with it."

Dwight fumbled with the catch of his bag.

"Why do you not come home with me when I go?"

"No. Not yet. There are some things I must still do."

"You can't undo what's *been* done, Ross. It's a question of adjusting oneself to a new situation."

"Well, that we shall see . . ."

The following day fog was rising from the river as Ross waited upon his patron. He found Lord Falmouth at home and willing to receive him. They talked in a back parlour, since Mrs. Boscawen was entertaining ladies to tea in the drawing room.

Lord Falmouth had shaken Ross by the left hand and dryly suggested they should take a glass of canary. He was wearing a skullcap, a plum-coloured coat shiny at the elbows, and black silk knee breeches and stockings.

"I trust your . . . self-inflicted wound is healing."

"Thank you, my lord. It is. Though it has been long enough about it. Dr. Enys tells me that only time stands between me and my ability to sign my name again."

"That will be of use to you when you return to your banking friends."

"Always supposing they still wish to retain me."

Falmouth handed the glass to his guest. "You were fortunate to bring your own surgeon with you. It is a refinement even I have not yet felt able to afford."

Ross smiled. "He's returning at the beginning of next week. After which I shall have to fend for myself or call in some mere London man." He sipped the wine, and there was a pause. "A lot has happened since I dined with you last, Lord Falmouth."

"So I have observed."

It was difficult to read the Viscount's expression. Never a man given to a show of feeling, he seemed now to be carefully avoiding it. His voice, apart from the little turn of sarcasm, was neutral, as if he waited for his visitor to declare his intent before committing himself to show his own.

"The story of what really happened is, I believe, well known by now," Ross said. "Yet it may be that the precise truth has not emerged in the telling; and I thought you should know it from me as soon as I was able to get out."

"If you're sure you wish to tell me."

"Why should I not be?"

"Because rumour is one thing, confession another. Some things are better left unsaid, Captain Poldark."

"I can assure you, my lord, that, except for this occasion, they will *remain* unsaid. But I represent Truro in your interest, and that interest, though I pay small heed to it sometimes, entitles you in this matter to know what was done."

"Very well." Falmouth went to the French windows, which looked out onto a conservatory, and shut them. "Say what you wish to say."

Ross told him the story of the duel. When it was done the other man refilled the glasses, frowning to see that none was spilled.

"So what do you want from me?"

"Possibly some advice."

"Of what sort?"

"I am known in Cornwall as a man of some temper. Now I am so known in London. The duel, of course, was fairly fought, but the mere fact that it was fought in a clandestine manner and that the law is not able to move against me—or *seems* not able to—gives it a shadier implication than if I were properly tried and served a sentence. You want someone to represent you in Westminster who is a parliamentarian, not a quarrelsome hothead. This stigma will linger in London for a while. I would have thought my proper course would be to resign my seat and for you to appoint someone more suitable in my place. After all, Truro is perfectly safe now and is entirely in your possession. There would be no need for an election. The matter could go through in a couple of months."

Lord Falmouth got up and pulled the bell. A man-servant came.

"Bring me a bottle of the older canary."

"Yes, m'lord."

"And take this empty one."

"Yes, m'lord."

Silence prevailed until the new wine came.

"This is better," Falmouth said. "It has a smoky flavour on the tongue. Alas, there's little more of it. My mother got it last year."

"Yes," Ross said. "It has more body."

"As for your problem, Poldark, are you telling me you are tired of Westminster and wish to leave any-way?"

"That was not what I said. But I think it may be, in the year or so I have sat in Parliament, that you have tired of me."

His lordship nodded his head. "That may be. We have not infrequently been at variance. But only in one or two matters—such as the Catholic Emancipation Bill—has there been a difference on an important issue. Where our differences *really* occur are not on issues but on principles."

"I'm not quite sure what you mean."

"Well, let us instance a single matter. You dislike what the French revolution has become and are pre-pared to fight it with all means in your power. But at heart I think you believe in the fundamentals of Lib-erty, Equality, and Fraternity yourself, though do not see it in those terms or say it in those words. Your humanity, your sentiment, respond to it and they are not sufficiently governed by your head, which would tell you that the achievement of those aims is impos-sible!"

Ross was silent for a while. "But if you take the emotion—the republicanism—the sense of violent revolution—out of them, do you not feel drawn to such ideals yourself?"

Falmouth smiled, tight-lipped. "Perhaps I have better trained myself, always to be governed by my head. Shall I say that I believe greatly in Fraternity, something in Liberty, and not at all in Equality."

"Which is precisely the opposite of what the French have now done," Ross said. "They have insisted so much on Equality that there is no room left for Liberty and little for Fraternity. But you haven't answered my question."

"Then I'll answer it now." His lordship paced about the room for a few moments, and took off his skullcap to scratch his head. "When I want you to resign I will tell you so. And when you wish to resign pray tell me. I like *some* character in a member, you know. But a stupid and unfortunately fatal affair of honour, much as it should be deplored, is not the grounds for such a decision. We all learn by our mistakes. I try to. I trust you will, Captain Poldark."

Ross put down his glass. "Thank you. That's what I wished to know."

"But go home," said Falmouth. "Go home at once. There's nothing important you can do here. And you know what the ancients said: 'When a man shall have been taken from sight he quickly goes also out of the mind.' This applies equally to the law. If they think of questioning you they may well do it if you are in George Street, but certainly will not travel three hundred miles to interview you on your estate in Cornwall."

"I see that."

"Then go tomorrow, or as soon as you can decently dispose of your affairs here."

Ross thought for a long moment. "My lord, I appreciate your thoughts for my welfare. It's considerate of you. . . . But I couldn't absent myself at this stage. I couldn't *skulk* away."

Viscount Falmouth shrugged. "There it is, Poldark.

Once again we disagree. And once again on a matter
of principle. You must be logical in life—not emotional."

II

So it was time to go out and about again, into the
public eye, in the Commons, into society. This in a
way was the acid test. Adderley had few friends but
many acquaintances. He was a "figure" who had been
seen everywhere. Now he was seen nowhere. In his
place, as it were, was the tall Cornishman with arm
in sling, sometimes, when appropriate, accompanied
by his pretty wife. Newcomers, strangers. Of course
Mrs. Pelham had them under her wing, but . . . Adderley was missed. There were side glances, whis-
perings in the background, conversations that dried up
when certain people approached.

To Ross's surprise, the Commons was easier. The
members seemed to take it as a matter of course that
an inveterate duellist would sooner or later come to his
end by the means he himself employed. Their chief
reaction was increased respect for the man who had
killed him. Either Poldark was a demmed good shot,
as the member for Bridgnorth put it, or else he had
been demmed lucky.

During all that very tense and disagreeable week the
Hoddy-Doddy song kept repeating itself in Demelza's
head, "Shepherd, I have lost my waist, Have you seen
my body?" Unforgettable in spite of its complete,
inane irrelevance to all her thoughts and fears.

Once they caught sight of George and Elizabeth at
a *soirée,* and Ross bethought himself of Adderley's
strange request. It was something that had to be fulfilled, however difficult and embarrassing the action was
going to be. Yet it must be inappropriate to hand
George ten guineas in view of a roomful of people,
and George might well think an insult intended. Also
both Ross—who was not at his most observant when
in company—and Demelza noticed how bitter they

were both looking. Nor could it have been anything to do with their own presence, for they had not been seen. Demelza had the impression that they did not speak to each other all night, and this was later confirmed by Caroline, who told her she had heard a rumour that they were on the point of separation.

"*Separation?*" Demelza said. "But she is going to have another baby!"

Caroline shrugged. "Something has happened this last week or so, I know not what. They were happy enough at my aunt's reception: I saw them laughing together."

"Who did you hear it from?"

"Mrs. Tracey called on them on Tuesday and she said Elizabeth was looking very ill, and that the feeling in the house was most unpleasant."

"Can it be because of Monk Adderley's death?"

"I would doubt it. I would think it must be something much more personal."

In the middle of the *soirée* a good-looking man of about forty called Harry Winthrop, who was a relative of the Marquis of Bute, came across and was attentive to Demelza. She was almost rude to him. That evening she came to a decision.

III

It was two days later that Ross saw George in the passageway leading to St. Stephen's Chapel. He was with another member, but there were few other people about. It was now or never. There couldn't be a less unsuitable time to discharge his unpleasant duty.

"George!" he called, and quickened his pace to catch up; and even as he moved he thought: I should have sent it; I should have sent it round.

George Warleggan turned, and Ross was startled by the look that came on the other's face when he saw who had addressed him. It was a look of such hatred that it stopped Ross in his tracks. If there was purer venom he had never seen it.

Had George cared so much, then, for Monk Adderley?

"Pardon me," George said to his companion. "It seems that I am being solicited in some way. I will rejoin you in a moment."

"Of course." The other man glanced quickly at George's terrible expression and at Ross's slinged arm and the scar on his face. Then he moved on.

"Well?"

Ross said: "As you know, I had a meeting with your friend, Captain Adderley. What occurred at it is not for me to say; but before he died he left a message with me through his friend Mr. John Craven. It is not a message I gladly pass on, since I have no wish to talk to you on the subject, but the last request of a dead man is something I can't ignore."

"Well?" George seemed to have difficulty in speaking at all.

"He commanded me to give you ten guineas." Ross fumbled with his left hand and got the ten pieces out of his fob.

"What—for?"

"I understand he made some wager with you and he lost. I have no idea whether it concerned me, and am not interested to know. I would suppose, since he employed me to do this, that it did. It would fit his sense of the appropriate."

Ross extended the money. George looked at it, then he looked at Ross. The glare in his eyes had not changed.

George put out his hand and Ross gave him the money. George counted it.

Then he flung the ten coins full in Ross's face and turned away.

Perhaps fortunately for all concerned John Bullock, the member for Essex, had just come up to speak to Ross, and he saw the occurrence and was able to grasp him by the arm.

"Steady on, boy, steady on. One quarrel is enough in a session. Let's not have another just yet."

Although nearing seventy, Bullock was a very strong

old man, and the grip he had on Ross's arm did not relax.

"You—saw what happened." Ross said, wincing as he moved his bad arm to wipe some spots of blood off his face. "You—saw what happened!"

"Yes, indeed I did. And a sorry waste of good gold it all seemed. If you will permit me I'll pick some of it up for you."

"I could . . ." Ross stopped. He had been going to say "call him out for this," but he realised what Bullock had instantly perceived. Whatever the provocation, a second duel now would finish Ross.

Another member had come up and was picking up the gold, which had rolled in various directions. Both members offered it to Ross, who was now standing in a dazed fashion staring up the long corridor and dabbing at his face. But he refused to accept the coins.

"The money belongs to Warleggan," he said. "I cannot take it. Pray give it to him. I could not trust myself near him at this time."

"I think," said Bullock peaceably, "it had better go in the Poor Box. I fancy not the task of distributing it to either of you."

IV

Ross said nothing to Demelza when he got home, and when she asked him what had bruised his face he said some apprentices had been fighting as he came through the notorious district of Petty France, and that stones had hit him.

A quiet evening, each busy with private thoughts, neither wishing to share them. All the splendid intimacy and happiness of the first week of the London stay was as if it had not been.

Just as she was getting into bed, Demelza said: "Do you feel safe now, Ross?"

"Safe?"

"From the police, I mean. It is three weeks. If they

had been going to charge you, would they not have done so by now?"

"I imagine so."

"Caroline was saying so today."

"I'm indebted to her for the reassurance."

"Ross, you must not be sarcastic with me."

"I'm sorry. No, I should not."

"Well I too was 'indebted for the reassurance,' which, it seems, comes not just from Caroline but from St. Andrew St. John, who is a barrister and should know a little as to how the law works. He said he thought the worst risks were over."

"I'm glad."

"*I'm* glad. And your arm is mending?"

"That too." He did not at the time notice her special need of reassurance.

Although they were in bed early Ross slept late. He dreamt horrible dreams of Monk Adderley—that he was a great snake and lay along the floor of the House wriggling and spitting venom. He heard someone screaming, and it was Elizabeth. Then he saw that she and Demelza were going to fight a duel and that he must stand between them to prevent it. And they discharged their shots and showers of coins hit him about the face and head. And then George was saying in a sneering voice: "Thirty pieces of silver. Thirty pieces of silver."

He woke from heavy sleep when it was full day. The curtains were still drawn but the rattle of the carts and the shouting outside told him it must be late. Demelza was already up, for her place was empty.

He raised his head and peered at the clock. Ten minutes past nine.

There was such a row outside that he drew the curtain aside to see what was about. A fight was in progress between two rabbit sellers and some ragged Irish labourers, who had tried to barter some not very fresh and probably stolen fish for the rabbits. That failing, they had tried to help themselves. A crowd of spectators—pedlars, barrow women, servants, apprentices, and all the flotsam of London—had formed round the struggling, cursing men. Whatever the outcome, neither the fish nor the rabbits were going to be saleable after.

Ross pulled the curtain further back and wondered where Demelza was. Then he saw the letter.

It just said:

Ross,

I am going home. Dwight is leaving this morning at seven o'clock from the Crown and Anchor, and I have asked him if I can go with him.

Ross, I do not feel I can stay in London any longer. Whether it be right or wrong I do not know, but I was the cause of the duel between you and Monk Adderley. For aught I know it might happen again. And again.

I should not have come, for I am out of my depth in London society, and my wish to be friendly and polite to everyone was taken to mean something more. It was even taken by you to mean something more.

Ross, I am going home—to your home and your farm and your children. When you return I shall be there, and we can see then what is best to be done.

Love,
Demelza

Chapter Nine

The hackney chairman said: "What number did ye say, my lady?"

"Fourteen," said Elizabeth.

"Fourteen. That be down at the other hend o' the street, my lady. 'Ave no doubt, Hi'll take ye there."

They jogged down the uneven pavement, thrusting

their way among pedestrians with a "By yer leave, sir! By yer leave!"

Pool Lane was a narrow twisting street making its way tortuously northwards from the Oxford Road and growing ever narrower as it proceeded, until, as they reached No. 14, a green door fresh-painted among many that were peeling, Elizabeth almost gave up and told the chairmen to carry her home. Only the memory of the last ten days drove her on.

Since Geoffrey Charles's innocent remark George had been insufferable. The terrible thing about the observation was that, although not strictly true—Valentine was a boy who seemed to change his appearance like a chameleon with his moods—once made it seemed to hang incontrovertibly in the air. It was as if it were a curse rather than a comment. As if the words spoken by Francis's son had been those of a Poldark recognising another Poldark. Something out of the grave. Of course this was wholly untrue—and would have been seen as such in a rational situation. But this was not a rational situation and never had been.

She was even more sick at heart because she saw that under his evil temper George too was sick at heart. Until the moment of Geoffrey Charles's declaration they had been happier together than ever before. Elizabeth was a woman who blossomed in society: though she had had little enough of it in her life, it was her natural element. Years ago when Francis was still alive and she was living a cloistered and poverty-stricken existence at Trenwith, while Francis gambled away what little money the estate brought in—George had visited her one day and said to her in his deferential voice how much it grieved him to see all her beauty wasted on a few relatives and the empty rooms of a decaying house, when she deserved, and would receive, the acclaim of society if it were ever permitted to see her. He had even ventured to hint that beauty did not last for ever.

Well, all these years later he had been as good as his word. Once before, when he had been member for Truro, she had been up with him for a short time, and that had been pleasant enough; but then he had been unsure of himself, defensive in society, jealous—or at least envious—of the way in which she moved in it as if it were her rightful place. This time had been different. Not only was he assured of his seat for just as long as he cared to occupy it: he owed it to no one but himself, and owed no one allegiance. Indeed, he brought to the Commons the vote of a second member. About a month ago, against his more cautious judgment, he had told Elizabeth of his plans and of the letter he had written under Mr. Robinson's direction to the First Lord of the Treasury, Mr. William Pitt. He had even showed Elizabeth a copy of it, and phrases still echoed in her mind. ". . . that I have settled and composed those matters in the county of Cornwall which in my conversations with Mr. John Robinson I have explained can be used as a means of supporting Government and your Administration. This I shall now uniformly do, as indeed shall be seen henceforth. And such Interests as I may take up will be those which you will call upon me to Support. I wish therefore before Parliament rises to have the honour of an audience at your earliest Conveniency, that closer arrangements may be made . . ."

The "audience" had not yet taken place, but Robinson had assured George that it would, and George had told Elizabeth that while the vulgar notion of a direct *quid pro quo* would not be raised, nevertheless it would be made known to Pitt that a knighthood for Mr. Warleggan would perpetuate the allegiance as no other form of favour was likely to do.

They had both been excited at the thought. To George it would be the accolade both in a literal and in a psychological sense. Once he was Sir George his cup would be full. He might even get a baronetcy in a year or two more, so that the title could be perpetuated. Elizabeth was full of satisfaction at the thought of being Lady Warleggan. Of course her birth assured her more firmly of her position than any mere title. Indeed it had been a tradition in the Chynoweth family—even a proud one—that they had been a line of landowners and distinguished gentlemen for a thousand years with never a title among them. But Elizabeth had been conscious ever since she married George of having lowered herself in the eyes of the county; this would make up.

So she had been convinced that the title if it came, and the new baby when it came, would cement their marriage as nothing before. And she was still beautiful—especially when her hair was done as it had been done at the party on the night of the opening of Parliament. Time might be shorter for her now than that day when George had spoken to her in the winter parlour of Trenwith; but there was still some left.

So everything had been pleasant and satisfactory to contemplate, and one woke in the morning with a good day ahead, one lay in bed before rising, making complicated and agreeable plans for the future.

And in a flash *nothing*. Nothing was satisfactory, *nothing* was pleasant any more. A thoughtless exclamation by her own son had poisoned the very well of their lives. They were back to the situation of three years ago when all the suspicion and distrust had festered and burst into a great quarrel between them. They were back only worse, with more to lose and more already lost. Everything they did now, every breath they drew, was contaminated.

Hence her visit today. One minute she thought herself insane to contemplate it; the next it seemed the only possible way out.

She had paid the chairman, and, with a veil over her face, was greeted by a thin Jewish boy in black silk coat and breeches. She gave her name—Mrs. Tabb—and was ushered in. Three minutes in a waiting room; then she was shown into the room beyond, and Dr. Anselm rose to greet her.

Franz Anselm, born in the ghettoes of Vienna, had arrived in England in 1770, a penniless young man of twenty-two, bringing with him a few guineas stitched into his shirt, and a case of medicines which were confiscated by the excise officers at Dover. He walked to London—as he had walked across Europe—and after a year of near starvation had found employment as a ward assistant in the recently established Westminster Lying-in Hospital. After five years there he had become assistant to a man-midwife called Lazarus, who worked in Cloth Lane, near Golden Square; and when Lazarus unfortunately cut his finger while dissecting a woman who had died of the childbed fever, Anselm came in for the practice. There, with no qualifications, but armed with a tremendous belief in himself, five years of pragmatic observation, an instinct for humanity he had got from his mother, and a copy of William Smellie's *Set of Anatomical Tables,* he had established a reputation.

He had moved to rooms at his present address fifteen years ago, and five years after that had bought the freehold of the house. From the poor women of the city he had made his way to the rich. Although he still had no letters after his name, more and more women came to him, or called him in. They liked him, were impressed by him, often just because he was not as other doctors. He had a new approach, a flexible conscience, an intimate understanding of and tolerance for the ways of the world, and a wide knowledge of continental medicine. Most valuable of all, still, was his mother's instinct for sick people.

At close quarters he looked even more ugly and intimidating than he had done at Mrs. Tracey's reception. His eyes were dewy black sloes peering out from the untrimmed, unkempt hedgerows of immense eyebrows. His upper lip and heavy jowls would not have looked out of place on an ape. The hair of his head might have been judged too woolly, too artificial, if it had been seen on a doll.

"Mrs.—er—Tabb," said Dr. Anselm in a very gentle, attractive voice that surprised coming from so big a man. "Have we met before?"

"No," said Elizabeth. "I have had you recommended to me."

"May I ask by whom?"

"I'd prefer—she'd prefer not to say."

"Very well. How may I be of service to you?"

Elizabeth licked her lips. She found she couldn't begin. He waited a few moments and then lifted his eyebrows.

"Perhaps I may get you something to drink, Mrs.—er—Tabb. A cordial, some orange juice? I don't keep spirits."

"No . . . thank you. What I have to say, Dr. Anselm, is—in the greatest confidence . . . you'll appreciate . . ."

"My dear madam, many titled people, including two duchesses and two princesses, have done me the favour of giving me their confidence. If I could not keep it I could not keep my practice, nor should I wish to."

It was a strange room she was in—too luxuriously furnished for good taste. It was as if Dr. Anselm had compensated not only his body for those thin hard years, but his senses also. The carpet was Arabian, of the most brilliant red and yellow, with an intricate geometric design. The curtains were French: heavily worked silk from Lyon. Tapestries covering the walls were French also, with scenes of the Old Testament. The chair in which she sat was of a luxury hardly met with in the furniture of the day. The chandeliers were Venetian. The only evidence of the use to which the room might sometimes be put was a long flat couch with a coverlet of pale yellow silk. She suppressed a shiver and hoped she might not be asked to lie on it.

"I am thirty-five," she said abruptly. "I married quite young. Then my husband died. I have remarried. Now I am with child."

Dr. Anselm's thick lips parted in a gentle smile. "So."

"Let me say at once that it is not illegitimate."

"Ah, so . . ."

"Also that I do not wish to lose the baby."

"I'm glad to know that. In any case, Mrs.—er—Tabb, if I observe you correctly, you are now—what—five months forward?"

"Six."

"Good. Good." He nodded his head and waited.

"I'm told," Elizabeth said, "that you have many abilities, Dr. Anselm."

"I have been told so."

"Well, for reasons I can't explain—don't wish to explain—I would like this to be a seven-month or eight-month child."

He looked his surprise and then away. There was a long silence. A French ormolu clock struck the half hour.

"You mean you wish to come to parturition before the appointed time?"

"Yes . . ."

"But you would like the child to be born alive?"

"Yes, yes. Of *course.*"

He put the tips of his hairy fingers together and stared down at the carpet.

"Is it *possible?*" Elizabeth asked at length.

"It is possible. But not easy. And there would be risk."

"To me or to the baby?"

"Either or both."

"How much risk?"

"It would depend. I would have to examine you."

Oh, God, she thought.

"Have you had other children?"

"Yes, two."

"How old were you?"

"My first—when my first was born I was twenty. My second—I would be twenty-nine."

"A considerable interval. Were they by the same man?"

"No."

"And now there is another interval—five and a half—six years?"

"It will be six years to the month if this child comes to its proper term."

"I see. Were there any complications at the birth of your other children?"

"No."

"And they were both full-term?"

401

She hesitated. ". . . Yes."

"When did you miss your first menses?"

"This time? In May."

"Can you be more specific?"

"It was the fourteenth. I particularly remember. Perhaps the thirteenth."

"Are your showings regular or do they vary in occurrence and length?"

"Regular. Sometimes they vary in length."

The chair creaked as Dr. Anselm reared his great bulk out of it and took his stomach across to a Chinese cupboard. He opened it and took out a calendar and laid it on the Louis Quinze desk. He dipped his pen in an inkwell and scratched some figures on a piece of paper.

"That means that you should come to your full term in February, most likely the early part. What you want me to do is advise you how you may have your child, alive and well, in December or January. Am I right?"

"Yes."

"Are you living in London? Would you wish me to attend you?"

"I had intended staying in London, but now I think I shall go back to—well, my house in the country."

Franz Anselm rubbed the feather against his chins, which, although shaved three hours ago, were already dark again.

"Mrs. Tabb. Before I go any further, may I ask you to consider what you are doing. Nature sets out immutable laws and is not lightly to be interfered with. Had you come to me with a two-month pregnancy I could have terminated it far more easily, and more safely, than what you are asking me to do. Indeed, although it is quite possible to do it, and although you look to be in good health, I would remind you that you are thirty-five, which is a disadvantage. Secondly, and more importantly, you would be asking me to prescribe a medicine whose effects I should not be in a position to supervise or oversee."

Elizabeth nodded, wishing she had never come.

Anselm said: "Indeed, I suppose I am right in assuming that you would wish this to appear a *naturally* premature birth, and that the presence of a doctor openly intending to produce this result would be contrary to your wishes."

She nodded again.

Silence fell in the room, but the bells of the hawkers outside were persistent.

"Sometimes there is little peace even at night," said Dr. Anselm. "The penny post comes at midnight and sets up such a clamour with his bell. Often, too, notices are read late in order to attract more attention. And some of the street men never seem to sleep."

Elizabeth said: "Dr. Anselm, I think I was wrong to come to you. I should not have done so had I not been in great distress."

"Please sit down. I appreciate what you say, madam. We must discuss this coolly and quietly for a little while, and then it may seem easier to decide what is to be done."

She subsided miserably and waited.

He passed across the room and came back with a glass of sweetened fruit juice, which she sipped. He nodded at that approvingly.

"A recipe of my own. Very soothing to the nerves. . . . Mrs. Tabb."

"Yes?"

"What I suggest—what I will suggest to you is that if my examination shows you to be in good health and the pregnancy—so far as I can tell at this stage—a normal one, I will make up a medicine for you, which you may take away with you today. It is a simple vegetable remedy, compounded of a distillation of a number of valuable herbs and of a fungus that grows on rye. If you take it as prescribed—neither more nor less; the amount will be carefully written down for you—and at the date prescribed—you are likely to produce a living child in the manner you desire. I shall put down two dates, one in December and one in January. It will be for you to choose, but I would certainly recommend the December one."

"Why?"

"At seven months the child, though less mature, is suitably positioned for birth. Towards the eighth month it turns and is not so positioned. There are far more children born alive at seven months than eight."

"I see."

"What I suggest is that you take this medicine away with you and keep it always by you. When the time comes you may decide not to take it after all, and then you will go to your full term as nature has designed. But if you are still of the same mind, then it will be available to you as required. I presume you will have a physician to attend you at the time?"

"Oh, yes."

"Good. Ah, so . . . Well, if there should be any complications—if, for instance, uterine spasms continue for long after the birth of the child—do not hesitate to take the doctor into your confidence. You could become ill yourself, and it would then be necessary for him to know what you had taken. After all, I am not the only doctor in the world capable of keeping his own counsel."

Elizabeth gave him a wan smile.

"However, that need not be and should not be. The fine blending of these herbs should prevent such complications."

"Thank you."

"Very well, then," said Dr. Anselm. "If you would kindly lie on this couch. I shall confine my examination to the mere essentials, so that it may be as little distressing to you as possible."

Chapter Ten

Demelza's long journey home with Dwight was one in which she was torn between a feeling that she had deserted Ross in what might yet be a crisis, and a stronger conviction that she could stay no longer with him in London. An impossible situation had been reached, and the only way was to separate. Whatever effect this might have on their future together, it could be no worse than the risk that would otherwise be run.

As they neared home, she tried to put aside all the bitterness and the heartache of a London visit which had promised and begun so well. However Ross felt when he returned—whatever was going to happen to their marriage—just now, within a day, within a few hours, within a few minutes, she was going to be reunited with her children and her home and her friends and servants and everything —except Ross—that she cared most about in the world. She must concentrate her thoughts on that.

It was strange coming back to Cornwall after her first time away. She saw again its barrenness, but also she instantly breathed in the soft air like a tonic. She understood the county's overall indigence and untidiness compared to the well-groomed and wealthy countryside through which she had passed. She felt once again that there was not the enormous gap in Cornwall between rich and poor. The great houses, with one or two exceptions, were much smaller than up-country, and there were many fewer. The poor in Cornwall, so far as she could judge, were no poorer, the gentry more on terms with their work people.

The only way from Truro was to hire horses, and

this they did. She wanted Dwight to fork off for Killewarren, but he insisted on seeing her home. So she came, and suddenly there was great commotion and squeals of delight, and her hat was knocked away and a pair of fat and a pair of thin arms were round her, and Jane and John Gimlett were crowding in and Betsy Maria Martin and Ena Daniel and all the rest. Presently Clowance burst into noisy tears, and when asked why, replied it was because Mama was crying. Demelza said, what nonsense, she never cried, it was because she had an onion in her pocket; but when they clamoured to see it she could only produce an orange. When Dwight turned to go she asked him to stay the night, knowing that no child waited to welcome him, but he shook his head and said he was anxious to see Clotworthy.

Over the next day talk never stopped at Nampara. The children were well, although Jeremy had been at death's door with a boil on his arm. At least, this was what Jeremy said, but it happened to be his favourite phrase at the moment. He had heard Mr. Zacky Martin use it, and liked it so much that he brought it in whenever possible. Clowance had actually *grown,* though without any sign yet of shedding her puppy fat. Neither of the children, Demelza thought, looked as *clean* as they ought. Although they had probably had more attention than when she was at home, they looked a little neglected and untidy. It was very strange. They lacked the lick of the mother cat.

Also things had not been so good among the servants while she was away. When she was at home complete tranquility reigned. Now it seemed that Mrs. Kemp had presumed too much (or done not enough), that Jane Gimlett had found Betsy Maria Martin disobedient (or had been too harsh with her), that John Gimlett had not told Jack Cobbledick something about the pigs that he should have done (or had to do something Cobbledick had neglected). And so backwards and forwards in respectful, or not so respectful, asides, until Demelza told each one privately that she wished to hear no more, that she was glad to be home, and that henceforward everything must return to its previous harmony.

All this should have helped her put events in London out of mind, or at least into the background. Instead contact with all the familiar things, all the preoccupations of a busy family life, accentuated her awareness of every detail of her stay in London, as a bright light will accentuate shadows. Production at the mine, as Zacky had written them, was up for the month of October and he now reported it up for November too. At the coinage in Truro their stuff had sold well, and prices generally had risen. Wheal Maiden was still barren of tin, but a modest amount of red copper, not dissimilar from that mined in the recently extinct Wheal Leisure, was now being brought up, also small quantities of silver and silverlead. These last were never likely to be found in such amounts as to justify the outlay of working a mine to bring them up, but as a by-product they were a small addition to the profit side of the ledger.

On the second day Sam called. He kissed his sister, an act which she always felt he performed with a proper mixture of respect and religious circumstance. She was his elder sister, and the wife of the squire; but she was also his daughter in Christ. She asked at once about Drake.

He said: "He's back in Pally's Shop, as your—as Ross instructed him—and working. The roof is repaired, the outside washed, some furniture bought and made, and what ye kindly sent by way of curtains, carpets, and mats have been put to the best use. His trade be back—that which he lost, I mean —and his fields are soon to be ploughed. But he have not yet climbed out of the mire of despond into which his spirit and his soul have fallen. I fear that the pains of hell have got hold upon him and that he is yet estranged from God."

"Sam," Demelza said; "as I have mentioned before my concern for Drake is not quite the same as yours. Of course I want him to be happy in the next world. But just now I am concerned with his happiness in this. I ask about his *spirits,* not his spirit."

"Sister," Sam said, "Drake is dull and quiet—and that is not his nature, as you well d'know."

"Is he seeing anything of Rosina?"

"Not's I know. I would reckon nothin 'tall."

Demelza got up and pushed a lock of hair away from her face. Sam looked at her in her cream dimity frock, with the keys dangling at the waist, and thought how young she still looked. But pale. And less pretty. As if something were dragging at her spirit.

He said: "Is something wrong wi' *your* life, sister? Are ye troubled of body or soul?"

She smiled. "A little perhaps of both, Sam. But it is something I cannot talk about."

"Tis easeful always for the soul to unburden itself to Christ."

"And that I cannot do neither. Though maybe more's the pity . . . But tell me of Drake. Did he ever say—did he never tell you what happened when he went Truro?"

"Mrs. Whitworth would not see him. She turned him away as if they was strangers. Drake said she had changed so's ye would not know her. Almost crazed she was, he says. And of course looking on Drake as far beneath her now. Ah, well . . . Twould have been a bad marriage whether or no, but Drake could not see that until it were too late. . . . Did I ever tell you two constables called? . . ."

"When? On you? What about?"

Demelza listened to Sam's story with a gathering coldness in her heart, half attending to the monstrous suspicion implied by the visit, half thinking of Ross wondering whether someone might yet call on *him.* If they did, and she were not there, what might he not be trapped into admitting? Her stomach turned over within her. Certain that if the Cornish law had taken the trouble to stretch out its fingers and touch Drake, then the London law, which must be so much more efficient and so much more severe, could hardly fail to move against Ross in the end. . . .

So I've wondered oft, if Lady Whitworth thought such a thing . . ."

With difficulty she brought her attention fully back to Sam. "What do you mean?"

"Well, Mrs. Whitworth—Morwenna—she did claim to be in love wi' Drake. That she should reject him just like that—so sharp, so unfriendly—I've thought since, if Lady Whitworth thought Drake might've had a hand in Mr. Whitworth's death, Morwenna might've thought the same."

"D'you mean that being why she turned him away?"

"Mebbe."

Demelza thought, and then shook her head conclusively.

"Whatever else, Morwenna, if she cared at all for Drake, must have come to know him well. No one who ever comes to know Drake well could ever suspect him of such a thing."

They moved on a few paces. How long now before Ross left London? Perhaps only a few days. Perhaps he had already left—if he was permitted to . . . What, she wondered, would her leaving him imply to him when he read her note? Their relationship at this moment seemed the most impossible of resolution that had ever been. Everything they did, said, thought, took place behind endless barriers of hurt pride and misunderstanding.

"What did you say, Sam? I'm sorry."

"I just wondered—when you've been Tehidy— I wondered if maybe you'd ever seen Emma?"

"I've not been to Tehidy while she's been there. Ross has been two or three times, but then he hardly knew her. Do you want me to ask?"

Sam squeezed his knuckles. "Nay. She's wed, and I pray she will be happy wed. Tis best left at that."

Demelza said bitterly: "There's a saying in London that hell is paved with good intentions. That seems to be what happens to all good intentions, both for my brothers and for myself."

Sam put a hand on her arm. "Never say that, sister. Never regret anything you do out of the goodness of your heart."

II

Two days later she walked the five miles to see Drake, feeling that life in London had been too sedentary, and that anyway perhaps the excercise would help to calm some of the crosscurrents in her heart.

Also they said Jud Paynter was very ill, so she could call on him on the way. She didn't want anyone *else* to die.

Up the nutty valley with the red stream bubbling beside her and Wheal Grace smoking; the clang of stamps, the braying of donkeys, the rattle of carts (was London after all that much noisier?), past Wheal Maiden, down towards Sawle Church, past the track leading to Sawle Combe. Goats were pastturing on the bare moorland, living comfortably on what no other domestic animal could subsist on. (She should really also call at the Nanfans', for Char had been ill.)

When she got to the Paynters' she was relieved to see Jud sitting up in bed and looking little different. Thinner, certainly—like a bulldog that had been pickled in spirit—but as full of complaints as ever and eating all that was put before him. Prudie admitted that he had been some slight, but then, she said, twas only gouty wind and bile, and it all came from him getting drunk last Wednesday sennight at Tweedy's kiddley, and then mistooken the road home and fallen into Parker's timber pond, and twas a pity he hadn't drownded there and then so he could have put an end on it.

Timber ponds were pools, or parts of a dammed stream, where wood was seasoned before use. The timber lying in them was very greasy, and Jud bitterly commented on the fact.

"I were feeling nashed afore ever this, I tell ee! Nay, Missus, twas naught to do wi' drink. *Sober* I were and walking home as slow as a dew snail. Hat on head, nose warmer in mouth, I were quaddling home as slow as a dew snail all along of me feeling slight from all the work I done that day teeling in widow Treamble. Gurt woman, she were, and her coffin, twas all we could do to prize un into the 'ole. They d'say she wouldn't go in the coffin proper way round so they 'ad to thrust 'er in backsyfore. And that's 'ow she'll *stay,* backsyfore till the Day of Judgment! And who d'know what the Lord God will say when He see a woman edging out of 'er coffin backsyfore? Shocked He'll be, I reckon, shamed, He'll be at such a sight! . . . Shouldn't wonder if the same thing don't 'appen to you, Prudie, when it come your turn."

"Twill not be afore I've seen *you* closed 'ome," said Prudie.

"Well, yur were I, Missus, walking 'ome, sober as a judge, or maybe soberer, and I come to this yur bridge—twas no more'n ten paces acrost—and I started acrost 'n, and by ivers, soon's I put foot 'pon the planchin, then the planchin began to give way! An' it slid, an' it slid, an' it slid, like you was on a frosty road covered wi' goose turds. Step I took, one 'pon t'other, each one rolling and slipping fasterer than the last un, till at last me feet flew from under me and plosh! I were in the water. Deep, deep, I sank, and a-swallowin' of un, and tasting like a drang. Twas a mercy I were brave 'nough to find me way 'ome! An I never been right since!"

"Never was right afore," said Prudie. "Nor never will be. Not till kingdom come. Nor after that. Long after that. When the sun d'grow cold Jud Paynter'll still not be right. 'Cos you wasn't *born* right, see!"

Demelza stayed for twenty minutes, hearing the gossip of the countryside, and then escaped into the more wholesome air outside and, when Prudie followed her, gave her her usual half guinea. Prudie was pathetically grateful, but long before Demelza was out of earshot she heard the rumble of argument begin again inside the cottage.

Through Grambler and past the gates of Trenwith, and the detour that everyone now accepted to avoid trespassing on Warleggan land. So towards Trevaunance Cove and Place House just out of sight over the headland. Here some oxen were being used to plough a field and she could hear the small boys who were driving them keep up a rhythmic chant of encouragement. *"Come* on, Fallow, *come* on, Chestnut. *Now,* then, Tartar, *now* then, County." *Come* on, Fallow, *come* on, Chestnut, *now* then, Tartar, *now* then, County." So the singsong drawl went on. She stood to watch them for a time. A ridge of cloud like a woolen blanket hung over the sea.

So down the hill to Pally's Shop.

Drake was shoeing a horse while the farmer waited. He gave her a quick smile and the farmer touched his hat.

"I'll not be long."

"Don't hurry," she said, and passed into the house.

III

They had taken tea and talked long and she was ready to go. He had said more to her than to anyone before; partly because she was his beloved sister whom he had not seen for two and a half months; partly because his last, and final, tragedy was now seven months old. Sick at heart with her own recent memories, she listened to his with the more sympathy.

"I shall never marry now," he said, "any more'n I believe Sam will. It is—over. I feel little of naught now. Like that time before, I work. And work and work. One day it seem me I shall be rich!" He laughed. "Maybe it is a good thing if you d'want to make money, to be crossed in love. You've little else to think on."

"You don't think about making money."

"No, I don't *think* about it: I just work and it come!"

"Drake, you remember the Christmas party of last year? Well, this year Caroline wants to have it there

—at Killewarren, instead of Nampara. But otherwise just the same. If she does have it—and we go— I want you to promise to come as you did before."

"*If* you go?"

"Well . . . it will depend. After London it will depend. I do not know how Ross will feel about a Christmas party . . ."

Drake looked at the expression on his sister's face and perceived the depth of the issues that waited for Ross's return.

Demelza said: "But even if we should not be there, Ross and I, or only one of us, I would still wish for you to go. I know Caroline will invite you and Sam. You must not feel any barrier between you because they are rich. They are my dearest friends."

"She've been very good to me. Any work she can she send over here. And sometimes when she was living down here permanent she used to come herself and chat and talk, just like we were equals."

"Well, then."

"Let us wait Christmas, sister."

She looked out at the day. The blanket of cloud had by now drawn itself over the land, putting the sky to bed. "I must go. I told them not to wait dinner for me."

"There's rain in the wind. Stay and eat wi' me."

"Not today, Drake. But thank you."

"I'll come partway home—"

"No, you'll lose custom . . ."

"Custom can wait."

So he walked back with her as far as the top of Sawle Combe. By now misty-wet had set in, and he watched her striding away into the damp grey afternoon, cloak over head, long grey skirt, sturdy shoes, until she was lost to sight among the pines of Wheal Maiden. Then he turned and walked home, bending his head into the gentle soaking rain.

When he reached home farmer Hancock was waiting for him, looking impatient. He had brought two oxen to be shod, and had sent a boy down this morning to tell Drake as much, and Drake had forgot.

So the next hour was busy, and when Hancock had gone Drake cut himself a couple of slices of ham he had bought from the Trevethans yesterday when they killed their pig. This, with bread and tea and two apples, made a good meal, and as soon as it was done another commission kept him busy till four.

So the days went. By now dark was not far off, and the two Trewinnard boys came in from working in his fields, soaked to the skin and anxious to be off home. He let them go, and walked to the gate of his yard to see them scuttling up the hill towards St. Ann's.

Work was less in the winter; few customers came after dark, and the long evenings which he had earlier spent by candlelight making spades and ladders and other things to sell to the mines, he now, since the fire, devoted to building furniture to replace the stuff that had been burned. This he found much more exacting, but it was one of the few things to give him a wholesome sense of satisfaction when done. To begin with he had used inferior wood, but recently he had bought some good oak and walnut, and he was resolved to make over again all the earlier pieces knocked together for quick convenience.

Well, it would not do to stand here endlessly with the wet dripping off his face. No one else was coming now. He had chickens to feed, and some geese he was fattening for Christmas.

He turned away from the gate, and then his sharp eye detected a man in a long coat coming down the hill from St. Ann's carrying a bag. He seemed hesitant, not quite sure where he was going, and sure enough Drake saw him stop at a cottage—the Robertses'—and, it seemed, ask the way. Mrs. Roberts was pointing down the hill. The man came on. He was not smartly dressed but he looked too respectable to be a vagrant or a beggar.

Drake went into the storehouse to get some meal for the chickens. He put it in a bowl to be able to throw it more easily, and fed a few of the chickens, watching them scuttle towards him on long rangy legs and then dart about the yard like thrown knives to jab at the food he scattered.

He heard the click of the gate and went out again. The figure at it said:

"Would you be so kind as to tell me . . . oh," and then in the smallest voice, "Drake!"

Drake dropped the bowl, which rolled on its rim into a corner, spilling the rest of the meal everywhere.

"Oh, my love . . ." he said. "Have you come home?"

IV

She sat opposite him in the tiny parlour, hair still lank from the rain, the lashes of her shortsighted eyes linked with tears. She had dropped her cloak, and sat there in her brown woollen dress like some tall damp bird that had come in for shelter but when it had dried and rested would take flight again. He had knelt to unbutton her black, blunt-toed wet shoes, but she had shrunk from his touch. She was holding a cup of tea, warming her hands with it and trying not to shiver.

"I left this morning . . ." she said, speaking rapidly, without pauses. "Early this morning; I thought at first I thought I should leave her a note; but that seemed—cowardly; I felt that, if I have sometimes been cowardly in the past, now was the time to stop; so I went into her bedroom before she was up and told her what I was going to do. At first she laughed—did not believe me—then when she saw I really intended she grew . . . swollen with rage; it was something—something my—something Osborne used to be able to do . . . to grow bigger in anger, in annoyance, in—in frustration."

He watched her in silence, hardly able yet to believe she was here.

"She said she would have me stopped; she said she would call the servants, get me locked up—then have me put away, she said, as Osborne had once tried to have me put away; I said she had no right

—no one had any right—I was a widow now; anyway, what did she care, I asked her, about me? What did she care? I was only an expense and a nuisance; I was going to leave her my son . . . my son."

Don't talk, Morwenna, if it upset you."

"I *want* to talk, Drake, I *must* talk. I must tell you everything I *can* . . ."

At that point she choked and was quiet for a while. The hot tea was burning colour in her cheeks.

"So when she had shouted at me for—for a long time, then she said, all right, I could go, but if I went, she said, I must take only what I stood up in, and if I went I must never come crawling back; I said I would go and never come back, I said . . . crawling or any other way. So then I left and walked to a farm nearby, and the farmer gave me a lift in his cart to Grampound, and there, after waiting hours, I caught the stage to Truro; then I had to wait again until I found a wagon coming this way; it came as far as Goonbell, and then—I walked from there; I had to ask often because I had really no idea—where you lived."

He stared at her and stared at her. The last time he had seen her close to like this, personally, in quiet conversation, was more than four years ago. He was recognising her all over afresh. Eventually she looked up at him and he looked away.

"You've eaten?"

"This morning."

"I've got some ham. And there's a morsel of cheese. And there's apples. Bread."

She shook her head, as if dismissing an irrelevancy.

He said: "Let me get ee a blanket to wrap yourself with."

She said: "Drake, I have to tell you about April."

"Does it matter now?"

"It does to me. I have to tell you. Even if it hurts you to tell you."

"Go on then. I mind for nothing of that, though."

She picked some strands of damp hair off her brow. Her eyes were like pools lying in shadow.

"You know I never cared for Osborne?"

"You hated him."

She considered this. "D'you know, when I was young I didn't know what hate was? I never—it never entered my being. Only after I was married. It's a terrible thing. It shrivels up all that's good in you. It's like a child becoming an old woman in a few months." She shivered. "I'd like to forget I ever felt that for *him*—or for any man. Drake, can I just say I never *cared* for Osborne?"

"So be it."

"After John—my baby—was born I was ill, and I was more ill and sick in spirit when I found that Osborne, while I was ill, had taken another woman; I cannot tell you who it was, but to me it was so physically degrading—so degrading—not that I ever wanted him *back!* . . . Oh, I am telling this so very badly!"

He got up and took the cup from her, refilled it and gave it back to her. He noticed again how she seemed to shrink at his touch.

"Then after some months—I can't recollect how many months—this other woman, she left, and he wanted to resume his relationship with me. I refused —and we had vile quarrels. I continued to refuse him, and made terrible threats. For a long time—I think it must have been two years, I did not let him touch me. . . . But then, only about six weeks before he died it—came about . . . well, he forced himself on me. And after that. Not just once, you see. When it had begun, it happened again and again . . ."

He clenched his fists. "Do you have to tell me this?"

"*Yes!* For I have to explain that when he died I felt *contaminated*—as if the mere thought of the contact between flesh and flesh—any flesh—would turn me sick and demented. Sometimes earlier when I had denied him he had called me demented—but I was far nearer to that just after he had died, after he had died, than at any other time in my life! Do you understand it *at all*, Drake? All that was—was beautiful between us, all that was tender, all that was true—all that perhaps there might be between any young man and any young woman—though I can scarce believe many felt it so deep as we did—all, *all* that was turned to ugliness, beastliness, vileness . . ."

She put the teacup down on the table, her hand not too certain. The fire Drake had lit was crackling with wood, and the hem of her skirt was drying.

She said: "When I was-about fifteen I went with my father once to St. Neot, where he was preaching. On the way home on the following day we happened upon a stag hunt, and I saw a young deer killed . . . I shall never forget it. Suddenly all its grace and its lissom beauty were stretched on a rock, and a knife came and slit open its belly, and all its entrails, its heart, its liver, its bowels, were pulled out to steam and stink in the sun!"

"Morwenna!"

"But it was the *same* deer, Drake, the *same* deer! And when you came I could see only the physical contact of two bodies which would turn my mind to the deepest revulsion, my flesh to shrivel and creep, my stomach to retch. So you see I was—a little—still am a little—demented."

"My love—"

"Also," she said. "I found—I knew that week that he died—that I was with child by him again."

"Then? . . ." He looked at her, instinctively glanced at her waist.

"I lost it two months ago. Oh, not deliberate. I did nothing. But I think perhaps the poor little thing knew that I . . . hated it. That word! I said I'd not use it again. I lost the baby. It just happened."

He breathed out slowly. "And so—now you have come."

"Now I felt I could at least come to see you."

"More'n *that,* I pray. Where else can you go?"

"To Trenwith."

He did not speak but went to the fire to stir it again, crouched there, then went swiftly down the two steps to the kitchen, cut a piece of bread and sliced some ham thinly upon it, brought it on a plate. "Eat this."

"I don't want it."

"Ye *need* it. Must need it after so long a fast."

Reluctantly she bit a corner, chewed, and swallowed, bit again. He watched her. When she had done she half smiled at him.

"Why Trenwith?" he asked.

"It is the best place to go. My cousin's father and mother live there."

"Do you want to see them special?"

"They were always kind."

"But you came here first."

"I had to see you—to explain."

"Is that all?"

"Yes . . . that's all."

A long silence fell between them.

Drake said: "When I came Truro to see ye, I thought to bring you away, to ask you to marry me so soon as ever twas decent after his death. I was—in such a hurry—an impulse—I should've know better."

"You were not to know what I have told you."

"But now . . . Will you marry me, Morwenna?"

She shook her head, not looking at him. "I can't, Drake."

"Why not?"

"Because of what I've told you. Because I feel as I do feel."

"What do that mean?"

"There's so little I can give you."

"You can give me yourself. That's all I want."

"That's just what I can't *do.*"

"Why not my love?"

"Drake, you haven't understood. Because I am still—contaminated—in my mind. I can't look on—on love—on what marriage means—without *revulsion.* If you were to kiss me now I might not shiver, for other people have kissed me. It could be just a salute. But if you were to touch my body I would shrink away because instantly across my mind would come the thought of *his* hands. Did you notice when you tried to unbutton my shoes?"

"Yes."

"Well, shoes particularly I could not—not stand. But *everything*. Because I *am* demented. A little. In that respect. The thought of—of lying with a man —the bodily contact—and what follows it . . . the— the very thought! . . ." She put her head down.

"Even with me?"

"Even with you . . ."

She took her glasses out of her bag and rubbed them on a handkerchief. "I had to take them off when I was walking here because the fine rain blinded me. Now I can see you better. Drake," she said in a matter-of-fact voice. "I must go. Thank you for— for welcoming me. After the way I treated you in April, you are so good, so kind."

He stood up, but not over her, keeping his distance. "Morwenna, I must tell you that just before he—Mr. Whitworth—died I had engaged to marry a girl in Sawle called Rosina Hoblyn. I'd thought that you were lost to me for ever. Kind friends thought my life was being wasted, lost. So twas. So I engaged to marry Rosina. But when I heard *he* was dead, I went to see Rosina and asked her to set me free. This she did, for she's a straight, honest, good girl. And I came Truro. And you turned me away. But when you turned me away I didn't go back to Rosina —even if she'd have had me. I resolved never to marry 'tall. I told my sister—she was over today— I told her only today that I should never marry 'tall. And that is the honest truth, without a word of a lie! So . . ." He looked down at her.

"So?"

"Would it not be better to marry me than to see me have no wife—all my days?"

She put her free hand hard to her mouth. "Drake, you still don't *understand*."

"Oh, yes, I reckon I do." He moved to sit on his haunches in front of her, but checked himself in time. He crouched some way away. "Be my wife in name—marry me—in church proper—that's all I ask. Love—what you call love—carnal love—if it d'come some day it come. If not, not. I shall not press. Twill be for you always to say."

She released her mouth long enough to say: "I couldn't *ask* it. It wouldn't be fair on you. You *love* me! I know that. So how could you—how could you keep a promise it wouldn't be fair to ask you to make?"

"When I make a promise I make it. Don't you love me enough to believe that?"

She shook her head.

"Look," he said, "why have you come here to-day?"

She stared at him.

He said patiently: "Was it not because ye wanted to see me?"

She nodded.

He said: "There's more to life than carnal love, isn't there?"

"Yes . . . oh, yes, but—"

"Be honest. Do you not really want to be with me? With me more than anyone else in the world."

She hesitated a long moment, then nodded again. "But—"

"Then be that not the most important thing of all? Being together. Working together. Talking together. Walking together. There's so *much* to love—even if it be not the love you mean. The sunrise, and the rain and the wind and the cloud, and the roaring of the sea and the cry of birds and the—the lowing of cows and the glow of corn and the smells of spring. And food and fresh water. New-laid eggs, warm milk, fresh-dug potatoes, home-made jams. Wood smoke, a baby robin, bluebells, a warm fire . . . I could go on and on and on. But if you enjoy them wi' the one you love, then it is enjoyment *fourfold!* D'you think I would not give all my life to see ye sitting smiling in that chair? What is life if you live it alone?"

"Oh, Drake," she said, tears suddenly running down

her face and over the hand across her mouth and onto the other hand. They splashed onto her frock where it was already wet with the rain. "Oh, dear—I was—I was—afraid of this . . ."

"Ye cann't be afraid of having what you most want in life."

"No . . . Afraid of my own weakness. Afraid I should never convince you. I love you, of course. I have said it so often to myself in the night. Often it has been like an anthem—giving me strength. But that doesn't mean I am a whole woman any longer. Drake, I am—damaged—and crippled . . . inside . . . in my *mind!*"

"There now," he said. "See, I'm not going to come nigh you, not even to wipe away your tears."

Chapter Eleven

Parliament adjourned on the twentieth of November, and was not to reassemble until the twenty-first of January. Those members who returned for the next session would come back into a new life, a new century.

With two months to kill, the Warleggans decided to return to Cornwall after all. Elizabeth was set on it now, and George made no objection. At the moment he seemed to have little interest in her, or the disputed child who travelled with them. Nor did he seem to care much about the child she now so obviously bore. Although their return was not hurried, there was none of the leisurely, triumphant progress of the journey up. If the coach jogged her it jogged her; if the length of the stages tired her they tired her; if the bedrooms were draughty they were draughty. They reached Truro on Sunday the first of December, but there was so much sickness in the town that Elizabeth said she would prefer to move to Trenwith. George said she must do as she pleased, he had business to attend to. (He had indeed, for some of the tennants at St. Michael were being obstinate and refusing to move.) Elizabeth drove to Trenwith on the fifth, taking Valentine with her.

Ross saw Caroline on the twenty-first, and she said, could he wait a few days for her and they would travel down together? Her maid would be with her, she pointed out, so they would be fully chaperoned, unlike *his* wife and *her* husband. Ross had been helping John Craven tidy up Monk Adderley's estate and to settle up some of the debts he had left, so he agreed. If he were yet to be visited and questioned, well, it would happen—another day or two would not make the difference—he had become fatalistic about it. But as each day followed the other there was still no summons, no knock upon the door from anyone representing the Crown. Once he called on Andromeda Page, but she had already taken up with a young earl recently down from Cambridge and had little time to waste on a lost lover. Thus passes away the glory of the world . . .

On Saturday the thirtieth of November on the same coach, departing from the Crown and Anchor in the Strand at seven o'clock in the morning, Ross and Caroline and her maid left for Cornwall. In spite of the pretence to the contrary that he kept up even with himself, he was glad to be away. . . . When he came back, *if* he came back, the thing would be too far in the past.

On the sixth of December Demelza received a message delivered by one of the Trewinnard twins, and she at once rode to Pally's Shop. Drake met her at the gate. His face told her everything.

"Is she? . . ."

"Inside. I said I'd asked ee to come."

As he helped her off her horse he held her hand a moment longer than necessary. "Sister . . . treat her kind."

Demelza smiled. "Do you think I should not do?"

"No . . . That's why I sent. But I think—"

"Think what?"

"That if anything goes amiss she'll just flee again. Just go . . ."

Morwenna was in the upper room peeling potatoes. She stood up at once and took off her glasses. Demelza smiled at her and she half smiled back and smoothed down her apron, looking tall and uncertain and out of place.

"Mrs. Poldark . . ."

"Mrs. Whitworth."

"Please—sit down."

"I think," Demelza said, "it would be better if we used our first names."

They sat down, Morwenna employing the bowl and the knife and the basket almost as a line of defence.

Demelza looked round the shabby little room. After a moment she said: "Drake badly needs someone to look after him."

"Yes . . ."

"He says he wants you to look after him."

"Yes."

"Do you want that, Morwenna?"

"I think so . . . It is just that I don't know if I am fit."

"Are you ill?"

"Oh, no. I'm strong. Physically I'm strong."

"Then? . . ."

Drake came in with the inevitable tea and for a few minutes they sat drinking it and not talking much. Then Drake, with considerable tact, edged Morwenna round to repeating some of the conversation that had passed last night.

At the end of it Demelza said quietly: "Drake has been very miserable, Morwenna, ever since you left—all these years. He's only been half a person. Now you have come back to him, do you not think it a pity to separate again?"

"Yes . . . But—"

"You have told him how you feel about marriage, and he fully accepts that if you marry him now his

424

marriage shall not be a full one—unless you should ever change. He swears he will respect your wishes."

"Yes, he does."

"Do you believe him?"

Morwenna looked at Drake.

"Yes . . ."

"So will you marry him?"

Morwenna looked round the room, her eyes half seeking some escape. At length she licked her lips and said: "I know I only want to be with him for the rest of my life . . ."

"I don't think," Demelza said, "that there can be a much better reason for marriage than that."

Morwenna said desperately: "So long as he *understands*. I'm not *normal* any longer. I'm not! I'm not!"

Drake said to Demelza: "I explained to her last night. Just being with her is better'n anything else that could be."

Demelza said: "You'll excuse me for mentioning this, but being a blacksmith's wife is that different from being a vicar's wife. There's no social position, like, and there may be work—hard work with hands. Drake could not afford to keep a servant. You *have* thought on that?"

"That!" said Morwenna contemptuously. "I was the eldest of a family of girls. And my mother was never strong. I was the strong one. So I learned to cook and to look after a house. Of course we had servants, but they didn't do all . . . These last years I've lived the life of a lady—cooked for, waited on, treated as a person of importance. So little have I had physically to work. But in my mind and soul I have envied the tween maid, the gardener's daughter, the beggar at the door; I would rather have swept the streets than been in my position! Do you think I would not work now?"

"To be with Drake?"

She hesitated again. "Yes."

"You could wash his clothes—scrub his floors?"

"No need for that," said Drake.

"Of *course*," said Morwenna. "It's nothing—nothing."

Demelza nodded. "And you will not mind if your mother is upset?"

"I'm near twenty-five," said Morwenna harshly. "It is not anything any relative would say that would make the difference."

So young, Demelza thought, and glanced from one to the other. Morwenna looked much older than that, much older than Drake. That was what suffering did. But who knew what happiness might do? Demelza had been against this match almost from the first. Not on personal grounds but on the grounds of Morwenna's unsuitability, her genteel upbringing, her connection with the Warleggans. Yet . . . Drake's eyes. A difference here from yesterday.

"So you'll marry him, Morwenna?"

"I thought I had answered."

"Not yes."

"Then . . . yes."

It had taken a time to reach this word, as if Morwenna had had to plough through fields of reservations and restraints to reach it. Drake stirred and let out a low breath.

Demelza said: "I'm that glad for you both."

"How soon can we be wed?" Drake asked.

"It will take a while. Morwenna, why do you not come and stay with us at Nampara? We should be happy to have you."

"I'd better prefer she stayed here," said Drake.

Demelza smiled. "It's for Morwenna to say. If you are going to go on living in this district, maybe you should consider what people will say."

"I don't care," Morwenna said.

"I can get Mrs. Trewinnard to come in and sleep," said Drake. "If need be I can sleep in the Trewinnards' cottage."

"Whatever you say, Drake," Morwenna said.

"It *should* be Morwenna's decision," Demelza insisted.

Morwenna hesitated. "I'm sorry. Sometimes I have difficulty in concentrating. . . . I'll stay, Demelza. Thank you. I'll stay here."

Demelza kissed her. "When you *are* married, and Drake knows you're safe caught, then I hope he'll bring you to Nampara and you can meet Ross—properly and to get to know—and we can have—other happy times together."

She went out. After a moment Drake came after her and laid his cheek against hers.

"Bless you, sister. Bless you, and can ye do something more this morning?"

"What is that?"

"Come with me to Parson Odgers. Tis some awful to think we must wait three weeks! Is there no way to cut the waiting short?"

"Does it matter?"

"I'm scared for her," he said. "It's just the way you said—safe caught. She's *not* yet safe caught—not till we're wed. I'm scared something may happen. I'm scared she may just change her mind and move on."

II

Mr. Odgers said: "Well, Mrs. Poldark, ma'am, I would be happy to oblige you if there were a way within the canon laws of the Church, but as you know, ma'am, there is none. It is Friday now. In order to convenience you I can call the banns for the first time on Sunday, though strictly speaking one needs more notice. But beyond that . . ."

The little clergyman had been flushed from the kitchen where he had been helping his wife salt a piece of pork. His manner was ingratiating but his feelings mixed. In fact he was deeply shocked. Being a fair man, he would if pressed have been willing to admit that it did not amount exactly to blasphemy that this dean's daughter, the relict of his ex-vicar, on whom he had been accustomed to lavish all the courtesy and deference her station deserved, should now be about to throw the whole of her position away and marry a common smith, and a dissenter at that, but in his view it came very near.

Had that been all, Drake's welcome would have been of the coldest. However, that was not all. Accompanying him was Captain Poldark's wife, and Captain Poldark was a member of Parliament with the "ear" of Viscount Falmouth, and now that the living had again, unexpectedly, even providentially, become vacant, there was still just one more chance, one very last chance, that it might be offered to Mr. Odgers. So he could not afford to offend in the smallest way Captain Poldark's wife.

Captain Poldark's wife wrinkled her brows and said: "Isn't there something, Mr. Odgers, I've heard about or read about called a special licence?"

"Ah, yes, ma'am. That is only obtainable from the Archbishop of Canterbury. But a licence, ma'am, a licence as distinct from a special licence, can be obtained from the Archdeacon of Cornwall, or from his representative, his officer in the county."

"And who would that be?"

Mr. Odgers scratched under his horsehair wig. "The Archdeacon normally, I believe, lives in Exeter, except when he is on one of his—er—visitations. But his court is in Bodmin. I believe if you were to go there, if the young man were to go there"—he couldn't bear to address him by name—"and someone were to go with him to swear a bond, then, I believe, ma'am, a licence might be granted, and then I could perform the wedding soon after receiving it."

Demelza looked at Drake. "That would be about five and twenty miles. Fifty there and back. Would you wish to go so far?"

Drake nodded.

"What do you have to do?" she asked.

"You would have to swear an affidavit that there are no lawful impediments. Or *he* would, ma'am. And take a witness that he is resident in this parish. He *is* in this parish, is he? Yes, just." Mr. Odgers admitted this resentfully. "He would need money. I think it is two guineas, but I am not sure. And the person accompanying him would have to be prepared to be jointly bonded with him in some considerable sum."

"Can a woman act in such a way?"

"Oh, yes. But not his—not his intended . . ."

"I was thinking of myself."

"Mind," said Mr. Odgers, "you had best wait till Monday, to make sure of finding him in. The clergyman, I mean, who acts as the archdeacon's surrogate. Weekends and Sundays are busy times, and he might be away."

Outside again in the windy morning Demelza said: "Well, that's the best we can do."

"You'd lend me a horse?"

"Oh, yes."

"And come yourself?"

"I think. I'd be better than Sam. Being married to Ross gives me a sort of . . ."

"I know." He kissed her. "I'll not forget this."

It would be good to get away for a day; it would be some activity. This waiting for Ross was pulling unbearably at her nerves.

"By the way," she said, "does Sam know yet?"

"Not yet. Could you tell him? I think, I reckon you'd do un better'n me."

III

Torrential December rain flooded the road near Marlborough, and Ross and Caroline's coach was held up for a day. Sunday the eighth they spent in Plymouth and knew that tomorrow they'd be home.

They had dined together each day and supped together pleasantly each evening and had talked of many subjects from the insanity of the Czar to the tax on horses; but they had kept off personal issues. Ross found Caroline an agreeable companion, witty when she talked but economical of speech. She didn't have Demelza's small conversation.

They were sleeping at the Fountain Inn, and dining in one of the comfortable boxes with the red plush seats and walnut tables; and eventually it was Ross who for the first time drew aside the polite veil that had existed between them. He reminded Caroline of the meeting he had contrived between Dwight and herself at this inn. It was scarcely more than six years ago, in fact.

"It seems half a lifetime," said Caroline. "And must seem more still to Dwight, covering as it does not merely his captivity in France but four years of marriage to me!"

"I have often wondered," Ross said, "at my arrogance in bringing you together almost by force, at my supposing I knew better than you and he whether you should become husband and wife."

"The trouble is, Ross," she said, "that you're an arrogant man. Sometimes it is a great virtue and sometimes not."

"Well, which was it on that occasion?"

She smiled. She had changed for supper into a gown of cool green velvet, her favourite colour, because it contrasted with her auburn hair and brought out the green in her eyes, which could often with other colours look plain hazel or grey.

"A virtue," she said. "Dwight is the only man I've ever wanted to marry . . . Though perhaps not the only man I've ever wanted to bed."

Ross cut up a piece of the mutton on his plate and added some caper sauce.

"I don't think that makes you unusual," he said.

"No . . . we all look elsewhere from time to time. But then we glance away."

"Usually . . ."

She ate a little, picked at her meat.

She said abruptly: "Dwight and I, you and Demelza; do you realise how moral we are by the standards of today?"

"No doubt."

"No doubt at all. So many of my friends in London . . . But forget London. This county we live in. Add up the number of affairs that are going on, some secret, some blatant, among our friends, or their friends. And the same, though perhaps to a different pattern, among the poor."

Ross took a sip of wine. "It has always been so."

"Yes. But also there has been always a small core of real marriages existing amongst the rest—marriages in which love and fidelity and truth have maintained their importance. Yours is one and mine is one. Isn't that so?"

"Yes."

Caroline took a long draught of wine, half a glass as against Ross's sip. She leaned back against the red plush. "For instance, Ross, I could lie happily with you tonight."

His eyes went quickly up to hers. "Could you?"

"Yes. In fact I've always wanted to—as perhaps you know."

"Do I?"

"I think so. I believe you could take me as few other men could take me—matching my arrogance with your own."

There was silence between them.

"But . . ." she said.

"But?"

"But it could not be. Even if you were willing. I have the instinct of a wanton but the emotions of a wife. I have too much love for Dwight. And too much love for Demelza. And perhaps even too much love for you."

He raised his eyes and smiled at her. "That's the nicest compliment of all."

The colour in her face came and went. "I am not here to pay you compliments, Ross, but only—I'm only trying to say some things that I think you should hear. If we got rid of Ellen—as we easily could—and spent *all* night making love, and if then the first time I went to Nampara I told Demelza about it, do you think she would be hurt?"

"Yes."

"So do I. But I am a good friend of hers now. We are deeply attached to each other. Perhaps in time she would forgive me."

"What are you trying to say?"

"I'm trying to say that if I told her what had happened between us she would be hurt. But no more so, I believe, than you hurt her in London."

Ross put down his knife. "I don't understand that at all."

"You killed a man because of her. Oh, I know it was his challenge. And I know the quarrel was about some seat in the House. And I know you disliked each other from the start. But it was really because of her that you killed him, wasn't it?"

"Partly, yes. But I don't see——"

"Ross, when you fought Monk Adderley, it was not really him you were killing, was it."

"Wasn't it?"

"No . . . it was Hugh Armitage."

He took a gulp of wine this time. "Damn you, Caroline, it was a plain straightforward duel——"

"It was nothing of the sort, and you know it! You killed him because you couldn't kill Hugh Armitage, who died anyway. But Hugh was a gentle, virile, sensitive man—the only sort Demelza would *ever* have, could *ever* have felt deeply drawn to. You must have known from the beginning that she wouldn't have spared so much as a *thought* for a wild worthless rake like Monk Adderley."

"Sometimes one doesn't think these things out."

"Of *course* one doesn't think them out—that's the trouble! Yours was a totally emotional act. But you were fighting the wrong man just the same."

Ross pushed his plate away and put his fingers on the table.

"And don't get up and leave me," she said "for I should consider that a piece of very ungentlemanly behaviour."

"I have no intention of getting up and leaving you. But I can listen better to your lecture if I am not eating."

"The lecture is over; so you may enjoy the rest of your supper in silence."

"After that I'm not sure that I want to enjoy my supper either in silence or in seasonable conversation."

"Perhaps I should not have spoken."

"If you believed it, then you should. I am trying to think hard of what you've just said, to be—rational about it instead of emotional. D'you know you're the second person in two weeks to accuse me of making emotional decisions. You'll never guess who the first was. But so be it. Let me think . . ."

She toyed again with her meat for a few moments, broke a piece of bread with her long fingers but made no move to eat it.

He said: "There may be some truth in it. How am I to be sure? Certainly I've felt a lot, and thought a lot, about Demelza and Hugh these last two years. When I first found out about Demelza it was as if I had lost some belief—some faith in human character. It was not so much her I blamed as—as something in humanity. You must not laugh at me for sounding silly and pompous."

"I'm not doing so. But if—"

"It was like finding an absolute flawed. If something has driven me of late, there may be jealousy in it, but it is not *just* jealousy. At times I have discovered a new lowness of spirit, a new need to revolt, to kick against the constraints that a civilised life tries to impose." He stopped and regarded her. "Because what is civilised life but an imposition of unreal standards upon flawed and defective human beings by other human beings no less flawed and defective? It has seemed to me that there is a rottenness to it that I have constantly wanted to kick against and to overset." He stopped again, breathing slowly, trying to marshal the complexities of his own feelings.

"And this has all come—this has derived from your estrangement from Demelza?"

"Oh, not in its entirety. But one and the other. One and the other. You called me an arrogant man just now, Caroline. Perhaps one aspect of arrogance lies in not being willing to accept what life sometimes expects one to accept. The very *feeling* of jealousy is an offence to one's spirit, it is a degrading sensation and should be stamped on." He tapped the table. "But so far as Demelza and Monk Adderley were concerned,

I think you do me some injustice. Demelza *did* give him encouragement, of a sort. She was always exchanging asides with him, making another appointment—or at least permitting him to. And she allowed him to paw her—"

"Oh, nonsense!" Caroline said. "It is Demelza's way to be friendly—to flirt a little out of sheer high spirits. Whenever she goes out, as you well know, some man or another is always attracted by her peculiar vitality and charm. When she is enjoying herself she can't resist giving off this—this challenging sparkle. And men come to it. And she enjoys that. But in all *innocence,* Ross, for God's sake! As you must know. Are you going to challenge Sir Hugh Bodrugan to a duel? He has made more attempts on Demelza's chastity than any other two men I know. What will you fight him with—walking sticks?"

Ross half laughed. "You must know that jealousy flares only when there is risk."

"And do you seriously think that Monk Adderley constituted a risk?"

"I . . . thought so. It was not as simple a choice as that. And in any event he challenged me, not I him."

Caroline shifted her position, and stretched. "Oh, that coach has tired me! . . . One more day and we shall be home."

The waiter came and took away their plates but left the knives and forks for use again.

Ross said quietly: "Yes, I could sleep with you."

She smiled at him.

He said: "And for the same reasons will not."

"Thank you, Captain."

He said: "You've *always* been my firm friend—from *so* long ago. Almost before we knew each other well at all."

"I believe I fancied you from the beginning."

"I believe it was something more important than that, even then."

She shrugged but did not speak as the waiter came back. When he had gone again she said: "Perhaps I have been hard on you tonight, Ross. . . . What a thing to say! Hard on *you! Strange* for me to be in this position! I've never before dared! Well, I understand —a little—how you must have felt about Hugh and Demelza. It has been—irking, festering in your soul for two years. And the rest too, if you will. I don't deny that a single disillusion, if deeply felt, can lead to a general disillusion. Well . . . But now the blood is let. Even if it be the wrong blood. Let us not discuss any more the merits or demerits of your quarrel with Monk Adderley. It is over and *nothing* can revive it. Well, so is your quarrel with Hugh Armitage. So should be your quarrel with humanity. And so should be your quarrel with Demelza. She has been desperately affronted by what happened in London. The rights and wrongs of it do not matter so much as that you killed a man because of her, *and* that you risked everything, your life, her life—in a way—for a senseless quarrel which to a well-bred person may seem the ultimate and honourable way of settling a difference but to a miner's daughter, with her sense of values so firmly and sanely earthy, looks like the petulance of a wicked man."

"God," said Ross. "Well, I will keep that in my heart and let that fester a while."

"You spoke to me straight six years ago," said Caroline. "I speak to you straight now."

"Out of love?" he asked.

She nodded. "Out of love."

Chapter Twelve

Early on the Monday morning Demelza and Drake left for Bodmin. Morwenna stayed at Pally's Shop. Mrs. Trewinnard had been spending each night in the cottage; during the day the Trewinnard twins were there to answer the bell. Morwenna had shown no desire to go out, being content to sit and sew or to help with the cooking or the housework. She and Drake had talked little, being content to exchange the occasional commonplace, each a little shy of the other. She was like a wounded wild animal he was trying to tame: he made no sudden move or attempt to touch her lest she take fright. At first he had thought her unwell, in spite of her denials, but she was not. Her spirit, he decided, was clouded and needed above all time to recuperate and rest.

They had not even been beyond the fences that marked the five acres that he owned. He showed her these with pride, and she asked him about his work, and when he was working watched with seeming interest. Sometimes she was downstairs when people brought things to the smithy, but she did not come out. They had not been to church yesterday, but at Demelza's suggestion the banns had been called for the first time. It did not matter that the news was out, and it was safer not to miss a week in case there should be some holdup at Bodmin.

On Saturday Sam had come to see them, and had been much taken with Morwenna's quietness and modesty, also by his brother's obvious elation. Drake knew he could not object to the wedding but had feared the qualifications in his voice and manner. They were not there. Indeed Sam at once perceived in this silent, quietly elegant girl potentially suitable material for conversion to his own flock. Admittedly, her all too close connections with the Church proper put her provisionally out of reach of the sort of Christian Message Sam brought; but she had suffered as a result of her first marriage, and might now very well not only prove to be a brand ripe to be snatched from the burning but a means of returning Drake to full membership of the Connexion.

Anyway that was in the future. For the present Sam looked on his brother's face and saw that it was good, and praised the Lord for something that was both a carnal and a spiritual joy. It was selfish and unworthy, he knew, to feel a little twist inside him as he tramped away to think how good it would have been if he could have had Emma too.

Monday was fine but heavily gusty. John Gimlett, who fancied himself a weather prophet, said there would be rain later, once the sun got round to the butt of the wind. What he should have noted was the way, far out in the distance, the sea tramped, glittering in the sun. Sea birds were coming inland.

Drake and Demelza left at eight, at about the time Ross and Caroline were passing through Liskeard. At eleven Elizabeth called to see Morwenna.

She was upstairs working on the curtains that Drake had inelegantly hemmed when one of the indistinguishable Trewinnards put his beak round the door and piped: "If ee plaise, ma'am, thur be a laady to see ee."

Elizabeth came up the steps. Morwenna flushed, rose defensively, looked around as if seeking a way of escape, and, finding none, accepted the kiss. Elizabeth was her dearest cousin, who had connived at her marriage with Ossie. Although the chief pressure had come from George, Elizabeth had connived. However, over the last year or more Elizabeth had shown real sympathy. And after John Conan was born she had been the one to insist that Morwenna was not being treated properly by Dr. Behenna and that Dr. Enys be called in. She had also helped in whatever way she could after Ossie's death.

In the hostile life of the vicarage Morwenna would have greeted her as a friend. In this warm quiet retreat where, cocoon-like, Drake was hiding her, Elizabeth represented the enemy.

Elizabeth said: "But the banns were called yesterday! How could I not know? Is Drake not here?"

"No, he's out. Will you sit down?"

They seated themselves and looked at each other, Morwenna's eyes not really seeing anything. After a few moments she remembered herself and said:

"Can I get you something—tea or hot milk? I'm afraid there's nothing stronger."

"No, thank you. Though I shall be glad to rest a few minutes. The wind is so blustery."

Morwenna looked at her cousin's figure. "You did not, surely, walk, now you are—"

"Of course. It does me good." Elizabeth unbuttoned her dark fawn cloak and allowed the hood to fall back. She tried to arrange her hair. "It is not very far to Trenwith, you know. Scarcely two miles. Perhaps you did not come this way when you lived there."

"Sometimes. Though I scarce remember this part. Most often it was the other way. Geoffrey Charles so often wanted . . ."

"I know, my dear, I know. That is all over and done with. It was a very sad period in our relationship. We did not know. We did not understand."

Morwenna thought how much older Elizabeth was suddenly looking. But perhaps it was the pregnancy tiring her, bearing her down.

"And now," Elizabeth said, "you are to marry Drake after all. And you are to live here?" She looked around. "Are the Poldarks pleased?"

Morwenna flushed: "I hope so."

"Have they not said so?"

"Captain Poldark is still away. I hope they will never have any reason to feel ashamed of me."

"That I would have thought very unlikely. And Lady Whitworth?"

"She was not pleased."

Elizabeth smoothed her frock to conceal the bulge that was there. "It must have been so very trying, living with her. One of the most formidable of old women . . . But you just told her you were leaving and left?"

"Yes."

"And—John Conan?"

Morwenna winced. "Yes also."

"You did not mind leaving your own *son?*"

"Yes . . . and no. Please do not ask me any more!"

"I'm sorry. I didn't wish to distress you."

"No . . ." Morwenna folded the curtain and put it down. "You see, I never felt he was really my child,

Elizabeth. He was *Ossie's* child. Ossie's son. And I am convinced he will grow up exactly like his father!"

Outside someone was ringing the bell for attention. The wind leaned against the cottage and made it creak.

Elizabeth said: "You could never accept Ossie, could you. I'm—when I got to know him better I felt I could understand that. But I never liked to ask more personally at the time. If you ever want to talk about it . . ."

"No."

Elizabeth said: "But it must have been a great sacrifice to leave your only child. . . . You did not think to bring him?"

Morwenna stood up. "Elizabeth, in whatever way I cared for him as a baby—and of course I cared then—I do not want him now! He is a *Whitworth!*"

Elizabeth stared out of the small window at the tossing trees. For no very good reason except the bitterness in Morwenna's voice, a reflection of something else seemed to show in the defective pane. It was a bottle of cloudy brown medicine that had come in the coach all the way from London, jogging in her luggage but not breaking. It had become a symbol, a bitter symbol of the disintegration of her own marriage. *He is a Whitworth! He is a Poldark!*

"You will not, of course, stay here all the time until you marry?"

"There is a woman comes in every night. I am—chaperoned."

"No, no, Morwenna, you must stay at Trenwith! It is only proper. You could have your old room."

"Oh, no, thank you!"

Elizabeth frowned, a little offended. "You were married from Trenwith last time. Why not this?"

"And have Mr. Warleggan give me away?"

Elizabeth looked up at this sarcasm from so gentle a creature.

"Mr. Warleggan is in Truro and like to remain there. He may come for Christmas. Shall you be able to be married before Christmas?" Elizabeth counted.

"Yes, just. What day is Christmas Day—Wednesday? You could be married perhaps Christmas Eve."

"Perhaps." Morwenna could not bring herself to explain where Demelza and Drake had gone today. Elizabeth would say, what is the hurry; you are both still young; after waiting all this time, where is the haste? She might even persuade Morwenna. That was the worst danger—that her opinion would prevail.

Elizabeth said: "I had hoped to see Drake. Will he be long?"

"Quite a time, I fear."

"I wanted to meet him again so that there should be no hard feelings between us."

"I don't think there is," said Morwenna. "I think he admires you. For what you did for him once."

Elizabeth coloured. "I had forgot that . . . It was little enough." She rose. "So I must see him some other time, for I think we're in for a storm and I should not want to be caught in it. Morwenna . . ."

"Yes?"

"Would you not come to Trenwith sometime? My mother and father are both still there and are both much devoted to you. They're very frail now, but I'm sure they would want to see you before your marriage —just to wish you well."

"Of course." The two women kissed, with a slightly greater warmth, at least on Morwenna's side, than when they had met.

They went down into the kitchen and Morwenna opened the door. It was torn from her grasp and flung back on its hinges. The wind gulped its way into the kitchen, knocking over a bottle and a pair of scales.

"My dear!" said Elizabeth. "It has doubled in force since I came. Fortunate that it will not be entirely in my face as I go home."

"Wait a while. This is perhaps a brief violence and will subside."

"I've lived too long on this coast to believe that! It may well blow for twelve hours. No, I can manage."

"You might fall. In your condition . . ."

"Would it matter?"

Morwenna drew a little back to look at her cousin. "I don't know what you mean."

Elizabeth tried to cover the slip. "I mean I think it would do me no harm."

"But did you not fall last time?" Morwenna's naturally warm nature forced its way through the veil of preoccupation that was obscuring her mind. "Wait. I'll come partway with you."

"No, no. Look, it is just by the door where it is so bad. Once out in the yard . . ."

"Two will be stronger than one. I'll get my cloak."

"As they were struggling out of the yard Morwenna called to one of the Trewinnard boys. "I am just taking Mrs. Warleggan back to Trenwith."

"Ais'm."

It was a long struggle, with a raving southwest gale just gathering strength and buffeting them this way and that. Quite clearly Morwenna could not turn back until Elizabeth was safely home, right up to the door of Trenwith. There Elizabeth said, since Morwenna had come so far, surely she would just slip in for a moment to greet her father and mother. Morwenna said, well, just at present she would really rather not. Elizabeth said, I think they would be hurt to know you had come right to the door and not seen them. With a shiver of remembrance, Morwenna stepped into the big, picture-hung hall. Then, with the wind ranting outside and rattling the great leaded window as if it would pull it down, she accepted their invitation to stay to dinner.

II

The gale of December the ninth, 1799, was little worse than a half dozen others that might occur most years; but it was distinguished by the great seas it brought in. The worst of the storms had been far out in the Atlantic, and the coast suffered the effects. Nine ships of varying size were wrecked, mainly along the south coast, and particularly in the area of the Manacles, but a few came to grief along the north coast. Hendrawna Beach drew a blank.

Various people were converging on the area of Sawle-with-Grambler as the day progressed. Ross and Caroline had caught the new express coach that left Torpoint at seven-thirty and was due in Truro soon after midday. The gale delayed the coach, and two o'clock had gone when, after a brief and early dinner at the Royal, they mounted their hired horses for the last stage.

Demelza and Drake had reached Bodmin in fair time, but the Reverend John Pomeroy, rector of Lesnewth, vicar of Bodmin, and the Archdeacon's representative, was out and did not return until noon. Although he then raised no obstacles to the issue of a licence, it was time enough when the formalities were completed; and even then Drake had another call to make before they turned for home.

The other notable riding towards the north coast was Mr. George Warleggan.

The first to reach his destination, if one excepts Caroline and her maid, whom he left at the gates of Killewarren, was Ross. Like his wife's a few weeks earlier, his arrival was unannounced and unexpected. The first person who saw him was a thin, long-legged eight-year-old boy staggering across the garden carrying a ball of twine. His scream was lost in the scream of the wind, but soon he was in his father's arms and soon there was all the confusion that had attended Demelza's return. In the midst of it Ross asked where his wife was and was told that Mama had gone off with Uncle Drake early this morning and had said she would not be back to dinner.

"Daddy!" Jeremy shouted, above the chatter of his sister and the welcome of the servants. "Daddy, come and look at the *sea!*"

So they all went to look, at least as far as the stile leading down to the beach; further it was unsafe to go. Where the beach would have been at any time except the highest of tides, was a battlefield of giant waves. The sea was washing away the lower sandhills and the roots of marram grass. As they stood there a wave came rushing up over the rough stony ground and licked at the foot of the stile, leaving a trail of froth to overflow and smear their boots. Surf in the ordinary sense progresses from deep water to shallow, losing height as it comes. Today waves were hitting the rocks below Wheal Leisure with such weight that they generated a new surf running at right angles to the flow of the sea, with geysers of water spouting high from the collisions. A new and irrational surf broke against the gentler rocks below the Long Field. Mountains of spume collected wherever the sea drew breath, and then blew like bursting shells across the land. The sea was so high there was no horizon and the clouds so low that they sagged into the sea.

As he steered his chattering family back into the house Ross tried to discover what their mother was about being away all day in this fashion, but nobody seemed to know. Then Jane Gimlett drew him aside and whispered in his ear. Ross nodded and looked out at the lowering sky. Once again something important had happened in his absence. She should have been home before this, and in less than an hour it would be dark.

Gimlett had taken his horse to the stables, and, after a glass of ale, he patted his children's eager faces and said he was going out and would be back in half an hour and, alas, it was too windy for them to come with him. So he went up to the mine and saw Zacky Martin and some of his other friends, and as he moved to return to the house he saw Drake riding away up the valley. Avoiding a meeting at this stage, he stood behind one of the sheds until he was past and then walked down.

Demelza, having heard of his arrival, had come quick again to the door and was peering into the dark afternoon looking for him. They saw each other, and she came as far as the edge of the garden to meet him; almost breaking into a run but then checking herself.

She stopped, uncertain.

He said: "Well, Demelza . . ."

"Are you—" she said. "Did anything happen?"

"When?"

"After I left, of course."

"No, the incident is dead."

She said: "Oh . . ."

"An unfortunate choice of words, perhaps."

"No," she said. "The incident is—dead."

"Though it will live a long time in my mind."

There was a pause.

He bent and kissed her. Her lips were cool and tentative.

"Have you been back long?"

"Less than an hour. I came with Caroline. The coach was late."

"What a day . . ."

They stared about them, glad of a subject they could share without emotion. Foam blew in soap suds about the garden and hung in tattered streaks from brambles and branches like the seeds of wild clematis.

Ross said: "This is why some of those pretty trees from Strawberry Hill would not grow here."

"Even those that are growing here look in a poor way."

"When I got home Jeremy was trying to tie some of them up."

"Was he? He loves plants. This morning it was only normal gusty. I have been to Bodmin with Drake."

"Jane told me."

"I'll explain it all later. Have you eaten, Ross?"

"Briefly and early. But I can wait till supper."

At the moment each was content with a neutrality founded on the exchange of commonplaces, the incidence and occurrence of mundane things. If there was to be war or peace between them, love or lost love, agreement or disagreement, affinity or misunderstanding, it must yet wait a while to emerge. The sharp edges could be cushioned for a time by the routine of home.

They turned and went into the house together.

With the licence in his belt Drake was meanwhile

making his way towards Sawle. Demelza had lent him Judith until tomorrow, so he was in time at Parson Odger's cottage to catch him and his eldest son hammering at a piece of guttering that had come down in the gale. Drake was feeling so benevolent to the world in general that he said he would come up so soon as ever the gale had abated and replace all that piece over the front door with a piece of new. What they were putting back, he said, had gone poor and would hardly see the winter out.

He did not intend this as an ingratiating gesture, but Parson Odgers did seem to feel that there might be more in the young man than he had previously noted; he peered at the licence through a pair of broken spectacles, said all was in order and when did they now wish to be wed; next Monday? Drake said, could it be earlier than that? Parson Odgers said, well, there was nothing to stipulate that it should *not* be earlier; when did the young man suggest? The young man suggested tomorrow. Odgers winced as if he had been trodden on and said, impossible, he was busy tomorrow; he had appointments, all sorts of things to see to; couldn't manage that. Perhaps, if he rearranged his schedules he might be able to fit it in on Wednesday morning. Drake, having observed the unintended effect of his offer to replace some of the guttering, said, well, if by some chance Mr. Odgers could fit them in any time tomorrow, didn't matter whether twas early or late, he would, could, easily repair the whole of the guttering of the cottage before the end of the winter. He'd got some very suitable iron that could soon be knocked into shape and given a coat of paint before it was put up. Heavy stuff that would last for years. Mr. Odgers coughed into his woollen scarf and said: "Two-thirty, then.

"Mind you're not late," he added, as Drake turned happily away. "I can't celebrate after three. It's against the law."

"Thank you, Mr. Odgers. Rest sure we'll not be late. Reckon we shall be in church soon after two."

"Two-*thirty*, I said! And that, of course, is dependent on the gale. In this climate my poor church has so much to stand."

As he mounted Judith, Drake offered up a silent prayer that Sawle's leaning spire should resist at least one more storm. The gale was becoming a little less violent with the onset of dusk. That was not saying much; Judith staggered under the constant buffeting, and even here, two hundred feet above the sea, puffs of foam drifted like ghosts, dodging and dipping in the wind.

It had been a long day for Drake following other long days, but there was no fatigue in any of them. He had slept barely three hours any night since Morwenna came but he had felt no sleepiness during the day, nor did now, nor would when he put his head down. If there had been need he would cheerfully have ridden the fifty miles to Bodmin and back all over again. Life was in him like a burning, glowing spark; every moment, every thought added breath to it, fanning it alive. Ross had said to him once: "Nothing should be able to destroy your life like that." But it had. Perhaps equally nothing—no one person—should have been able to *make* his life like this—to make it over again, in Sam's terms. But it was so. And if the depths were too deep, surely no heights could be too high. There might be a moral law against misery: there was none against happiness.

Nor did he feel any serious doubts about Morwenna's love for him. At the moment he had no thoughts beyond securing her in wedded companionship: let the rest come if or when it would. He was prepared to be as patient as he promised—to wait for months or years. What did it matter if it *was* half a marriage? There was a proverb that among the blind the one-eyed man was king. Until a few days ago he had been blind.

At the top of the last long hill he dismounted, for Judith was very tired. He led her down the narrow track, noticing with some surprise that there seemed to be no light in Pally's Shop. Indoors it must surely be dark by now, and Morwenna, if she were sewing, should not be straining her eyes. A worm of alarm moved in him. But then, of course, she might be at the gate waiting for him. She should be the one who might be worried.

But she was not at the gate. The place looked deserted. The Trewinnard boys normally worked from dawn until dusk, but on a day like this he would have sent them home by three. Had they gone? And had Morwenna gone? He jumped off the pony, looped the reins over the post, and ran into the house.

"Morwenna! Morwenna!" Through the kitchen up to the parlour, and then partway up the ladder to the bedrooms. Nobody. The fire was out. Nothing. He was back to what he had been a week ago. He climbed the rest of the way and looked in at the bedroom where she had been sleeping. There was her bag, her nightdress, her slippers, her brush and comb. So at least she could not have—

"If ee plaise, sur." One of the Trewinnards, he didn't know which. "Mistress Whitworth, sur, she'm gone out."

"*Gone* out? Where?" Relief of a sort.

"Gone Trenwith."

"Trenwith?" No relief now.

"Mistress Warleggan came for she this morning. Mistress Whitworth say she will walk her 'ome, as Mistress Warleggan be carren a baby, and in this gale o'wind."

"When was this, Jack?"

"Jim, sur. Jack be gone. We tossed a coin to see who'd stay till one of ee was 'ome. Oh . . . dunno. Aven no wa-atch. Twould be afore noon, reckon."

"Did she say—*anything* more—how long she'd be?"

"Nay, sur, naught more'n I d'say. She just say she be gwan walk Mistress Warleggan 'ome. I reckoned she'd be no more'n a 'our."

"Thank ee, Jim. Go home now."

"Ais, sur."

Barely stopping to slam the door behind him, Drake ran for the tired pony, clambered on its back, dug his heels in, and turned madly up the hill towards Trenwith.

Chapter Thirteen

As soon as she sat down to dinner Morwenna regretted the decision to stay. It had been very hard to refuse and would have seemed like a rebuff to the two old people welcoming her. It would, too, have been a rebuff to Elizabeth, who, however misguided earlier, had made what amends she could. Especially she had befriended Drake on an issue of great importance to his survival as a smith. It was good also to see that darkly attractive little boy, Valentine Warleggan, again. On their visits in Truro Morwenna had seen a good deal of him and become fond of him. He sat beside her at the meal, and plied her with more food and drink than she could eat.

That was all right; but this house was darkly reminiscent of trouble and bitter scenes and heartbreak. Merely being in it put back the clock to the time when she was Geoffrey Charles's governess and an impressionable girl in her teens, likely to be overborne by her elders. It served to undermine her conviction now. Now that she was here, nothing seemed as definite, nothing as decided. She told herself that this was a weakness within herself, created by the nervous strains of these last years; irresolution was not deep in her temperament. Yet it was deep in her consciousness.

Nor, now that she had stayed, did she feel she had had the need to for fear of offending the old Chynoweths. Though they knew her to be a widow and had had a child of her own, they were not really interested in her or concerned about her affairs. The four years since she left Trenwith as a modest bride might have contained a whole lifetime for Morwenna; to them it was a few months in a repetitive existence whose monotony was only broken by the variety of the ailments they suffered. And their welcome to her was not really based on any personal warmth but on the recognition of a familiar human being who in the past had always been willing to sit and listen sympathetically to their complaints.

They had finished their main course and the heavy dishes were just being borne away when George arrived.

First it was a noise at the door and distant voices and the sound of feet. Then voices nearer and the clop of hooves on the gravel near the window. Elizabeth rose, her face flushing, put her hand on the back of her chair. George came in.

He was in tall boots and a snuff-coloured riding suit, and he was handing his cloak and hat to a servant as he entered. His hair was blown about by the wind, and he put up a hand to smooth it. His face was unusually red from its buffeting.

"Well, well," he said. "The family at dinner. Am I late?"

"Not in the least," Elizabeth said. "It can all be brought back straightaway. Stevens, Morrison . . ."

"Yes'm."

"And Morwenna," said George, looking across as he greeted his mother-in-law. "I had not thought to find you here."

"Just a visit," said Elizabeth. "What a day! What brought you in such weather?"

"Impulse. And I felt I should look to my affairs—"

"Papa! Papa! Did you get near blown away?—"

"And Valentine," said George sarcastically. "What a happy family!"

"Papa! Did you see the sea? It is e-*nor*-mous! Tom and Bettina took me to look down into Trevaunance Cove!"

"It is almost six months since I was here," George said, "and sometimes the presence of the owner has a salutary effect on the servants." He sat opposite Morwenna and glanced around him. "Ah . . . well, no, I think the cod is not for me, Stevens. Nor the fried beef. Was the goose good?"

"I did not eat it," said Elizabeth. "Father . . ."

"Eh? What? Oh, yes, the goose was fair enough. We'll need bigger than that for Christmas, though. There's few enough of any size about. The bad spring seemed to start 'em off late."

"Papa! They say the roof came right off Hoskin's cottage! Just like stripping a wig off a bald man! That's what Bettina said. Just like stripping a wig off a bald man!"

"Are you settling down with Lady Whitworth?" George asked Morwenna, ignoring the little boy. "No doubt you will find the life somewhat constricting."

"Well, no," said Morwenna, and stopped.

"Papa!—"

"Valentine," Elizabeth said, "please do not talk so much at the table. Allow your father a little peace."

"Peace," said George, still not looking at Valentine, "is something we prize only when it is lost. Like faith, like trust, like confidence." He began his dinner.

Elizabeth motioned to the butler to bring in the next course for the rest of them. It consisted of cherry tarts, mince pies, apple fritters, and a plum pudding, with cream and custard and jelly. Dinner went on for a while to the sound of the buffeting wind. George's presence was big and alien and dominant in the room, like that of a king who had just come into a group of his subjects. Everyone strove to behave normally and no one quite did.

Morwenna looked at Elizabeth, caught her eye, and indicated that she would like to leave. Elizabeth made a little warning negative movement of the head.

"From what I could see," said George, "the gardens are in poor state. What have the men been doing?"

"It is difficult to keep a place tidy at this time of the year. And in this wind. I see a branch of the fir by the gates is hanging."

"The whole tree should come down. Have the apprentices arrived?"

"Yesterday in the forenoon."

"They cost me fifteen pounds each. It was too much, I thought, coming from a poorhouse, but the overseers said they were apty young boys."

"They seem so. But one, George, one called Wilkins, I would not allow in the house as he hadn't had the smallpox. He will have to sleep in the village."

"Oh, George," said Mrs. Chynoweth, digging into her immediate memory and struggling with her unruly tongue. "Did you th-know that our little Morwenna is to wed again?"

Morwenna stared at the old woman in horror: during the whole of her visit this had not even been mentioned before. She had been given no idea that Mrs. Chynoweth even knew.

"No," said George, and laid down his knife to take a sip of wine. "That might be a way out of your present difficulties. Who is to be the man?"

"Papa," Valentine said, "I have been doing some painting in that picture book you bought me in London. You have to have the book quite flat or the colours run. I'll show you when I get down. Mama, might I get down?"

"No, dear, not yet . . ."

"The United States," said Mr. Chynoweth, half waking from a doze. "That's what they call themselves. A democracy. Hah! But what does their president say about it, what does he say? Eh? I'll tell you. He says, 'Remember, there never was a democracy that did not commit suicide.' That's what he says. What's his name? I forget. Adamson or Adams or some such."

An accumulation of the gale leaned against the house and seemed about to push it over. A footman came in and took away plates.

Elizabeth said: "That silver coffeepot we bought in London: one of the hinges of the lid is defective, I believe. I think we should take it back."

"I paid twenty-six pounds for it," said George.

"Your old horse, Kinsman has been ill with the butts," Elizabeth said. "A bottle of Daffy's Elixir has brought him a little better, but I fear it is partly his age."

"Let him be put down," said George.

"Papa," said Valentine, "the day we arrived such fun! We had scarce got into the house when a hawk was chasing a sparrow and the sparrow flew into the big hall through the open door and hid under the sideboard with the hawk following right into the house. Such a commotion! All the servants beating about! And in the end away flew the sparrow with the hawk still after him!"

There was a silence while they all listened to the wind.

Elizabeth said: "Farmer Hancock called yesterday. He was concerned to renew the lease on the 30 acres that you rent him. He says at present he pays thirty-five pounds a year."

"Hancock should know better than to call on you with his troubles," said George. "Tankard will be here next week."

"I didn't know that. I didn't know, of course, that you were coming."

Silence again.

"Who is to be the man?" George asked Morwenna.

Morwenna looked at him with sightless eyes.

"Lucy Pipe came back with the th-news from th-church yesterday," said Mrs. Chynoweth. "Th-some name. A carpenter or a smith or th-some such. Not a good match, I th-should say. I don't know what her mother will think."

"Is it Carne?" George said, still looking directly at Morwenna.

"Papa," Valentine said. "When dinner is over, will you come up and let me show you—"

"Stevens," George said, turning to the butler, "please take this child away."

There was a brief stormy interlude while Valentine, tears in his eyes but not falling, was led away.

After the commotion had settled George said: "Is it Carne?"

Morwenna continued to look back at him. "Yes," she said.

II

Near Trenwith gates a gust of wind almost had pony and rider over, so Drake jumped off and ran beside Judith up the gravel drive. It seemed a long way, but his anxiety swamped fears of meeting the gamekeepers. He reached the front door. He hitched Judith to a post and pounded on the door. It was no time now for courtesy or finesse.

A man at length opened it, and held it open a bare three inches as the wind thrust to be in.

"Yes?"

"Is Mor— Is Mrs. . . . Is— I came for Mrs. Whitworth."

The light showed up Drake's clothes. "Go round to the back door."

This door was closing. Drake put his foot in it. "I've come to see Mrs. Whitworth. Miss Chynoweth that was. She did say as she were coming here about noontime." He hesitated. "Be Mrs. *Warleggan* here?"

"You get round to the back, my man, where you belong, or else . . ."

"Can I see Mrs. Warleggan, please."

A struggle developed in the doorway. A door beyond opened, and more light came out.

"What is it, Morrison?"

"A man, sur—"

The door went back and the wind screamed like mad children and rushed round the hall.

"Begging your pardon, Mr. Warleggan," said Drake, his face tight. "I've no wish nor want to intrude, but I've heard that Morwenna's come up here and I've come for her."

"Carne," said George. "You are trespassing on this property. The law of trespass is a severe one, and I am a magistrate. I give you three minutes to be off my land." He took out his watch. "Then I'll send my gamekeepers after you."

Elizabeth came out of the room behind him. Her face was stretched with controlled emotion.

"Oh, Drake is it?" she said. "You must have—"

"Ma'am, I'm seeking Morwenna. If—"

"She's gone. Not ten minutes since."

A child was shouting upstairs and a door banged violently.

"Gone? Where? Where, ma'am?"

"She left. I thought she was—"

"On her own?"

"Yes, she would not stay—"

Drake said: "I just come from my shop. I've not seen her on the way."

"You have two minutes," said George. "And if you doubt my wife's word I shall rescind that, you insolent puppy. As for that dim-sighted slut you intend to marry, I'll see she never enters this house again. Nor will she have any connection with anyone here! D'you *understand*! If she comes on this land I'll have her whipped off for a beggar!"

"Drake," said Elizabeth. "If you came by the drive ... She may have taken the shortcut."

"Only ten minutes since?" He hesitated. "Thank ee, ma'am. *Thank* ee, ma'am."

Trembling with anger and anxiety, Drake turned again and went out. Before he was through the door it shut behind him, knocking him down the steps. He grabbed Judith and mounted her again, riding now into the teeth of the gale.

Elizabeth must be telling the truth. But even if she'd left, had she gone home? She might have wandered off somewhere. Even towards the cliffs. If George had treated her as he had treated him she would be desperately distraught. And the dark, and the low clouds, and this vile wind ...

Kicking at the ribs of the pony, he reached the gates and began the struggle home.

Now that the tide was ebbing there was less spume

to contend with; but still bits of twigs and dust and other light refuse flew intermittently, getting in Judith's eyes and making her ever more nervous. Few people were about even though it was yet early evening. Few would stir in such weather. A cottage here and there in the sheltered declivities of the land showed a gleam of light. Past Trevaunance the wind slackened.

Judith reared and nearly unseated him; it was a badger scuttling like an evil spirit across their path. Suppose Morwenna had fallen and he had missed her in the dark. He was superstitious about calling her name aloud as he rode. It might drive her away. She might not recognise his voice and cower in a ditch till he was past. Still worse, distressed by whatever had been said at Trenwith, she might have returned to the nervous mood in which she had rejected him in April, and refuse to answer.

He had to *see* her first, to see something moving. He prayed silently, but altogether without words.

The moon was rising, so it was not properly dark. The wind boomed overhead as if in an echoing, hollow tunnel from which all life had long since fled. The few harried trees nodded their heads against the breaking clouds. The land crouched in ungainly lumps and shadows, unfamiliar in the half-dark.

Down the last hill, which was the sharpest of all, and he got from the pony again as they went down, slithering and slipping among the mud and the stones. Pally's Shop was still in darkness. A single light gleamed on the opposite hill. And then he saw her.

There was no doubt at all in his mind because she looked exactly as she had done when she first came last Thursday. Tall, mannish in her long cloak, with a shuffling walk. She was at the gate of smithy.

He dropped the reins and ran on and called her name, but it was too gentle and the wind snatched at it and bore it away.

"Morwenna!" he shouted.

She heard him this time and turned, but with the

cloak over her hair it was too dark to see her face.

"Drake."

He said: "I been *searching* for you and *searching* for you everywhere."

"Drake," she said, and hesitated, and then went into his arms.

He said: "I just been to Trenwith. They said you'd just left . . ."

"I was looking for you. I thought you weren't home." She was trembling and out of breath, exhausted.

"I must've missed you. Ye must've come through the wood."

"I came through the wood."

"Never fear, my love. Tis all past now. There's no need to worry no more."

He carefully did not kiss her or hold her against her will. But he noted that at this moment she was clinging to him.

III

George found Elizabeth in her bedroom, whence she had gone after quieting Valentine and talking to him and admiring his painting. George moved around the bedroom for a few moments, picking up one or two things and looking at them and then setting them down.

He said casually: "It is good to be in this house again. Having been absent so long one forgets its virtues."

Elizabeth did not reply, but examined a tiny blemish on her face.

George said: "A disagreeable ride and a disagreeable welcome. I fear I lost my temper downstairs."

"There was nothing disagreeable until you made it so."

He turned his head slowly, viewing her with quiet hostility. "You feel perfectly content that your cousin should be marrying that insolent, down-at-heel Methodist?"

"Not happy, no," said Elizabeth. "But before this we attempted to guide her, and perhaps we guided her wrong. Now there is nothing to be done. She is a woman—no longer a girl—and a widow, without ties, except those that her mother-in-law has accepted. We cannot control her, and it is stupid not to admit the fact."

"Stupid," he said. "I see. And is it not stupid of you to have invited her here?"

"I hardly expected you to arrive today."

"And that excuses it?"

"I don't consider any excuse is necessary," she said quietly.

"Ah, so that is it."

"Yes . . . that is it."

George recognised the steely sound in Elizabeth's voice which meant that she was willing for once to do battle. He realised that at this moment her anger was greater than his own. His had reached its peak downstairs when he had turned Morwenna out of the house, and was evaporating now into a sardonic ill-humour.

"You think it right that she should answer me in the way she did—that girl, that woman?"

"Do you think it right to say what you did to her? Implying that Drake Carne might have had some complicity in Osborne's death!"

"I said nothing of the sort. If she chose to take it that way . . ."

"You know it was investigated and proved he was far away at the time."

"Oh, proved . . . One can prove anything. After all, Carne, it seems, stands most to gain by the event."

"Sometimes I cannot understand you, George. You seem . . . driven on by something."

"Oh, yes, driven on. Sometimes I am driven on."

She took up her brush and began to touch the sides of her hair with it, arranging and adjusting the fine strands.

He made an effort. "I hope you've been well." But the words were cold.

"Quite well. Though scenes such as those downstairs make me feel no better."

"I'm sorry."

"Are you?"

He analysed his thoughts. "I am sorry that you upset yourself over what I said. I am not sorry to have turned that impudent creature out of the house, even if she is your cousin. Nor am I sorry to have sent her dishonest dandy boy packing."

"On the contrary," Elizabeth said. "I felt—degraded."

George flushed. He was struck in his most vulnerable point. No Achilles could more obviously have possessed a heel through which his pride and confidence would escape.

"You have no *right* to say that!"

"You think not?"

"I *say* not."

He hacked the curtain aside and looked out. The moon was making the night light, and in Elizabeth's room, which overlooked the small courtyard, the wind was not strong enough to create a draught through the leaded panes. One more effort at some sort of conciliation.

He said with a dry laugh: "I have ridden here especially to see you, and we quarrel over two trivial people who concern us very little at all."

"There is one who does concern us both."

"Who is that?"

"Valentine."

He let the curtain fall. Elizabeth was sitting at her dressing table in a long flowing robe which hid the child she was bearing, and her slim shoulders and straight back seemed almost as girlish as when he had first seen them twenty years ago. The usual mixed emotions struggled within him when he looked at her. She was the only human being who could disturb him in this way.

"I have been—busy—scarce time to eat. I came here to *rest*. Valentine's prattle—annoys me."

"It is only the prattle of a normal boy. He was vastly upset tonight at being so dismissed."

George did not speak.

"Have you been in to see him since?" Elizabeth asked.

"No."

"Then you should."

George's neck stiffened all over again. Another reprimand. Ever since he came in this room everything she said had been a reprimand. As if *she* were the master. As if *hers* were the money, the mines, the bank, the properties, the membership of the House, the business connections! It was *insufferable!* He could have struck her. He could have squeezed her neck between his fingers and silenced her in half a minute.

She turned and half smiled at him. "You should, George."

His feelings broke then, like a wave against the immutable rocks. And the immutability lay in his concern for this woman and what she thought of him.

"Elizabeth," he said harshly. "You know at times I am in torment."

"Because of the thoughtless words of *another* child?" She was bringing the issue into the open.

"Possibly. Partly. Out of the mouths of babes and sucklings . . ."

So you think Geoffrey Charles in idleness points the truth, while all I have sworn to you before is false?"

He lowered his head like a goaded bull. "One does not *always* see these things in such precise terms. Let us say that at times I have been in torment; and then —then I speak my mind without concern for the courtesies of polite conversation. Then, no doubt, you reflect on the hazards of having married a black-smith's son."

"I did not say that."

"You said as good as that!"

"No, I did *not*. And if you are in torment, George, how do you think I feel when you come into this house and ride roughshod over everyone and are violent to my cousin and cruel to our son? *Our* son, George! *Our* son! No, I do not think I have married a blacksmith's son, I think I have married a man who still carries a terrible weight upon his shoulders, a terrible evil weight of jealousy and suspicion that *nothing* and *nobody* can remove! Not anything I say! Not anything I have sworn! Not anything I may *do!* You will carry this black load for evermore and ruin the rest of our married life with it! . . . If there *is* to be more to our married life? . . ."

George looked into the darkness of his own soul and knew that she spoke the truth. He collected his temper, struggled with it, strove to put it aside. "Yes, well; we have had all this out before."

"So I had thought!"

"It is not a pretty subject. Old Agatha laid a curse upon our marriage, I believe, and—"

"Agatha?" She turned swiftly. *"Aunt* Agatha? What has she to do with this?"

He brooded a moment. "I had not intended ever to tell you . . ."

"I think it is time you told me, whatever there is to tell!"

He still hesitated, plucking at his lip. "No matter now."

"Tell me!"

"Well, the night she died she—when I went up to tell her she was only ninety-eight and not a centenarian as she pretended—she turned on me—I believe it was out of spite, out of revenge . . ."

"What did she say?"

"She said that Valentine was not my child."

Elizabeth stared at him, her face bitter.

"So *that* was where it all came from . . ."

"Yes. Most of it. All of it, I suppose."

"And you believed *her?* You believed a half-demented old woman?"

"She said you had not been married long enough to bear the child to its full term."

"Valentine was *premature.* I fell on the stairs!"

"So you said . . ."

"So I *said!* You still think, then, in spite of *everything* I've told you, that I have been living a deliberate lie ever since Valentine was born? That I never *fell* down the stairs, that I made it all up, to pass off Valentine as your child when he was *not!* Did Aunt Agatha tell you all that too?"

"No. But that was clearly what she meant. And why should she say anything of the sort?—"

"Because she *hated* you, George, that is why! She hated you just as much as you hated her! And how *could* she hate anyone more than you, when you just ruined her precious birthday celebrations! She would say anything, anything that came into her head to damage you before she died."

"I thought you were fond of her."

"Of course I was!"

"Then why should she say something that might spoil your life just as much as mine?"

"Because hurting you was more important to her than anything else at that moment. It *must* have been! It was a *vile* trick of yours to ruin everything for her—"

"No trick! It was the truth!"

"Which no one need have known but for you! If you had come to see me first I would have besought you to say nothing about it. The celebration would have gone off, and everyone would have been happy, and in a few months Aunt Agatha would have passed peaceably away, content with her great triumph. But no! You had to go up and see her and tell her—you had to exact your cheap and petty revenge on her! So she tried to fight back, to hit you back with any weapon she had. And she could see that you were happy in your child; this was your great pride, that you had a *son,* a son to follow you and succeed to all your possessions. So she had to try and destroy *that.* I don't suppose it ever entered her head to consider me—or Valentine. Her one aim was to revenge herself on *you!* . . . And she did, didn't she? She succeeded!" Elizabeth laughed harshly. "She succeeded more than she could ever have imagined! Ever since then the venom has been working in your veins, and it will go on working till the day you die! What a revenge, George, what a revenge she scored on you, all because of your mean little triumph! Every day you've lived since then has been destroyed by Aunt Agatha!"

The sweat was standing out on his face. "God damn you, how dare you say anything like that to me! Mean and petty, you call me. Cheap and petty. I'll not suffer such insults!" He turned as if to walk out of the room. "I sought to set things to rights about her age, that was all. Trust a Poldark to be cheating—"

"She didn't know it!"

"I suspect she did." At the door he turned again, came back to the dressing table. "And what you have said to me tonight, Elizabeth—apart from such unforgivable insults—is totally untrue! It is not true that Agatha has poisoned my life ever since she died. Elizabeth, stop laughing!"

Elizabeth had her knuckles to her mouth, trying to control her laughter, the hysteria. She hiccuped, and coughed and laughed again, then retched.

"Are you ill?"

"I think," she said, "I'm going to faint."

He came quickly behind her as she swayed, caught her shoulders, then round the waist. As she slipped out of the chair he gathered her, picked her up with a grunt, looked down at her clouded eyes, carried her to the bed. She lay back, colour returning slowly, her fine fair hair, a little brazen from its recent tintings, coiled about her as it had fallen down, gleaming in the candlelight like a tarnished lake.

"What is it? What's the *matter?*" His anger was different now, deriving from alarm and not ill-temper. But it sounded little changed.

"It's nothing."

"It must be something! What can I get you? I'll ring for Ellen."

"No . . . The smelling salts. The drawer . . ."

He got them and waited. For a while neither spoke, and the interval allowed their passions to cool. Presently he moved away, stood with his back to the fire staring across at the bed.

She took another sniff and sighed. My child moved —and there was pain."

"You'd best have a doctor," he said shortly. "Though God knows who to have in this benighted district! Choake is a cripple now, and that fellow Enys is too superior by half . . ."

"I shall be all right."

"We'll go back to Truro so soon as Christmas is over. Or before. It's safer with Behenna close by."

"You upset me greatly," she said. "I was very well."

He thrust his hands into his pockets. "It seems that I am a bad influence."

"Indeed you are."

"So I should go again, eh?"

"I don't wish you to go, but I cannot stand another scene like this."

"You perhaps would rather prefer I behaved like your first husband, going with light women, drinking myself stupid, gambling my money away . . ."

"You know I would not."

"So there are disadvantages to the fact that I care, eh? That it matters to me what you do and what you have done?"

She did not reply, and he stood over her, the conflict in himself still unresolved but aware that he could air it no farther. His anxiety about her health made it necessary for him to make a peaceable end of the quarrel, but he did not know how.

"I'll go and see Valentine," he said grudgingly.

"Thank you."

"This damned house is *unlucky*," he said. "Always it seems our misfortunes have come here."

"What misfortunes have we had?"

"It is a wrong word. Everything I say today seems wrong . . ." He struggled with his resentment. "You know my—my fondness for you never wavers."

"It is hard to believe that!"

"Well, it's the truth!" Suddenly angry again, he shouted: "You *must* know it, Elizabeth! You're the only person I've ever cared about!"

"There's one way you can prove it."

"How?"

"Include Valentine in your love."

IV

After he had gone she lay and dozed for a while.

She had genuinely felt ill and been afraid she would faint. The child had been very restless, and the passion of the quarrel had exhausted her. But after about an hour she got up and went into the next room and took a bottle out of her valise.

She knew it was nearly time for tea but she had asked not to be disturbed, and anyway she was not thirsty. She carried the bottle back to the bed, with a spoon, and unscrewed the cork and sniffed the reddish-brown liquid inside. A rather musty smell, as of stale mushrooms. Then she put a spot on her tongue. It was not particularly unpleasant.

After seeing Dr. Anselm she had been on the point of throwing the bottle away. Eventually she had decided to keep it, but was sure she would never take it. As the time for taking it drew nearer this resolution had hardened. As she ailed frequently in small ways she had a decent respect for her own health, and she had no wish to damage it. Dr. Anselm had not disguised the fact that there was some risk, though he had not specified what the risk precisely was. Risk to the child, for one thing. She had no wish to risk its life. She hoped for a daughter. It seemed sometimes that she was surrounded by men. A little girl would be a joy and a comfort.

But George's manner tonight had shown that, even

if he tried, he could *not* relinquish his old suspicions. Would a seven-month child now lay them for ever? He could not fail to be impressed. He could not possibly know of any artificial means she had resorted to to induce it. It *must* destroy his suspicions—surely. Even if Valentine grew up dark and tall and bony. A *second* premature child. He *could* not continue to harbour the old jealous fevers.

So, if she took the risk and all was well, she gained a stability for her own married life, but still more she was likely to ensure a normal life for Valentine. If he lived as he had lived intermittently these last years, as George's suspicions waxed and waned, he would grow up a nervous wreck. But if this ghost were laid for ever he could look forward to inheriting all that the Warleggans had built up for him. Nothing was dearer to Elizabeth's heart than the friendship which had grown between her first and her second son. If her first son—for whom she still cared most—was poor, and her second son was rich, and they loved each other, there could well be some interchange of interests and property which would enable Geoffrey Charles to live at Trenwith as its squire in the manner to which he should be entitled. Valentine, of course, was still very young and this was all in the future; but she would look forward to that future with a different vision if Valentine's position as George's heir were assured.

And this was the way of assuring it? It seemed so. There seemed no other.

She unstoppered the bottle again and put a drop of liquid into the spoon. It was quite a small bottle and it carried no label. The instructions were on a separate piece of paper in her handbag, and she knew them by heart. "Eight tablespoons of the liquid before retiring, during the second week of December. If the medicine fails to act, do not repeat."

V

A good deal later that evening, when the children were in bed, Ross asked Jane where his mistress was.

"She was out back somewhere, sur. Looking to the pigs, I b'lieve. But I think she've gone out by the back way. She thought to see the sea."

Ross put on his cloak and went to look for her. Whereas two hours ago he had hardly been able to stand, now it was only the occasional gust that made him stagger. The clouds had broken up and a brilliant moon two days from full was riding the sky.

He saw her standing by the old wall under the shelter of an outcrop of rock. It was the first place he looked because it was a favourite spot of hers from which to see the stretch of Hendrawna Beach.

He came up behind her, trying to make a noise with his boots so that he should not startle her. But all the same she started up.

"You made me jump!"

"I thought you might be here."

"Yes, I just came for a few minutes. I often do when you're away."

"I would have thought you'd have had enough fresh air today."

"I really came to look. Look at it."

With the tide more than half out, the beach lay tattered and broken in the moonlight, and covered with froth like the remnants of milk which has boiled away in a saucepan.

Ross said: "Thank God I didn't come home by sea."

"Thank God you didn't."

They stood there quiet for a while.

She said: "Nothing happened in London? There was truly nothing?"

"Nothing."

"That's . . . good to know."

"Mrs. Parkins was upset when you left so sudden. She thought you did not like the room."

"I trust you told her different."

"I told her you did not like me."

". . . That would not be exactly true."

Conversation dropped.

He said: "Drake will wed tomorrow?"

"He wants to. If Mr. Odgers will do it."

"He'd better. For us."

"Has he any hopes this time? Mr. Odgers, I mean."

"I think I have contrived it. But of course it must come through the patron, so he must hear it officially first."

"I'm *that* glad! Especially for Mrs. Odgers and the children. It will mean him getting—what?"

"Two hundred a year. It will multiply his present stipend nearly four times."

"I'm glad," said Demelza again.

For a few moments the wind shouted them down.

"But much more I'm glad for Drake," she continued. "Much, much more, of course. You would not believe the difference in him. He's a new man. All the way home he was singing."

"D'you think it will work?"

"I do now. Now I've met her properly. But I think in any case, Ross, if two people love one another the way they do, then it's best to marry whatever the future bring. Even if it all goes wrong in a few years, nothing will take away the years they've had. Being in love is the difference between being alive and not being alive."

"Yes," said Ross.

After a minute Demelza went on: "Drake is very—right thinking. Today, because we were going to Bodmin, we *had* to call and see Morwenna's mother on the way home and ask her for her permission. I tried to put him off, but no. That's why we were so late back."

"Did she give it?"

"I wish I knew the word to describe her. Is it 'pretentious'?"

"I would think it likely."

"Of course, at first it was all distress. 'My little Morwenna, throwing herself away . . .' But—for Drake's sake, Ross—I had to put on a pretence myself. I pointed out that Drake, in spite of him not being smart in dress or speaking, is no common smith. After I'd told her that his brother-in-law was a mine owner, a member of Parliament, and a partner in the new Cornish Bank in Truro she began to come round."

Ross grunted. " 'Pretence' is the word."

"No, Ross, not all. But it all ended quite comfortable with her wiping away her tears and saying she was too prostrate to see us to the door, and Drake having the impudence to kiss her, and then he kissed both Morwenna's pretty sisters, and they saw us away. So perhaps in a fashion it was a good thing to do after all."

"That other sister of hers," said Ross. "I think I saw her in Truro today. *She's* a strange creature, if ever there was one. Dowdy clothes and a dowdy walk, but . . . somehow she draws the eye."

"Morwenna can draw the eye," said Demelza. "After all, she drew the eye of Ossie."

"To everybody's ultimate ruin . . . But *she* does it in all modesty . . . Not the other sister . . . Not she. Are you cold?"

"No."

"Demelza . . . I have brought you a small present."

"Oh? Where? Where is it?"

"I'll give it to you tomorrow—or whenever the wedding is."

"Why do I have to wait?"

"I had intended it for Christmas. And then I had intended it for tonight. But then I remembered other times I had given you presents, and it seemed to me that this was too easy a way of buying myself back into your favour . . ."

"Do you think you need to?"

"Well . . . what was done in London was not well done."

She said: "Is it then perhaps your own favours that you should first seek?"

"Maybe. Maybe it's the same thing. But in either case it is too easy a way of setting things to rights. A present, a little money spent, and all is forgiven and forgotten. It won't do."

Moonlight briefly flooded the scene, and she looked up at the scudding sky.

She said: "I left you. I left you when I should not have done—while there was still danger."

"Perhaps it was the only thing you could do."

"At the time it seemed so. But afterwards, when I got home I thought different. That too was not well done."

He said: "In the past sometimes, when we have had great differences, there have been occasions when we have talked them out. We have talked and argued back and forth, and in the end I believe come to some acceptable conclusion. But other times nothing has been said. Nothing much but a word or two of regret or understanding. And that too has served. I am not sure which is the proper way here. Sometimes I think talking, explaining, creates as much misunderstanding as it clears anyway. And yet we cannot resume, cannot go on as if nothing at all had happened."

"No, I don't think we can, Ross."

"What can I say to put it right? . . ."

"Perhaps not much. Perhaps that is the wisest. For what can I say in my turn?"

"Well, I don't know. In our lives before this we've each given the other cause for deep offence. This is not worse, and should in ways be less bad. Yet it cuts as deep."

"It cuts as deep."

They had reached the heart of the issue.

"This time," Ross said, "I'm the chief offender—maybe the only one. At least I plead no excuse."

"Oh, Ross, it is not—"

"Perhaps in the end one measures the quality of one's forgiveness by the quality of one's love. Sometimes my love has been lacking. Is yours now?"

"No," she said. "Nor ever will be. Tisn't love I lack, Ross; but *understanding*."

"Understanding comes from the head; love from

the heart. Which have you always believed to be the more important?"

"It isn't quite as easy as that."

"No, I know," he acknowledged slowly. "I *ought* to know."

The clouds were flying so fast it looked as if the moon were being thrown across the sky.

"Perhaps," she said, "we both care too much."

"It's a signal failing in two people who have been married fourteen years. But I think if we can admit that, it is a long way towards understanding."

"But caring," she said. "Doesn't that mean thinking of the other? Perhaps we have each done too little of that."

"In other words our love has been selfish—"

"Not *that* much. But sometimes—"

"So we must be more tolerant, each of the other . . . But how do we achieve tolerance without indifference? Isn't that a worse fate?"

After a minute she said: "Yes."

"Then what is your answer?"

"My answer?"

"Your solution."

"Perhaps we must just go on living—and learning, Ross."

"And loving," said Ross.

"That most of all."

Chapter Fourteen

Drake was round at Nampara by seven-thirty. Having told them the time of the wedding, he went off to see Sam. Demelza rode to see Caroline and asked her if she could borrow a dress for Morwenna, since Caroline was about the right height. She bore this away to Pally's Shop.

Problems here, for Morwenna, although she looked slim enough, was like her sister Rowella and fuller in the right places than she appeared, and Caroline's frock would not button. This had *all* happened before, but only Morwenna knew it. Four years ago sew and stitch, sew and stitch—then it was altering Elizabeth's wedding frock for her. So another marriage now, in even greater haste, *same* church, *same* cleric—only the man was different. A tight hold, keep a tight hold on overstrung nerves. But her quarrel with George Warleggan last night—the vile things, the evil insinuations against Drake—somehow it had broken some mental block—not the effect Mr. Warleggan intended. She had *defended* Drake—would with her life—and in so doing became clearer in heart and mind. Marriage —this marriage—was still a haven to be sought, where she could at last be at peace. But the conflict last night had emptied her heart of doubt.

Drake, with more subtlety than Demelza had given him credit for, was careful not to crowd her or fuss over her. He never asked her what had taken place at Trenwith. He went on with his work throughout the morning, and cooked them a light meal at twelve, and stared up at the cumulus castles over the sea and reckoned it would not rain until nightfall. So time passed, and the frock, a cream grosgrain with a few dashes of crimson ribbon, was somehow made to fasten, and Drake changed into his new jacket and soon after two o'clock they all rode to the church. Waiting for them was Ross, and the two children and Mrs. Kemp to keep them in order, and Sam, and his mate Peter Hoskin, and Jud and Prudie—uninvited—and Caroline—unexpected—and three or four others who had heard about it and drifted in.

And at two twenty-five the Reverend and Mrs. Odgers came and the ceremony began, and in what seemed no time at all it was all over and the indissoluble bond was sealed. The married couple signed the register, and a few minutes later they were all standing in the crowded graveyard with its silent stones leaning this way and that, like broken teeth, the names on them erased by the wild weather and the occupants below long since mouldered and forgotten.

Demelza, wearing a new and rare painted cameo on her breast, repeated her invitation to Drake and Morwenna to come to Nampara for tea and cakes, but she knew they would refuse. Ross kissed Morwenna, and then Demelza did, and then Caroline and then Sam; Drake kissed Demelza and then his brother; Caroline also kissed Demelza and left Ross to the last. Much handshaking followed, before Mr. and Mrs. Drake Carne moved off on their ponies for the short ride home.

"So it is done," Demelza said, holding to her hat, which threatened to take off. "It is done, Sam. It is what they have desired most in the world ever since they first set eyes on each other."

"God have set them to grow in beauty side by side," Sam said.

Demelza watched the two figures dwindling in size as they passed the gates of Trenwith. In ten minutes they would be home, alone, happy in their new-found isolation, sipping tea, talking—or perhaps not talking —wishing only to be together in companionship and trust. She turned to look up at her brother, who was shading his face with his hand, to follow the departing couple. The rest of the group were dispersing. Mr. and Mrs. Odgers, having taken obsequious leave of Ross, were on their way back to their cottage. Caroline was talking to Ross. Jeremy was picking some moss off a tombstone and trying to read the lettering. Clowance was hopping from one curb to another. Mrs. Kemp was talking to an acquaintance. The sky was streaked as if broom-brushed; the cumulus clouds had faded into the sea, which roared as if it had swallowed them.

Clowance stepped on one curb near where Jud and Prudie were waddling off.

Jud said: "Careful, 'ow ee d'walk, my 'andsome. Put your feet wrong round yur, and a gurt big skeleton'll jump out an' bite yer toe!"

"Big ox!" said Prudie. "Take no 'eed of 'm, my dee-er. Step just wher ee d'wish—there's naught'll disturb ee."

They passed on, growling at each other, leaving Clowance thumb in mouth staring after them. When they had gone a distance she tiptoed carefully to the edge of the path and hurried back to her mother.

Demelza led her to Ross.

"Where's Dwight?" she said to Caroline. "I had hoped you would both come to tea."

Caroline wrinkled her brows. "I was telling Ross. Dwight was to have come with me but at midday he was summoned to Trenwith, and I have seen nothing of him since."

"Probably one of the old people," Demelza said. "Dr. Choake is now so crippled with gout . . ."

"No," Caroline said. "It was Elizabeth."

There was a short silence.

"Did they say what it was?"

"No . . ."

Ross took out his watch. "Well, he's been gone three hours."

"It might be to do with her baby," said Demelza.

"I wondered that," said Caroline. "I hope not, because it would be premature . . . though I understand Valentine was premature."

There was another silence.

"Yes," said Ross.

II

George had found Elizabeth lying on the floor of her bedroom about ten o'clock that morning. She had fallen in a faint but not hurt herself. He got her back to bed, and he was all for summoning a doctor at once, but she assured him she had come to no hurt. Only the fact that Choake was immobile and his dislike of Enys persuaded George to acquiesce.

But an hour and a half later she complained of pain in the back, and he at once sent a man for

Dwight. Dwight came and examined her and told him she was in the first stages of childbirth. George sent a man galloping to Truro to fetch Dr. Behenna.

This time, however, Dr. Behenna was going to be far too late. Pains were constant, with scarcely any intervals of any length, and contractions were regular and severe. At three o'clock Elizabeth gave birth to a girl, weighing just five pounds, wrinkled and red-faced and tiny, with a mouth that opened to cry but seemed only capable of emitting a faint mew like a newborn kitten. It was hairless, almost nailless, but very much alive. Elizabeth's wish for a daughter had come true.

There was no proper nurse present, and Dwight had to make use of Ellen Prowse, Polly Odgers, and the slovenly Lucy Pipe. But all had gone well, there were no complications, and when he had tidied up a bit he went down to inform the proud father of his fortune.

George had endured horrible conflicting doubts and fears since ten this morning, and when Dwight told him he had a daughter and that mother and child were doing well, he went across and poured himself another strong brandy, the decanter clicking on the glass as he did so. For once in his life he had drunk too much.

"May I offer you something, Dr.—er—hm—Dr. Enys?"

"Thank you, no." Dwight changed his mind in the interests of neighborliness. "Well, yes, a weak one."

They drank together.

"My wife has come through well?" George asked, steadying himself on a chair.

"Yes. In one sense a premature child is less strain on the mother, being that much smaller. But the spasms were unusually violent, and if this is the result of her fall she will have to take the greatest care over the next few weeks. I would advise a wet nurse."

"Yes, yes. And the child?"

"The greatest care for a while. There's no reason at all why she should not do perfectly well, but a premature child is always more at risk. I presume you will have your own doctor . . ."

"Dr. Behenna has been sent for."

"Then I am sure he will be able to prescribe the correct treatment and care."

"When can I go and see them?"

"I have given your wife a sleeping draught which will make her drowsy until this evening, and have left another one with Miss Odgers in case she needs it to-night. Look in now if you wish, but don't stay."

George hesitated. "The old people are just starting dinner. If you would care to join them . . ."

"Well, it's time I was home. I have been here near on four hours and my wife will be wondering what has become of me."

George said: "They are safe to be left now—without a doctor, I mean?"

"Oh, yes. I'll call again about nine this evening if you wish it. But I presume Dr. Behenna will be here before then."

"If he left promptly when summoned he should be here within the hour. Thank you for your prompt and efficient attention."

After Dr. Enys had been shown out, George hesitated whether to go in and tell the old people that they were grandparents again; but he reasoned that although they knew Elizabeth was in labour they would not expect anything so soon, and Lucy Pipe could be sent down to tell them later. His overmastering need was to see Elizabeth.

He put his glass down and went to the mirror, straightened his stock, patted his hair. He wiped the sweat from his face with a handkerchief. He would do. He had not felt like this before, so damnably anxious all day, now so damnably relieved. It was not right that one should be subject to this sort of emotional stress; it made one feel vulnerable and ashamed.

He went up and tapped on the door. Polly Odgers opened it and he went in.

Elizabeth was very pale, but in some respects

looked less exhausted than she had done after the long labour of Valentine's birth. As always her frail beauty was enhanced by recumbency. It seemed natural to her deceptive delicacy to be at rest. Her hair lay gilt-picture-framed about the pillow, and when she saw George she took a handkerchief to wipe her dry lips. In a cot before the fire a tiny thing kicked and stirred.

"Well, George," she said.

George said: "Leave us, Polly."

"Yes, sir."

When she had gone he sat down heavily and stared at her; emotionally tight.

"So . . . all is well."

"Yes. All is well."

"Are you in pain?"

"Not now. Dr. Enys was very good."

"It has all happened the second time. Just as before. And so quickly."

"Yes. But last time it was eight months. This time it is seven."

"You *fall*," he said accusingly, "always you fall."

"I *faint*. It is some peculiarity. You remember I even did it this year when the child was first coming."

"Elizabeth, I . . ."

She watched him struggling with words but did not help.

"Elizabeth. Aunt Agatha's venom . . ."

Elizabeth waved a weary hand. "Let us forget it."

"Her venom. Her venom has . . . Since she died— as you said yesterday—it has affected half my life."

"And half mine without knowing the cause."

"I am a self-sufficient man. Self-contained. As you know. It is very difficult for me to—to unburden myself to another. In such cases suspicion flourishes. I have given way to suspicion and jealousy."

"From which I have had small opportunity to defend myself."

"Yes . . . I know. But you must appreciate that I have suffered too." He hunched his shoulders and stared broodingly at her. "And what I said that night two years ago—oh, it's true enough. Love and jealousy are part of the same face. Only a saint can enjoy one without enduring the other. And I had good reason for suspicion—"

"Good reason?"

"Thought I had. Helped by that old woman's curse, so it seemed. Now at last I can see I was wrong. Clearly it has done damage—to our marriage. I trust it's not beyond repair."

She was silent, luxuriating for a moment in the absence of pain, of travail, the laudanum working gently to blur the sharper edges of existence. George had drawn his chair closer and was holding her hand. It was very unusual in him. In fact she had never known it before. So is the hard man tamed.

She said quietly: "It is for you to decide," knowing of course what his decision would be.

He said, with a new note of resolution: "We have a full life ahead of us, then. Now that we—now that I can put this out of my mind. However much I may regret that it was ever allowed to enter—it *happened*. I cannot—no one ever can—withdraw the past. Elizabeth, I have to say that I have been at fault in all this. Perhaps now—from now on . . . some of the unhappiness can be forgiven . . . the disagreeable times forgot."

She squeezed his hand. "Go and look at our daughter."

He got up and moved over to the cot. In the shade of the cot, just out of range of the light of the fire flames, a small red face blinked its unfringed blue eyes, and the tiny mouth opened and closed. He put down a finger, and a hand no bigger than a soft pink walnut closed around it. He noted that she was much smaller than Valentine had been. But then Valentine had been an eight-month child.

He stood a while, swaying a little on the balls of his feet, not so much from inebriety as from the satisfaction that was flooding over him. He was moved. It was something very basic in his nature that resented the emotional strain put upon him by marriage and parenthood. A part of his character would have been far more content with figures and commerce all day long, like Uncle Cary, not these terrible tug-of-wars, these battlefields of sensation that plagued him on the level of his personal existence.

Yet because of them he was living more deeply, and when, as now, there was a gratifying outcome to it all . . . He went back to the bed.

"What shall we call her?"

Elizabeth opened her eyes.

"Ursula," she said without hesitation.

"Ursula?"

"Yes. You called him Valentine, so I think it is my turn. My godmother, who was also my great-aunt, was called Ursula. My great-uncle died when she was thirty and she lived as a widow for thirty-eight years."

"Ursula," said George, and tried it over on his tongue. "I would not quibble with that. But was there something especial—about your godmother?"

"I think she brought the brains into the Chynoweth family. That's if you think we have any! Though much older, she was a friend of Mary Wollstonecraft, and she translated books from the Greek."

"Ursula Warleggan. Yes, I am not at all unpartial to that. Valentine Warleggan. Ursula Warleggan. They would make a famous pair."

Through a haze of sleep Elizabeth noticed the pairing of the names with special satisfaction, and silently blessed Dr. Anselm for his assistance in bringing about such a result.

George knew it was time to go. But he had one more thing to say.

"Elizabeth."

"Yes?"

"Yesterday when I came, my visit was not without purpose. I had something to tell you."

"I hope it is good."

"Yes, it is good. You'll remember I called to see Mr. Pitt in the morning of the day before we left London."

". . . I knew you were going . . . But you did not tell me afterwards."

George grunted and turned the money in his fob. "No. Well, there was that reason. As you know. I trust it will never exist again. It is our duty to see that it never exists again . . . But I have to tell you now that my interview with the Chancellor was very agreeable and very useful. I gave him my promise of full support, and he was gracious enough to accept my expressions of loyalty."

". . . I'm glad."

"Well, that was three weeks ago. Yesterday morning I received a letter from John Robinson. He was able to tell me that Pitt has found it possible to agree to my request—my solitary and only request—and will be pleased to recommend to His Majesty that I receive a knighthood in the new year."

A faint breath of noise, like a tiny sigh, came from the infant in her cot, registering her first comment upon this strange new world.

Elizabeth opened her eyes wide, those beautiful grey-blue eyes that had always fascinated him. "Oh, George, I am so *very* gratified!"

George smiled freely; a rare occurrence for him. "I suspected you would be—Lady Warleggan."

There was a light tap on the door. It was Lucy Pipe. "If ye plaise, sur, Dr. Behenna be downstairs. Shall 'e come up?"

"No. He shall not come up. First your mistress must sleep." The head hastily withdrew. George said: "You must sleep, my dear." His voice carried more warmth than had ever been heard in it before.

Eilzabeth's eyes drooped. "Yes."

"Sleep well, Lady Warleggan," George said, bending and kissing her.

"Thank you, Sir . . . Sir George."

III

Dr. Behenna was not a little put out after his long and tiresome journey to be told that the child was already safely delivered and that mother and child were doing well. He was still more put out by George's refusal to allow him to see the patient. In most households he would of course have tramped straight up and into the bedroom; but with the Warleggans and their *nouveau riche* insistence on their own importance in the world he had to go more carefully.

And when Mr. Warleggan eventually condescended to come down Mr. Warleggan was adamant. His wife had successfully borne her child and now must sleep. Miss Odgers was with her and would summon them if the need arose. George knew that Behenna was one of those men mentally incapable of tiptoeing into a bedroom, so for the time being he must be confined to the ground floor.

To assuage him he led him into the dining room, where the old Chynoweths were dozing over their brandy and port, and the kitchens were alerted to serve a late dinner for two hungry men.

Mrs. Chynoweth was naturally delighted to learn that she had a granddaughter, and like Dr. Behenna took umbrage that she was not immediately allowed upstairs. Mr. Chynoweth was too far gone to rejoice, and presently laid his head on the table and snored through the rest of the meal. It was a large table and they were able to eat at the other end.

George was never a great talker, and Dr. Behenna was still nursing his grievance, so the dominating voice at the table, often the only one, was the aristocratic but thick-tongued and slurred voice of the grandmother, Mrs. Joan Chynoweth—née Le Grice, as she pointed out—one of the oldest and most distinguished families in England.

"Rubbish," Jonathan Chynoweth was heard to exclaim under his breath, having caught enough of this through his drunken doze. "Very or-ordinary sort of family. Came from Normandy only a couple of centuries ago. Very ordinary."

His wife went into lengthy speculations as to a suitable name for the child. George ate on, remembering the previous occasion, after Valentine was born, when there had been a similar conversation as to what *he* should be called. Only then it had been his own father who had been here; and curled in an armchair like an ancient crone, putting in her asp-like suggestions from time to time, had been that evil, festering harridan, Agatha Poldark.

George was not a superstitious man, but he recalled his mother's dread of the old woman; in an earlier age Agatha would have been one of the first to face the ducking stool and the fire. Well deserved, for no black succubus could have done more to harm him. Even his father's bronchitis had seemed to stem from that night when the fire had smoked as if the draught had been supernaturally reversed. He had been a cursed fool himself to have taken heed of the vile old woman. Even on the day of Valentine's birth she had pointed out that he had been born at a moon's eclipse and therefore would be unlucky all his life.

Of course from the very beginning she had hated George—before even he had begun to notice or to hate her. As the living embodiment of the four generations of Poldarks she had outlived, she had above all resented the arrival of this upstart—allowed here at first on sufferance because he was a school friend of Francis—she had witnessed his insignificance and gradual growth to significance: she had watched and come to detest his progress until he became first the owner of Francis and then the owner of this house. It had been just as intolerable for Agatha to witness as it had been stimulating and satisfying for George to experience.

Although the edge of pleasure wore blunter with repetition—as all pleasures did—he still knew the satisfaction of coming into this gracious Tudor manor house and gazing round and remembering his first visit here as a youth of eighteen, unpolished, unsophisti-

cated, unlearned in the nicer manners. Then the Poldarks had seemed immeasurably superior to him, and
immensely secure in their position and their property.
Charles William, Francis's father, fat and impressive
in his long vermilion coat, with his belches, his unstable humours, his patronising friendliness; and
Charles William's widowed sister, Mrs. Johns; and *her*
son and daughter-in-law, the Reverend and Mrs. Alfred Johns; and Francis's elder sister, Verity; and Ross,
Francis's other cousin, the dark, quiet, difficult one,
whom George had also known at school and had already learned to dislike; and the relative who was
always absent, Ross's father, because he had got into
so many disreputable scrapes that he was not mentioned in the house. Over them all Aunt Agatha had
presided, half doyen, half neglected maiden aunt, but
embodying some watchful spirit to which the family
paid tribute.

Now all, all had gone. Verity to Falmouth, the Alfred Johnses to Plymouth, Ross to his own lair, the
rest to the grave. And he, the rough unlearned youth,
owned it all. As he now owned so much in Cornwall.
But perhaps this estate was the property he valued
most highly.

"Ursula," he said, thinking aloud.

"Eh?" said Mrs. Chynoweth. "Who? What do you
say?"

"That is what she is to be called."

"The th-child? My granddaughter?"

"Elizabeth wishes it. And I like it well."

"Ursula," said Jonathan, raising himself an inch or
two from the table. "Ursula. The little she-bear. Very
good. I call that very good." He laid his head peaceably to rest.

Mrs. Chynoweth dabbed at her one good eye.
"Ursula. That was the th-name of Morwenna's grandmother. She was Elizabeth's th-godmother. She died
th-not so long ago."

George stiffened but did not say anything.

"Not that I cared for her so vastly," said Mrs.
Chynoweth. "She thought th-too much about the rights

of th-woman. My—my father once th-said—my father once th-said: 'If a woman do have blue stockings she must th-contrive that her petticoat shall hide 'em.' *She* didn't. She never—never hid them."

"I'll trouble you to pass me the mustard sauce," said Dr. Behenna.

"Why do you say 'the little she-bear'?" George asked Jonathan, but his father-in-law answered with a snore.

"I believe that is what the name means," said Dr. Behenna. "Do I understand, Mr. Warleggan, that you are offering me hospitality for the night?"

"The little she-bear," said George. "Well, I have no objection to that. And that name Ursula Warleggan runs very well." He looked coldly at the doctor. "What was that you said? Well, yes, of course. Naturally you shall stay the night. It is not a ride you would wish to undertake in the dark, is it?"

Behenna bowed with equal lack of warmth. "Very well. But as I have so far been prevented from seeing my patient I wondered whether you wished to avail yourself of my services at all."

George said impatiently: "God's life, man! The child has been born scarce more than three hours. Dr. Enys gave my wife a draught and they are now both sleeping. Of course you may see them when they wake. Until then I would have thought it simple medical sense to allow them to rest."

"Indeed," said Behenna pettishly. "Just so."

"Even I have th-not been allowed to see them," said Mrs. Chynoweth. "And after all th-a grandmother should have certain rights. But th-dear Mr. Warleggan will decide . . . You decide most things, th-George, and upon my soul, that is the way it should be in a th-properly conducted th-household."

George reflected that it had never been so in his mother-in-law's household, where she had always held the reins over Jonathan. Nevertheless at Trenwith she had a proper view of the importance of her son-in-law in her world today. Without him they would both have long since mouldered away at their old home, Cus-

garne; here they lived in comfort and idleness, warmed
and fed and waited on, and would do so till they died.
Mrs. Chynoweth had never been a woman to ignore
the practical realities of a situation.

All the same, he well knew that Mrs. Chynoweth
would once have been horrified at the thought of her
beautiful young porcelain daughter forming anything
so degrading as a union with the common Warleggan
boy.

So time had moved on and values shifted and
changed.

Elizabeth slept right through until after supper,
when she woke feeling much refreshed, and all the
people who were waiting to see her were permitted to
see her. Ursula was also inspected and admired. Dr.
Behenna restricted his examination to the briefest and
professed himself satisfied. At midnight they all retired to rest. At three A.M. Dr. Behenna was wakened
by Ellen Prowse, who told him that her mistress was
suffering severe pain in the arms and legs.

Chapter Fifteen

It was not until the Thursday morning that George
sent for Dwight. Caroline, feeling neighbourly, was at
that time just pinning on a hat to call on Elizabeth
and admire the baby. She now unpinned it and let
Dwight go alone.

Dr. Behenna was with George in the hall, but they
were not speaking to each other.

George was pale and had not slept. "Mrs. Warleggan is in great pain and has been now for thirty-six
hours. I should be glad if you will go up and see if
you can aid her."

Dwight looked at Behenna, who said stiffly: "The
premature labour has brought on an acute gouty condi-

tion of the abdominal viscera which is manifesting itself in severe cramp-like spasms of the extremities. All that can be done is being done, but Mr. Warleggan feels that, since you delivered the child, you should be brought in for further consultation."

Dwight nodded. "What have you prescribed?"

"Some bleeding. Infusion of the leaves of *Atropa belladonna*. Salt of wormwood and ammoniac. Light purges to reduce the excessive pressure of the nerve fluids." Behenna spoke with keen annoyance—one did not usually give away the details of one's treatment to a rival—and Dwight was surprised that he was being so frank.

An old woman came out of one of the rooms and limped across the hall; Dwight hardly recognised her as Mrs. Chynoweth.

He said to Behenna: "Would you lead the way, sir?"

When he got in the bedroom Dwight stared at Elizabeth in horror. She had aged ten years, and her face was thin and etched with pain. Dwight sniffed slightly as he came into the room. Then he went to the bed.

"Mrs. Warleggan. This is a sad change. We must get you well soon."

"Of course we will get her well soon!" Behenna was right behind him. He despised doctors who let their patients know how ill they looked. "A few days and you will be about again."

"Now tell me, what is it? Where is your pain?"

Elizabeth moistened her lips to speak, and could not. She stared up at Dwight. Dwight bent his head close to her mouth. She said: "My—feet. All my body—*aches*—I have never felt so ill—or felt such *pain*." Her tongue, he saw, was swollen and coated with a dark reddish stain of blood.

"You have given her opiates?" Dwight asked Behenna.

"Some, yes. But it is more important at this stage to increase the elasticity of the veins and to clear the effete matter rioting in the bloodstream."

"So *cold*," whispered Elizabeth.

Dwight glanced at the fire blazing in the hearth. Lucy Pipe was sitting beside it gently stirring the cot. He put his hand on Elizabeth's brow and then felt her pulse, which was very rapid. The fingers of one hand were blue and swollen.

He said: "Perhaps I might examine you, Mrs. Warleggan. I will try not to hurt you."

He pulled the bedclothes gently back and pressed light fingers on her abdomen. She winced and groaned. Then he pulled the sheet further back and looked at her feet. He closed his hand on the right foot. Then he looked at the left foot. Then he stroked each leg up as far as the knee.

He straightened up and the bedclothes were put back. He knew now why Dr. Behenna had been so frank about the details of his treatments. They were doing no good.

A faint cry came from the cot.

He snapped: "Get that child out of here!"

"Oh," said Elizabeth, suddenly more alert. "Oh, why? Why? Why?"

"Because you must have perfect rest and quiet," Dwight said gently. "Even the smallest noise must not disturb you."

George had come into the room and was staring down at his wife with a concentrated frown of one who fears he is being bested at some game of which he does not know the rules.

"Well?" he said.

Dwight bit his lip. "First I will give you something stronger to ease the pain, Mrs. Warleggan. Dr. Behenna is correct in supposing it to be a condition of the blood. He and I must work together to help alleviate this condition."

"What is the cure for it?" George demanded.

Dwight said: "We must take one step at a time, Mr. Warleggan. Let us aim first at the alleviation. Afterwards we can attempt—the rest. I shall give her a strong opiate at once, and then we must try to bring greater warmth to the limbs. But in the gentlest possible way. Are you thirsty?"

"All . . . all the time."

"Then lemonade—as much as she can drink. She must have warm bricks to her feet and her hands rubbed lightly. But only *warm* bricks, changed hourly. Above all we must try to restore her body heat. It is of the utmost urgency. I want the fire built up and the window a little open. You will be staying, Dr. Behenna?"

"I have patients in town, but they must wait."

Dwight smiled at Elizabeth. "Have patience ma'am, we will try to help you as quick as possible." He turned. "Then we must wait, Mr. Warleggan. There is nothing more we can do at this stage. Dr. Behenna, may I have the favour of a word with you in private?"

Behenna grunted and inclined his head. The two men went off into Elizabeth's dressing room, with its pretty pink hangings and elegant lace table covers.

Behenna shut the door: "Well?"

Dwight said: "I take it you don't *believe* this to be a gouty condition at all?"

Behenna grunted. "The excessive excitability of the nerve fluids suggests a severe gouty inflammation which may well predispose towards the symptoms we are now observing."

Dwight said: "You have clearly not ever been in a prisoner-of-war camp, sir."

"What do you mean by that?"

Dwight hesitated again. He dreaded even formulating the words. "Well, it appears plain to me. Can you not smell anything?"

"I must agree there is a very slight disturbing odour which I did not notice until this forenoon. But that . . ."

"Yes, *that*. Though God in His heaven only knows what may have brought her to such a condition!"

"Are you suggesting, sir, that my treatment is in some way responsible?"

"I am suggesting nothing—"

"I could as well suggest to you, sir, that had I been here to deliver the child this condition might not have supervened!"

Dwight looked at the other man.

"We're both physicians, Dr. Behenna, and I believe equally dedicated to the succour and cure of human ills. Our treatments may differ as widely as two languages, but our aims are similar and our integrity, I trust, is not in question. So I'd suggest to you that there is nothing I could have done in delivering a child in an uncomplicated birth, or anything you could have done in prescribing the treatments that you have described to me, which would or could produce the symptoms Mrs. Warleggan is now suffering from."

Behenna paced about.

"Agreed."

Dwight said: "Contraction of the arteries, restricting and then inhibiting the blood supply. This is what appears to be occurring. Particularly and most dangerously restricting the blood supply to the limbs. There appears to be no *reason* for it! The birth, as I have told you, was unexceptional: premature but otherwise only distinguished by the fact that the uterine spasms were very rapid and over-emphatic. But I took that to be a characteristic of the patient—after all, a woman I delivered last week gave birth to a child in fifty-five minutes from having complained of the first pains. It was that, I thought, or an outcome of the fall she had had and not indicating any pathological complications. Now this . . . the cause is obscure; the disease hardly so."

Behenna said: "You're going too fast and too far." He glanced at Enys.

"I pray I am. Indeed I do. We shall know soon enough."

"I trust you do not intend to publish your suspicion to Mr. Warleggan."

"Far from it. In the meantime, though you may doubt my diagnosis you do not, I trust, disassociate yourself from my treatment?"

"No . . . It can do no harm."

II

Ross was in Truro all day Friday, the thirteenth, attending his second meeting at the Cornish Bank as a partner and guarantor. The duel was not mentioned, though everyone must have known about it for the simple reason that no one remarked on the stiffness of his right hand. Movement was returning, but he still had difficulty in signing his name.

For the most part the talk was double Dutch to him, though he maintained a polite attention. On matters of broad policy he found he was of some general use, and, although Lord de Dunstanville must have had many other ears to the ground in London, Ross was the only member of Parliament present and could contribute here and there.

After it was over he supped and slept with Harris Pascoe in Calenick, where for the moment he was continuing to live with his sister. The old premises of Pascoe's Bank would be sold or pulled down, and Harris was looking for a smaller house in Truro, near the centre, whence he could walk daily to the new bank. He had fitted well into his reorganised life, and although he lacked the prestige of being entirely his own man, he was saved much of the anxiety, and, as he said to Ross in his usual deprecating way, this was no bad thing for someone of his age and disposition.

Ross left on the Saturday morning and was home by midday. It was the darkest day of the year, of the whole winter, for although no rain fell the world was sunk in cloud, and dawn and dusk were nominal terms to indicate grudging changes in visibility.

As soon as he got home Demelza told him she had heard Elizabeth was still gravely ill. They had heard yesterday through Caroline, and Demelza had been to Killewarren this morning to inquire.

"It was the nearest I could go," she said. "If we were neighbours in any proper sense . . ."

"Did she say there was any change at all?"

"Not for the better. Dwight was at Trenwith then."

"Is the child alive?"

"Oh, yes, and well, I believe. Premature but well."
They met each other's eyes but said no more.

Dinner was usually taken with the children, and, now that Mrs. Kemp was becoming something of a permanent resident, with her too; so there was no lack of talk. Clowance, from being a silent child, was now vying with Jeremy in an ability to keep up a non-stop conversation whether anyone was listening or not.

Ross did not eat much, and halfway through the meal he said in an undertone to Demelza: "I think I must go."

Demelza nodded. "I think you should. Only I'm afraid for you."

"I can look to myself."

"If you were to meet Tom Harry in the grounds—and you with your weak arm."

"He could not stop me on a horse. And at a time like this George must surely admit me."

"I . . . wouldn't rely on it, Ross."

"No." Ross bethought himself of their last meeting. "I can only try."

"Should I come?"

"No . . . If there have to be insults I can swallow them, on such an occasion as this. But if you were insulted I could not."

"Take Gimlett with you."

"I don't think he would terrify a mouse. Tholly Tregirls is the man, but I can hardly draw him out of his kiddley just to accompany me on a social call."

"A sick visit," said Demelza.

"Whichever you say . . . I think I'll go now, while the daylight lasts—such as it is."

Demelza said: "I'll light the candles."

To the accompaniment of a dozen questions Ross got up and went for his cloak and hat. As he left he kissed Demelza, which was unusual for him in mid-afternoon.

She said: "Don't stay too long, or I shall worry. For your safety, I mean."

He smiled. "For my safety."

Outside he cast a glance at the sea, which had now lost all its wildness. It was coming in like an oilcloth that was being lifted by a draught, only the edges frayed with dirty white. Sea gulls were celebrating the darkness of the day.

When he turned in at the gates of Trenwith a number of lights already flickered in the building. Few houses, he thought, responded more quickly to mood than Trenwith. When he had been here on that summer evening eighteen months ago it had been pulsating and gay; now it looked still and cold, as cold as the Christmas when he had visited Aunt Agatha.

There were no gamekeepers about. He dismounted and knocked on the door. It was opened almost immediately by a manservant he did not know.

"Are you the—oh . . ."

Ross said: "I came to inquire about Mrs. Warleggan. Is Mr. Warleggan in?"

"Mrs. Warleggan . . . Well . . ."

"My name is Poldark."

"Oh . . ." The man seemed frozen.

"What is it?" said a voice behind. It was George.

His face was in the shadow but his voice was at its coldest.

Ross said: "I come in peace, George. I come simply to inquire after Elizabeth. I trust she's better."

There were noises inside the house but it was difficult to identify them.

George said: "Turn this man away."

"I came to ask how she was," Ross said. "That is all. I think at times of sickness one should be able to set aside old feuds—even the bitterest of feuds."

George said: "Turn this man away."

The door was shutting. Ross put his foot in it and his good shoulder against it and shoved. The manservant staggered back and collided with a table. Ross went in. There was only a single candle guttering in the great hall. It looked like a wobbling yellow eye in the iron-grey daylight.

Ross shut the door behind him. "For *God's* sake, George! Have we to be so petty as to quarrel like

mangy dogs at a time of *sickness?* Tell me she is better. Tell me she is about the same. Tell me what the
doctors say, and I will *go!* And go gladly! I have no
business here but that of a long-standing relationship
—with this house, and those in it. I am related by
marriage to Elizabeth, and wish her only well . . ."

George said: "God damn you, and your family, and
your blood to all eternity." He choked and stopped as
if he was ill himself.

Ross waited, but no more came. The manservant
had recovered himself and was rearranging the table
he had upset.

Ross said: "I will not go till I know how she is."

"Elizabeth?" said George. "Oh, Elizabeth? . . . Elizabeth is dead."

III

In the silence that followed, the manservant slid
away silently and was gone from the hall.

The hall itself was like a church, echoing and cold;
sickly light from the multi-paned window falling upon
the great table, the empty hearth; and the one candle
burning.

Ross said: "It . . . you can't . . ." He took a breath.
"She can't . . ."

"Two hours ago," said George in a detached voice;
"she died, holding my hand. Is that any pleasure to
you?"

Ross recognised now the sound he had heard earlier. It was someone crying, a woman, almost a wail,
like a Celtic keening. No one would have recognised
Mrs. Chynoweth, whose voice for some years had
been muffled and halting.

"Elizabeth is . . . I can't—believe . . . George, this
is not some . . ."

"Some jest?" said George. "Oh, yes, I jest from
time to time, but not on such a trivial subject as the
loss of a wife."

Ross stood as if his limbs were unable to make any

concerted movement. He licked his lips and stared at the other man.

"Go on, you scum!" George shouted. "Go up and *see* her! See what we have brought her to!"

A man came out of the winter parlour. At another time Ross would have recognised him as Dr. Behenna.

"Mr. Warleggan, I beg of you not to upset yourself further. No more could have been done, and there is nothing to do now—"

George turned. "I have Captain Poldark here. Captain Poldark, M.P. He doubts my word that my wife —whom he long coveted—is dead. He thinks I am jesting. I have invited him to go up and see."

"Mr. Warleggan, if I might suggest—"

"Where is she?"

George looked at Ross. "In the pink bedroom overlooking the courtyard. You must know your way about this house, since you have always felt it belonged to you. Go up and see her for yourself. There is no one with her. No one will stay with her."

"Captain Poldark—" Behenna began, but Ross was already making for the stairs.

He went up them, stumbling here and there. It was dark in the interior of the house, and another solitary candle burned at the end of the long passage. Past Verity's old bedroom, past Francis's bedroom, past Aunt Agatha's bedroom. Shadows barred his way. He stumbled against an ancient tallboy. The floorboards creaked under his tread. Past the bedroom where he and Demelza had once slept and made love. Up five steps. Those five steps that Elizabeth had fallen down before the birth of Valentine.

He came to the door. He could not bring himself to open it. It was the room in which he had come to see Elizabeth seven years ago—a meaning from which so much mischief had sprung. Suddenly as a non-believer and a non-Catholic he wanted to cross himself.

He opened the door, and the stench hit him like a wall.

The bed was there, and Elizabeth was on it, and two candles burned. The fire still flickered in the grate.

The curtains were drawn but a window was slightly open. The only movement in the room was a stirring of the pink curtain in the evening breeze. On the table by the bed were an hourglass, a bowl, a tall painted feeding bottle, two lemons. On the dressing table was Elizabeth's necklace of garnets, a glass containing three leeches, a pair of scissors, and a bottle of water and a spoon. Before the fire were her slippers, and a kettle hissed faintly on the hob.

He hung on to the handle of the door and retched. She did not move to greet him.

He retched again and again, and pulled out a handkerchief and put it to his nose and mouth. He stared at his first love. The candles dipped in the draught of the open door.

He walked slowly to the bed. Death had removed all the lines of pain and fatigue and fever. Except that her skin was yellow. Her hair, unbrushed but curiously tidy, still framed that pale patrician face. Robbed of expression, her face in repose retained the old sweet beauty so many men had admired. You could have supposed that at any moment her eyelids would flicker open and her lips would curve into a welcoming smile. Except that her skin was yellow.

And under the sheet, and barely contained by it, lay all the horrors of corruption, mortification, and decay. It was creeping up by every minute that she lay there. How far had it already reached? She had decayed while still alive, so that burial was already days overdue.

He swallowed back vomit, and took the handkerchief from his mouth and kissed her. Her lips were like soft cold stale putty.

Handkerchief back, he heaved his heart out against it and almost fell. The room swung as he caught at a chair. He turned and fled. The bang of the door behind him sounded hollow; the door of a sepulchre. A sepulchre that needed sealing off from all that was still alive.

He reeled along the passage and down the stairs without looking at George, who stood there watching him. He went out of the house and found his horse, and leaned his head against the horse's neck, unable to mount.

IV

George said: "Tell me the sum I am in your debt and I will pay you."

"In due course. I'll attend to it in due course."

"Let me know when you want your horse brought from the stables."

"As it is again night," Dr. Behenna said stiffly, "I should prefer to sleep here. Also, I think it advisable to look at the baby once more before I go."

"She's not unwell?"

"Not at all. But I am not sure if the wet nurse is not a thought clumsy. These country girls . . ."

"She was the best to be found at such short notice."

"Oh, quite. I've given Mrs. Chynoweth a strong opiate, and she should sleep sound now. The women are upstairs now?"

"The women are upstairs."

"I think the casque should be closed as quick as possible."

"I'm sure they will feel the same."

Somewhere in a nearby room Valentine was arguing with his nurse. He did not yet know anything except that Mama was unwell.

George went prowling round the cold shadowy silent house. This thing that had happened to him was contrary to all his previous experiences of life. In forty years he had suffered few setbacks, and they had all been man-made and capable of reversal. Most of them *had* been reversed in the fulness of time. One accepted a rebuff, a defeat, and then carefully gauged the size and quality of the defeat and set one's mind to arranging future events in such a way as to overcome or circumvent it. Of course from time to time he and his parents had had minor or more than minor ailments, and one accepted that in due course one would grow old and die. But in forty years he had not *lost* any-body—certainly nobody important.

This total defeat was something he found difficult—impossible—to accept. From the age of twenty Eliza-beth had been his goal—for long quite out of reach, beyond all possibility of attainment. But he had at-tained her, against all probability, against all the odds. This had been his greatest triumph. Since then, though he had allowed suspicion and jealousy to rage in him and impair his life with her, it had been rage against his *own,* it had been bitter anger within a circum-scribed area of personal possession. So when on the rare occasions jealousy had broken into bitter quarrel, he had been prepared to back down at the last under her threat to leave him. He might be miserable *with* her, and fiercely intent on making her life miserable too; but there had never been any question in his mind that he was ever going to be *without* her.

For she was the person he had been working for—to please, to offend, to observe, to criticise, to consult, even to insult, to show off to others, to buy things for, above all to *impress. There was nobody else.* And now, and now when Aunt Agatha's spleen had just lost its venom, when the poison barb had at last been with-drawn and they could live in a greater amity together, when they had a *daughter* to add to their son, when life could really begin anew, when—*especially*—he was on the point of achieving that ultimate pinnacle of distinction, a knighthood—he, George Warleggan, the blacksmith's grandson—a knighthood—Sir George . . . Sir George and Lady Warleggan . . . coming into a reception . . . everyone would look—one of the wealthiest men in Cornwall and one of the most influ-ential, member of Parliament, owner of a parliamen-tary borough, and a *knight;* and on his arm the fair-haired gracious aristocratic Elizabeth: Lady War-leggan . . . and at this stage she had been *snatched away*.

It was not *bearable.* He stared around him at the room he found himself in—it was a guest room and he did not know why he had come in here. It was next

THE ANGRY TIDE

to Agatha's old room, and he quickly went out and
entered hers. She had cursed him, she had *cursed* him!
—all this time her curse had lain on him, and now,
when he had been about to cast it off, she had cursed
him afresh, and his life was laid waste.

Most of the furniture was unchanged from when she
had died—this was the bed she had died on. He kicked
violently at the dressing table, splintering one of the
legs. Then he pushed it over and it fell with a crash,
smashing the glass and scattering toiletries about the
floor. He wrenched open the door of the wardrobe
and tugged at it. Slowly it toppled and fell with a re-
sounding thud, bringing over a chair and breaking a
wooden table in its fall. The candle he had brought in
lurched on its shelf and nearly fell too.

This was a cursed house, and he would willingly
have burned it down—the candle to the curtain and
to the corner of the bedspread—there was plenty of
ancient timber which would soon ignite: a fitting pyre
for Elizabeth and all the cursed and twice damned
Poldarks who had ever lived here.

But in spite of his insensate anger it was not in him,
not in his nature to destroy property, especially property
which more than ever now was by rights his. He stared
around the room, his hands still trembling with passion, and tore off the walls two pictures which had belonged to Agatha, dashed them to the floor. He thought
tomorrow night—or perhaps even tonight—he would
go to Sawle Church and desecrate her grave—have
two men smash the headstone, dig up the rotten powdered corpse and *throw* it around and *throw* it around
for the crows to pick. Anything, anything, to revenge
himself for this unrevengeable injury he had suffered.

He tremblingly took up the candle again and went
out of the room, dripping tallow on his fingers and all
over the floor. He stood outside, unable to contain his
anger yet unable to find a subject on which to vent it.
He would have gone again in to see Elizabeth, but
knew it was better to wait until the two women had
finished laying her out and the room had been heavily

scattered with chloride of lime. He did not know whether he could bear to go in even then.

She had left him. She had *left* him. He couldn't *believe* it.

He could not tolerate the thought of returning to the rooms downstairs where he might encounter that inept quack, Behenna, or, worse, Elizabeth's doddering, feeble-faced father. If he saw him he would cry: why are *you* alive? What good are *you* to me? Why don't you and your miserable wife die too?

A girl had come out of a door and was staring at him. It was Polly Odgers.

"Beg pardon, sir. I didn't rightly know if anything was wrong . . . I mean *more* wrong. I heard those noises—crashes and the like. I didn't rightly know what they were."

"*Nothing,*" he said between his teeth. "It is nothing."

"Oh . . . Thank you, sir. Excuse me." She prepared to withdraw.

"Did it wake the child?"

"Oh, no, sir; she's a proper little sleeper. And hungry with it! She's grown, I believe she's grown in just four days!"

He followed her into the room. Mrs. Simons, the young wet nurse, bobbed him a curtsy as he came in.

He stared down at the child. Ursula Warleggan. But Elizabeth had left him. This was all that was left. She had left him Ursula.

He stayed motionless for a long time, and the two young women watched him, careful not to disturb his thoughts.

He had held her hand while she was dying. When Behenna said there was no more hope, he had come into the loathsome, nauseous room and sat down beside her and held her hand. One hand was badly swollen but the other as pale and slim as ever. He had thought her unconscious, but her fingers had moved in his. It was her left hand, and his ring was on it, his ring proclaiming his pride and his capture, which he had put on her finger in the dilapidated old church of Mylor by the river Fal less than seven years ago. With what pride and triumph. And now it had come to this.

Once towards the end she had come round and tried to smile at him through her parched and discoloured lips. Then the smile had disappeared and a look of dread had come over her face. "George," she had whispered. "It's going dark! I'm afraid of the dark." He had held her hand more tightly as if with his firm grip he could keep her in this world, hold her against the drag of all the horrors that drew her to the grave.

He thought of all this, standing staring down at the child which was all Elizabeth had left him. He was no philosopher and no seer, but had he been both he might have wondered at the fact that his fair-haired, frailly beautiful wife had now borne three children and that none of them would come to resemble her at all. Though Elizabeth had been constitutionally strong enough, perhaps some exhaustion in the ancient Chynoweth strain was to be the cause of this virtual obliteration of her personal appearance in any of her children, and the dominance of the three fathers. Geoffrey Charles was already like Francis. Valentine would grow ever more like the man who had just left the house. And little Ursula would become sturdy and strong and thick-necked and as determined as a black-smith.

The child stirred in her sleep; still so tiny; still so frail. "Look after the children," Elizabeth had whispered. Very well, very well: he would do that; but what was the use of *that*? It was his *wife* he wanted: the person you did things *for*, the cornerstone. All his labour, all his scheming, all his organising and amass-ing and negotiating and achieving . . . without her it was all in *vain*. He could have kicked this cot over like the furniture in Agatha's room; turned it upside down with its frail contents, as his life had been overset, killed, made empty by a solitary stroke of malignant fate. He blamed fate, never knowing that he should have blamed himself.

Polly Odgers leaned forward and pulled a corner of the blanket further from the child's mouth. "Dear of'n," she said.

"Ursula," George muttered. "The little she-bear."

"Please?"

"Nothing," said George.

And for the first time he had to take a handkerchief to wipe his eyes.

Chapter Sixteen

Ross walked home beside his horse. Shock and horror had made his limbs so weak that to go home slowly step by step with Sheridan beside him was more instinct than choice.

He walked through Grambler village and past Sawle Church out onto the moorland. A wind was soughing over the land.

This was the most familiar way in the world to him; he had run from one house to the other in childhood and in boyhood; he had ridden this way and walked this way more times than he could estimate. But it was Sheridan who knew the path tonight.

One or two people passed and called good night. It was a Cornish custom, not always mere friendliness but often curiosity to identify the other in the dark. Tonight he did not reply. The horror was on him. As a soldier he had seen enough, but this was different. That she should have decayed like that while still looking so beautiful was something he would never be able to rid himself of. This was what love came to. This was what beauty came to. The worm. God in Christ!

He shuddered and spat. The sickness lay in his stomach like the gangrene she had died of.

He came up to the Meeting House beside Wheal Maiden. There was a light in it. Probably Sam. Perhaps a few faithful members of the class praying or listening to him read. Perhaps he should go in, kneel in a corner, ask for guidance and pray for humility. That was what all men lacked. Humility and perspective. But the latter was dangerous. With perspective one could always perceive the end.

Something moved. "Is it you, Ross?"

"Demelza,'" he said. "What are you doing here?"

"I thought to come this far—just to watch for you ... Why are you walking?"

"I—wished to take my time."

She said: "I know what's happened. Caroline sent Myners over to tell us."

"I'm glad you know."

They turned and began to walk back. She said: "I'm that sorry."

He said: "Let us not talk about it."

They went down the valley. As soon as they reached home she went in and hustled the children out of the parlour, and he sat before the fire and drank the brandy she brought. She helped him off with his boots.

"Do you want to be alone?"

"Not if you'll stay."

So she told the children to be quiet in the kitchen, and fetched her sewing and took a chair on the other side of the fire. He drank brandy for about an hour. She had a couple of small glasses. At last he looked up.

"I'm sorry," he said.

"Do you want supper?"

"*No*. No food. But take some yourself. Are the children in the dining room?"

"I don't know. I'm not that hungry."

"It's been a dark day," he said. "Sometimes I think there are days in December when the human spirit is at its lowest. This is such a one."

"With good reason. Did she—"

"I'd—rather not talk about it."

They sat for about another hour. He had stopped drinking but lay back dozing, with his head against the back of the high chair. She went out and said good night to the children and cut herself a piece of bread and cheese.

When she went in again he said: "I think I'll go for a walk."

"At this time?"

"Yes . . . it might help. Don't wait up."

"You don't want for me to come with you, then?"

"I think I shall go too far."

She said: "Remember to come back."

When he got out the three-quarter moon was rising, invisible and smothered in cloud, but lightening the way. He went on to Hendrawna Beach, where the tide was far out, and began to walk across it. The sand broke under his weight, as crisp as frost. His own shadow, vague as a ghost, moved about his feet.

He went the way Drake had walked in his tribulation some months ago, but at the Holy Well he deserted the beach and climbed the rocky steps beside it till he reached the old path that the pilgrims had used centuries ago. Up and down, skirting the sandhills, with the sea murmuring just below, he stumbled on, passing the Dark Cliffs and Ellenglaze, skirted Hoblyn's Cove and dipped into the valley beyond. Except for the solitary crofter or gypsy, this was empty land, wind-swept and sand-swept, barren of vegetation except the marram grass and a few patches of gorse and heather. Not a tree. It was years since he had come this way. He did not remember ever having come this way since he returned from America sixteen years ago. There was nothing to come for. Except when, as now, he was trying to escape from himself.

Once or twice he sat down, not so much to rest as to think; but as soon as he began to think he was up and off again. As the night progressed so the sky lightened, and now and then the moon appeared, veiled and warped and wasted with age. The cliff edges became sharper, like the faces of old men as the flesh shrinks from them. In some of the smaller, darker coves seaweed slithered on the rocks and stank of the sea's decay.

It was hours before he turned about and began the long tramp back. But now it was a question of making his tired body take over from his tired mind. Or accommodate his conscious thinking to ideas only of muscular effort. Back on the beach at last, he lengthened his stride to beat the tide as it came in. He rounded the Wheal Leisure cliffs with water splashing above his knees.

Day was just creeping up into the sky as he sighted Nampara. It came reluctantly, like someone drawing back the curtains in a shrouded room. Fine rain was beginning to fall. He found his way over the familiar stile, into the garden, past the lilac tree, and let himself into the house. He moved silently into the parlour, chilled with the sea water clammy about his legs and thinking some remnants of the fire might still be warm.

The fire was still in, though low, and as he crouched before it someone stirred in his armchair. He started and then saw who it was.

He said: "I *told* you. You should have gone to bed."

She said: "Why should I?"

They stayed in silence for a time, while he put pieces of coal on the fire and then used the bellows to blow it up.

"Are you cold?" he asked.

"Yes. Are you?"

He nodded and went to open the curtains. The sickly daylight showed that she had not undressed but had a blanket over her knees and a wrap round her shoulders.

"Let me get you some breakfast."

He shook his head. "You have something."

"No, no; I'm not hungry." She stirred. "You're wet."

"No matter. I'll change in a while." He poured himself a glass of brandy to try to take the stale taste of other brandy from his mouth. He offered her one but she refused.

"Have you been walking all night?"

"Yes. I think these boots are nearly through."

He pulled them off, crouched again by the fire. She watched the warmer light play on his features. The brandy went down, burning deep. He made a face, and shivered. "Have you been asleep?"

"Sort of."

"But waiting."

"Waiting."

He subsided against the back of the other chair. "This is the end of the century, you know. It seems —appropriate. In a few weeks it will be eighteen hundred."

"I know."

"For perhaps very good reasons, it seems just now to be the end of more than the century to me. It seems to be the end of life as we've known it."

"Because of—Elizabeth's death?"

He baulked at the word. "Not altogether. Though that, of course."

"Do you want to talk about it now?"

"No—if you don't mind."

There was silence.

She said: "Well, the end of the century does not mean the end of our lives, Ross."

"Oh . . . it's a fit of deepest depression I am in. It will look different in a month ot two. I'll recover by and by."

"There's no hurry."

"Perhaps there's always hurry."

He shovelled more coal on, and a puff of smoke blew into the room.

She said: "Go and sleep before the children wake."

"No. I want to talk to you, Demelza. What I've been thinking. Not long ago you lost someone you —loved. It—bites deep."

"Yes," she said. "It bites deep."

"Yes . . ." He reached for the brandy and then put it in the fireplace untasted. "Though I once loved Elizabeth, it's been the *memory* of that love that bit deepest tonight. Sometime this month or next I shall be forty. So there's always hurry. It is the memory—

and the fear—of the loss of *all* love that bites deepest."

"I don't quite see what you mean."

"Well, in some ways my grief is a selfish grief. Perhaps that's what Sam preaches. One can attain no goodness without subduing the self."

"And do you wish to do that?"

"It's not what one wishes, it's what one should do."

"Self . . ." said Demelza. "Is there no difference between self and selfishness? Is there no difference between—appreciating all the good things of life and—and exploiting the good things for one's own advantage? I think so."

He stared at her with her dark hair falling carelessly about her shoulders, and under the wrap her canary silk frock, and her hands never quite still, and her breast rising and falling, and the dark vivid intelligence in her eyes.

He said: "What I have seen last night—makes me sick at heart—sick for all the charm and beauty that is lost—in Elizabeth. But most of all it makes me afraid."

"Afraid, Ross? What of?"

"Of losing you, I suppose."

"There's little chance."

"I don't mean to another man—though that was bad enough. I mean just of losing you physically, as a person, as a companion, as a human presence being beside me and with me all my life."

Her heart opened to him. "Ross," she said, "there's no *chance*. Unless you throw me out."

"It's not a chance, it's a *certainty*," he said. "Seeing Elizabeth like that . . . We are at the end of a century, at the end of an era . . ."

"It's just a date."

"No, it isn't. Not for us. Not for anybody; but especially not for us. It's—it's a watershed. We have come up so far; now we look down."

"We look onwards, surely."

"Onwards and down. D'you realise there will come a time, there will *have* to come a time, when I shall never hear your voice again, or you mine? It may be sentimental to say so, but this—this fact is something I find intolerable, unthinkable, beyond bearing . . ."

Demelza moved from her chair suddenly, knelt to the fire and picked up the bellows and began to work them. It was to disguise the tears that had lurched to the edge of her lashes. She realised that he had reached some ultimate darkness of the soul, that he struggled in deep waters, and that perhaps only she could stretch out a hand.

"Ross, you mustn't be afraid. It's not like you. 'Tisn't in your nature."

"Perhaps one's nature changes as one grows older."

"It mustn't."

He watched her. "Aren't you ever afraid?"

"Yes. Oh, yes, Maybe every moment of the day if I allowed myself to think. But you can't *live*, not that way, if you think like that. I'm here. You're here. The children are upstairs. That's all that matters at this moment, at this time. The—the blood is in my veins. It's in yours. Our hearts beat. Our eyes see. Our ears hear. We smell and talk and feel."

She turned and squatted beside him on the carpet, and he put his arm round her, staring sightlessly into the dark.

She said: "And we're together. Isn't that important?"

"Even when it is like it was in London?"

"That mustn't ever be again."

"No," he said. "That mustn't ever be again."

"Of course there has to be an end," she said. "Of course. For that is what everyone has faced since the world began. And that is—what do you call it?— intolerable! It's intolerable! So you must not think of it. You must not face it. Because it is a—certainty it has to be forgotten. One cannot—must not—fear a certainty. All we know is this moment, and this moment, Ross, we are *alive!* We *are*. *We* are. The past is over, gone. What is to come doesn't exist yet. That's tomorrow! It's only now that can ever be, at any one moment. And at this moment, *now,* we are alive and together. We can't ask more. There isn't any more to ask."